Vaulted Eagles

by
Rayzor Dent

PublishAmerica
Baltimore

First printing

This is a work of fiction. Names, characters, places, and incidents either are the product of the author's imagination or are used fictitiously. Any resemblance to actual persons, living or dead, events, or locales is entirely coincidental.

PublishAmerica has allowed this work to remain exactly as the author intended, verbatim, without editorial input.

Hardcover 978-1-4560-3478-8
Softcover 978-1-4560-3479-5
PUBLISHED BY PUBLISHAMERICA, LLLP
www.publishamerica.com
Baltimore

Printed in the United States of America

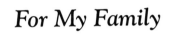

For My Family

Acknowledgements

I love the Southwest. The big country, the traditions, the people and the sunsets are all part of my soul. It is a shame that most Americans know so little about the vast expanse of our nation that stretches from Texas to the Pacific Ocean. I wrote this fictional book, built around many actual events and characters, in an attempt to provide an entertaining vehicle for others to gain an appreciation for this area and its remarkable history.

Many people made the epic journey with the characters in this manuscript as I wrote the words. Without their help and support, I could not have survived that trip. While I offer my sincere thanks to everyone whose comments and advice helped make my story better, I must specifically mention a few who contributed significantly.

Jo Ann Corbet, my English teacher at Monterey High School in Lubbock, Texas, has been a mentor and friend for over 40 years. She has always championed my efforts and she remains a champion editor of my efforts.

Other important editors and critics were Terri Ackers, Jan Hensen, Jan Clute, Betty Halff, Melissa Martinez, Dane Hooks, John and Suzanne Stowe along with Bill and Barbara Galuhn. Having had the valuable experience of critiquing me since childhood, my sister, Kay Sutherland, was also a very important part of that support team.

My heartfelt thanks go to Corinne Joy Brown, an accomplished writer, novelist and lecturer in the Western genre, for her unselfish willingness to help less experienced authors. Throughout the creation of this book she has been an excellent teacher, brutal editor and exceptional friend.

I must also thank the Daughters of the Republic of Texas for access to their Library and their excellent library staff members Elaine Davis, Leslie Stapleton and Martha Utterback.

It is to, and for, my family that I am most thankful. I dedicate this work to them. My children, Amanda Maeyaert and Travis Dent, have helped and encouraged me with this book since the first sentence was written. They have been invaluable because they read, and edit, with their hearts as well as their minds. I think they get that from Nancy, their mother.

Nancy has been the love of my life since we were both 18 year old freshmen in college. As with every other important thing in my life, I could never have written this book without the love, support and help of my best friend.

Prologue

"Pa's comin'!...Pa's comin' in!...He's all right!...I can see him!" Sam screamed so loud it made his throat hurt as he ran down the hill toward the homestead. He barely kept his balance as he ran yelling and whistling, flailing both arms at full length, waving his thick old wool hat in his right hand.

He continued the headlong descent frantically trying to get the attention of his mother and big brother. Sam was almost half way to the corrals when he knew they heard him, because they each dropped their chores and came running. The young man then spun around and ran back up the hill toward his father.

Sam had been on top of the hill west of the family's small rustic Texas home most of the morning. He and his best friend, his sister Mary Elizabeth, were working on an old dead tree trying to trim it out and get it ready to pull down to chop for firewood.

The big oak had been struck by lightning in a bad thunderstorm the summer before. The family had already gathered and used the big limbs that had exploded out of the top of the tree, but the lightning had also split the massive trunk almost completely down the middle. It wouldn't be easy, but once they dealt with it, that stout old tree would give them enough fuel to keep their family warm the rest of the winter.

Mary Beth was the first one to see their father. Like most children raised in the colony, she and Sam had been trained to always keep one eye on their work and the other watching for Indians - or now Mexicans. While Sam hacked away at the tree with their ax, Mary Beth noticed a man walking in the sunlight two hills over. When the figure got closer they both recognized their father's distinctive long-legged gait. Their Pa, and most of the other men they knew, had been gone for three months fighting the Mexicans at San Antonio de Bexar.

"Sam, go get Momma!" Mary Beth had barked over her shoulder to her little brother as she started off the hilltop in a dead run to greet her Pa.

Samuel Austin Stevens was sixteen years old and the youngest of the three Stevens children. Mary Beth (she was only called Mary Elizabeth when she was in trouble) was two years older. Their brother, Luke, was almost twenty.

As with many pioneer families, the five in the Stevens clan were very close-knit and proud. They had carved a home in the wild heart of southern Texas with their own muscle and sweat, and because of their isolation, the children had grown up knowing few companions but one another. Although Sam loved and hero-worshipped his older brother, he often felt Luke treated him like a kid, especially when Pa was gone. Sam didn't like it when Luke tried to take over for Pa and acted like he was an adult.

Mary Beth, on the other hand, never treated Sam like a kid. Of course when he was a little boy, Mary Beth had taken care of him and looked out for him. But now they were equals, at least that's how Sam saw it.

They did most everything together and still horsed around and wrestled when Momma would tolerate it. The two of them would stay up late at night sometimes just talking. Mary Beth was the only person in the world who knew Sam's dreams and deepest fears.

Jonathan Michael Stevens' eye caught something moving on the hill three quarters of a mile ahead and he instinctively stopped. As he squinted into the distance he realized the far away object was his precious daughter running to him. His whisker stubbled chin wrinkled up and Jonathan's vision of the excited girl blurred through his rising tears.

He had left San Antonio de Bexar, and all the bloodshed, over a week ago. Although he was sore and stiff and completely exhausted from the hundred and forty mile trek home he raised himself tall, wiped the tears from his eyes, and started to run to Mary Beth. He had vowed to himself to make it home to his family for Christmas and, as near as he could figure, this day was December 21, 1835.

Jonathan and the other Texas volunteers had just defeated General Martin Perfecto de Cos and the twelve hundred Mexican soldiers who had taken San Antonio de Bexar, the western gateway of the *Camino Real* through Texas. The Mexicans had fortified the old *Mission San Antonio de Valero* that everyone now called the *Alamo*. It had been a very long siege.

As a Captain in the volunteers, Jonathan had been away from his family since late September. In the end, after all that fighting and dying, once the Mexicans were defeated the Texians let them all go back to Mexico. The Mexicans surrendered most of their equipment and weapons, but neither army had enough supplies to sustain a large group of prisoners.

Jonathan had been mad about the futility of the whole mess all the way home. He and the other Texians, as they called themselves, had always done everything the Mexican Government had asked of them. They had become Mexican citizens, sworn their allegiance to Mexico, and even changed their religions to Catholic.

The colonists had tamed the wild country between the Colorado and Brazos Rivers, clearing the land and creating homes and commerce. They had always worked within the government's systems and even helped frame Mexico's Democratic Constitution.

But that had all changed because of one man. He was a power hungry liar who lived thousand miles away in *Ciudad Mexico*. Although the man had a long fancy name, most of the Texians just knew him as… Santa Anna.

Santa Anna had been overwhelmingly elected President of Mexico a couple of years before. Jonathan and the majority of the other colonists had supported him because he ran as a liberal promising to unite the country under the Democratic Constitution of 1824.

However, once he was elected and in power, the first thing the bastard did was abolish the Constitution. Then he took away the power of the Mexican States and the rights of the people, and consolidated all government authority under his autocratic rule.

Now the Anglo colonists and the *Tejanos*, the original Mexican nationals living in Texas, were rebelling. It was obvious that under Santa Anna's dictatorship they could lose everything they had worked so hard to build. After the Siege of Bexar, Jonathan knew there would be a war and there was nothing he, or anyone else, could do about it.

He wished his friend, Stephen Austin, was here. Austin was a good man and a good leader. They had elected him their Commander at San Antonio de Bexar, but Stephen had to leave for Washington back in November. Although there were many good men among the Texians, and Jonathan knew most of them, he was concerned about just who would be able to lead the scattered, ill-equipped settlers in a real war.

When he and Mary Beth were seventy yards apart Jonathan stopped and laid his long heavy rifle in the tall dry grass. The slings of his possibles bag and his bedroll were crisscrossed around his chest and he started stripping them off over his head. He dumped them on the ground and reached out just as Mary Beth ran into his arms and almost knocked him over.

He hugged her tightly to him and kissed her long black hair on the side of her head. The tears flooded his eyes again, and he said in a husky whispering voice, "Oh, God, I've missed my babies!"

"Pa," Mary Beth said, hugging her father as tightly as he was hugging her, "you're home! I've been so worried about you. Thank goodness you're home. Are you all right?" She started to pull away to look and see if he was hurt.

Her Pa grabbed her back and held her. "I'm fine, darlin'. Sound as a dollar. God, I missed you." Then he put his hands down to her waist and held her there as he moved back to arms length and looked into her pretty face. "I've been worried if y'all were all right? How's your Momma and the boys?"

Just then Jonathan looked up and saw Sam running to him and his wife with Luke starting down from the top of the hill. He squeezed his lips tightly together and Mary Beth watched them quiver as tears started down her father's face. She had only seen her father cry once or twice before in her life. Her throat tightened up and tears filled her eyes as she put her arms tightly around her Pa again.

Sam ran into his father's arms the same way Mary Beth had saying, "Pa, you're home, you're home! Did you get hurt?"

Pa wrapped his arms around the boy. "I'm fine, Sam. How's my Frog Ears?" That was the name his Pa had called him teasingly when Sam was little. "Lord, I'm glad to be back here with you, son!"

Jonathan raised himself slightly, and while he held onto Sam with his right arm he reached for Mary Beth with his left. She put her arms around the two men and the three of them hugged together for a moment. Then Pa said, "Grab my gear, let's go see your Momma and Luke!"

By the time they reached Momma, all Jonathan's tears were replaced by his familiar big broad smile. Sarah, his wife, was the one with tears streaming as she ran into her husband's strong open arms. "Oh, Jonathan" was all she kept saying over and over. Luke stood back slightly and let his parents embrace and kiss. After a while, Pa looked up at Luke and said, "Hey, son." Then he released Sarah and stepped to the young man who was just slightly taller than his father. When he and Luke hugged, Jonathan thought to himself how hard the boy's muscles were. He was very proud of the man his eldest had become and he said, "Thanks for takin' care of your Momma and everything, son. I know you did a good job."

"Are you fit, Jonathan?" Sarah asked her husband as she hugged his back while he still had his arms around Luke. "You didn't get hurt did you?"

"No, I'm fit as a fiddle, lady," Jonathan replied. He turned and kissed her again. "Just plum wore out."

"Is it over?" Sarah asked looking straight into Jonathan's tired eyes.

"Well, we kicked the Mexicans out of San Antonio, but it's not over," Jonathan replied slowly. "I'm afraid it's just startin', honey."

Then he looked around at his three children who were standing close to him and realized they were scared by his words. He grinned at them all and looked to the top of the hill toward home.

"Let's go home," Pa said loudly and enthusiastically. "I've been dreamin' about sittin' in front of our fireplace with y'all and sleepin' in my warm bed with your Momma for a hell of a long time! There'll be time for me to tell you all about everything."

With that the two boys picked up their father's trappings and they all started up the hill toward the homestead. Jonathan was between his two girls with an arm around each one's waist. Half way up the hill Sarah asked, surprised she had just thought about it, "Where's *Rojo Grande*?"

Her husband replied, "Well, I made it back, but old Big Red didn't. He got shot in a skirmish Will Travis got us into last month. Funny thing was, we were out stealin' the Mexican's horses when it happened. We got close to three hundred of their horses and mules that day, but not a one of 'em was half the animal old *Rojo* was."

He looked at his son. "Sure am sorry about losin' your horse, Luke."

Jonathan had taken the big horse Luke raised from a colt to the fighting because it was the best mount of the ten horses they owned.

Luke replied sincerely, "Pa, it was just a horse. I'd give ten thousand horses to have you home safe!"

"But he sure was a good one, and got me through some tight spots," Jonathan continued. "I had one of the Mexican horses 'til he went lame about three days ago. That's when I had to start walkin'."

Jonathan thought of how he had left San Antonio de Bexar with twenty of the men in his command. They were all volunteers that he knew from the colony. Three of the men were sick from the cold and lack of food, and two men were wounded. When Jonathan's horse went lame late on the fifth day, he had cut its throat and they all ate the animal that night. The next morning Jonathan split from the group to take the most direct route home because he was on foot. He saw no reason to tell his family about any of it.

When they got to the top of the hill Jonathan stopped. The others kept going a few steps then halted. They looked back all wondering if something was wrong.

Pa was just standing there looking down at the familiar spread with a closed mouth smile on his face. He had shivered through many lonely nights longing to see this sight, and said wistfully, "You know, I'm not sure a person ever truly knows how important his home and family are in this life, 'til he thinks he might not ever see them again."

Sarah turned herself to him and kissed Jonathan on the lips. Then she said, "Thank God you're back. Let's go home, Mister."

PART
ONE

1

The old cowboy looked around the room one last time to make sure he hadn't forgotten anything. This little room between his bedroom and the kitchen had become his office of sorts. It's where he had put his old roll top desk, ancient wooden file cabinet, telephone and Internet connection. It's where he had also poured the concrete vault.

The room sure looked a lot better than it usually did. It was neat and clean in preparation for his guests. The rest of the house looked good too, but it always did, because he still had Rosalee come by and clean for him.

Rosalee had done the housekeeping for the old man and his wife for over twenty years. When she first started as a shy young newcomer to the United States, she didn't speak any English. Although her English had improved substantially, Rosalee continued to speak only Spanish to the aging *Patron* whenever she worked here. Once a week she did his laundry and cleaned every room in the house - every room but his office. She wasn't allowed in there.

Without the normal clutter of books, pictures and papers scattered about, it was easy for him to see this was the last of it. He walked to the vault and started the closing process.

The big homemade safe wasn't fancy, but it served his purpose well. He had used wooden two-by-four studs to reframe the inside walls and ceiling of the small room's old closet. He then ran three-eighth inch steel rebar rods vertically and horizontally between and through the studs. Next he fastened half-inch plywood to the studs with long wood screws to make the existing closet's new interior walls and ceiling, and then pumped the voids around the rebar full of concrete.

He sealed the doorway with the kind of tamper-proof steel door that is normally used on the exterior of commercial buildings. The old fellow knew someone, who wanted to badly enough, could probably break into his stronghold - but they'd have hell doing it. Also, first, they'd have to find it.

Along the wall where the closet was located, the elderly fox had put oak veneered wood paneling. A section of the paneling, held perfectly in place by several strong magnets glued to the back of the panel and attracted to the steel door, hid the vault.

There was no knob on the solid door, just an industrial style Schrade lock. He set the tempered steel deadbolt, then stowed the only key behind the sweatband inside his hat. As he positioned the false-front oak panel the stout magnets clicked it loudly into place onto the heavy steel door.

After that part was done he lifted, one side at a time, the Navajo rug. He stretched his body as high as he could reach in order to hang the top outside loops of the hand-woven piece on the long nails he'd hammered into the wall just outside the perimeter of the false door panel. The colorful tapestry he'd had for at least forty years was the perfect wall decoration for a western man's office. It was also just the right size.

Once the rug was hung, the old man stepped back and checked to make sure it was straight. He was tired and his back hurt. It was a part of getting old he didn't like much. With the end of a forefinger that was still tough, but thin-skinned with age, he bumped up the brim of his Stetson. He took in a deep breath, just before he carefully picked the last precious pieces from the worktable and carried them out of the room.

In the garage, he gently laid them on the open tailgate of his pickup. When he'd dragged the worn steamer chest out of the vault, and found it was too heavy for him to carry by himself and load into the truck, he had methodically removed each thing from inside it. Once he'd manhandled the empty chest out of the house and into the bed of his pickup, he carried the individual items separately and cautiously out to the vehicle and reloaded them into the special container.

On knees a little bowed and tender from too many years on horseback, he gingerly crawled into the bed of the pickup. He put his left hand on the top of the antique steamer chest and used it for support to help get to his feet. His fingertips felt dull as he fumbled with the trunk's brass latch before it opened.

For a moment he stood in the back of his pickup and looked down on the tailgate. On the side of his face he felt heat from the bare, hundred watt bulb screwed into the single white porcelain socket mounted to the middle of the ceiling. It was the only light in the garage.

Even in this poor light, and through the plastic, their beautiful rich color shown through. The old man was struck by how shiny they were. He marveled again at their weight as he picked them up.

Partner smiled and gently put them into their place inside the strong, ninety year old chest.

2

"Welcome to New Mexico!" was the greeting Partner gave with his broad smile as he raised himself tall. The eighty-three year old wore a freshly starched shirt and pressed western cut trousers. He gave a quick tip of his gray felt cowboy hat to the young lady before he opened the short wooden gate into the small manicured courtyard entry of the old adobe home.

Partner lifted both arms wide to the girl and her approaching husband as he said, "*Mi casa - su casa.* My home is your home, Amanda."

The New Mexico native and his wife had greeted their many guests, especially the out-of-staters, into their home that way for so many decades that it had become a tradition. Unfortunately, Partner didn't get to do it very often these days. He seldom entertained anymore.

The old man lived by himself now in Mesilla, New Mexico. Ellen, his wife and best friend for over fifty years, had died of cancer four years earlier. It was a mean thing that took her in only eight months. Because of their age and perspective on life they had handled it well, but her passing left a mighty big hole in Partner's world.

Through the seasons of their long marriage he and Ellen had discussed the reality that the one left behind would have the hard part; so Partner did find some comfort in knowing that his lover had been spared this end of the deal. Of course, things would have been different if they'd had any living children, but their grandson, Sammy, was the only immediate family left.

The elderly man put his arms around the young woman and hugged her. As her husband approached, Partner reached for his grandson with one arm and kept his other still tightly around his brand new grand daughter-in-law. He pulled the two together and hugged them both in his arms as he said, "Aghhh, I'm so glad y'all made it in. I didn't think y'all would ever get here!"

Amanda, a proper Bostonian who had just spent seven hours in a car, was being hugged by an ancient western guy she didn't really know. Her reaction was a little stiff.

Sammy, in the other arm, hugged his grandfather enthusiastically. "It's so good to be back in this old desert with you! Been a long time. Thanks for havin' us, Partner."

"Tell you what, Sammy boy, I damn near threw a party the night you called a few months ago and said y'all would be drivin' to California for your honeymoon and wanted to come through and stay here a day or two." The old man grinned as he pulled away and bumped up the brim of his Stetson with his thumb. "That's the best day I've had...in I can't tell you when. Well, 'til today, I guess."

Partner chuckled and shrugged his shoulders. "And, hell, poor Rosalee has been scrubbin' this whole house ever since I told her you two were comin' in."

"How is Rosalee?" Sammy asked sincerely as he stepped back, too, and smiled as he looked into his grandfather's face.

"Oh, she's fine, son. Got her kids in the college here, so we're all real proud of 'em. And, her health is good. 'Course, she 'mothers' me too damn much, but other than that she's just fine. She'll be pleased that you asked about her."

Partner turned and looked at the pretty bride he'd met at the couple's rehearsal dinner in Boston the week before and said, "Amanda, you 'bout to starve, dear?"

When she smiled back and said, "No, I'm OK, thank you." he looked at his grandson and continued, "Sammy, let's get all your gear into the house. I'll give y'all a quick tour of the new place, and then we'll feed you two a good supper.

"We're goin' to eat at the Double Eagle tonight, if that suits you. They're holdin' the Carlotta Room for us. We'll have our cocktails over there."

"That's great!" Sammy said. "Amanda, you'll love that place."

"Well, then let's get you settled in." Partner said patting his grandson's back as he and the young man turned toward the car. Partner suddenly hesitated and turned back to the young woman. He cocked his head slightly to one side and said, "Amanda, you're not afraid of ghosts, are ya', darlin'?"

3

Partner opened the heavy wooden door to his home and let his house quests walk in ahead of him. As soon as Sammy was inside he sat down the two bags he carried. He started walking around in amazement, swiveling his head trying to take everything in at once.

"The place looks awesome, Partner!" Sammy said as his eyes danced around the new interior. "I can't believe you're living here now. What a difference!"

The transformation was remarkable.

The old building with its two feet thick adobe walls had belonged to someone in Partner's family for four generations. It was originally the family home built by his great grandfather in the late 1840's, but over the years the building had served many different functions.

Most recently, for some thirty-five years prior to her death, it had been Ellen's dress shop. It was a block off the Mesilla Plaza and in the early 1960's, before the mall, fancy mail order catalogs and the Internet; Ellen opened the store as a place for the local ladies to buy nice clothes.

Mesilla and the adjoining town of Las Cruces weren't very big back then. Actually, they still aren't. Although Las Cruces is the second largest city in New Mexico, its population is under 100,000 and Mesilla has dwindled to fewer than 2,000 souls. But for over three decades, whenever a woman anywhere in the county wanted some nice clothes or needed something special for a social function, she always went to Ellen's store.

The store had become a public institution. It was not only a place to see the latest fashions, but because it was a cozy space to meet with old friends it was also the perfect spot to catch up on all the local goings on. The store was called simply, "Tia's".

In Spanish *Tia* means "Aunt", which is what every child who ever knew her affectionately called Ellen. Over time just about everyone in town knew Ellen as *Tia*, partially because so many of her customer's children grew up and became store customers themselves. Sammy had always addressed his grandparents as *Tia* and Partner.

"So you like the place all right?" Partner asked grinning and sat down the two smaller bags he carried. He was proud of what he had done remodeling the store back into a home and his grandson's reaction pleased him.

"Amanda, I guess Sammy told you we used to have a pretty good sized place down by the river where I could keep my horses and Ellen had her big gardens. After my wife died, I sold the house. It was just too big, and with her gone it was hard for me to enjoy it much.

"Besides, I always hated gardenin'. I knew if I let all her gardens go to seed, she'd have my hide the next time I see her."

Amanda hid a smile while Sammy laughed and said, "You better believe she would, Partner."

"Let me give y'all a quick tour around here and then we'll come back and get your bags and get you settled in." Partner said, and began showing them the refurbished old home.

A fair piece of Partner's life had been spent in the construction industry, so all the work on the building he had done himself with sometimes a friend or two, and a hired hand with a strong back when absolutely necessary. As they started off in the "great room", Partner explained to Amanda that the long exposed pole beams across the ceiling were called "*vigas*" and the little sticks laid in patterns atop the *vigas,* which had originally supported earth roofs, were called "*latillas*".

While they walked through the home Amanda was struck by how deep and massive the walls were. Some of the thick doorways were arched, and some had huge rough timbers exposed across the top of them. Partner explained to her how the adobe mud bricks were made and then stacked and covered with a fine plaster.

There were little arched recesses, which he called "*nichas*", built into the walls in strategic places throughout the house. The *nichas* held religious figurines, small pictures, and all sorts of other interesting looking things that Amanda found fascinating.

The home was well decorated, which Amanda hadn't expected for a widower living alone. It was also very warm and masculine; that seemed to fit her new grandfather-in-law. The furniture was heavy, functional and comfortable looking. There were western paintings, some of cowboys and some of brilliantly colored open landscapes, throughout the home.

Amanda didn't really like mounted animal heads, but the ones Partner had in some of the rooms were beautiful and seemed just the right touch for those spaces. In the great room a big bear skin rug in front of the crackling fire in the grand stone fireplace had made her think, for just a split second, of turning all the lights off and curling up there with her new husband.

Like Partner, Sammy was also very proud of what the old man had done. As they went along Sammy bragged on the craftsmanship when he could, and he could see Partner's touch in the planning that had gone into every detail. He realized this project had given his grandfather a way to help deal with losing *Tia*.

"This is y'all's room." Partner opened a heavy wooden door he'd had hand carved by an old Mexican craftsman in *Juarez*. He led the two newlyweds through the arched doorway. As they entered the room single file, Sammy was behind Amanda with a hand on each side of her thin waist.

He went right and Amanda went left as they walked around surveying the large bedroom and adjoining bath. The furniture, antique looking heavy pieces from Mexico, was all new. There was a king sized bed with lots of pillows and a huge fur elk hide laid like a comforter across the foot of it.

"Jesus, Partner, this is great! Can we just move in and live here with you?" Sammy said obviously impressed. He pointed to an inlaid stone hearth he'd never seen before. "And I can't believe you built that fireplace in here."

"Well, actually, my great grandfather apparently did that when he built the original part of this house. I stumbled on it when I was doin' the remodel." Partner said smiling. "I just uncovered it and dressed it back up a little."

"Wow, I'll bet that old fireplace could sure tell you a story or two, couldn't it?" Sammy said while he looked at Amanda and then at his grandfather.

"Yep. No doubt about it, son." Partner answered.

4

While the two young people took a few minutes to freshen up after their long drive, Partner sat by himself in the great room enjoying the moment. This was the day he'd looked forward to more that any Christmas when he was a child.

He heard their bedroom door open and looked up. When Amanda entered the room walking in front of Sammy, Partner stood. He gave a long authentic World War II wolf whistle and said, "You may not know how fast word gets around town here, but I'm liable to get awful popular when everybody finds out I went to supper with the prettiest girl in New Mexico."

Amanda balked for a moment at the compliment and then smiled. "Thank you." She said quietly.

"Amanda, I hope you'll be comfortable here." Partner smiled warmly and looked directly into the girl's eyes. "Wish Ellen was around. She always enjoyed seeing to house guests.

"It's a real shame she's not here to tell me about everything I haven't done right to make things ready for you. But, I do want you to feel at home and know that I'm so glad you're here. If there is anything at all you need or want while you're here, you let me know."

"That's very kind of you, Mr. Stevens. Thank you."

Partner turned to the small table next to his chair. He moved his Sunday cowboy hat out of the way and picked up a cream colored shawl. He spread it open.

"Here, try this on." He said and wrapped the soft material around Amanda's shoulders.

"This is so beautiful." Amanda said, grabbing the ends in each hand and looking down at the shawl as she crossed her arms.

"I'm glad you like it." Partner said smiling. "We'll be walkin' tonight and the desert can get a little cool in the evenings. Ellen always enjoyed that shawl this time of year, just to keep the chill off. She'd be proud for you to have it."

Amanda's eyes opened wide and she protested, "Oh no, Mr. Stevens, I can't accept this! I…"

"Too late," Partner interrupted, "it already fits you. Besides, that thing has been needin' another pretty girl to keep warm." As far as he was concerned that was the end of it, and he turned to walk to the door as Amanda looked up at her husband.

It felt good to walk outside in the cool winter air at twilight. There was the most wonderful smell, which Partner explained as the juniper and piñon wood burning in fireplaces in homes all over the valley.

"If you want to smell somethin' really good, Amanda, you'll have to come stay with me in late August and September. That's when our green chile comes in season and everywhere you go around here you smell roasting chile. It's one of my favorite times of the year."

Although she didn't say anything, Amanda had a strange feeling she was visiting a foreign country. The streets were narrow and somewhat uneven, almost like places she had visited in Europe. The houses were made of plastered mud with very few visible roofs. Everything here was so different from what she had grown up around back East.

They only walked a few minutes to the restaurant, but it gave Amanda a chance to ponder on the character she had recently inherited as a grandfather. She noticed that Partner didn't walk fast, but he walked strong and steady, which was impressive for a person his age. Most of the adults she had known either never made it to eighty-three, or were feeble by the time they got there.

Partner obviously wasn't feeble. She actually thought he was attractive, for an old fellow. He had almost a full head of silver gray hair and a big matching mustache that never seemed to have a hair out of place. Although he was a little stooped, he still stood almost six feet tall.

She had met him for the first time when he flew to Boston for their wedding. Partner had been quite a hit when he walked into the opulent rehearsal dinner in his tailored western cut suit, shiny boots, and big gray Stetson hat. Amanda had only known the old cowboy for a week and a half, but she was beginning to really like him.

The evening was beautiful as they walked and talked past the stuccoed adobe buildings that were crowded closely one next to the other. Some of them, like Partner's home, looked almost new with fresh coats of stucco, while others had obviously gone a long time since their better days.

Then, like a small clearing in the forest, they came upon the Mesilla Plaza. It wasn't big, but it was obviously the town's center-point. The rectangular Plaza was surrounded with narrow worn brick streets and, on three sides, with old western looking store fronts.

At the north end a weathered church made of pale yellow bricks stood like a tired old castle. It had a high pitched roof down the middle with two tall pointed tin roofed spires on either side. Although it wasn't a big church, it dominated the small plaza. Amanda thought of how the little plaza fit this place just as much as the quaint little town squares in her small New England towns matched their settings. She also noticed how uncrowded the streets were. They had only seen a few other people on their walk.

The three of them turned into a narrow courtyard that had white wrought iron tables and chairs on either side of a center walkway. Painted on the corner of the adobe building was a small sign which read "Double Eagle Restaurant". They walked past the empty tables toward the soft comforting sound of water trickling from a wall fountain which was made of blue and gold Mexican tile.

Partner opened a plain white wood framed glass door just to the right of the fountain. Amanda was so shocked by what she saw inside the building that her mouth flew open.

5

They entered a restaurant as lavish as any Amanda had ever been to in Boston. It was richly appointed with stained glass, tapestries and huge oil paintings. The entry area was filled with rich looking carpets and beautiful antique furniture sitting areas. Amanda simply couldn't believe this was the inside of the plain adobe mud building she had just walked into.

A well dressed lady looked up from an ornate antique breakfront and said, "Hello, Mr. Stevens, are these your special guests we've been looking forward to?"

Partner beamed, "They sure are, Lucy. This is my new granddaughter, Amanda, and her new husband, my grandson, Samuel."

Partner knew that was the name his grandson really went by. Partner and *Tia* were the only ones, except the boy's father and a few of the close old family friends, who ever called him Sammy.

"Kids, this is Lucy. She runs the place."

The nice looking woman smiled and said, "It is such a pleasure to meet you both. We've all been looking forward to your visit. Welcome to New Mexico and the Double Eagle. I hope you enjoy your stay here.

"I guess you know your grandfather exaggerates a bit sometimes. I'm just your hostess for the evening. But if you need anything while you're here, don't hesitate to let me know."

Partner winked at them all and said, "Like I said, Lucy runs the place here."

Sammy said, "Isn't this place beautiful, Amanda? Look at that bar."

To the left of the entry area was a long room that looked narrow because it had a massive carved wooden bar running down the entire length of one side. Behind the bar were two sharp looking college age men in crisp white shirts and black slacks. Behind the two bartenders were large mirrors, tall carved wooden columns with ornate connecting facia, and rows of fancy glasses and liquor. Amanda felt like the setting was straight out of an old picture book.

Partner waved at the two bartenders and said, "Howdy, boys."

They each replied, "Hey, Partner. Good to see you."

As Lucy announced their table was ready and started to show them out of the bar, Partner said loudly to his two guests, "Y'all watch out for those two scallywags behind the bar. They'll get you in trouble - and don't ask me how I know that."

They followed Lucy to a private room on the far side of the restaurant. It was a charming room with more antique furniture and paintings. Lucy seated them at the round oak table that stood in the middle of the room.

The small area felt warm and cozy. There was a fresh cut flower centerpiece on the table and perfectly laid place settings. The feeling reminded Amanda of dinners in Boston at her favorite grandmother's home.

Once they were alone in the room Partner turned to them and said, "This place suit you two O.K.?" After the two young people raved a bit, he went on, "Well, I's hopin' you'd like it. The owner's an old friend. He'll probably stop in to say hello or have a drink with us if he's here tonight. Do you remember this place, Sammy?"

"Of course I do, Partner. You and *Tia* brought me here a lot."

As Sammy finished his sentence Lucy entered the room carrying a tray of drinks. A waiter followed behind with a tray of food.

"My boss isn't here this evening." She announced. "But he asked that I start your evening with these drinks and special *hors d'oeuvres* whenever you arrived. He said to tell you that they are with his compliments and best wishes to welcome the new bride and his old Indian friend."

While Lucy served margaritas to the two young people and whiskey to Partner the old man turned to his grandson. "You remember when you were an Indian, son?"

Sammy, and Amanda, immediately knew the answer. Sammy had often told Amanda about his summer trips to New Mexico when he was a child.

Sammy's father, an Air Force pilot, was killed in a plane crash when Sammy was six years old. His wife moved to Philadelphia, where her family lived, and raised her son there. But, while Sammy was growing up, his mother always sent him to New Mexico every summer to spend time with *Tia* and Partner. Those times were some of Sammy's best childhood memories.

Before every visit *Tia* would call and ask Sammy what he wanted to be for the summer, then she and Partner would set the stage and plan the adventures for his trip. When he wanted to be an Indian, *Tia* made a fringed costume which she soaked in tea so it was stained to look like buckskin. Partner fashioned a headdress from wild turkey feathers and built a tee-pee in the backyard out of long poles and canvas tarps. Sammy got to be an Indian the whole trip, even when they went out.

The year he wanted to be King Arthur, Partner made a suit of armor out of left over junk and plumbing parts from his workshop. Together they created all sorts of wooden swords and lances while *Tia* fancied up one of Partner's old bathrobes and became Merlin the Magician.

Of course some of the most fun, and authentic, masquerades were the years when Sammy decided to be a cowboy. They had all the genuine trappings and real horses. One of those years Partner arranged for them to go on an actual round-up at a friend's ranch.

Unfortunately, like the real cowboys and Indians, King Arthur and Merlin, those days faded away. There came years, as Sammy grew, when the demands of adolescence kept him from coming to New Mexico at all. His last summer trip was between his junior and senior year in high school.

The highlight of that trip had been going into the Gila Wilderness Area with Partner and a couple of other men. The Gila was the first Wilderness Area established in the United States, and by law, the only way to access it is on foot or horseback. It wasn't very far away, so they had taken both horses and pack mules. They spent a week camping, fishing and exploring the wilderness. Sammy had fallen in love with that spectacular, rough country.

Now that Sammy was back in New Mexico with Partner, he realized he had let some very unimportant summer jobs and insignificant college events cause him to lose a wonderful part of his young life. He truly loved *Tia* and Partner. He felt ashamed that the last time he had been to the Mesilla Valley was for *Tia's* funeral.

"I'd love to be an Indian again, even for just a little while," Sammy said.

"I know what you mean, son." Partner answered smiling. "Wouldn't we all. You used to have some grand times here in the summer."

Then he looked at Amanda and said, "Has Sammy told you about the things his grandmother did when he came out for summer visits?"

Amanda said, "Oh, yes, I've heard many stories about his make-believe characters and how she spoiled him rotten. She must have been a wonderful woman.

"Of course, Samuel doesn't play make believe anymore." Amanda stopped and gave a warm grin to the old man. "But, he is *still* spoiled rotten."

"Hey!" Sammy protested as his grandfather laughed out loud.

Partner raised his glass and made the first, of his many, toasts that evening. "To my new granddaughter and our good fortune to have you as part of our family. I'm glad you're here, darlin'."

He turned to Sammy and said. "I think you got a keeper here, boy."

6

Just before dinner was served, the hostess stepped into the doorway to check on the guests. Partner looked up and said, "Lucy, how's Carlotta doin'? Anybody seen her around lately?"

He turned to his grandson and said, "You remember Carlotta?"

"Yeah, when you asked Amanda if she was afraid of ghosts. I don't really remember the story, but I remember the ghost."

Partner saw Amanda sitting back in her chair looking at the two of them with widening eyes. He looked back to the hostess and said, "Lucy, Amanda didn't know I's bringin' her to a haunted house for supper. I was just fixin' to tell her about Carlotta when you came in. How 'bout tellin' her the story."

Partner winked at Sammy as Lucy began her performance. With much dramatic flair, perfected from countless repetitions of the story, Lucy proceeded to tell Amanda about the ghost that haunted the restaurant.

"She has only been seen a few times in the middle of the night by employees working late, and it's always when they are alone. She does, however, let us know she's here by moving furniture around after everyone has left, turning over place settings when there is nobody here, and leaving unexplainable spills in the kitchen after everything has been cleaned.

"Look at those two chairs against the wall." Lucy said pointing to the matching antique chairs upholstered with burgundy colored velvet. "We had those chairs reupholstered eight months ago. They stay in this room and have never been used by customers or employees. The cushions on those seats are crushed, and the velvet is worn out just as it would be if someone sat there every night! Sometimes we come in and find those chairs moved around."

Amanda looked at the faded and obviously worn chair seats as Lucy continued, "At one time this part of the building was the residence of a very wealthy Mexican family. The matriarch was a mean, domineering women whose son fell in love with a servant girl - a *peon*.

"*Peons* were people, who could actually be of any nationality, bound to their Mexican masters to work because of some indebtedness. It was Mexico's version of indentured servitude.

"One day the mother walked into her son's room and found him in bed with the young maid. The woman flew into a rage and murdered the girl, Carlotta, in this very room!"

The storyteller could tell Amanda was spellbound, so she paused for effect. "We think our ghost is that poor murdered *peon* girl, Carlotta."

Lucy walked to the doorway and took a framed black and white photograph off the wall. She said, "Take a look at this," as he handed Sammy and Amanda the picture. "Partner knows these people. The man there was our Dean of Arts and Sciences at the University. Read the letter he sent with that picture."

Sammy held the frame between them as he and Amanda looked at the three by five inch photograph and read the letter that was matted with it. In the letter the man explained that this picture of he and his wife was taken at a dinner celebrating their wedding anniversary. He was attesting to the identity of the photographer, what camera was used, and the fact that there was nobody else in the room or any special film processing.

Amanda immediately recognized that the two people in the picture were sitting in exactly the same places, at the same table, in the same room as she and Sammy. Behind the man and his wife in the black and white picture was the ghostly silhouette of a woman standing between them. The back of Amanda's neck tingled and she involuntarily looked over her shoulder. Sammy looked, too.

"Strange feeling, isn't it?" Lucy asked smiling. "Don't be scared though. I think she's a nice ghost. As a matter of fact, I haven't lost a customer yet."

Sammy and Amanda had caught each other's eye as they turned back from looking over their shoulders. They both laughed and Partner said, "Hope y'all got a kick outa' that. It's the closest thing to a floor show we get around here!"

Lucy was pleased with the effect of her story, and like any good performer, decided to leave with the audience wanting more. "I must let you all get on with your dinner now, so you'll have plenty of time to visit.

"I understand you two aren't going to get to stay for very long on this trip. It's been so nice seeing you both and do come back real soon." With that she gave the small group a big smile, and then she left the room.

That began a most wonderful evening for the three of them in their little private room. They spent over two hours there with never a dull point in the conversation or the superb food and drink. It was turning into one of those special nights they would each remember for the rest of their lives.

7

Amanda talked for most of the early part of the evening. Partner made her feel comfortable and important by asking questions about her, her family, and her goals and dreams. He knew the story of how she and Sammy met and dated through college, but this was Partner's first opportunity to actually get to know Amanda.

She had some grit and a sense of humor, this pretty young girl from Boston, so Partner took a shine to her right away. At one point he also described her Boston accent as "a hoot".

As the evening progressed Partner satisfied himself that the two young people were truly a good fit for one another. He was generally a pretty sound judge of people and relationships, after eight decades of experiencing both.

The thing that pleased him most about what he saw between the two newlyweds was their friendship. Sammy and Amanda had dated, and then gone steady, for a long time. Through the course of it all they had apparently shared enough experiences and time together to become best friends. That made Partner happy.

Of course he could also see the lustful sparkle in their eyes, especially after they'd had a little wine. He was seasoned enough to know that one can lust with a lot of people, especially at their young age. But he also knew that when people share those kinds of feelings with their best friend, it becomes a special kind of love that makes magic. That is what he had with Ellen, and Partner could sense that magic between Amanda and Sammy.

"So tell me about this thing you're doing with the museums now." Sammy said as he reached for his wine glass. "I told Amanda you were a big wheel out here doing projects for the governor."

"It ain't that big a deal, Amanda," Partner said turning to her. "I'm just on the Governor's Advisory Committee for the Museums of New Mexico. I suppose they put me on there because they think I've been alive through most of the history of New Mexico. The Governor says I bring an interesting perspective to the committee."

Partner raised his eyebrows which wrinkled his forehead. He got a silly smirk on his face and said, "Besides, the Governor thinks I'm colorful.

"The way that really works is, I gave him a campaign contribution the last time he was runnin' for office. It's the same out here as it is in New York, Massachusetts or anywhere else. I guess puttin' me on his committee was him just sayin' thank you.

"I sure have enjoyed it though and I've learned a lot. My family has lived in what is now New Mexico for a long, long time, and I've always been real interested in our history. This museum job has given me a chance to meet some damn good historians and have access to an unbelievable amount of information. It's been kinda' fun."

"Samuel and I went to museums quite often when we were dating," Amanda said smiling. "I thought it was because they were inexpensive, and he was always out of money. I didn't realize it was something in his gene pool."

"Oh gee, that's very funny." Sammy replied sarcastically.

Partner chuckled and said, "Well, there are a lot a museums back there, and a lot a history.

"Pilgrims, Boston Tea Party, the American Revolution; everybody knows about those, and their history is a big deal back where y'all grew up. But most people don't realize even half the things that went on in this part of the country. Some of it's pretty amazing.

"For example, Amanda, I've got a meeting next week in Santa Fe at a museum called 'The Palace of the Governor's'. It was built and was the capitol of this whole part of the country *10 years before* the Pilgrims even landed at Plymouth Rock, in what is now Massachusetts.

"It is the oldest continuously occupied government building in the United States, and a year or two ago we got it designated as a 'National

Treasure' by the *politico's* in Washington. It's the only official National Treasure west of the Mississippi."

Partner grinned and winked at Amanda as he nodded toward Sammy. "Sammy didn't know I knew all this stuff. He probably thought I napped through all those committee meetings."

"I'm not sure I like the way you two are starting to gang up on me," Sammy said. Although he couldn't have been happier that two of the most important people in his life had finally met and were hitting it off so well. He always knew they would like each other.

Actually, seeing Amanda warm up to his grandfather, and watching Partner lay the 'ol Stevens' charm on his bride, confirmed to him that he had done the right thing bringing Amanda to New Mexico. It also made him feel like a jerk again for not introducing them sooner and for letting so much time disappear without being around Partner. Sammy wagged his index finger at them and said, "Just remember, I'm the one who brought you two together!"

They finished dinner with coffee and some very sinful desserts. As they left the restaurant, saying good-byes to all the staff along the way, Amanda said, "That was the best dinner I can remember. Thank you so much."

Partner put his Stetson on with one hand while he reached around Amanda with the other. He gave her a small one armed hug and said, "You're very welcome, darlin'. It was my pleasure. I can't tell you how glad I am that you're here - both of you."

With that he reached over and gave Sammy a hug, too, as he said, "I think we should stroll the Plaza. I could sure use a little walk and a cigar after that supper. Whatdayathink?"

The night air was crisp and clear as they went back outside onto the Plaza. The wonderful smell of the burning piñon and juniper was still coming from chimneys somewhere. There were only two other sets of people window shopping the stores and strolling the sidewalks as Partner stopped to light his cigar.

He held the medium sized stogie in his mouth with his left hand while he fished a wooden kitchen match out of his pocket. Partner jerked his thumbnail across the top of the match to light it. As he started making small white clouds of smoke and the match flared higher with each draw, he asked Amanda between puffs, "You feel like promenadin' the Plaza with an old man and his smelly cigar?"

"Actually, I love the smell of cigars. My father smokes them occasionally, over my mother's objections," Amanda replied.

They started walking around the Plaza and Partner said, "Yeah, I know, Ellen wasn't too keen on me smokin' these damn things either.

"Sure is nice out here tonight. Since I can't ride horses anymore this is usually how I take my exercise now, just walkin' around these old streets - talkin' to the ghosts."

Sammy stopped and pulled Amanda's hand, which stopped her. He stood up straight, cocked his head to one side, and with concern looked at his grandfather.

"When did you start talking to ghosts, Partner?" The boy said in a slightly patronizing voice.

8

"Now hold on a minute, son," Partner said, surprised at the question. He started laughing as he continued. "I don't really *talk* to ghosts. I may be old, but I'm not addle brained - yet. It's just a figure of speech."

He stopped laughing and settled into a normal conversational tone. "What I do is walk around this tired, forgotten little old town and think about all the things that have happened here. Sometimes I think about the changes this valley, and my family, have seen since the first ones of us came out here.

"There are times, in my mind's eye, when I can almost see the cowboys and Indians, the priests and the politicians, the gunfights, the bullfights, the floods and the droughts. And we've been a part of it all."

Amanda was touched by the emotion in Partner's voice. This was something he obviously cared deeply about and wanted to share with them. She took his arm just above the elbow, the way a lady grabs an escort, and said, "Thank you for letting us come visit. When I was a little girl I always wanted to see the Wild West. Now I think maybe I'm here."

"I'd say you're smack dab in the middle of it, dear," Partner said. He was glad she was interested. "See that building there? Billy the Kid was jailed there, and that one's where Pat Garrett brought Billy in for trial and he was sentenced to hang."

Amanda smiled at Samuel as she walked holding his grandfather's arm. She knew how much Samuel and Partner meant to one another, and she wanted them both to know she was interested in everything the old man was telling them.

Partner continued, talking slowly, as they kept walking. "That cantina on the corner there was once the depot for the Butterfield Stage.

The mules were kept back behind it. They used mules instead of horses 'cause they did better on poor food and little water.

"The Butterfield ran 3000 miles from Tipton, Missouri, where the railroad stopped, to San Francisco, California in 25 days. They traveled night and day and the high point of the journey, the biggest town they went through on the whole trip, was Mesilla, New Mexico. Of course Mesilla was a lot bigger then, and that was prior to the American Civil War.

"The entire time that the Butterfield Stage Line was operational they never once missed their 25 day schedule. Well, at least not until a shave-tail Army lieutenant put Cochise, the Apache Chief, on the warpath out here. That's what took the Butterfield Stage out of business."

"When I was little, Partner and *Tia* always made stories and books come to life for me." Sammy said. "Whenever I came here I always thought there were cowboys and Indians behind every mesquite tree. When I was 10, Partner and I decided the two of us were just born about a hundred and fifty years too late."

"I remember that." Partner said, obviously recalling the happy memory. "I'm not sure the old West could've handled a pair of 'Rounders' like us though.

"Amanda, stand right there," Partner said and took her hand off his arm. He positioned her and Sammy next to each other.

"You are standing in the exact spot where the Gadsden Purchase was consummated in 1854. My great grandfather, Samuel Austin Stevens, was probably standing right over there when it was signed. Do you remember what the Gadsden Purchase was?"

"I remember it from school." Amanda said feeling like a student caught in a pop quiz without studying. "But I honestly have no idea what it was."

"Well, the United States border was about 50 miles north of here. This used to be Mexico." Partner said squinting his eyes in thought. "A fellow named Jefferson Davis, who wound up being the President of the Confederacy, pushed to bring the railroad out west here. They found they couldn't get the railroad across the mountains up north and stay on United States land.

"So, the U.S. brought their best negotiator, a fellow named Gadsden, back from France to negotiate with Mexico. He negotiated with Santa Anna, a sorry son-of-a-bitch, who had just declared himself President of Mexico for life.

"Excuse my language, Amanda. But Santa Anna was about as sorry as the *politicos* ever come. He was a bad man...real bad.

"Anyway, the Union bought all the land south of the Gila River, from here to California, for ten million dollars. It was about 30,000 square miles. Pretty good deal and it was signed right where you're standin'."

"This is so fascinating! I can't imagine all those things going on here," Amanda said, honestly impressed. She thought of her first impression of the quiet little plaza she had walked into just before dinner.

"Amanda, you wouldn't believe the things this little old town, and this Mesilla Valley, have seen," Partner said wistfully. "If there really are ghosts, I'll betcha there are a lot of 'em walkin' around this old plaza."

His cigar had gone out and he fired up another wooden kitchen match. "I hope all these ghost stories aren't going to keep you up all night."

"No, sir," Amanda said. "After seven hours driving today, and those killer margaritas, I think I shall sleep just fine."

"Good." Partner said. "We're going to get an early start in the morning. I didn't want to keep you two out very late tonight."

"Hey, Partner, what do you mean 'early start'?" Sammy quibbled. "We're on our honeymoon. You know, that's kind of like a vacation." Since junior high Sammy hated getting up early, especially if there was even a remote chance of sleeping in. "I think we should sleep in and take it easy tomorrow."

"Not a chance, Bub," Partner replied. "I've only got you two for a couple of days, and I'm not going to waste it havin' you wallow around in the bed sleepin' the whole time. You can sleep when the honeymoon's over.

"We're goin' out in the desert tomorrow. I gotta' show you some things. Besides," he turned to the girl, "I'll bet you've never had a real cowboy breakfast, have you, Amanda?"

"But, Partner, how early are we talking about here?" Sammy kept going.

"Oh, a little before daylight," Partner said. "I wanna' catch the sunrise out there."

"Partner, you gotta' be shittin' me. That's too early." Sammy whined.

Partner lifted the brim of his cowboy hat and looked his grandson straight in the eyes while he said, "Sammy, I don't have much time with you. I need to take you out there in the mornin'. It's important that we do it. You'll just have to trust me on this one, son."

9

After his shower early the next morning Sammy went through the dark rooms into the brightly lit kitchen to find Partner while Amanda finished getting ready. Partner poured him a cup of coffee and asked, "Think you're going to make it there, Sleepy Head?"

Sammy blew gently across the top of the steaming mug while he nodded his head. "Oh, yeah. Once I'm up and going, I enjoy the early morning. It's the getting up and going part I don't like." Then he tentatively took a test sip of the coffee, which turned out to be hot and strong.

Sammy leaned against the kitchen counter and continued talking to Partner, punctuating each sentence with short sips from the big mug of hot coffee. "Sorry I had my head up my ass last night. I'm glad we're taking Amanda into the desert. She really likes it here and I want to show her all I can before we have to go."

After sleeping on Partner's words from the night before, Sammy was vexed with an uneasy feeling he didn't like. For the first time in his life he felt that his time with his grandfather was limited. There had been an urgency in Partner's voice last night when he said it was important that he take them into the desert. It seemed something beyond just the fact that this was to be a short visit.

Sammy had never contemplated his grandfather's mortality before, even after *Tia* passed away, yet he had thought about it in the shower this morning. Perhaps that's what caused this strange feeling. Whatever it was, Sammy didn't like it at all.

"Hey, Partner," Sammy said softly in the early morning quiet of the kitchen after there had been a short silence between them. He looked up from his coffee cup at the old cowboy and continued.

"A lot of people couldn't believe what you've done with this place... with *Tia's* dress shop...but, I can. This really is incredible. I'm very proud of what you've done here, and...I'm sure she is, too. Just thought you should know that."

Partner looked down into his own mug of coffee. Sammy couldn't see his grandfather's face for the brim of the old man's work Stetson that he'd put on for their morning in the desert.

From under the hat Sammy heard the words, "Glad you like it, son. That means a lot to me...really does."

Partner coughed and cleared his throat. He pulled in a quick snort through his nose as he raised his head up to the boy.

"But, let me tell you somethin', son," his grandfather said in a strong voice as he wiped his thumb across one nostril and came back and wiped his other with the back of that same hand's index finger. "You wouldn't believe the crap I went through with 'The Historic Preservation Society' to get this job done!

"Never mind the fact that this is our property. And has been for a hundred and fifty years! Those pompous bastards wanted to control everything!

"I tell ya' what," Partner leaned back against the counter and blew out a deep breath. He took a slug from his coffee mug.

The old man looked across the kitchen at his grandson. Partner's eyes twinkled, reflecting the kitchen's overhead light as he grinned slyly and said, "Havin' *them* tell *me* about 'historic preservation', was like havin' some pious young preacher lecture *Jack Daniel* about how to make *whiskey!*"

Sammy blew all over the floor the sip of coffee he'd just taken.

Partner quickly threw down a cup towel to mop up the coffee while Sammy finished choking. As he moved the rag around the floor under his cowboy boot, Partner said. "We better start getting' on the road if we're gonna' get that girl out there for the sunrise.

"I hope I got everything in those ice chests." He looked around and pointed. "That one's the dry box with all the food, and the other one's got plenty of water, cokes, and beer. I assume you still like beer."

"You got that right," Sammy replied, still sputtering.

"Well, I suppose if I forgot somethin', we'll just have to learn to live without it." Partner said smiling.

Sammy laughed. He knew Partner had enough in those two chests to provision the three of them for a week out in the wild. The old bull had probably been planning and making lists for the outing for at least a month.

"What else do we need to load?" Sammy asked.

"Just those two ice chests," Partner answered. "I've been packin' and repackin' that truck for a week. I think I've got everything else we need already in there."

Sammy lugged the first ice chest into the garage and smiled when he saw *Tia's* Cadillac sitting next to Partner's well used truck. He maneuvered around the vehicles and saw that the bed of Partner's big pickup was packed like a tight jigsaw puzzle. Partner opened the pickup's tailgate and Sammy said sarcastically, "Godomighty, Partner, think you have enough firewood?"

"Well, I didn't know what the weather'd be like and I don't want Amanda to get cold her first time out. Besides, the firewood's like the beer; you can always bring some back home, but it's a bitch to be way out in the desert and run out. We may wind up bein' out there for awhile, ya' never know."

After the truck was loaded and Amanda was outfitted with one of Ellen's big palm leaf straw cowboy hats, they pulled out sitting three abreast in the cab of the pickup. Amanda, in the middle, was excited and thought of being a little girl when her Dad took just her on a business trip and they left very early in the morning.

The air was cold, but the truck heater made them warm and cozy. There was a full moon still fairly high in the west, and Sammy commented that it was almost like daylight. The moon actually cast their vehicle's shadow as they drove out of the sleeping little village of Mesilla and turned onto University Avenue which bled them into the city of Las Cruces.

Within five minutes driving on the empty streets they were passing New Mexico State University. Partner pointed to the large buildings and said to Amanda, "I guess Sammy showed you the college when y'all drove in yesterday. It was founded in 1888. Our family has a long history with that place."

Then he continued, sounding somewhat like a tour guide, "It's the land grant college for New Mexico - the old A&M system. President Lincoln signed the law that established the land grant colleges in every state in the union - *'to provide for the education of the children of the industrious classes.'* This one's turned into a damn good school."

Amanda looked out of the truck cab's front and side windows at the large old trees and multistoried buildings throwing shadows on one another in the bright moonlight. "When Samuel showed this to me as we were driving in," she said, "I had no idea there was a major university here."

"Where are you taking us anyway, Partner?" Sammy asked as Amanda was leaning across him still trying to look at the University campus.

"Right up there," Partner said, and pointed straight ahead at the Organ Mountains rising in the distance.

They were headed nearly due east, straight at the mountains which topped out at eight thousand feet above sea level with towering irregular rock faces that almost glowed in the bright moonlight. Sammy immediately thought of the large framed photograph of the snow-covered Organ's that his grandparents had given him as a high school graduation present. The picture had hung in his bedroom, from dorm rooms to apartments, ever since.

Amanda leaned forward to look at the high peaks and her big cowboy hat got tangled with the rear view mirror.

"The Organ Mountains are the tail end of the Rocky Mountain chain." Partner said smiling as Amanda adjusted the big hat. "The early settlers of the Mesilla Valley thought the jagged rock peaks of the mountains looked like the up and down columns of a giant pipe organ. Guess over time, that name just stuck.

"Anyway, we're goin' to my favorite spot at the base of the Organs." Partner said. "*Tia* and I took you there lotsa' times when you were little, Sammy."

"I remember it," Sammy said. "Amanda, wait 'til you see it. The view is unbelievable!"

"Yeah, I don't know what's prettier up there, the sunrise or the sunset." The old man said smiling. "Guess I've been tryin' to figure that out for a lot a years now.

"Amanda, my brother and I found this spot we're goin' to when I was a teenager. We were on horseback huntin' mountain lions in the Organs with my Dad and some other men. We got a big lion right before dark, so we spent the night way back in one of those deep canyons.

"The next morning, early, my brother and I took our horses and went exploring. I liked this little spot we found because I knew it'd be easy to get to from town.

"When I was a dapper young sport I used to take the ladies riding up there, so we could do a little spoonin'." Partner said as he turned to them with a smirk and a wink. "Then after I got married and Sammy's dad came along, I carved a little ranch road in there with my truck so I could take him with me when he turned six. About thirty years ago the county made a real road out of that trail I cut in there.

"Now the damned thing's paved pretty close up to my spot! Hell, there's a bunch of houses out there now, just south of where we'll be. You're not goin' to believe it, Sammy."

They were still on University land passing "A" Mountain, a huge rocky hill with rounded tops that made it look like a giant turtle crouched all by itself in the flats of the East Mesa between the Mesilla Valley and the majestic Organ Mountains. It was called "A" mountain because of the 100 foot tall white letter, which stands for the New Mexico State University "Aggies", laid out in rocks on the side facing the University.

In the days before it was considered hazing, the freshman class was expected to have an outing every year on the mountain and whitewash the rocks with paint. Partner thought about that every time he passed the mountain. He always thought those freshman class outings were fun because he and some of the other businessmen in town, who always donated the whitewash, were usually invited to some of the festivities.

"When did they pave this road through the...," Sammy started to say as their truck sped around the last part of "A" Mountain. He interrupted himself with, "Jesus Christ! Are those all houses out there?"

"Yup," Partner said. "That's what I was tellin' you about. Once they paved this stretch through the University's land, those houses started poppin' up like ticks on a dog. In your lifetime, son, this whole East Mesa - everything you see from here to the mountains - will be solid houses."

"That's gonna' suck!" Sammy exclaimed. "I hate that!"

"It's called civilization, Sammy boy," Partner said smiling. "You can't stop it. It's been goin' on in this Valley for a long, long time."

10

In another five minutes they left the blacktop and took a wide, obviously well traveled, dirt road for perhaps a half mile. Then Partner maneuvered the pickup off that road and onto the shadow of a two track trail that led through the brush into the moonlit desert. They crowned a small ridge and stopped on its point. After they crawled from the cab of the truck and its light went off when they closed the door, the three of them stood line abreast in the quiet darkness of the East Mesa and looked down to the valley below.

The full moon in front of them was still well above the straight dark stripe on the horizon that separated the Mesilla Valley from the vast expanse of the West Mesa. The moon was bright enough to illuminate the rolling desert and its creosote, cactus and mesquites from their spot by the pickup all the way to the valley floor. The urban lights reflecting the years of civilization that had taken over the valley sparkled like tiny stars clustered in a miniature Milky Way that stretched along the Rio Grande River as far as they could see from the Robledo Mountains north to the Franklin Mountains south. Amanda broke their silence when she said softly, "This is unbelievable. It is so beautiful."

Sammy inhaled a very deep breath through his nose. He could pick out the pungent aroma of the creosote and the almost sweet smell of the mesquite trees. He could also separate the scent he knew came from the dry desert grasses.

When he had let all the air out slowly he said, "I love the smell of the desert. There's nothing like it anywhere else. I feel like I'm home now."

Amanda stuck her nose high into the light breeze and gave it a try. "Oh, it does smell good," she said. "What is that?"

"Everything out here," Sammy replied. "One of the things I remember most about *Tia* was smelling everything with her. She and

I would close our eyes and smell all her garden flowers. Whenever we came out like this, she always picked wild plants and flowers and taught me to love the way they smelled so different from anything else in the world.

"You should be in the desert after a rain, honey. You can't believe how great all this dry thorny stuff smells."

Partner turned and walked to the back of the pickup. As he opened the tailgate and started reaching for things to unload, he said to Sammy, "First, let's get a garbage bag and pick up the souvenirs all the civilized people have left at our spot. I don't want Amanda to have to see a mess up here once the sun comes up. You don't need a light do you?" Sammy could see everything, including the garbage and beer cans, very well in the bright moonlight. He started policing the area.

"What can I do, Mr. Stevens?" Amanda asked.

"Well, Amanda, I guess the first thing you can do is start calling me Partner." The old man said grinning. "Now that we're sharing my grandson, *and* my special spot out here in the desert, I think you and I are liable to become pretty good *compadres*. But for that to happen, you're gonna' have to make the transition and call me what all my other *compadres* do. O.K.?"

Amanda smiled at him. She had wanted to call him Partner before but wasn't exactly sure if it was appropriate. Once again the elderly fellow had put her at ease and made her feel comfortable and welcome.

"It's a deal, Pahtnah!" She said and suddenly realized it didn't sound the same with a Boston accent.

11

Partner had the newlyweds help him unload the truck and set up for the cowboy breakfast he had looked forward to for so long. They pitched the firewood into two stacks. The juniper was in one pile for the campfire. The other pile was the mesquite Partner had brought to make good hot coals for cooking.

They set up tables and big folding chairs. As Sammy reached for what looked like a small old wooden steamer chest, he asked Partner where he wanted it. "Just leave that, son. We don't need it right now."

Sammy unloaded the Dutch ovens and ice chests while Partner started the fire for Amanda. With one wooden kitchen match, and a half pint of gasoline, Partner created a roaring fire instantaneously.

"Wow!" Amanda squealed when the gasoline burst into huge flames.

As the initial flash subsided and the big logs started to burn and crackle, Partner said, "We'll have a 'white man' fire up here this mornin', Amanda."

When she looked back at him uncertain just what he meant Partner continued, "An Indian always builds a small fire, gets close to it and stays warm. A white man always makes a big fire he can't get next to, then burns his front and freezes his butt."

Amanda laughed. "Well, I don't know about the Indian fires, but this one feels great." She had gotten cold standing in the light predawn breeze. She opened the palms of her hands to the fire and moved closer to the blaze.

She watched Partner and Sammy scoot around their little campsite. The two of them were moving around one another and passing things back and forth like a couple of big hairy ballerinas in a well orchestrated main stage production. It was obvious that they were not only having a ball being back together again, but she could also see that they were showing off for her.

Throughout Amanda's time together with Samuel, he had always gotten a far off look in his eyes and a heartfelt tone in his voice whenever he told her the many tales about his outings with his grandfather, especially the ones about their pack trip into the Gila Wilderness. Amanda understood how important it was for her husband to share this experience with her.

Within no time Partner had a giant dark metal coffee pot, straight out of the cowboy movies she had seen, sitting on a heavy steel grate above the campfire, and her husband was serving her a glass of orange juice. "Well, this is the kind of service I like." Amanda said loudly. "Now that I know you can do this, Samuel, I shall expect my coffee and juice in bed every morning promptly at seven."

"Hey, girl, don't push it," Sammy retorted sipping his own cup of juice "Or I'll leave you up here with the coyotes and mountain lions."

"Now, Amanda, there're two very important rules you need to know about when you're out here in the desert." Partner said in a serious voice. "The first one is:...", and he turned to Sammy to finish the sentence for him.

"You can do anything out here you're big enough to do!" Sammy said, proud of himself that he had responded by instinct. As a small boy, Sammy had felt grown up because of that rule his grandfather made.

Whenever Sammy wanted to do something new or different on his boyhood trips into the wild, Partner had always repeated that first rule. It had given the boy confidence and Sammy never knew that his grandfather watched him like a mother hen. Every time they went out when Sammy was young, Partner made him wear a big whistle around his neck. Sammy knew that if he got lost or in trouble, a blast on the big whistle would bring Partner - and the cavalry.

"The second rule is," Partner said, again in a serious tone. "The men's restroom is on this side of the road and the lady's room is on that side of the road."

He showed his big smile and inside Amanda was relieved. The one thing she had been worried about was having to go to the bathroom out there, especially with the two men around. She didn't like the prospect of doing it at all.

"Amanda, this is 'Little Joe'." Partner said and pulled what looked like a folding camp stool from the back of the pickup. He unfolded the legs and Amanda saw that the part one was to sit on was actually a small toilet seat.

"Ellen always said 'Little Joe' was one of her best friends out here in the desert. I'll put him over here on the other side of the truck with the toilet paper if you need to make his acquaintance. Is that O.K.?"

"Perfect!" Amanda said. Now she could enjoy the trip.

The coffee started to boil and gave forth a wonderful smell into the chilly clean air. Amanda sat in a chair while Sammy organized food on one of the tables. Partner laid out large cast iron cooking devices next to the fire pit. The brightness of the campfire had taken away their ability to see well by moonlight, but as she sat there Amanda realized she could see things outside the campfire's light more clearly.

Then Partner said. "Here she comes!"

The dawn started with brilliant rays of light blasting between the jagged peaks of the Organ Mountains and streaming across the sky above them. The rays reached out in front of them and made a band of light running north to south that illuminated the far off West Mesa.

Partner poured them all coffee. They watched while the line of light moved off the West Mesa and down into the Valley. It kept coming toward them.

As the darker side of the tier of light kept retreating across the valley floor, Amanda suddenly saw the Organ Mountains in its shape and realized the irregular line was caused by the shadow of the mountains as the sun rose behind them. The early morning sun generated colors she had never seen before, both in the sky and on the ground. While Amanda sat there truly in awe of the wonderful sight, Partner said, "That's the way she wakes the Valley up every mornin'."

12

"It'll take a minute to get some coals to cook with." Partner said and pitched another mesquite log onto the fire. "Think you two'll be able to choke down some breakfast this mornin?"

"I could eat the tires off your truck I'm so hungry," Sammy responded quickly. "Honey, you are in for the breakfast of your life. Partner is the best cook you ever saw!"

"Hey, Bub, don't count your cookies," Partner said, then turned to Amanda.

"I'm not that good a cook. But I've found that if you bring people way out in the desert and make 'em starve for a while, then you can feed 'em sticks or rocks or anything, and they'll swear it's delicious!

"How do you like your biscuits anyway, Amanda?" The old cowboy continued as he poked the fire with the shovel. "Sammy and I enjoy ours kinda' burned on the bottom and raw in the middle. Is that the way you like yours?"

"I'm not sure I've ever tried them that way, Partner." Amanda answered with a half laugh in her voice. "But with a side order of sticks and rocks, I know they will be delicious!"

With that Partner started his part of the morning's entertainment. Amanda sipped another cup of orange juice and watched what soon looked to her like an artist working in his studio. Partner moved skillfully around the big fire as he prepared two large, heavy black cast iron Dutch ovens. Amanda had heard of them before, but had never seen one, and certainly had no idea how they worked.

Next he put hot coals under what looked like a huge steel wok with legs on the bottom. She was told that the device was actually the disc from a farm plow that Partner had welded for just this purpose.

Soon Partner turned from working at one of the tables and held a pie in his hands. "I don't cook much anymore," Partner said to Amanda "And pies aren't usually on the breakfast menu. But, since I like pies and they're *my* Dutch ovens, we're havin' apple pie for dessert!" Then he gently placed the pie into one of the Dutch ovens.

Partner grabbed a long steel rod with a hook on one end and an elk horn handle on the other. He deftly hooked the Dutch oven's lid off the rocks by the firepit, slid it into place above the pie, then used the hook to grab the bucket style bale and lifted the whole device onto some mesquite coals he had shoveled out on the ground.

Next Partner picked up the shovel and scooped more coals from the fire and spread them just so across the top of the oven's lid. He realized Amanda was watching his every move, so Partner looked up and said, "Guess they don't cook much with shovels back in Boston, huh?"

"This is so fascinating," Amanda said smiling. "Thank you for doing this for us. I feel like I should be doing something." She wanted him to know she was willing to help.

Partner stood up, propped the shovel against a nearby creosote bush and said, "Are you enjoyin' the mornin', dear?" When Amanda nodded her head he continued. "Then you're doin' exactly what I want you to do. Now we'll let that pie get a little head start on things, and I'll have a shot of that orange juice Sammy's been hoggin'."

Partner pulled one of the big comfortable chairs next to Amanda's by the fire and looked up at Sammy for service. He was obviously in no rush. Partner had dreamed of this day for too long.

The three of them sat around the old fire pit and talked, while they watched the colors of everything all around them change by the minute as the sun kept trying to peak over the tops of the Organs. The far away mountains and hills to the west were well lit by then and Sammy said, "From up here I always feel like I can see forever. Back East you never see the sky like this."

Then he looked across to his grandfather's smiling eyes and continued, "I remember when I was little, and even when we were in school, there were times when the cities, and the people, and everything, would crowd in on me. *This* is where I would come in my mind. I'd come up here and smell the desert.

"Then I'd look up to the tops of these mountains, and I'd turn away to the horizon and see how far I could see. I'd try to picture every hill and remember all the stories you told about them.

"I guess having this place by the mountains, in my head as a sanctuary to escape, got me through a lot of bullshit over the years, Partner. You probably never knew that."

Partner rose to start the biscuits in the second Dutch oven and Sammy continued, "You know what I mean, Partner. It's a lot easier to deal with things - the world and all the petty stuff - after you get out in a place like this for a while. It's just hard to explain to people who have never done it or been out in big country like this."

"Yup, know exactly what you mean, son," Partner replied as he carefully placed the round pucks of dough gently onto the oven's blackened cast iron bottom. "That's pretty much the way I've always felt about this country. 'Course, your grandmother maintained that I's about half nuts.

"And now you'd better be careful. The way you're talkin', Amanda's liable to realize that you're about half nuts, too."

"Samuel's talked about New Mexico, and you, like this for so long." Amanda said. "It was just a little hard for me to understand.

"Now I can see why he feels this way. Being out here is so refreshing and different. But everything is so big, I don't know if it makes me feel important, or completely insignificant."

"I think we got a new convert, Sammy," Partner said shoveling the coals onto the lid over the biscuits. Then he turned to Amanda and said, "I'm glad you like it here, Amanda. I sure hoped you would." The old man kept working as he talked. He got the bacon and sausage from the dry box.

"I wanted to bring you two up here so you could see this whole valley and the country around it," Partner said stooped over the cooking disc. When the bacon and sausage were placed there they immediately started to sizzle and pop.

"Tend to these for a minute, Sammy," He said handing the young man a long handled spatula that had been laying on the fire ring of rocks.

"There's a lot of this country's past that makes more sense, too, when you can look at it from up here. You remember any of the landmarks, Sammy?"

"Yes, but I'd be embarrassed to try to tell Amanda about them with you around," Sammy replied honestly. It had been far too long since his last trip to the old man's spot. "Partner, go ahead and tell her about Pancho Villa."

13

"Amanda, see those three peaks close together on the horizon?" Partner pointed to the southwest. "Those are the *Tres Hermanas*, the Three Sister Mountains. They're about sixty or seventy miles away as the crow flies, so the visibility is only about a hundred miles today."

He winked at her. "The smog's pretty thick."

He looked back to the distant peaks and continued, "Just this side of 'em to the south is Columbus, New Mexico, where Pancho Villa made his famous raid. It's the only time the army of a foreign nation has attacked the continental U.S."

"I didn't know that about Pancho Villa." Amanda said. "And those mountains look so close."

"Yeah, they're not that far." Partner said and pointed to another hill down in the valley. "This big pointed hill across the valley is called Picacho Peak. In Spanish *Picacho* means 'peak', so I guess it's really Peak Peak."

Amanda gave a small giggle and Partner went on, "At the base of it on the far side was a way station for the Butterfield Stage. The stage raced from where we were in Mesilla last night to Picacho Peak for a change of mules, and then up a steep canyon you can't see from here to the top of the West Mesa. The climb up the canyon was so rough that most of the passengers got out and walked to the top. From there they went on to Massacre Gap back near those hills over there."

Sammy was watching Amanda soak up the old man's every word and he said, "How would you like to be in Apache country knowing that you were taking a stage coach through a place called Massacre Gap?"

"No." Amanda said quickly "Thank you very much!"

"There was a period in this valley when Indian raids were very common, and devastating." Partner said sighing.

The old fellow looked at his grandson. "How's your pig doin' over there?"

He had Sammy move the meat to the outer edges of the cooking disk and got the eggs from the dry box. Partner had cracked the eggs into a Tupperware bowl and mixed them with chopped green chile before he woke his two houseguests that morning.

Partner then took over the spatula and the cooking chores from Sammy. He added the eggs to the hot cooking surface as he continued to talk to Amanda.

"That pass you can barely see over there is where Pat Garrett, the man who shot Billy the Kid, was shot and killed. That happened nine years before I was born.

"Mr. Garrett had stopped his buckboard and got out to go to the bathroom. He was standin' there with his right glove off doin' his business when the fella with him shot him in the back.

"My Dad knew Pat Garrett and always said he was a mean son-of-a-bitch; not very well liked. I guess that was true, because the man who shot Pat pleaded self defense - and got off!"

"That's amazing!" Amanda said astonished at both the story and the fact that Partner's father knew Pat Garrett. "Your father knew Pat Garrett?"

"Oh sure," Partner replied as he motioned for Sammy to bring the plates to him. "He knew Pancho Villa, too. Pancho used to spend a lot of time in Mesilla buying arms for the revolution.

"You two hold your plates here and I'll serve your breakfast."

Partner dished up a large serving of everything onto each of the three plates. The young people bragged about how good it looked and smelled as they took their seats at the folding camp table. After they were seated, Partner hooked the bale on the Dutch oven that held the biscuits and carried it to the table.

He sat it down on the ground and carefully lifted the lid. Steam rose then cleared away. Amanda looked inside to see ten big, perfectly baked, golden brown biscuits. "Oh, my God," was all she could say.

"Hope these are fit to eat," Partner said and used his fingers to put a biscuit onto each plate. "You two get started, and I'll see how bad

I've burned the pie." Then he took the apple pie out of the remaining oven and placed it gently on the other table to cool.

When Partner sat at the table to join them Sammy said, "Thank you, Partner. This is super. It's the only thing I can think of worth getting up for at such an ungodly hour!" He turned to his wife and said, "How do you like your cowboy breakfast, dear?"

Through a mouthful of biscuit with honey Amanda mumbled, "Wonderful!" and gave a thumbs up sign as she swallowed. "This is the best breakfast I've ever had in my life! These eggs are delicious."

"Remember what I told you about the sticks and rocks?" Partner said with his head down and his eyes looking out from under the brim of his hat. "It works every time."

14

It was easy to eat too much of the biscuits and eggs, so none of them felt like dessert right away. While Amanda and Partner threw away the paper plates and cleaned the table, Partner had Sammy unload the small steamer chest and put it near the fire pit. Sammy was curious about what was inside but did not ask.

"Would you like some more coffee, Partner?" Amanda asked after the old fellow had pulled his chair to the fire by the chest and sat down.

"I'd love some, darlin'," He replied in earnest. "With a little sweet'ner in it this time, please."

"I don't see any sweetener over here," Amanda said as she looked around the two tables. "Where is it?"

Sammy answered her smiling, "There's a bottle of whisky in that cardboard box. That's the only kind of "sweetener" *real cowboys* use in their coffee. Actually, I think I'll have some of *sweet'ner* myself."

Amanda served the two men their coffee and sweet'ner then settled into her chair beside them.

"I still can't believe your father actually knew those men," Amanda said to Partner wanting to restart the conversation about Pancho Villa and Pat Garrett. "I mean, those guys were in books. We read about them in school, and he really met them."

"Well, that's actually one of the reasons I brought you two up here today," Partner replied very seriously. He looked at Sammy and Amanda and thought about how young they looked. So far everything on their visit had gone exactly as he had planned.

"There are many things I need to tell you," the old man said slowly. "And I think this is an appropriate place to do it."

Sammy and Amanda looked at each other wondering what was about to happen. Amanda reached for Sammy's hand, and they both sat and watched the old gentleman as he talked.

"You know my brother and I were the fourth generation of our family to live in the Mesilla Valley." Partner said looking off into the distance. "'Course, World War II took him a long time ago. He was a good guy; you'd have liked him.

"Then your dad was the fifth generation. You know, I think one of the hardest things I ever did in my life was put him on that plane in El Paso to go off to Viet Nam. When he made it through that mess then got killed in a plane crash here in the States, it nearly killed my soul."

Partner had practiced how he would start this conversation many times. Now he realized he was already into it, and fumbling, but he kept going.

"My son was my best friend, the best son a dad ever had." Partner stopped monetarily as tears filled his eyes and his lips squeezed tightly together. He wiped his right eye with the back of his hand then continued, "He and I always knew he would eventually settle back here."

"It's O.K., Partner," Sammy said in a soft, kind voice. "Is something wrong?"

Partner took a deep breath, to steady himself, and blew it out through his mouth. "Nope, nothin's wrong." He said then turned to look at them both and smiled. "Actually, life is just movin' along, the way it's supposed to. Thing is, life doesn't always move along the way we figure it's goin' to.

"You and I are the last ones in our family, Sammy boy." Partner picked up the coffee cup he'd sat on the top of the old chest and took a sip.

"Problem is, I'm eighty-three years old. Hell, I pro'bly ain't got but another twenty good years left in me."

Both the young people smiled as he continued, "But if I get run over by a beer truck tomorrow, it all dies with me. That's why I gotta' pass some things on to you, son."

"What do you mean, Partner?" Sammy said leaning forward in his chair.

"All the things our family has done, and seen, and built will be important to you someday. You and Amanda are starting your new life together, and you have to go live that life wherever it takes you. That's the way it's supposed to be.

"I realize that life probably isn't going to be around here, and that's O.K. - it really is. But the lives our people lived before us, and the things they did in those lives, cannot disappear. They cannot be forgotten."

Partner reached for the old wooden steamer chest and lifted its lid. The strong box held, at the top, several leather covered paper binders. Beneath the binders were rows of what looked like office files. They were interspersed with small plastic containers and rolled up cylinders of paper.

"This box holds the history of our family," he said. "It's everything I've been able to locate, from stories and letters to birth certificates and land deeds.

"Ellen got me started on this before she passed away. Each of these binders has the story and pertinent papers of a different generation. This will be important to you, and your children, and theirs…someday.

"Now you two get comfortable, and Amanda, why don't you slide that sweet'ner a little closer over here." Partner said as he pulled a heavy leather binder out of the chest and leaned back in his chair.

"I need to tell you both how this whole thing got started…"

PART
TWO

15

December 25, 1835

Jonathan awoke in the darkness. Christmas morning did not yet have even its first faint hint of light in the east. He tried to roll over and go back to sleep, but knew he couldn't. He was ready for it to be Christmas.

He laid there for awhile thinking about all the Christmas mornings the years had brought him with Sarah and the children. Jonathan smiled as he thought about how, when the kids were little, they always woke him very early by crawling into his bed with, "Is it Christmas yet?"

Then, as they grew, the early morning greeting became, "It's Christmas! You and Momma have to get up!" Over time there evolved a Christmas morning rule in their house that no child could get out of bed until the parents said they could, which was always after Sarah had made his coffee and Jonathan had set out the gifts. Now that his children weren't children anymore, Jonathan was always the one up early waiting for the sleepy young adults to stir.

He wondered what time it was and reached for the pocket watch he kept on the little table next to his side of the bed. As he held its face toward the fireplace glow, he strained to read what the little hands and numbers were telling him. They were just too fuzzy for him to read. His eyes weren't as good as they used to be, and he hated that.

Not long ago he could have read the small dial clear across the room by moonlight, but now he had to really squint to make out details. He supposed that meant he was growing old, and he damn sure didn't want to lay in bed and think about that. As he started to get up, Sarah rolled over and reached for him. He rubbed her shoulder and said, "Go back to sleep, honey. I'm just goin' to stir the fire."

Jonathan did stir the fire and put on another log. Then he quietly stoked the stove and started the coffee he had made ready before they went to bed. This would be a grand day, he thought to himself. He and Sam had gone out yesterday morning, and he let the boy shoot a yearling whitetail deer for their Christmas feast. It was hanging in the smoke house. As the coffee began to boil, Jonathan almost started to cut one of the cakes Sarah and Mary Beth had baked, but he didn't. Although he loved their baked goods more than anything, and they had baked enough to feed half the colony, there was no way he was going to start Christmas in trouble with both of his girls.

Instead, he grabbed a cold biscuit from the plate sitting on the table beside the cakes and pies. He then poured himself a cup of coffee and went to his big rocking chair in front of the warm rock fireplace. While Jonathan sat there watching the fire and waiting for the morning, he pulled his old watch from his nightshirt pocket. When he held it at arms length in front of the bright fire, he saw the time was twenty minutes past four. The old time piece was the only clock in their house. Jonathan always kept it on the table at his bedside and wound the stem every night when he went to bed. The only time it ever left the cabin now was in Jonathan's vest pocket on Sunday's when they went to church.

Jonathan sat there for a long time rubbing his rough, callused thumb across the smooth worn surfaces of the cherished old pocket watch. As he stared into the dancing flames all alone in the stillness of the Christmas predawn, Jonathan began to see back in time. He saw Moses Austin, the wonderful old gentleman who had given him the watch. He also saw the fire reflect back to him the circumstances that had brought him to this remarkable wilderness with his little family.

Jonathan was eighteen years old in 1809 when he went to work at the Potosi lead mines in Spanish Upper Louisiana in an area that had eventually been named Missouri. The owner of the mine, a robust man named Moses Austin, took notice that Jonathan was a hard worker. When he found out Jonathan could read and cipher numbers, he made him a foreman over men twice his age. Soon Jonathan was a vital part of the mine's operation.

Jonathan got along well with the experienced miners and smelterers the owner had brought over from England to improve the efficiency of the business. Over the years they all worked hard, played hard, and built the best lead mining enterprise in the country. During that time Jonathan had also built a very special relationship with Moses Austin.

The old man was like a generous father to him. He paid Jonathan well and every time Jonathan took on more responsibilities, he rewarded him more. Moses had a nice home built, not far from his own, for Jonathan when he and Sarah married. Moses' wife, Maria, helped Sarah through the delivery of all their children. After Luke was born, Moses had Maria send one of their slaves twice a week to help Sarah with the house chores.

But above all that, in Jonathan's mind and heart, Moses Austin had given the young man his friendship and respect. The two of them regularly talked for hours about everything from lead prices to politics and life with a good woman to life in the here after. Jonathan truly loved the flamboyant old coot who mentored him through the transition from boyhood to manhood.

However, because of Aaron Burr's conspiracy, the War of 1812 and the depression that followed, lead sales were lost. Things started to turn down. Moses' son, Stephen Fuller Austin, who was a couple of years younger than Jonathan, returned from school back east and started working in the business.

Even though Stephen was the well educated son of a wealthy influential man, he never acted like it. He had inherited enough of the old man's work ethic and heart to make him and Jonathan not only a good work team, but also friends. By about 1816 Moses had placed his son in control of the mining business, but because Stephen was also involved in politics and had become a member of the territorial legislature, Jonathan was the one actually running the operation.

In the midst of those difficult times, Moses and some other men founded a bank in an effort to increase the money supply in circulation, a concept Jonathan didn't totally understand. The Bank of St. Louis was the first bank west of the Mississippi, and it devoured most of the old man's time and attention. When the bank failed in 1819, it devoured most of his assets as well.

Moses had sold his fine home and moved to Herculaneum, a town he started in 1808 as a shipping point for their lead. Jonathan stayed in Potosi with the mine trying to keep it going, but the creditors eventually took it, and Jonathan was out of work. While Moses tried everything conventional to work his way out of debt, Jonathan struggled to provide for his young family. The two stayed in contact, but both their lives were bleak.

For a time Jonathan took a job delivering freight by wagon team. He used it as an opportunity to see his old friend more often, and Moses used those times as an opportunity to have the young man as a sounding board for his business ideas.

On one of those trips around the Christmas of 1819, Moses lit up like a bright chandelier in a great ballroom when he told Jonathan of a plan he had developed to make money by settling an American colony in Spanish Texas. He walked around the room, waving his arms in commanding gestures, as he described the possibilities of the venture in the enthusiastic voice Jonathan hadn't heard for a long time. Jonathan remembered thinking his old friend was the sort of man who would always sound the charge, when most were looking for a foxhole.

They both struggled through the winter and, that spring in March, Moses Austin declared bankruptcy. His son, Stephen, left for Arkansas to explore business opportunities for the family there. Jonathan was forced to move his family out of their comfortable home into a plank board shanty while he desperately worked at any job he could find trying to make a living.

Early in May, Moses came to see Jonathan and Sarah. He explained that he was going to San Antonio de Bexar in the Spanish Territory of Texas to pursue his colonization idea. He tried to persuade Jonathan to join him on the journey because he said he needed an honest man with backbone and spirit to accompany him on the adventure. They both knew Jonathan couldn't leave his wife and babies, but Jonathan needed the confidence of the offer, and Moses needed Jonathan to know he wanted the young man involved in the enterprise.

Jonathan always had faith in the dear old man, but in his heart he didn't know if this time the master wasn't just chasing smoke in a hailstorm. Even so, were it not for Sarah and the babies, Jonathan would have joined the quest and traveled to Texas, or Hell, with his mentor. But in those hard times Jonathan's responsibility was to stay and provide for his family, and Moses certainly understood and respected his position. Moses disappeared from their lives for almost a year.

In late April of 1821, Moses sent for Jonathan and Sarah. Jonathan borrowed a wagon and took his young family to Herculaneum. Maria came running out to meet them as he pulled the wagon up to the front of the Austin's modest home.

"Thank God you came!" Maria said wringing her hands in her long apron, "Oh, thank God you came! Moses is in a real bad way, Jonathan."

Jonathan jerked the wagon's brake handle into position, wrapped two loops of the team's leads around it, and jumped out of the wagon all in one quick smooth motion. As soon as he hit the ground he put his arms around Maria, and she started to cry into his broad chest. "Oh, Jonathan, he's getting worse." She sobbed, "You've got to help me with Moses. We can't lose him! He will listen to you. I know he will."

Jonathan held the woman and patted her back gently, letting her cry. He looked up to Sarah who was still sitting in the wagon holding their infant, Sam. "What happened, Maria?" Jonathan asked softly. "Tell me what's going on. Sarah and I are here now and we'll help you. Everything is going to be all right. What's happened to Moses?"

Maria tried to compose herself. She had always been a strong capable woman, able to deal with any situation no matter how demanding, but now she was unable to stop crying. She stepped back from Jonathan and took several deep breaths to steady herself while she looked away from the two young people. When she turned back and looked into their faces, her chin crumpled up and she started crying again.

She had held back her tears, trying to be a strong refuge for Moses, since the day he returned from his long Texas journey so ill he could barely stand. Maria had also stayed up day and night nursing her husband, catching only occasional cat naps in the big chair she had moved next to his bed. Her body, and her spirit, were depleted. Now that Jonathan and Sarah were there her body knew it could rest and her spirit knew it could cry. As she wept, Jonathan reached for her and held her in his strong arms once more.

Between her sobs, Maria began explaining the situation. She told them that Moses had been gone for ten months on his quest to obtain a grant from the Spanish government to start his colony of Americans in the Texas wilderness. It had been too long and difficult a journey for her sixty year old husband. On his way out of Texas, Moses had contracted pneumonia from exposure during four weeks of wet and cold weather. The last week of the ordeal Moses had survived by eating roots and berries.

Moses' will and determination were the only things that took the old man back to his Maria. He was so weak and fevered when he got to their home, he collapsed on the front porch.

Initially, with rest and Maria's nursing, Moses had gotten better. However, just as Moses was beginning to show signs of recovery, he received word that the Spanish government had approved his grant for the colony.

Moses then completely disregarded his health and devoted all his energies to what he called the "Texas Venture". His body had become so debilitated that Moses lost ground rapidly to the pneumonia. By then he had already sent for Jonathan.

Maria lifted her face and looked into Jonathan's eyes. Jonathan felt an awful pang deep inside his chest when he saw how frail and hollow her look was. "Go to Moses, Jonathan," she said. "He's been so anxious for you to come. It will give him peace to know you're here." Then she turned, smiled dimly at Sarah and the children and continued, "I'll help Sarah with our little ones."

Jonathan walked into the darkened room and saw the man who had been such a strong Father to him lying weak and pale in sweaty sheets. The bubbling sound that came from deep within Moses' chest, as he labored hard for each breath, made Jonathan bite his jaws down tight enough to almost break his back teeth as he desperately tried to hold back his tears. There was a dank odor in the still room and Jonathan sensed he was smelling death.

Moses opened his eyes and turned his head to look at Jonathan, then smiled. The old man's big smile that normally lit up whole rooms, was now just a warm glow. "I'm glad you're here, son." Moses said in an unsteady but peaceful voice as he started to raise himself on his pillows. "We've got a lot of work to do. We're goin' to Texas!"

The sound of his friend's voice made it even harder for Jonathan to push the tears back again. "That's what I hear." Jonathan said trying his best to sound normal. "But don't you think I oughta' get you out of those bedclothes first?"

Moses started to laugh. Then suddenly he went into a massive fit of coughing. He coughed uncontrollably long and hard and deep. Moses could barely catch his breath between the spasms, and Jonathan bolted to the bedside. Moses motioned with a weak hand for Jonathan to stay away as he clasp a large handkerchief over his mouth. Jonathan's stomach almost turned when he saw the huge globs of phlegm Moses expelled into the handkerchief.

When the coughing finally stopped, Moses laid back on the pillows exhausted. He motioned with a shaky hand toward the water pitcher on the night table. Jonathan poured a glass half full and helped Moses take a few sips. Moses then settled back onto the pillow and rested.

After awhile Moses looked up and said, "Thanks for coming, Jonathan. I haven't been doing too well." Then he smiled weakly and continued, "Guess you pro'bly noticed that."

Jonathan pulled a chair to the bedside and put his hand on the old gentleman's arm just below the elbow as he said quietly, "Well, I do remember you bein' a little taller than this, but you're gonna be just fine. Sarah and I are both here now, and we're all going to get you back on your feet. You need some more water?"

When Moses shook his head and said, "No," Jonathan continued. "Maria said you've been pushing it awful hard. You gotta take care of yourself, Moses. I'm here now and you know I'll handle anything you need done. But you've got to rest up and get yourself well. That's your most important job now."

Moses smiled peacefully and nodded his head. Then he closed his eyes.

"Glad we got that settled", Jonathan said as he rose and started to leave the room. "You sleep now, and I'll bring Sarah in to see you after while."

Moses turned his head on the pillow and said, "Thanks for coming, son. I'm glad you're here. We've got a lotta work to do." Then he went to sleep.

Over the next three days Moses' spirits were lifted by Jonathan's presence, but his physical condition continued to deteriorate. The coughing spells became more violent and frequent, sapping more of the tired old man's strength each time. But despite his weakening state, Moses' eyes lit up and his heart emitted energy each time he told Jonathan about the wonders and opportunity he had found in Texas.

After sunset on the third day, Maria came to Jonathan and said, "Moses is asking for you, Jonathan."

When Jonathan entered the room Moses' trembling hand motioned him to the bedside. Jonathan pulled a chair close and sat next to the bed. As Moses spoke softly, desperately working for each breath between phrases, Jonathan leaned forward to hear.

"Jonathan, I think I've about used up this old body." Moses said with a hint of a smile on his face. "I'll be leaving it behind pretty soon."

The side of Jonathan's face protruded slightly as his jaw muscles tightened again trying to fight back his tears. Then his chin wrinkled up and tears burned his eyes as he realized the old man had called him in to say good-bye.

Moses' words were slow and calm. "Son, I'm not goin' to see my Texas Venture through, but it's the best thing I've ever done in my life. I've talked to Stephen about it, and I want you and Maria to ask him to pursue it for me. Will you do that?"

"Of course, Moses," was all Jonathan could get out in a squeaky voice as his throat burned from holding back his body's need to cry out loud.

"There's a couple more things, Jonathan", Moses continued as he struggled for air. "I want you to help Stephen with this endeavor. The two of you have always been friends and you work well together.

Stephen likes you and he'll need a strong man he can trust. If he will take on this task, I'll rest better if I know you'll be there to help him."

Jonathan nodded.

"I've written down that you and Sarah are to receive 20,000 acres of your choice in the new colony. That's ten percent of the land grant." Moses said, and then went on saying, "You are also to have a share in the eventual profits of the Texas Venture. Stephen will be happy to agree to that." Though his eyes were terribly bloodshot from all the coughing, Moses could see clearly that Jonathan was taken with what he had just heard. Moses smiled.

"In that drawer," Moses gestured mostly with his eyes toward the small night table, "is five hundred dollars for you and Sarah. I wish I could do more. That money is to help you start a new life."

Tears began to roll down Jonathan's face. He realized he would never again talk to one of the most important people in his life, and his whole body felt heavy. His nose was dripping and as he wiped it with his hand he said, "Dammit, Moses, don't you leave me. Hell, I pro'bly can't even find Texas without you."

Moses smiled weakly and said, "Just head south. It's pretty big, you can't miss it."

"Oh, Moses, dammit" Jonathan said wiping his nose again.

"Now don't be sad, boy." Moses said. "Here, I want you to have this." Moses pulled his right hand from under the covers and opened it palm up to Jonathan. It held his gold pocket watch.

Since Jonathan was eighteen years old, he had seen Moses pull that watch from his vest pocket a hundred times a day. The old man said softly, "Whenever you look at this watch, Jonathan, I want you to think about the time you and I have shared as friends."

Jonathan's right hand was shaking as he took the pocket watch and squeezed it tight. He cupped his left hand around the back of Moses' hand and held his friend trying to pour life back into him. Jonathan's voice was only a whisper through his tears as he said, "Thank you, Moses."

Moses looked straight up into Jonathan's eyes. The young man felt that Moses was looking directly into his soul when he heard the soft words. "I have to rest now, son." Moses' eyes closed and Jonathan quietly left the room.

Jonathan startled when he felt the light tapping on his shoulder. He turned around in his big rocking chair to see Sarah and his three grown children smiling down at him. Mary Beth giggled and said in a pretend little girl voice, "Is it Christmas yet?"

16

"It's Christmas! Smile to the peons, you pig's ass!" Ines said to her husband through her big smile. Like a skilled ventriloquist, her lips and her teeth barely moved when she addressed him. Anyone standing even five feet away saw only her gracious smile as she waved to the crowd. However, the disgust and anger in her voice carried her words like a double edged sword. They hit their mark and sliced into the peacock of a man standing next to her, cutting short the angry thoughts that had preoccupied him.

Antonio Lopez de Santa Anna Perez de Lebron, Ines' husband, the President of Mexico, snapped back into the moment and smiled and waved sanctimoniously to the crowd gathered for Christmas Mass. Ines and her husband had just stepped out of the President's ornate coach and were standing on an elevated walkway at the edge of *Ciudad Mexico*'s ceremonial plaza, the *Zocalo*.

Santa Anna stuck out his chest, and with a grand upward swing of his left arm, flipped back the elegant cape he wore over his shoulders. It was a dramatic move he had perfected in front of the big mirrors in his palace. As the rich black material flew up and back over his shoulder, it showed the bright red underside of the cape, and he knew it had the desired effect. He stood there like a matador while the crowd cheered.

Ines continued to smile and looked at him, but she didn't see the matador. She saw the peacock.

Cardinal Eduardo Bustamante, Mexico's highest ranking Roman Catholic priest, watched the spectacle from across the Zocalo. He stood at the front door of the National Cathedral with his assembled underlings waiting for the arrival of *El Presidente* so they could start the Christmas Mass. From the top steps of the Cathedral he was above the people gathered in the plaza and could see the elaborate arrival clearly.

The Cardinal had survived Mexico's independence from Spain and had made it through the many different changes in the country's leadership that had followed. He had dealt with countless difficult situations, protecting both the church and his position in it, because he was practical enough to realize that, at his level, he was more politician than priest. Actually that was his job now in serving the Church, and he was good at it. But for the first time in the thirty years he had been in the priesthood of Mexico, he was scared.

Bustamante had dealings throughout his adult life with many men who had risen to powerful positions, both in the church and in government. Many of those men displayed human shortcomings like arrogance, vanity, or even deceit. But Bustamante had always been able to function with them by overlooking those human frailties and finding out what was truly in the other man's heart. What he usually found in those hearts were basically good men with noble desires and purpose who were wrapped up in the turmoils or conflicts of the day. He then used that knowledge to his advantage, both for the church and for himself.

As the Cardinal watched this president walk toward the Cathedral, waving and smiling to the tumultuous crowd along the way, he finally realized why Santa Anna was so dangerous. Bustamante had never, in the many years he had known the man, been able to see what was truly in his heart.

The sun flashed off the medals and braiding of Santa Anna's flamboyant military uniform as he strutted across the expanse of the Zocalo. The Cardinal thought of quicksilver. He mused to himself that perhaps that was what filled Santa Anna's heart. Then he thought, "No, there's a chameleon in there." He smiled at the picture that thought created in his mind.

The smile left his face and he realized that was exactly why he had never found the man's true heart. Santa Anna's career and his rise to power had been a maze of dramatic shifts in allegiance to people and causes. He served only himself and was a master at telling whatever person or group he was addressing - exactly what they wanted to hear.

Bustamante remembered back to the spring of 1822, after Mexico won her independence from Spain, when he first met a new Brigadier General named Santa Anna. That was the priest's first recollection of the man. He remembered it because of the story about how Santa Anna fought for Spain against Augustine de Inturbide, then in the middle of the campaign as military advantage changed, he switched sides and fought for Inturbide and the rebels. When Inturbide became the new Republic of Mexico's first Head of State, he rewarded Santa Anna with the promotion to General.

As these new pieces to the puzzle began to fall into place in Cardinal Bustamante's mind, his eyes watched the peons throw ferns into Santa Anna's path for him to walk on as he paraded across the Zocalo. Bustamante thought of his Lord Jesus, and he shuddered inside. He also watched Ines walking the measured two steps behind her husband. The priest in him sensed her unhappiness through the smiles she gave the throngs of well wishers.

Recent events started flashing through the Cardinal's mind while the dignitaries kept slowly proceeding toward him from across the plaza. Santa Anna had been elected President of the Republic less than two years ago on his promise to unify the country under its democratic constitution. He had abolished the constitution and was now a virtual dictator. Once he was in complete control, some of his first initiatives were to reform the church, the state, and the army.

Earlier in the year the liberals in *Zacatecas* had defied his authority and his attempt to reduce their militia. Santa Anna was merciless. He led his army on an attack that crushed their militia, and then followed his battlefield victory with a harsh crusade of repression. The stories of devastation, torture, and executions in *Zacatecas* that reached the Cardinal were horrifying. In the church Bustamante had personally taken confessions from returning soldiers atoning for obeying direct orders to rape and plunder.

Bustamante had fought with all his powers against Santa Anna's takeover of all church property. When the President's reforms also infuriated vested interests in the army, he blamed the actions on his vice-president. Santa Anna had just led a bloody coup against his own government to reassert his authority. The whole country was in fear and disorder, and now there was talk of revolt in the Texas Province.

Suddenly Bustamante wondered if the man approaching him even had a heart. As Cardinal Bustamante said, "Feliz Navidad, Your Excellency," he looked into the dark eyes and shook the cold hand of Santa Anna. He knew he was right to be afraid.

As Santa Anna held onto the Cardinal's hand, he turned to wave to the crowd, showing them all how he embraced the Mother Church. "Wonderful crowd, Cardinal Bustamante," Santa Anna said smiling. "You may proceed with the mass." Then he held out his arm for Ines, which she took dutifully, and marched into the cathedral.

Cardinal Bustamante oversaw the service in the National Cathedral for the upper classes while other priests held Christmas Mass in the Zocalo for the working classes. The Christmas ceremony had always been the Cardinal's favorite service because the story of Christ's birth gave people hope in their lives. However, he kept being distracted by the thoughts he'd had before the mass.

Ines was also distracted. Although she tried to make them leave her, the feelings of fury and resentment would not go away after she entered the cathedral. She wanted to find peace in the church, but no matter how much she tried to concentrate on the service, the rage she felt kept returning. She found herself wishing that her husband, Antonio, would take his precious army to Texas and get himself killed. Then she silently asked God to forgive her.

Antonio had been furious ever since the news arrived about General Cos' defeat at the Siege of Bexar in the Texas Province. The tantrums he threw in front of his staff were almost unbelievable. His initial response was to have General Cos executed for cowardice, but he had been convinced by others to at least get the General's full report first.

He worked himself into screaming fits of rage. Antonio paced frantically around the palace damning the trespassing American colonists and the treasonous *Tejanos* as he swore oaths of retaliation and retribution. He gathered the country's most respected military leaders and demanded maps and immediate battle plans. They all scurried around like frightened children in an orphanage who were terrified by a cruel headmaster.

Unfortunately, Antonio's cruelty wasn't restricted to his subordinates. He had always been abusive, but this time Ines didn't know if she could take it. He had already beaten her twice since the news about Texas arrived. Both times were in their quarters after the servant's work day had ended so her screams went unheard. Although they were severe beatings, Antonio was always careful not to leave a mark that would show in public. As she sat in church Ines' body was so sore and bruised beneath her clothing, that she worried if she would be able to rise by herself when the service ended.

She hated the life she had with this man. He wasn't just cruel to her physically. Antonio had begun to taunt her with his mistresses. Ines knew about four of the whores through reports from her spies, but she believed there were more.

Last night Antonio hadn't even come home. He spent Christmas Eve with one of his whores, then came to the palace late for Mass smelling of the other woman. He told Ines he had been detained all night with "Affairs of State". She had to wait, as did a thousand people in the Zocalo, while the arrogant bastard changed his clothes and primped. Ines looked at the suffering Cristo behind the ornate altar and begged Him to give her strength and peace.

Santa Anna dropped his smile after he took his special seat in the church. He knew the people would think his solemn expression was simply his concentration on the sermon. That freed him to concentrate on the important things.

He had already decided that he must be the one to lead the army against the traitors in Texas. There was obviously no one else capable. If the example in *Zacatecas* had not been enough of a lesson for the liberals, then he would have to teach them again in Texas. Besides, he hated the Americans, and this would give him a chance to quell their lust for Mexico's land once and for all. Santa Anna looked at the image of Christ hanging on the cross mounted to the wall behind the altar and knew he was doing God's Will.

Santa Anna smiled. He would lead a massive army to Texas on his greatest crusade. When he found the traitors who defied his power - he would open the gates of Hell!

17

It was a blue bird morning, this Christmas in the colony, bright and clear. With Pa home all the anxiety and fears were gone, and that released their hearts to just celebrate the day. It was something they all needed. Laughter had started the day when the tight little family made Pa jump awake from his daydream in the big rocker. The tone was set for a real holiday - laughter and happiness.

All the boys wanted to get into the Christmas cakes right away, but Momma wouldn't allow it. She had made some as gifts for their friends, and the rest were for Christmas Dinner. Although Mary Beth stood firmly on Momma's side, the coaxing and begging of all the boys began to wear down Sarah's resistance. Her favorite little devil, Sam, turned his head downward and looked up at her from under his eyebrows with his beautiful big brown eyes.

He said, in his mock statesman voice, "*Now, Sarah*, it seems to me a shame, that *all* those wonderful cakes should go to people who may not even *appreciate* the fact that you are the *most wonderful cook* and *most beautiful woman* in *all* of *Tejas*."

"You boys are not getting into the Christmas cakes," Sarah responded firmly as she crossed her arms in front of her chest. "You can talk all the sweet molasses words you want, but Mary Beth and I made these cakes special – just for company."

Sam continued with, "You know, of course, Christmas is a time of giving and sharing. Now what better way would there be to celebrate this joyous season than *giving and sharing* those spectacular cakes with the three men you adore?" The boy cocked his head slightly to give his best little puppy expression as he looked into Sarah's eyes.

"Sam, you are such a shameless rake!" Momma said with exasperation on her forehead, but a smile on her lips. "You boys may start that one, but that's all the breakfast you're getting. The next meal in this house is Christmas Dinner!"

While Pa and Luke quickly picked up the cake Momma had pointed to and carried it to her for slicing, Sam snuggled up to his mother in the kitchen and put his arms around her. She gave the tall boy a sideways stare with a very unconvincing stern look on her face. Sam kissed her on the cheek and backed up to look at her with his head again cocked to one side.

When he said, "You really are the most wonderful cook and most beautiful woman in all of Tejas," her scowl exploded into a warm smile.

Though all her children were special and had their own unique qualities and position in the family, Sam had always been the one who could make her laugh or melt her heart with just a word or a look. It wasn't merely the fact that he was her youngest, although sometimes she thought that perhaps she had babied him too much. Sam simply had a special sparkle that drew Sarah to him. He was a blend of just enough rascal and just enough sweetheart.

Sarah hugged the boy, then pushed him away and said loudly trying to protest the fact that she had given into the men, "Sam, you *are* a rake! I pity the poor woman who falls in love with you. She will have a scoundrel for a husband!"

"Now, Sarah...," Sam said cocking his head to the side again and looking at his Mother with his big wide eyes. "Why would I ever want to get married? I've spent sixteen years just getting you and Mary Beth broken in. Havin' to break another lucky woman in properly would be just too much work."

Pa and Luke both giggled, then pulled their heads down into their shoulders and winced their eyes at Sam, knowing he had just pushed right to the cliff edge of Momma's good nature - again. Momma swatted Sam on the bottom with the side of the big knife she had picked up to slice the Christmas cake and pushed him toward the door saying, "You better go fetch some water before I break you in properly with my rolling pin, young man!"

"Yes Ma'am, Momma," Sam said smartly as he picked up the wooded bucket by the wash basin. He danced lightly across the house with the water bucket for a partner. Before he reached the front door he said gallantly, "It is always my duty, nay, my pleasure, to cater to your every need and indulge your every whim!"

Pa stepped in saying, "Son, you'd better go fetch that water before Momma boxes your ears for your breakfast."

Sam held the bucket by its rope handle and raised it high as though it were a salute to his family. "I shall return!", he said dramatically, and wheeled around and pranced out the door.

"Jonathan, what *are* we going to do with that boy?" Sarah asked in a good hearted tone not really wanting an answer.

"Let's sell him to the Indians," Luke said as he took his first giant sized bite of the cake Momma had sliced.

"I don't think they'd take him," Mary Beth said laughing while reaching for her slice. "But let's eat all the cake before he gets back!" Luke and Pa laughed and nodded approval of the plan as they each reached for another slice.

"Y'all are awful!" Momma exclaimed, putting her hands on her hips. "How could you even think of doing such a thing to your baby brother?" Then she took three slices of the cake and put them on a separate plate which she hid in the cupboard. She grinned back at them and said, "I should have thought of it. It's a grand idea!"

Pa was laying out the presents when Sam returned with the heavy bucket of fresh water. "Did ya' check the fire out there, Sam?" He asked as the boy carefully lugged the full bucket into the house.

"Yes, sir!" Sam chirped. "Added three more big logs. We'll have some good coals…" Then he stopped in mid sentence. "What happened to all the cake?!"

When they almost had Sam convinced the family had eaten all the breakfast cake, Momma took out the three slices she had hidden in the cupboard. She poured him some coffee to have with his cake while the others continued to razz the boy. Then Mary Beth said, "We've wasted enough time. Let's open presents!"

The family gathered around in front of the rock fireplace and took turns opening the simple presents they had given one another. They were mostly small items, either home-made or bartered for with traveling merchants. The most exciting gifts were the ones Pa had carried back the whole way from Bexar carefully rolled up in his bedroll.

He brought Momma several yards of pretty blue cloth for a new dress. He gave Mary Beth some new combs and a half dozen bright ribbons for her long hair. Luke got a pistol and lead balls taken from a Mexican army officer Pa disarmed after the surrender. And Sam got a knife with a leather sheath that had belonged to their old friend, Jim Bowie.

They were all thrilled with the nice gifts, but Sam whooped like an Indian and danced around the room waving the sheath in one hand and the knife in the other. Although he was well liked by the whole family and had stayed in their home often over the years, Colonel Bowie was a hero to Sam. He was a handsome and bold adventurer who always made a point of making Sam feel important. Jim Bowie was one of the only adults in the world, other than Pa, who had ever asked for or cared about Sam's opinion on things. He also told some wonderful stories. Sam could sit for hours listening to Bowie's tales of lost gold mines, Indian fights, and far away places like New Orleans.

Sam knew this wasn't the big knife Colonel Bowie always wore at his side, because Sam had seen and held that knife many times. That was the one he called his "fightin' knife", after the one that had made him famous in Louisiana. This was the one Colonel Bowie called his "workin' knife". It was made just like his fightin knife but small enough to use all the time for regular things - when he wasn't fighting Indians or killing people.

The boy passed his newest, most prized possession around for all to see while Pa told the story of how he came by the knife. Pa explained in some detail the events of a poker game one night in Bexar in which he won the knife from Bowie. A few days after the card game, when Bowie was sober, he tried to buy the knife back.

Jonathan smiled and looked at Sam. "When I told him that I was giving that knife to you for Christmas, son, ol' Jim just smiled and nodded his head. He said, 'You tell my good friend, Sam, that I'm proud for him to have that knife. You tell him that if he takes good care of that knife, she'll take good care of him'."

As Jonathan watched the joy almost bursting out of his youngest, and looked around at the happy faces of the others, he remembered the vow he'd made to himself and God. "Lord, I will make it home, if you will just give us this Christmas together."

18

"…and green grow the violets!" Gabriel gave a strong finish to his song with his rich deep voice as he sat on the wagon seat and flipped the reins to slap the mules' backs. "C'mon mules," he said, just to make sure he had their attention. Gabriel loved to sing. He always sang when he worked with the others. But when he was out by himself driving the big wagon with nobody else around, he could sing as loud as he wanted.

He smiled when he figured the mules probably liked his singing, but he didn't care if they didn't. They were just mules. Singing always made him happy and made the days go easier. That's why he enjoyed it. He liked that song too, because it was pretty.

All the people in the colony sang *Green Grow the Violets*. They sang it so much that the Mexicans started calling them all "green gros". Gabriel thought that was funny.

He reached into the pocket of his old threadbare coat and pulled out a rag that held the last piece of his Christmas cake. He had made it last for almost two weeks, savoring every taste, and hoarding each crumb like it was gold dust. Of course he had shared some with the others on Christmas night, but the cake had been made special just for him. All Gabriel really wanted to do, was make it last.

He never had much of anything that was just his, not even a last name. He was merely Gabriel. He was a Negro slave who had been owned by the Cavanaugh's so long he could barely remember being bought with part of his family twenty years before when he was 10 years old.

On Christmas day Gabriel got to go to the Stevens' place with the Cavanaugh's because he drove the big wagon. He had always liked the Stevens folks and had helped them work their fields and harvests sometimes. They were people he was glad to help out with anything they needed, whenever he could. Their young boy, Sam, was Gabriel's good friend. They fished and hunted together whenever they could both cut loose from their chores.

Gabriel knew about Baby Jesus and loved the story about Him being born. That's why they had Christmas. He also knew that if he stayed a good man, he'd get to meet Jesus someday. The best part about that was Jesus didn't care if he was a Negro, and He'd make it so Gabriel wasn't a slave anymore.

Although he didn't understand why all the black people had to be slaves for white people in this life, he suspected Jesus had His reasons. But it was sure something they were going to talk about - when he met Him.

Gabriel put the mules' reins between his legs and pinched his knees together to hold them. With both hands he carefully unfolded the rag that held his cake. He looked down at that last crumbly morsel wondering if this was a good day to finish it. The cake was dry and falling apart, and Gabriel knew he couldn't make it last much longer. He sat up straight in the wagon seat, took a deep breath, and smiled. He was by himself, driving the big wagon, and singing as loud as he wanted. As he looked around at the clear pretty morning, he brought the cake up to his mouth and stuck his tongue into the crumbs.

Gabriel was the lead man now on the Cavanaugh's plantation. He was physically a big man and strong like a bear. He either knew how to do all the jobs on the plantation, or could figure out how to get them done, and all the others listened to him. Nowadays Master Cavanaugh usually just told Gabriel the tasks he wanted accomplished and Gabriel took it from there.

Building a plantation in the wilderness was grueling hard work, especially for slaves, but the Cavanaugh's were better Masters than some. Gabriel was thankful for that. He had heard stories that were so awful from slaves of other plantations that he sometimes had bad dreams.

That's why he figured he had a good life, all and all, and he tried to be happy. "The works gotta git done, might as well enjoy it," he always told the others. But, of course, some work was plain easier to enjoy. Gabriel had two jobs that were just his, and they were the most pleasurable things in his life. They were taking care of the Master's hunting dogs and driving the big wagon.

The Cavanaugh's kept a small band of hunting dogs that Gabriel tended to everyday. He trained them and fed them and was in charge of them when the Master wanted to go out hunting. Gabriel loved every one of those big dogs like they were his children. Whenever they got onto a snake or javalina tore one of them up, he nursed them night and day. He was also the one who buried them when their time came.

His other best thing was driving the big wagon. The Cavanaugh's had the largest wagon in the colony. It was made back in Tennessee out of solid oak timbers, and it had carried them all the way to Texas. It was one of the family's prized possessions, and Gabriel always kept it in good repair. They had traces to hitch two mules, four mules, or even six mules depending on the load.

Gabriel was the only Negro entrusted with driving it, and that made him feel important. The Master sent him to the settlement once, sometimes twice, a week with the wagon to deliver the molasses and whiskey they made on the plantation. That's where he was headed this morning.

"Lordee! That's mighty fine cake Missus Stevens. And I sure do thank ya fo' it!" Gabriel said loudly into the morning air. The cake was so stale and dry it had very little taste left in it, but that wasn't an issue with him. In Gabriel's mind, as he thought back, that cake was as moist and tasty as it had been on Christmas Day.

Right in the middle of the big feast and celebration with all the neighbors at the Steven's place, Missus Stevens had called Gabriel to the front porch where she stood with her family. He took off his hat, the way he was supposed to, and walked up onto the porch to see what she needed him to do. As he stepped up saying, "Yes, Ma'am, what is it I can do fo' ya?", Captain Stevens stuck out his hand.

"Merry Christmas, Gabriel," the Captain said smiling. While they shook right hands he reached up and put his left hand on Gabriel's shoulder. "I'm glad you're here to share it with us. And I want you to know I appreciate you lookin' in on my family while I was away. You're a good man!"

Gabriel felt blood rushing into his face and ears. He knew he should say something, but he didn't know what to say. He looked into the other man's eyes, and as he nodded his head slightly, all that came out was, "Cap'm."

Then Missus Stevens turned around and picked up something from the seat of the chair behind her. When she turned back to face him she held his cake in her hands. "Merry Christmas, Gabriel!" the whole Stevens family said at one time and the two boys started patting him on the back.

The big wagon squeaked along slowly as Gabriel swallowed the last crumbs of his fine gift and smiled. Then he took a deep breath in through his nose and started to sing with a loud booming, "Green Grow..." He stopped suddenly when he saw five riders coming in from the west. He instinctively slapped the mules with the wagon reins to keep them going.

The horsemen were too far away at first, but as he watched he could tell they were riding to him. By the time they were a half mile away, he knew the men were Mexicans by their saddles and the way they sat on their horses. Gabriel was scared. If these were bad men, he couldn't out run them in his heavy wagon, and bad men would kill for a lot less than a wagon half full of whiskey.

When the riders were a hundred yards away, he recognized the man in the lead. He didn't know the man's name, but Gabriel knew he was an important *Tejano* from San Antonio de Bexar. As the men rode closer, he noticed that both the men riding in front were dressed better than the three behind.

Gabriel stopped the big wagon as the *Tejano* and his band approached. He stayed in the wagon's seat, but he took off his hat and held it across his chest while he tilted his head down slightly. He kept his eyes looking up at the man he'd recognized and said, "Mornin', Sir."

"*Buenos Dias*," the man said as he pulled up his horse and patted the fine animal's neck. "I know you. I've seen you before."

Gabriel responded, "Yes, sir, I'd be Gabriel. Missir Angus Cavanaugh's man." He turned and pointed behind him toward his home. "From up on the Cavanaugh Plantation yonder."

"Where are you going now, Gabriel?" The man asked.

"I's just takin these tradin' goods into the settlement, Sir." Gabriel said as politely as he could. "Then I has'ta git back to the plantation."

The man turned in his saddle and looked toward the settlement. When he turned back to Gabriel he said, "I'm going to send a man with you to talk to the people in the settlement. Gabriel, I want you to give a message to your Master when you get back to the plantation. Can you do that for me?"

"Yes, sir!" Gabriel said quickly and sincerely, because he sensed this was an important matter.

"Tell Angus you met Juan Seguin and his cousin Maximilian," he said making it obvious that he knew Gabriel's boss. "We're on our way to meet with Governor Smith and General Houston. Tell him we're going to Jonathan Stevens' hacienda to spend the night, and we'll meet with him and any of the other settlers there at eight o'clock in the morning. Can you remember that?"

Gabriel nodded his head and said, "Yes, sir, every word."

After he had repeated the message back to Señor Juan Seguin, almost verbatim, the *Tejano* smiled. He tipped his hat and nodded to the black slave and said, "Then you go on with your business, Gabriel, and I'll go on with mine. *Vaya con Dios.*"

19

Cardinal Bustamante took his seat in the reviewing stand which sat atop high wooden scaffolding on the military parade grounds a half mile outside *Ciudad Mexico*. The sun was barely showing over the horizon and the morning air carried the whisper of a chill with it. The large open field before him was filled with groups of soldiers standing straight and tall in lines and rows, making the men look like crops on several different farms ready to be harvested.

As he sat there not listening to a General making the preliminary speeches and introductions, the Cardinal became mesmerized by the faces. There was a sea of faces in front of him all looking up to the stanchion where he sat with the other dignitaries. In the dawn's breaking light he studied those faces.

He could see bright-eyed young men lusting for adventure and tired older men dreading the thought of it. With a priest's insight he saw the ones who didn't yet shave and were so scared they were about to cry. That insight also showed him the ones with young families scared their babies would never know a father. He knew that beyond all the faces close enough for him to see clearly, there were more lines and rows of those same faces all looking up to the platform.

This was the main body of the massive army Santa Anna had conscripted to take to Texas and put down the uprising there. More columns from other parts of Mexico were to join this force along the way. Cardinal Bustamante had spent most of his life looking at large crowds from the pulpit, but as he saw thousands of men who were being pushed into battle in a far away land, he felt a strange anxiety about being in front of all those faces.

There had been no denying Santa Anna his army. He wanted it large and he wanted it immediately. Every able-bodied man within searching distance who couldn't buy or talk his way out of service had been conscripted. They were melded in with the standing army and any training they had not gotten in the past couple of weeks they were expected to get along the way. By the time they made the thousand mile trek to the fighting, those who survived, would be ready.

Santa Anna could feel the sun lighting up the tall reviewing stand while the field below him was still shadowed by the trees to the east. This was the moment he had planned. He sat straight and commanding because he knew all the men's eyes were on him. He cleared his throat as the signal for the General to stop talking and introduce him. He waited for the General to sit, then the President stood. With his chest high he turned toward the sun to catch all the light possible so its rays would dance and sparkle off the medals, buttons, and gold thread of his parade uniform. To the ranks below, especially those in the back, the flashes of light coming from Santa Anna's body made it look like he was the sun rising. When the whole army cheered, he savored his moment and his intelligence, then slowly turned to them and raised both arms high over his head. Santa Anna felt his body fill with power as he basked in the praise. When the cheering subsided, he spoke with distinctly measured words and syllables that were paced so the dense still morning air carried his loud voice to every ear.

"Brave soldiers of Mexico, we have been called upon to defend our beloved country!

"We are the only ones who can stand against the traitors and evil Norte Americanos who are stealing our land and our freedoms.

"We must protect our homes, our families, and our very way of life from the evil ones who are trying to take them from us!"

He paused to let the army cheer, and they did.

He turned his head down purposefully and looked at the sword sheathed on the left side of his waist, then he slowly raised his face back up and looked at the masses. He boldly grabbed the scabbard with his left hand and took the weapon's handle in his right. With one grand lightening sweep, he jerked the sword from its scabbard and raised it high above his head, pointing to the heavens so the morning light would catch the blade. Santa Anna turned his hand until he could see the thin band of bright light on the crowd that was being reflected like a signal mirror off the saber's shiny blade. He turned his hand maneuvering the reflection across every line and row of men.

As he finished panning the army with his sword's light he said, "I ask God to bless this sword!" He tilted the saber horizontally and took the blade in his left hand. He held the weapon high over his head with both hands and said loudly, "Pray with me!" and he dropped himself dramatically onto one knee as he turned toward Cardinal Bustamante.

The Cardinal rose and stepped to a position in front of the heartless man who looked like a saint kneeling with his body bowed low holding a shiny offering over his head. Bustamante did as he had been instructed. He blessed the sword. Then he blessed the equipment, the animals, and the mission itself. His final blessing was on the soldiers.

A huge army of men was below him kneeling with their heads bowed, but still all he could see were the faces. As the priest said his closing words, a feeling came over him that he would carry those faces with him the rest of his life. "Father, go with these men. These are the fathers, the husbands, the sons of Mexico. Bless them. Amen."

Santa Anna waited for the priest to be seated. Then he stood. He raised himself erect before the army and held his sword's handle hiding his own face with the blade straight up into the air as though he were making a parade salute. With an exaggerated movement he kept the weapon vertical while he made a large sign of the cross in front of his body with the handle. After he brought the handle back to its starting point in, he thrust the sword as high as he could reach into the air.

"Brave soldiers of Mexico; you are the sword of God!" He exclaimed boldly. "God has called upon me to carry His sword! I will carry God's sword to Tejas and defeat the evil there!" He stopped, hoping for a cheer, and it came from the army in a deafening roar.

"Will you go to Tejas with me to fight the evil?!" Santa Anna screamed at the crowd and they screamed back that they would.

"Will you be the sword of God?!"

When the army cheered back, the leader pointed his sword to the north and commanded, "On to Tejas! On to God's Glory!"

He marched off the platform and down the stairs where his great white horse was being held for him. After he mounted the animal and pranced it across the front of the assembly, he drew his sword again, waved it over his head, then pointed it northward. Santa Anna paced his horse off the parade grounds, and the battalions started moving in ranks to follow him.

20

"Good afternoon my good friend, Jonathan Stevens." Juan said with a broad smile after he'd dismounted from his horse and handed the reins to his *vaquero*.

"*Buenas tardes buen amigo mio, Juan Seguin.*" Jonathan responded stepping off the covered front porch of his homestead. He showed the visitor his big smile as he walked toward the man. They exchanged a strong warm shake with their right hands while they each clasped the other's shoulder with their left. The two had been friends for a long time.

The Seguin's were an influential family in San Antonio. Juan's father, Erasmo, had been the postmaster there for over 25 years. Erasmo was the man appointed by the governor to inform Moses Austin that the application for his colony had been approved. Erasmo and his son had not only befriended Stephen Austin and Jonathan upon their arrival to Tejas, but they had also become invaluable supporters. Erasmo spent a year in *Ciudad Mexico* as a Texas delegate to the congress that wrote the Democratic Constitution of 1824, and there he also served on the committee that wrote the liberal National Colonization Law. Juan was now one of the harshest critics of Santa Anna's centralist policies.

Inside the house Mary Beth was in a flush. When she heard someone approaching she had looked out the window and seen Juan riding in. Although she knew he was married, Juan Seguin was the most handsome man she had ever met, and he always displayed impeccable manners, especially to her. She felt that she probably looked like an overworked farm hand and would rather die than have Juan see her like this. As Sarah started toward the door to go outside and greet their company, Mary Beth almost knocked her over running the opposite direction to find her combs and hair ribbons.

Sarah walked through the doorway wiping her hands on her long apron. When she stepped off the porch into the late afternoon sun, Juan turned from Jonathan and faced her. He removed his hat and bowed his head respectfully. He raised his twinkling eyes back to Sarah and popped open the familiar grin she knew well, but hadn't seen for a long time.

"I see the beautiful flower my friend brought to Tejas continues to bloom," he said sincerely. "*Grande Dios*, Sarah, you are prettier each time I see you!"

Sarah smiled and blushed and opened her arms wide to embrace the charming man who had been such a friend and ally since their arrival to this wild country. "Oh, it's so good to see you, Juan." She said as she hugged him quickly and gave him a light kiss on the cheek, then stepped back and continued, "It's been way too long. What brings you here? Can you stay with us?"

"I would be most grateful if my men and I could stay the night, if it is not too much of an imposition," he answered looking to both Sarah and Jonathan.

Jonathan spoke up saying, with equal amounts of jest and respect, "We'd be honored to have the *Mayor* of San Antonio de Bexar share our humble shelter."

Juan quickly responded in-kind saying, "I'm not the *Alcalde* anymore. Thanks to your friend Stephen Austin, I'm a Captain in the 'Army of the People', just like you. Remember?"

Jonathan put his arm around his friend's back and grabbed his shoulder, telling Juan how glad he was to see him and have him stay, as Mary Beth walked out of the house. She had removed her soiled apron and straightened her dress. After combing her thick long hair, she had tied it with her brightest ribbon, then pinched her cheeks to give them some color. An eighteen year old girl walked off the front porch, but the sunlight she stepped into lit up a strikingly beautiful young lady.

"*Ay Dios Mio!*" Juan gasped and left his mouth open as he saw Mary Beth. "Sarah, this can't be your daughter!"

"She's grown up hasn't she, Juan?" Sarah answered proudly.

Mary Beth walked across the yard and reached out to shake hands with their guest saying, "It is so good to see you again, *Señor* Seguin."

Juan held her fingertips in his as he removed his hat, then bowed low and kissed the back of her hand. "*El gusto es mio, Senorita.*" Juan said gallantly. Then he looked up to her and said, "I prefer that grown ladies call me Juan."

Mary Beth beamed and blushed as Juan turned back to Jonathan and said smiling, "Now you have two beautiful flowers blooming in your Texas garden, *amigo.*"

While all the men made sure the *Tejanos'* tired horses were well fed and cared for, Momma had Sam kill and dress three chickens. She and Mary Beth set about preparing a large meal and heated water that was taken to the barn so their company could freshen up. Sarah had made it clear to Jonathan that she didn't want any news discussed until they could all talk together.

Just as Jonathan finished saying the supper blessing, Juan's cousin, Maximilian, arrived from the trip he had taken to the settlement with the Cavanaugh's slave, Gabriel. Jonathan knew the man from the Siege of Bexar, but there was a round of introductions for the rest of the family who had never met Max. Although he wasn't as handsome, Maximilian was every bit the gentleman his cousin was.

"Thank you for your hospitality, Captain Stevens," Max said as they started the meal. "It is very kind of you to share your home with us."

"We're glad to have you, Max. Now that you know where the place is, you're welcome here anytime," Jonathan said.

"Thank you," Max said then smiled. "I know my cousin enjoys your company, but I do believe the real reason we came this way is your wife's cooking." He turned to Sarah and continued as he gestured to all the food on the table, "Mrs. Stevens, I can see now why this is all Juan has talked about for the last hundred miles of our journey. This meal is delicious. Thank you."

Sarah enjoyed the compliment and said, "It's a pleasure to have you, Max. Please, have another biscuit."

More pleasantries were exchanged for a while then the conversation turned to the purpose for this trip. The table talk stopped, and Sarah quit eating as Jonathan asked their guests probing questions. Mary Beth grabbed Sam's hand under the table while they all listened to the answers.

Juan spoke solemnly. "We know Santa Anna is gathering an army, and he will probably be the one leading it to Texas. It will be a large force. You can count on that. We don't know when they will start marching this way. I doubt they have left yet, but they could be here by April or May.

"Jonathan, you know Colonel Neill to be a good man and a very capable soldier." Juan said and Jonathan nodded. "He's been given command of the garrison at Bexar. He is fortifying the old Spanish mission, the Alamo, that General Cos held during the siege last fall.

"They have built ramparts and installed some twenty-one artillery pieces of various calibers, but they are horribly under-manned and under-supplied. There is no way they could withstand an enemy attack."

"How many men does he have?" Jonathan asked.

"Not many", Juan replied, "Less than a hundred. And the men haven't been paid in months. Those of us in town who are not loyal to Santa Anna have been scrounging food for the soldiers because they don't even have basic victuals. I don't know how Neill is keeping the men at their posts."

Jonathan bristled. "What about General Houston and the provisional government, aren't they going to send reinforcements and aid?"

"Jonathan, I've received word that General Houston wants to withdraw the cannons and munitions of war to Gonzales and Copano. He plans to blow up the Alamo and abandon it because he doesn't think it can be manned by the volunteers."

Jonathan sat quietly and listened to his friend continue.

"Of course, it is my town, and I don't want it left defenseless in the path of the Mexican army. But Jonathan, you know as well as I that the Alamo at San Antonio de Bexar is the only fortifiable position between Santa Anna and your homes here in the colony. It is the gateway to Texas and it cannot be left unguarded!

"That is why we are going to meet with General Houston and Governor Smith. Someone has got to convince them to fortify the

Alamo so that blood thirsty lying bastard, Santa Anna, doesn't destroy this whole country!

Juan turned to Sarah and tilted his head down to one side. "Forgive my language at your table, Sarah. My passion overtakes my manners."

"What's the Governor's position on this, Juan?" Jonathan asked stoically.

"We don't know." Juan said quietly to his friend. "He may be our only hope."

Although all the *Tejanos* slept well that night, the Stevens family didn't. The *Tejanos* were tired from their journey and comfortable from the Stevens' hospitality. They would all be ready tomorrow for another day of hard riding. The Stevens family spent the night trying to absorb the supper table news, each in their own way.

Pa grew angrier through the night over the stupidity and futility of the situation created by men he didn't even know. Each time he rolled over, Sarah was also awake. She was worried for her husband's life and the safety of her children. Luke was mad and anxious to right the wrongs that were being inflicted on his family and homeland. Mary Beth and Sam, who each slept on quilt pallets close together on the floor, talked in whispers late into the night, and were scared.

Shortly after breakfast the next morning, Angus Cavanaugh arrived with his two sons. He was a heavy man in his mid-fifties with somewhat of a coarse nature. His head was bald under the big black hat he always wore, but his face sported a thick beard that was changing from red to gray. His huge nose was also mostly red from years of sampling the whisky he made. His two strong sons were in their late twenties. Both had bright red hair and fair skin. The three Cavanaugh's were part of Jonathan's volunteer company from the colony.

By eight o'clock men and several women with children from twelve other families had gathered in front of the Stevens' home. Sarah and Mary Beth passed through the crowd serving hot coffee as Juan stepped onto the front porch. The good looking man stood tall and turned to face the assembled pioneers. His eyes seemed to meet each of the fifty odd pairs of eyes looking back at him. Each pair was wondering what the news was and what the *Alcalde* had to say about it.

Almost all the grown men in the crowd had served with Juan and Jonathan at the Siege of Bexar. The few who didn't actually know *Señor* Seguin, knew he was a man to be respected. Before he spoke, the yard became so quiet that the sounds of the squeaking leather from the horse's saddles and harnesses, as the animals shifted from one foot to the other, seemed very loud. Juan's full voice filled the clear crisp morning air.

"Thank you for coming. It is good to be back here with my friends, the sound people of the Austin Colony. I bid you all a good morning.

"I realize you are here anxious for news, so I shall get right to it. War with Mexico is inevitable. It is coming to us all."

Juan paused, his sad eyes surveying the crowd. He saw families look at one another and many of the women either reached for their husband's arms or pulled their children closer to them. Juan set his jaw before he took in a full breath and continued. "The years of hard work building our dream for a free and democratic Mexico are all gone now because President Santa Anna betrayed us. You all know of his despicable actions eliminating our Constitution, the rights of the Mexican states, and the rights of the citizens.

"He is no longer the president of a free and democratic country." Juan's right hand rose and he clenched his fist. "He is a maniacal dictator who intends to crush our spirit of freedom under the heavy boot of the Mexican army!"

Using his clenched fist to emphasize his words, the *Tejano* seemed to look directly into the eyes of each person in the crowd as he said slowly, "By defeating General Cos at the Siege of Bexar last fall, the people of Texas sent a message to Santa Anna telling him that we are a free people and we will fight against his tyranny to keep our freedom."

Juan opened his hand and gestured palm open to the gathering. "You women and children here today should be very proud of the men standing with you. Captain Stevens and I served at Bexar with most every man here. Their bravery and fortitude defeated a well trained force many times the size of ours. Texas has virtually no standing army. These brave men volunteered to risk their lives to keep their families and all the families of Texas free.

"When we face the Mexican army again it will be these strong men and other volunteers from other families all over Texas who will make the difference. These volunteers are 'The Army of the People'. They draw their strength and courage from their families and their determination to raise those families in a free Texas!"

As Juan paused momentarily, Sarah reached for her husband's hand and squeezed it. Jonathan turned to her and smiled then faced Juan again.

"We know that Santa Anna is raising a large army and we think he will be the one leading it to Texas. He intends to bring the atrocities he perpetrated on *Zacatecas* to our homeland. His army will probably be here by mid to late spring.

"Colonel James Neill is in command of the garrison at San Antonio de Bexar. He is fortifying the old Spanish mission we took from General Cos last fall. The Alamo is now bristling with cannons in preparation for Santa Anna's arrival.

"There is some concern at the capitol that our volunteers will not be able to man the Alamo when the time comes to defend Texas against the enemy. We have received word that General Houston is considering demolishing the Alamo and withdrawing the garrison with its weapons to the southeast. At this point I am not sure if he and Governor Smith have made a final decision on the plan."

There were quiet grumblings within the crowd as men turned to one another with questioning looks on many of their faces. Juan pointed to the other *Tejano* standing just off the porch to his right and continued.

"My cousin, Maximilian, and I are on our way to seek an audience with General Houston and Governor Smith. We intend to explain to them, in the strongest of terms, how important it is to stop Santa Anna at the frontier before he enters the front door of Texas.

"He cannot be allowed to reach your homes and penetrate into the heart of our country! Our volunteers can defend Texas at the Alamo! With enough support from the provisional government we can defeat

Santa Anna's army and win our independence from his corrupt amoral dictatorship forever!

"I know this because I know the people of this frontier and the strength they possess." Juan never took his eyes from the assembled pioneers as he stepped off the Stevens' front porch and walked closer to them. "You and I, all of us together, are brothers and sisters of the frontier. You are people of character. You came to this wilderness, and with your brave hearts and strength of soul you created farms and ranches and plantations and...homes. Your families, with sweat and tears and blood, have tamed this beautiful land and made it into a homeland you can be proud of!

"My family and our ancestors before us have done those same things with this land. This place demands people of strong character with hearty souls. People who lack those attributes have no place here. The land will not forgive and the residents will not tolerate lesser people. That is why you were welcomed here."

Seguin walked slowly back and forth in front of the group and seemed to look into each of their hearts as he spoke from his own. "You brought to this wilderness your brave spirit that honors your ancestors. You did not come here to take - you came to build. You didn't come to enslave - you came here to be free.

"My ancestors were Mexican and Spanish. Your ancestors were English and Dutch, Irish and German. Those differences have not divided us because they are not important here. Those are not issues significant to free men and women building a new country in this wilderness. On the frontier in Texas we measure a man by his heart - not his heritage!

"Here we speak Spanish, English, and German. Our different languages have not divided us nor diminished our efforts to help one another build and grow. Our different tongues have not stopped the spirit of Texas, nay; they have become part of our spirit! On the frontier in Texas we measure a man by his deeds - not his dialect!

"In the days ahead the full measure of every man and woman here will surely be tested. That is when the strong character and strength of soul you brought to this great wilderness will prevail. It will not matter whether we have called ourselves Texicans or *Tejanos* or Colonists because all of us, together, truly are brothers and sisters of the frontier fighting to be free."

The handsome *Tejano* stepped up onto the front porch as he clasp both hands together to emphasize his words. "The bonds we have forged in building our lives upon this great land, and facing its challenges together, are what make us one people. We are Texans! We must stand shoulder to shoulder and fight for a free Texas!

"We did not master this vast wilderness to have our homes and freedoms taken away by a vile dictator and a wretched government that operates a thousand miles from here. When I meet with General Houston and Governor Smith, I will tell them that the men and women of Texas are willing to fight for our freedom!" He clenched his right hand again and raised it to the crowd. "I will tell them that when the time comes the volunteers of 'The Army of the People' will go to the Alamo, and defeat Santa Anna!"

Loud cheers rang through the cool morning air so suddenly that some of the horses spooked and pulled on their tetherings. Women, many of them with tears in their eyes, hugged the men standing next to them. Men yelled and whistled with clenched fists waving in the air.

Sam felt like he stood three inches taller. The fears he shared with Mary Beth the night before were gone. He was ready to take his new Christmas knife from the scabbard on his belt and join the fight.

Juan was exhilarated and pleased with the scene before him. He had managed to give the right words to the thoughts he'd had on the long journey from Bexar. He was still standing on the front porch of the modest homestead when his friend, Jonathan, walked up to him smiling and shook his hand. Jonathan said, "Well done, my good friend."

21

Traveling with an army was tedious. The larger the force the more slowly they moved. Although he loved the sights and sounds and smells of war, Santa Anna hated moving with his army. He hated the pace and he hated the monotony. He longed for a diversion and cursed himself for the lack of judgment in not taking even one mistress on this campaign.

He looked ahead at the small hill he'd been watching since noon the day before. He judged it to be perfect. It was not too high, so the men would be able to see him clearly. The battalions would move along its west side so the morning sun would be at his back, and he wouldn't have to look into it while he waited for them to pass.

"Keep your columns moving!" he ordered boldly to the generals plodding their horses along slowly on either side of him.

Santa Anna spurred his great white horse and galloped ahead veering right toward the small hill. He rode to the top of the little rounded knob that was completely bare of any vegetation except its tall yellow grass. It did not give him enough elevation to see the very back of the long winding procession below him, but it served his purpose well.

When he stopped he struck a stately but comfortable pose atop the large white gelding. His mounts were the only pure white horses allowed in the field. Aside from accenting Santa Anna's elegant military uniforms, he felt that the animals' color symbolized to the ranks his position as a pure divine leader. He also knew that in the heat of a battle his soldiers would be able to readily see the big white horse and would rally around, and protect, the person sitting on it.

To his admirable Mexican army marching proudly below his vantage point, Santa Anna knew he would look like a god astride the great mythical Pegasus silhouetted against the morning sky. To the heavily loaded poor conscripted souls who raised their tired eyes to *El*

Presidente as they passed on their endless trudge through the dessert - he did.

Santa Anna could see the heads of his soldiers turn to look up at him as they route stepped in loose ranks at his feet. Turning his own head, he surveyed the vast countryside. He ruled everything he could see and everything beyond the horizon in every direction.

I am invincible! He thought, as the majesty of the moment inspired him.

Looking off into the distance in the fair morning sun he began to think about his last great campaign in *Zacatecas* against those who defied his power. The silver rich state was now his, and there was no more disloyalty. In his mind he relived the brilliance of his battle plan and the crushing defeat of those who had dared to oppose his will.

As his army approached *Zacatecas*, Santa Anna had ordered several of his best officers to leave ranks and go to the city feigning defection. They swore to the people their allegiance to the Constitution of 1824 and their hatred for Santa Anna. Because they were trained military leaders, they were given command positions with the *Zacatean* rebels. Santa Anna led his large force toward the city then swung around and attacked from the rear. With his own officers leading much of the *Zacatean* militia, there was a wholesale slaughter of the armed resistance in less than a day.

It took two more days to kill another twenty five hundred men, women, and children of the city who had not participated in the fighting but were deemed, without trial or hearing, sympathizers to the resistance. He had made specific examples of the foreigners, especially the American and English. Those men were bayoneted in front of their families and the women stripped naked, raped, then paraded through the streets to be raped again. He unleashed his mighty army on a looting and pillaging rampage, and then set the once beautiful city to the torch. It had been enough of a lesson for all of Mexico - except Tejas.

Now he had to teach the traitors in that province a lesson. He would eliminate the *Norteamericanos* completely. Then he would deal such harsh punishment to the rebels that he would never again have to worry about insurrection in Tejas. The corners of Santa Anna's mouth turned up as he thought of the irony because Tejas was, after all, where he had learned his skills at putting down insurrections.

Every officer and foot soldier passing the base of Santa Anna's mound felt the eyes of *El Presidente* watching just him. However, in reality, Santa Anna's eyes had lost their focus on the current day. Instead his eyes were watching himself, as a sixteen year old boy, being appointed a cadet in the Fijo de Vera Cruz infantry regiment under the command of Joaquin de Arredondo. He watched his early years flash by as he was schooled by the legendary General Arredondo. He then saw the events that took them to Tejas one hot summer to deal with a minor rebellion led by American adventurers and Mexican dissidents.

General Arredondo sprung a trap on the rebels at the Medina River near San Antonio de Bexar. The fighting was bloody, but short lived, and they took more than a hundred prisoners. Santa Anna was standing with the group of soldiers holding the prisoners when his mentor rode up and dismounted.

General Arredondo walked straight to Santa Anna, and after returning his salute, congratulated him on his action in the battle. Then in a smooth nonchalant manner with no emotion whatsoever showing on his face, General Arredondo pulled the pistol from his belt and shot the closest prisoner through the neck. The unsuspecting man was standing only four feet away. The General saw the surprise on Santa Anna's face so he looked straight into his eyes and commanded, "Kill them all."

It took over an hour for Santa Anna and three other men to kill the prisoners shooting at point blank range. Santa Anna steeled himself so he displayed the same emotional response as the General. Initially it was distasteful. Then it became drudgery. Finally, he made it a challenge to accomplish a quick kill. In the end he was enjoying it.

The rest of that day and the next, on General Arredondo's orders, they arrested anyone even remotely suspected of supporting the rebellion. They consolidated the prisoners into a makeshift jail in a building at San Antonio de Bexar. With over two hundred prisoners, Santa Anna used his boot and shoulder to cram the last ones in. By the next morning, when the soldiers dragged the prisoners into the town plaza for execution, over a dozen had already died of suffocation.

After the public executions, General Arredondo set his troops to the task of punishing the civilian populace for allowing the rebellion. He gave his consent for the soldiers to loot and rape in the streets. As an insult, he had the women of the town's leading families taken to his encampment area to do laundry and cook for his officers.

General Arredondo and Santa Anna were the only two left at the officer's mess table that night at supper while the town was being sacked by their troops.

"Do you think my methods too harsh?" Arredondo asked after their meal was served.

"It is not my place to say, Sir." Santa Anna responded.

"This is a hard lesson. You must learn it and never compromise!" The leader said, pointing an index finger at his inexperienced charge to emphasize the point. "Antonio, our empire is vast and growing rapidly. We are responsible for its rule and order, as well as its defense. This pocket of disobedience is like a plague. If it is not burned out, and removed completely, the plague can spread. If it spreads, it can kill. It can kill our government, and our power.

"There can be only one response to a rebellion. It must be swift and it must be complete." The general's eyes looked like they were on fire from the reflection of the candles on the table as he continued. "You must exterminate the perpetrators and anyone connected with them! Then you must humiliate the women and families that are left behind. It is an extremely important weapon. It is a weapon of war! They must fear you down to their very souls. They must fear you to the point that they would kill their own children rather than face your wrath! You must understand, there is no compromise!"

"I understand." Santa Anna said looking directly into the fire in the General's eyes.

A woman in her early twenties walked past the other end of the table carrying a plate of bread to serve. She was attractive and both the men noticed her. Arredondo said, "She's the daughter of the town's doctor. Take her to your tent and teach her a lesson. Teach her to fear the great General Arredondo and his men."

Santa Anna looked with uncertainty at the General.

Arredondo smiled and said, "That's an order, Antonio."

He watched as Antonio walked to the pretty woman and started talking. Then he grabbed her arm and she resisted. With a wave of the General's hand, two soldiers appeared and dragged the lady to Antonio's tent.

Santa Anna felt his loins stir as he sat in his saddle on top of the strong white horse and noticed his army still passing slowly below him at the bottom of the hill. He was excited at the thought of what he'd done with that doctor's beautiful daughter so long ago. She was the first woman he'd ever forced his way with. In that moment, he longed to be nineteen years old again.

22

Luke was poking the branding iron into the fire coals, while Pa and Sam released the yearling they had just branded, when he saw riders coming from the east. "Must be Juan and Max headin' back already", he said to Pa pointing them out below the midmorning sun.

"Wonder how things turned out with the Governor?" Pa said squinting toward the horsemen, trying to make them out. "Sam, ride in and tell your Momma we'll probably have some extras for dinner. I think Juan and Max are coming back from their parley."

"That's not Juan and Max," Sam said to his Pa. Even at that great distance Sam could tell the people approaching were not the men who had stayed at their home last week. "I can't see who they are, Pa, but all those men are Anglos." Then the men and horses disappeared below the horizon as they rode behind one of the hills between them and the Stevens.

The three stood watching for the riders to reappear. Luke was the first to find them again and said, "There they are. Pa, the one in the lead is Jim Bowie."

Jonathan still couldn't make out details on the riders when Sam piped up. "Pa, it is Jim Bowie! You think he'll stay the night with us?"

"Don't know, son," Pa replied straining his eyes into the distance. "But if that is Bowie, you'd better hurry back to your Momma and tell her we're definitely havin' some extras for dinner."

Momma and Mary Beth were frantically making flour tortillas, and the big pot hanging in the fireplace was boiling the extra beans they'd put on when Pa led Jim Bowie through the front door. Pa said grinning, "Sarah, I found an old Indian fighter wanderin' around lost out there. He looks pretty bad, think you can feed him?"

"If he'll eat tortillas and Mexican strawberries," Sarah turned and said with her pretty smile, "I sure can." Then she sat down her work and wiped her hands in her apron as she walked quickly across the floor to their guest. "Jim, how are you?" She said, and then as she gave the man a big hug continued, "It's good to see you here. Welcome."

"It's good to be here, Sarah. Seems like I don't get this way very often anymore. I swear it is a shame that you are livin' way out here with the likes of Jonathan. You ought to just run away with me, and we'll go to New Orleans or someplace civilized where the world truly appreciates a woman as beautiful as you," Jim said after he had gotten his hug and stood back looking at Sarah.

She responded, "Well, if I'd known such a gallant gentleman was ridin' this way, we'd have more than a frontier dinner of bread and beans. But I promise I'll make it up to you at supper, if you'll stay the night with us."

"I'd rather spend the night sharing company with you and your kids and havin' a hand a cards with your old man than anything else in this world, Sarah, but I can't," Jim said. "And I'm sorry about comin' in unannounced, but I'm on some important business. I've gotta make some more miles before dark."

"How far you going, Jim?" Jonathan asked.

"I'm headin' to San Antonio de Bexar, Jonathan. Need to get there as soon as I can. Sure do appreciate your hospitality though."

"You will have some dinner won't you, Colonel Bowie?" Sam asked, afraid that his hero would ride off immediately.

"Well, Sam, if you could spare some of those Mexican strawberries for me and my men, and maybe some water and shade for our wore out ponies, I suspect we could probably take an hour or two rest." Bowie said smiling at his young friend. "Besides, I need to find out how many panthers you've skinned out with that new knife of yours."

The midday meal was ready by the time the men finished tending to the visitor's horses. Momma had Sam set wash basins on the front porch so all the men could wash up outside before dinner. She and Mary Beth had made plenty of tortillas for everyone, but she had to stretch the pot of beans a little to make sure their guests had enough to eat.

After the meal was devoured and Sarah had been thanked several times by each of the members of Bowie's group, the dinner dishes were left to be done later. They all went outside. Bowie's men scattered out under the trees and laid down to take naps while their leader sat on the front porch with the Stevens family to visit and share news. Jonathan started with the story of Juan and Max's recent trip.

"Yeah, I know about all that," Jim said. "I saw 'em both before I left. They're pushing Houston and the Governor pretty hard. That's why I'm on my way to San Antonio. The General wants me to go look at the situation at the Alamo and see what kind of shape I think Neill is in out there."

"Juan says they've made a good fort out of it," Jonathan said. "But they need men and supplies desperately."

"Well there's the rub, Jonathan," Jim said lifting his head and looking into his friend's eyes. "Houston doesn't think we can hold it against Santa Anna, and he doesn't want to waste the men and the powder. He's trying like hell to get an army put together, and Smith is trying like hell to get a government put together. Everything is spread awful thin, and Santa Anna may already be on his way out here."

Sarah sat up straight and said, "But, Jim, doesn't he think that Santa Anna has to be stopped before he reaches the homesteads and all the settlements?"

"Sarah, this is big country," Jim responded. "Right now the General figures we're too strung out. I believe he's thinking that the farther Santa Anna gets into Texas the farther he'll be strung out, and the better chance we'll have against him. That is, of course, if *we* can gather and bunch up a big army."

"What do you think about that, Jim?" Jonathan asked.

"Hell, I don't know, Jonathan. This whole damn mess rankles me!"

"Does the Governor agree with General Houston?" Jonathan went on.

"He hasn't said one way or the other. I know there's Houston and Seguin and everybody else workin' on him, but I don't have any idea which way he's leaning." Jim answered and moved forward to put his forearms on the table.

"All I know is it's got me in a hell of a pickle. I've got to get to the Alamo pronto and decide if it's going to be worth tryin' to make a stand there. Houston gave me these orders," Jim said reaching into his pocket and pulling out some papers. "The gist of 'em is if I get there and see things his way, I'm supposed to blow up the Alamo and take all the men and canons to Gonzales and Copano. James Fannin has a garrison forming down in Goliad and some of it might need to go there. Hell of a pickle, ain't it?"

Jonathan shook his head and pursed his lips together which showed his friend he sympathized with his awkward position. Then he said, "You know all the folks out here, Jim. You know they'll fight and fight hard, but unless there is some help with men and supplies from Houston there's no way to hold back a big Mexican army."

Bowie could see the concern of a father and husband in Jonathan's face as he continued. "Jim, you've heard what that animal did in *Zacatecas*. That's the part that scares me. If he gets down into this country and on into the settlements east of here, Santa Anna's goin' to leave all of Texas a burnin' wreck. He'll destroy everything he's allowed to get to."

"I've been thinkin' about that a lot, too, Jonathan." Bowie sighed. Then he slapped his knees with his hands and took a deep breath as he stood. "Well, guess I'd better saddle up and get on to it. Wish these were different times."

That night in bed Jonathan told Sarah he wanted her to take the children and go east to someplace safer. After he gave her all his thoughts about the idea, she pulled him to her and said, "Honey, we're here now together and we're safe. There may come a time when we will have to leave this place. We don't know that. But we will stay in our home with our family for every minute God gives us together. This is our home and the children and I will not leave it unless there is no other option. We will just have to see what each new day brings."

A week and a half later the day brought more riders to the Stevens' homestead. Jonathan and the boys were working in the barn and the women were in the house when they all heard the horses approaching.

William Travis rode in with thirty mounted Cavalry. Will was a twenty-six-year-old Lieutenant Colonel in the regular army. He and Jonathan had become friends during the action they saw together at the Siege of Bexar.

"Mornin', Will," Jonathan said to the young Colonel as he and the boys walked out of the barn. Jonathan finished wiping his hands on an old rag and reached up to shake hands with the mounted soldier.

"Good to see you, Jonathan," Will responded smiling as they shook. "You look well."

"I am well. Thanks. What brings you out this way? Get down and rest a while," Jonathan said, "and let me introduce you to my family."

Lt. Col. Travis dismounted and handed his horse's reins to one of the still mounted men. Then he said in a very official sounding voice, "Sergeant, take the men down to the creek there and have them water their horses and check their gear. I need a little time with Captain Stevens."

As the horses and men made their way down to the creek, Will met the family and Sarah invited him into the house. Mary Beth brought coffee and cups to the table while Pa sat down across from the guest and said, "What's afoot, Will? Tell me what's going on."

"Jonathan, Governor Smith has ordered us to help man the Alamo at San Antonio de Bexar. I understand you're aware of Colonel Neill's situation there." Travis thanked Mary Beth for the coffee then continued. "The Governor asked me to recruit a hundred cavalry to start reinforcing the garrison. When these thirty were all we could raise I pleaded with him to reconsider, but he insisted that I carry out his orders."

"Is he going to send more men and supplies?" Jonathan asked.

"Yes, as they become available," Will answered sipping the hot liquid. "The Governor has rejected General Houston's plan to abandon the Alamo and wants to stop Santa Anna on the frontier. Jonathan, the volunteers are critical. You know that without a large volunteer army we cannot survive."

Jonathan nodded his head and Sarah and the children sat quietly.

"We must have your men, Jonathan. I told the Governor I'd mobilize your forces on the way to San Antonio. I need you to gather your company and report to the Alamo as soon as possible."

Two days later, at nine o'clock in the morning, Jonathan's entire company from the colony was assembled in front of his house. Some of the families had come along also to see their men off. Most, however, had said good byes at their homes and left their families there. Sarah noticed several of the men going were Luke's age or younger, but Jonathan had insisted that Luke stay to take care of the family. Luke was sulking over it, but Jonathan was firm. He told Luke he would send for him if he was needed.

Angus Cavanaugh, the coarse natured man who was the Stevens' nearest neighbor, got off his horse and handed the reins to one of his stout red headed sons. He walked up to Sarah and Mary Beth and did something neither of the women had ever seen before. Angus removed his big black hat.

As he held it across his chest the sincerity in his voice and in his piercing green eyes kept them from even noticing the man's big bald head. Quietly but firmly he said, "I told my lead man, Gabriel, to check in on y'all. You get word to him if you need anything. He's a strong man. I told him he was to do anything he had to so as to take care of your family."

"That's very kind of you, Angus," Sarah said smiling. "Thank you. We'll be just fine. And we'll help keep an eye on your people too. I want you and those boys to be careful, you hear me?"

When Jonathan was sure all the men were ready, he turned to his family. He hugged his children tightly one by one and said to each, "You take good care of your Momma and each other. I love you so much." Then he reached for Sarah. He kissed her and hugged her tightly to him. "You take care of my babies." He said into the side of her head as his voice started to quiver. "I love you more than anything in this world, Honey."

"I love you, too," she said softly. Then with strength in her tone she said, "You take care of yourself, mister. I'm going to see you real soon."

The families waved, some cheering and some crying, as the brave pioneers from the Austin Colony rode off to the Alamo.

23

Sam sat by himself warming in the afternoon sun on the hill west of the homestead. His chair was the big stump left from the old oak that had been struck by lightning last summer. He went there everyday now either after or between his chores to watch for his Pa, and think about things.

His world had been changing and he was having a hard time sorting it out. With Pa gone everyone in his family seemed to be working harder than normal, not because they needed to in order to keep the place up, but because they all wanted to be occupied with something besides worry. Sam didn't understand why there had to be a war. He didn't know why his Pa and all the other good men he knew had to go so far away and fight real soldiers in a real army.

Some days, sitting on his stump all alone, he cried. He wanted things to be like they were before. He wanted things to be the way they should, with just his family and no war.

Other days he wanted to hate. He wanted to get his gun and knife and ride to the front lines and kill all the ones responsible for the bad things that were changing his life. Then he would find his Pa, bring him home to the family, and things would be the way they were before.

That was the way he felt today. But as the anger started to boil up inside, he thought of his Pa and the conversation they'd had the day before he left for the Alamo. They had walked up to this same spot on the little hill and spent a long time talking together, the way they always did, just the two of them. Sam turned slightly and could almost see his father sitting there beside him as he remembered virtually every word of their last talk.

"Sam, you're pretty much grown now," his Pa had said. "And I swear, I'm so proud of the man you've grown into I could just bust sometimes." The honest tone in Jonathan's voice made the adolescent's heart swell.

"I know this is hard on you, son, but I need you to stay strong for the others, especially your Momma. She's gonna have a tough time with this, and I need you to help me keep her spirits up. While I'm gone make her smile whenever you can. You're pretty good at that, you know."

Sam's lower lip started to stick out and tremble and tears flooded his young eyes. He sounded almost like a little boy when he said in a weak and shaky voice, "I don't want you to go, Pa."

Jonathan put his arm around the boy and held him. "I know, Sam. I don't want to go. There's just some things in our lives we don't have much control over. This is one of 'em."

"But you don't have to go, Pa. We need you here," Sam said. His voice was shaking between short sobs while tears ran from his eyes and his nose started to drip. "What if you get hurt? There's lots of other men that can go!"

"None of us want to go, Sam. There's not a man on this frontier who wants to leave his home and go do this, but it's our place. And you know I couldn't let another man go in my stead, not when his home and family are just as important to him as you are to me."

Pa released his strong arm from around his son's shoulder and turned to face him. He put his rough hand gently under Sam's chin and raised the boy's face up to look at him. Pa grinned and said, "And by the way, I don't plan on gettin' hurt. You see, I don't think there's an army big enough to keep me from comin' home to you and your Momma."

Sam sputtered a quick smile through his tears and started taking short breaths in through his mouth because his nose had stopped up. "But, Pa, why does all this have to happen? I hate the damn Mexicans for doing this!"

"Well, son, it ain't their doin'. I don't think the Mexican people have anymore to do with this mess than you and me."

"Then why, Pa?" Sam blurted in a mad teary voice with his throat burning.

"I wish I could tell you, Sam, but I don't know. I've been wonderin' that same thing since before we went to Bexar last fall. All I know is the Mexican people are good people. They're just men and women, husbands and wives and families, just like we are tryin' to live their lives and work and be happy. I don't think they want to be doin' this anymore than we do. And you gotta remember, son, we're Mexican citizens, too. You and me both."

Sam's sobbing short breaths started to lengthen in through his mouth as he looked up into his father's kind face and listened to him continue.

"I've been around lots of different kinds of people in my life and so have you. Juan Sequin's a Mexican and you don't hate him. He's a fine man. Look at all the Germans and Irishmen here. They're good people all and a lot different than we are. Ol' Angus Cavanaugh is kind of a strange duck, but we could never have picked a better neighbor."

"Guess what I'm tryin' to say, son, is I don't think it matters where a man is born or what the color of his skin is. That's not what makes him good or bad. Hell, look at Gabriel. He's a Negro slave. But he's been a good friend to you, and I'd judge him to be as good a man as any white man I've ever known. Better than a lot of 'em."

Jonathan looked up to the blue sky trying to find the right words to give his sixteen year old son. He turned back to the boy and said, "God made most people good. I truly believe that. Problem is there's some bad people in this world, too. This man Santa Anna is as bad as they come, and he's the one's got this whole deal stirred up. If it wasn't for him none of this would be happening."

Sam's tears had stopped, and Pa put his arm around his son again. The boy put his head against his father's shoulder and listened as he kept talking.

"Your Momma and I brought you children to this wild place to make a new life and grab onto the chance for our family to own land and live free. And by God, that's what we've done.

"But bein' free doesn't mean just gettin' to do whatever you want. A whole country of people couldn't work like that. Bein' free means gettin' to have a say in the laws you live under and which men make those laws.

"That's part of what this Santa Anna is takin' away from us. He wants to be a king or emperor or somethin' and take away our say in things. He wants to rule us. Does any of this make sense to you, Sam?"

Sam leaned back from his Pa slightly and looked at him. "I understand what you're saying, Pa, but I don't know why it has to be this way. Why is he doing this?"

"Well, like I said son, there's some bad people in this world and that son-of-a-bitch is rotten. That's all I can figure. And he's the worst kind. He's a bad man with power," Pa said looking into his boy's tear streaked face.

"But we're not going to let him get away with it. I promise you that," Pa said with a nod of his head and a soft smile.

"Sam," Jonathan sighed leaning forward and putting his hands just above each of the boy's knees while he kept looking into his son's eyes, "I know you're scared, and truth is, I am, too. And I'm tellin' you, I don't want to go fight in this damn war. But a man's always gotta' do what's right and sometimes that's not an easy thing. Sometimes, like we're doin' now, that means fightin' against what's wrong. It means standing up against the bad ones and not lettin' 'em have their way."

Jonathan sat up straight and took a deep breath. He said calmly, "That's why we're doin' this, son. If there was a different shot, I'd take it."

Sam looked at his father. "I guess I know that, Pa," he said as the tears returned and blurred his eyes. "Just want you to be careful while you're whippin' Santa Anna."

Pa grabbed the boy into his arms again and said, "I will, son, you can count on it.

"You remember all this for when your time comes though. As you go through life your whole world will change, at least a time or two. I know mine has. Everybody's does.

"But no matter how much the world around you might get twisted up or look different, there's one thing you can hang onto. Right and wrong, *never* change. In your life, when it's your turn, a good man like you can't let the bad ones win. Will ya' promise me that?"

"I promise, Pa," Sam said with all his heart and hugged his father.

Sam rose from the oak stump and stretched. He suspected he should go back to see if Momma needed help with any of the chores. He looked at the empty spot where his father had sat the day before he left and said out loud, "I promise, Pa...and I swear, I'm so proud of you I could about bust sometimes, too." He turned to walk back down the hill. That's when Sam saw the dust.

Way off in the distance to the west was a small lineal cloud rising from the earth. It was too far to see how many, but somebody was definitely riding hard toward the homestead. Sam ran off the hill to tell the others.

The first thing Luke and Momma did was make sure all the guns were loaded. Luke stuffed the pistol Pa had given him for Christmas into his belt and said, "C'mon, Sam!" They both shouldered a powder horn and possibles bag and dashed off the front porch carrying their rifles toward the hill.

They ran all the way to the top. When they got there and dropped their hands on their knees, breathing very hard, they scanned the distant countryside. Sam knew where to look so he was the first to find the plume again and pointed it out to Luke. "There they are!" he said still huffing for breath.

Both the young men's heads bobbed up and down while their lungs tried to get all the pure Texas air they could hold. Their eyes, however, never moved from the line of dust streaking toward them. As the dry reddish brown dirt was thrown high into the air from the horse's driving hooves, it was magnified by the angle of the late afternoon sun behind it. That made it large and very visible at this great distance, but whatever created it was still just a speck.

"How many you think?" Luke asked Sam as they caught their breaths and watched.

"Can't tell," Sam said like a grown up. "Not many. Maybe just one or two."

"If they're bad ones, Sam, you stay up here and hide. I'll go down with Momma and get the girls hidden. Then you sneak down from behind. I'll talk to 'em loud and armed from the front porch. If there's trouble, we'll get 'em in a cross fire," Luke said and turned to look straight into his little brother's eyes. "Can you do that?"

"I'll have the one closest to you in my sites before you start talkin'," Sam said so seriously he could feel the hair on the back of his arms start to stick up.

The boys watched. They had both caught their breath and were now just sweating. The pointed cloud approaching them never stopped nor slowed. It just kept coming.

Finally Luke said, "It's a lone rider. There's only one man."

"You think it's Pa?" Sam wished out loud.

"Can't tell yet, but he's ridin' hard. Run down and tell the girls it's only one man comin' in. I'll stay up here and watch."

Both the women wanted to go to the top of the hill and wait for Pa, but Sam convinced them to wait. "If it's Pa then Luke will let us know in plenty of time to get up there and meet him," he said. "But if it's someone else, we may need to stay close to the house." Momma respected her boy's judgment so she and Mary Beth started puttering around the house picking up and cleaning. Sam watched the hill and they all waited.

Before long Luke came walking down the hill. The three from the cabin ran through the front yard to meet him and find out what was going on. "Is Pa comin' in?" Mary Beth said frantically. She was frustrated and mad because she hadn't been out there with the boys. Sometimes she hated being a girl and being forced to act like one.

"No, it's not Pa," Luke said firmly when he was close enough for them to hear without having to scream. He had already dealt with his disappointment and tried to give the others a moment to deal with theirs. Then he said, "It's Juan Seguin, and he's ridin' hard. Somethin's up. Mary Beth, get him some fresh water ready. He's gonna need it when he gets here."

24

Juan forced his spent horse to run all the way up to the front of the Stevens' homestead. The horse was covered in lather that was mostly brown from the dirt of the obviously long and tough ride. Juan and his clothes were also covered with dusty grime. As he jerked the poor animal to a hard stop Juan said through several tries at coaxing the words out of his parched throat, "Sarah, I need a fresh horse and some food and water!"

Sam grabbed the fidgeting horse's reins close to the bit holding him still while the others walked closer, and Juan started to dismount. Juan's legs were unsteady from the rough ride and he stumbled when he put his weight on them. Luke caught the man and kept him from falling. As the strong young man held their friend so he could get the feeling back in his legs, Sarah reached for both of Juan's hands and said, "What is it, Juan? What has happened?"

"Santa Anna's army has already reached the Alamo!" Juan said, still breathing hard. "They've sent me to get reinforcements. The fighting has begun."

Sarah's right hand flew to her mouth as she involuntarily sucked in a deep breath. The hand stayed there as though it was supposed to hold back a cry or a scream. Then Sarah closed her mouth and bit her teeth together hard for a moment. She started breathing deeply in through her nose and her eyes narrowed a little. Her hand moved itself away from her mouth and she said firmly, "Luke, catch a good horse. Sam, get the saddle off this one. Mary Beth, get some food together. Quickly children! Juan, here's some fresh water for you."

The children jumped into action, and Sarah led the exhausted Seguin to the front porch. Sam tied the wheezing horse and tried to calm it while he removed the saddle. It was not the well bred mount Juan had been riding before, and Sam figured it was probably one of many Seguin had traded out since he left San Antonio de Bexar.

Sam tried to listen, but there wasn't any conversation on the front porch. Momma let Juan gulp down some water and splash his face. She told him to rest and she'd bring food and a wash basin.

While he pulled the ornate Mexican saddle off the worn pony and laid it to the ground, Sam never took his eyes off Juan. The man moved to one of the short backed chairs on the front porch and flopped down. He then raised himself to stretch and pop his spine over it. The look on Juan's face as he groaned told Sam that their Mexican friend's back was probably ruined from this ordeal. Juan got up from the chair and laid down flat on the coarse plank floor of the front porch with his knees up in the air. By the time Momma walked out of the house a half minute later with the wash basin and a towel, Juan was sound asleep.

They all moved about quietly at their tasks while the Mexican slept. After the boys had saddled the new mount, Momma put the cold biscuits and jerky she had wrapped into the saddle bags. Sam walked the over-ridden horse Juan had come in on trying to cool it down and save it. When Mary Beth brought a big plate of bacon, beans, and fresh tortillas onto the front porch, Sam tied the suffering horse to the corral fence and went to join the others.

"Juan, here's some food and coffee for you," Momma said softly as she tried to gently wake him.

Seguin's eyelids popped open and he started taking in fast deep breaths as he burst out of his dead sleep with a momentary confusion about where he was. He looked around quickly through bleary bloodshot eyes at the four Stevens' standing over him. "How long have I been asleep?!" he asked immediately with almost a sense of panic in his voice.

"It's all right, Juan," Momma said with her kind inflection. "You've only been asleep for a little bit. Just long enough for us to get everything ready for you. Now sit up and eat some food."

Both the boys grabbed an arm and helped the stiffening man to his feet. Juan's whole body hurt as he tried to clear his head and make his way to the chair and small table they had prepared for him. Before he had anything from the table he drank down two more large dippers of water from the wooden bucket sitting on the floor next to his chair.

Juan finished his last swallow. He took a deep breath and started to return the dipper to the bucket when Sarah asked, "How is Jonathan? Have you seen him?"

"Please forgive my rudeness, Sarah. Your husband is fine. Jonathan and I have seen each other every day since he and his men arrived at the Alamo. He sends his love and asked me to give you this." Juan reached into the inside pocket of his jacket and produced a folded piece of paper. "I promised him I would get it to you."

Sarah opened the note and read it. Her children watched as she stood there with tears filling her eyes, then rolling down her cheeks. Each grown child desperately wanted to ask what the letter said, but didn't.

When she finished her hands shook slightly as they helped the piece of paper find its original folds. She held it between both hands as though she were holding Jonathan there, then slipped the note into the front pocket of her apron. Sarah looked up at the children and smiled sadly saying, "Pa sends his love."

Luke sensed his mother needed to sit down and slid one of the chairs close to her next to Juan's small table. A little unsteady, Sarah sat into the chair then looked up to Mary Beth and asked, "Honey, would you bring me some coffee please?" As her daughter started into the house, Sarah turned to Juan and said, "Tell me what's happened. I want to know everything, Juan." Then as though catching herself she reached down and nudged the plate of food in front of the *Tejano* and said, "Oh, please, you need to eat while it's hot. I'm sure you must be starving."

The hungry man picked up a piece of the coarse fried bacon and crunched two bites into his mouth as he also reached down for a tortilla. "This is so good. Thank you very much," He said while the manners deep inside him tried to control his body's starving urge to stuff everything on the plate into his mouth all at once.

After he had quickly eaten several more bites of the beans with bacon and two tortillas he said, "I will try to remember everything for you, Sarah." Juan reached for the coffee, trying to slow himself down. This was the first food he'd had in two days, and it was nearly making him light headed. He drank some of the strong black coffee then stretched his back up straight.

Sam sat on the porch's rough floor while Luke and Mary Beth each pulled a chair closer to their guest and sat. Juan leaned forward and started eating again more slowly. They all listened while he began to recount all the details he could remember about what had happened at the Alamo.

"When Max and I returned from our trip to meet with the Governor and General Houston, Jim Bowie and his men were already in San Antonio. Jim expected to destroy the Alamo and remove the garrison. That is basically why Houston had sent him.

"By the time we got back, however, Jim had already made up his mind to the contrary. He saw the fortifications and Colonel Neill had been very persuasive. He convinced Jim the Alamo was the best hope for Texas to halt Santa Anna's advance before he destroyed the settlements and the interior.

"You can't imagine how glad I was to see him so committed to the endeavor. Jim showed me a most passionate letter he wrote to Governor Smith. He commended James Neill for his outstanding leadership and told the Governor that he and Neill would never surrender the post. I sent my best *vaquero* as a courier to personally deliver that letter to Governor Smith.

"Apparently it made a difference because within a couple of weeks William Travis arrived with thirty cavalry on direct orders from the Governor. Three days after that Jonathan came in with his company from here. A couple of days later David Crockett, the famous Indian fighter and Congressman from Tennessee, arrived with a group of American volunteers.

"As men kept coming, Will Travis told everyone the government would send more supplies and men as they became available. We were building the Alamo into a true fortress.

"Then things started to change." Juan paused and reached for his coffee as he looked around the small group. "About three and a half weeks ago, Colonel Neill got word that illness had taken over his family and he was needed there immediately, so he left on furlough to Bastrop. He was to be back within twenty days.

"He left Travis in charge as acting post commander. I honestly don't think he was trying to slight Colonel Bowie with his decision. Jim is certainly older and more experienced, but he's commissioned as a volunteer officer, just like Jonathan and me. Travis has a regular Army commission, like Colonel Neill."

Juan drank the last of the coffee and sat the cup back on the small table. Sarah remained motionless and never took her eyes from Juan's face. Mary Beth refilled the *Tejanos'* cup from the black metal coffee pot while he started speaking again.

"At any rate, the men didn't like it at all. They followed Neill because they knew him and he had proven himself, but the volunteers didn't know William Barrett Travis from a sack of beans. They insisted on electing their officers the way we have always done before. Travis agreed, and of course, the regulars voted for him and the volunteers all voted for Jim.

"The night after the election Bowie got quite out of hand with his celebration. In Bexar that night Jonathan told him he was making an ass of himself and I thought the two of them would come to blows."

Juan reacted to the surprised expression on Sarah's face with a slight nod and a half smile as he continued saying, "Jonathan let it pass though and returned to the fortress, which was probably a good thing for Jim because he was exceedingly drunk. Through the course of the night, however, Jim did manage to distress literally every local in the town.

"I understand you've met Will Travis." Juan said slowly as he tilted his head down slightly and cast his eyes up as he looked at Sarah. When she gave an understanding nod he said, "In my opinion, he is a good man. However, you may have noticed, he is yet a little stiff and proper for our frontier environment. He was appalled at Bowie's behavior. Maybe he hasn't been out here long enough, but he tried to make quite an issue out of his impression of Jim's lack of propriety.

"As it turned out none of that lasted very long because within a day or two we learned Santa Anna had reached the Rio Bravo with a large army. Thank goodness those two men were bigger than their petty differences and locked onto the important issue. They agreed that Bowie would command the volunteers, and Travis would command the regulars until Colonel Neill returned. They jointly signed all orders and correspondence.

"We continued to prepare the fort because both Bowie and Travis figured Santa Anna couldn't reach Bexar until March fifteenth. The bastard arrived eleven days ago on February twenty-third."

Juan stopped eating for a moment and looked around at everyone. "His army kept coming and coming. All that day and the next more and more gathered, and they still kept coming. Santa Anna sent a contingent under a white flag to meet with us. Their officer presented Travis and Bowie written terms of surrender then returned to their side to await our answer.

"Travis fired a cannon shot as our reply!"

He tore a tortilla in half and leaned forward. Juan ate more slowly and continued.

"Will has actually taken full command of the Alamo for all practical purposes. Jim is extremely ill and is now bedridden. He had the men help him to his feet to receive the Mexican envoy and stood there like a rock while the officer presented their terms, but as soon as the gate closed behind the Mexicans, Jim collapsed."

"What's wrong with him?" Sam blurted out.

"I don't know what is wrong with him, but he is in a bad way. Jonathan and I both noticed how much more he had been coughing over the past several weeks, but he is now bringing up blood and also has fever. Something is very wrong deep within his chest.

"Bowie is a natural leader though and continues to put on a strong face for the men. Sometimes he has his bed carried outside so that he can talk with the troops and help boost their spirits." Juan looked at Sam then at his mother. "You know Jim well so you'll understand that even though he is quite ill, he is still a unique character.

"Through all this Will Travis has performed and conducted himself well. He has gained the respect of all the men now. After Santa Anna's army started to form, Will gathered everyone into the main yard."

Juan paused again and sat up straight in his chair. "He faced the entire assembly and spoke boldly about how critical the situation was, and then he drew a line in the sand with his saber. He gave every man the option of leaving with no disgrace, or staying to defend the Alamo. He asked those who would stay to cross the line and stand by him."

Emotion caused the *Tejano's* voice to falter and tears came into his eyes as he turned to Sarah Stevens. "Your husband was one of the first to cross the line." Juan turned to Sam as he said, "Jim Bowie had four men carry his bed across." He then looked from face to face. "Every single man, save one, crossed the line and stood by Travis. I have no words for the feeling in my heart, but if I live to be a hundred, Sarah, I swear to God I will never forget that moment!"

Juan cleared his throat and took in some deep breaths. He reached for his coffee and took a couple of large sips before he leaned forward and continued telling the story as he started eating again.

"After their main body assembled, the Mexicans started hitting us with cannon fire. Although they have continued the cannonade around the clock since they started, we actually haven't sustained much damage. Apparently they don't change the elevation of their artillery.

"There has also been no assault against the Alamo. We assume they believe it would be too costly because of our array of cannons. When I left four days ago, we had not lost a single man. They, on the other hand, have lost many. Whenever a Mexican gets within five hundred yards of our walls, one of Davy Crockett's Tennessee riflemen shoots him. Those fellows and their long rifles are incredible.

"Our overall situation, however, is most desperate. We must have reinforcements. Colonel James Fannin has a large garrison in Goliad, and we have sent word for him to come to our aid immediately."

Juan turned to Sarah's eldest. "Luke, your father asked that you go to Goliad and join Fannin's force. Hopefully they will be on the march to San Antonio by the time you reach Goliad, but you should be able to catch up to them."

With the *Tejano's* words Sam felt his heart stop as he looked at his brother. Then Juan turned to him and said, "Sam, he said that you are to take care of 'his girls'." Sam nodded.

Juan turned to Sarah. "Travis sent Maximilian and me to gather reinforcements and get correspondence to the government. Neither of us wanted to leave the Alamo, but Jonathan and Jim maintained that as Mexicans we'd have a better chance of getting through or surviving if we were caught. Max left his oldest son there.

"Once we got through Santa Anna's lines, we split up in order to reach more people. Max went south toward Goliad, and I came this way. If he makes it by here, tell him I left on my way to the Governor's. If he doesn't catch up to me, tell him I will meet him at the Alamo."

Juan stopped talking and looked down at his plate while he used the last tortilla half to sop up the remaining bean juice from his meal. He knew he had told them about everything important. Everything except the red flag. The huge, horrible red flag that Santa Anna had hung from the church tower in San Antonio de Bexar for the men inside the Alamo to see.

It was the battle field flag that meant - No Quarter. If Santa Anna took the Alamo, every man would be put to death. There would be no prisoners taken. As he looked up at his friend's wife and children, Juan knew that was information they didn't need.

With that Juan stood and, as he stretched his back, Sam heard several vertebrae crack. "I must be on my way now." He said looking around at the little family that had quietly been digesting his every word. "The men are depending on me."

"Juan, do you think there will be time and enough men?" Sarah said hoping for the right answer as she remained seated and looked up at the *Tejano*.

Juan looked straight into her eyes. "There has to be, Sarah."

25

The room felt closed in with its low ceiling and thick walls as Jonathan stuck his head and shoulders through the narrow doorway. The original parts of the Alamo were three times Jonathan's age, but this dark room his friend was in seemed even older than that. There was also a bad smell to it. The yellow light from the single oil lamp on the small old wooden bedside table gave the whole place a musty feeling.

"You feelin' all right, Jim? Brought my deck. Thought maybe you could use a hand a cards tonight," Jonathan said boldly with his broad smile as he strutted into the room. Angus Cavanaugh followed in quietly behind Jonathan.

"If I had the strength to lift up my fightin' knife, I'd slit my own damn throat," Bowie said as he raised himself weakly onto the pillows that he started to move against the rough wooden headboard. "But I don't. I suspect I could pro'bly still lift a few paper cards though, and maybe choke down a hand or two. It's good to see you boys.

"Angus, I'm glad you're here 'cause I wanna thank you for that whiskey you gave me. I swear you make the finest whiskey in Texas! That is definitely the best medicine I've had since I started gettin' sick. Ain't sure it's makin' me well, but at least I feel a lot better while I'm laid up."

The whiskey maker smiled at the compliment and said, "Glad you like it, Colonel Bowie. Sure wish I had some more here with me to give you."

"Well, don't worry about it, Angus," Bowie smiled. "While I's layin' here thinkin', I decided that as soon as we get this little spat with Santa Anna over I'm movin' to the Colony, so I can be closer to you. I figure, chances are, I'm not gonna ever get to see the Pearly Gates.

But if I had a neighbor that could make lots a whiskey like that, you know, that'd be close enough to heaven for me."

Angus Cavanaugh laughed out loud and pushed the brim of his big black hat up with his thumb. Suddenly he felt more comfortable and was honored that the Colonel liked his whiskey. He had met Bowie before, but didn't know him well, and was still somewhat awed to be in the presence of such a famous man.

Jonathan laughed, too, and said, "Now hold on there, Jim. You know we're pretty particular about who we let settle in the Colony. We've got rules about morals and character and things. Besides, Angus has only got one plantation. I'm not sure he could make enough whiskey to keep up with you."

Jim's mouth started into the comfortable laugh Jonathan had enjoyed over the years, but as the laughter started its way out, the coughing took over. The sick man almost retched with its violence. For an instant Jonathan's mind flashed to Moses Austin, as he hurried to Jim's side and put his hand on his friend's back.

Eventually Jim quit coughing and eased himself back onto the pillows. He was pale and his eyes were dark and sunken. Jonathan helped him hold a glass of water and take a couple of sips. As he finished, and Jonathan put the glass back onto the table, Jim said in a flat voice, "Ga'damn I'm glad that's over. It's the shits, ain't it?"

"Are you gonna make it, Jim?" Jonathan asked softly.

Bowie grinned up at his friend and said with more strength in his voice, "Yeah, I'm fine. Thanks. That's just somethin' I do every now and then to keep myself from falling asleep. You boys still feel like playin' some cards?"

Jonathan and Angus pulled two worn ladder-back chairs and another small table to the bedside. As they maneuvered around in the small dark room Jim asked, "What's happenin' out there, Jonathan? It's been kinda slow in here. All I get to do is listen to those blame Mexican cannons and wait around to catch a cannon ball in my lap!"

"Well, Jim, things are gettin' a little bleak out there," Jonathan sighed as he sat down with Angus and pulled the well-used deck of cards from his pocket. "We got word back that Fannin's garrison from Goliad likely won't come. Guess Fannin was bein' mealy mouthed about not havin' proper orders, and sounds to me like his feet have turned real heavy and grown roots.

"'Course we haven't heard anything from Juan and Maximilian's sortie. Hopefully they've got reinforcements on the way. We still haven't lost any men, but the cannons are startin' to have their effect. They're beatin' down our north wall pretty bad. We have got to have more men, and we've got to have 'em soon. Wanna play stud or draw?"

As Jonathan started dealing out three hands of draw poker Bowie said, "I been hoardin' the last of Angus's whiskey. You boys want a taste?" After they both declined, he continued, "Well, hope you don't mind if I have a swallow. I've been sick you know. An' I don't feel like an ass whippin' in cards either, Jonathan! You should take a little pity on a dyin' man."

Jonathan smiled as he picked up his cards. "Well, if you weren't such a sorry card player, it'd be easier for me to let you win once in a while."

The card game in the dingy little room improved Jim's spirits and gave them all a way to escape the slowly passing time and the tension of being surrounded by a Mexican army that outnumbered them twenty to one. As they played, the three men talked some about family and home, but mostly they kept to light-hearted card table chatter telling of other times and reliving better days.

They each took turns winning through several hands, then Bowie got suddenly quiet. He raised his palm toward Jonathan in a signal to be silent as he turned his head slightly to one side and cast his eyes upward. "You hear that, Jonathan?" Bowie asked seriously.

"I don't hear it, Jim. What is it?"

"The cannons have stopped."

The three men sat quietly and listened. None of them moved. They listened so hard that soon they could hear one another breathing, and the flicker of the flame from the small oil lamp. In its yellow light the room seemed even smaller than before. For the first time in twelve days the slow constant rumble of cannon fire was missing.

Bowie broke the silence. "They're repositioning their troops. They may be gittin' ready to hit us tonight. Better go find Will and see what's goin' on."

As Jonathan and Angus grabbed their gear and started out the door, Jim said, "Send somebody back down here to let me know what's happenin'. Good luck, boys. Go get 'em!"

* * * *

"You were right standing up to the President the way you did, Sir," Lieutenant Bernillo attempted to flatter General Martin Perfecto de Cos, the commander who had sworn an oath to the Texians that he would never return to Tejas under arms after his defeat at the Siege of Bexar.

The two had just left the Officers Call at Santa Anna's command tent and were now in a fast walk through the encampment toward their battalion. General Cos kept his focus straight ahead as they briskly marched past rows of tents, small fires, and cone shaped stacks of rifles. The young Lieutenant stayed up with the quick pace, but stumbled several times as he kept turning his body toward the General trying to talk to him.

"This is foolish, Sir. You know we should not be attacking the Alamo. It makes no sense at all! I mean from a military standpoint, of course," Bernillo chattered in what sounded like a plea for the General to do something. Cos gave no indication that he even heard the twenty year old, but his eyes cut a sideways look at him as they walked. General Cos did not like this junior officer he'd been given.

Lieutenant Denicio Bernillo's father was a medium level politician in *Ciudad Mexico*. When the call-to-arms went out for this campaign, the man had traded enough influence to get his son an officer's commission. Although Cos had never met Denicio's father, he held contempt for most politicians. In his experience they had no scruples and cared only about advancing their own careers and interests. Traveling a thousand miles with the younger Bernillo had confirmed General Cos's thoughts on that subject.

"Sir, you said so yourself, the Texians have gotten no reinforcements and there are none in sight. All we have to do is wait for their supplies to run out and they will have no choice but surrender. I agree with General Ripperda. It is insane for us to be forced into the teeth of their cannons and rifle fire. We could all be killed. Sir, we have the advantage. We do not need to attack!"

As that last word left Denicio's lips General Cos stopped himself by planting his right foot. He swung abruptly to face the surprised underling. Cos's upper body leaned forward and his eyes squinted into a hateful glare. The General moved only his lips, while his crooked teeth stayed clenched together, as he growled at the Lieutenant in a voice that made the bottom of the young man's stomach feel as though it was falling away.

"Listen to me you whimpering whelp! The officers have given the President our opinion. He has made his decision. Our orders are to attack! Now you will shut your mouth and carry out his orders! If I hear you say one more word about it, or if you hesitate one step on the field of battle, I will kill you myself! Do you understand me, boy?"

Denicio gulped before he got out a quick, "*Sí, General.*"

Cos wheeled around and started back to his battalion. Lieutenant Bernillo stood alone trying to make his quaking legs move again. Before they did, he threw up.

* * * *

Jonathan was standing on the ramparts of the north wall an hour before daylight when the first wave of white trousers on the Mexican uniforms appeared through the darkness. When they got within range the Alamo's cannons fired. The grapeshot they were filled with ripped through enough bodies to devastate the first ranks and make them stop.

There were so many of them it made Jonathan think about the ocean many miles to the south. In the blackest part of the night that comes just before sunrise, the massive lines of churning white clad legs looked like a foamy wave coming onshore in the darkness. It stopped, and started to recede, as the pieces of metal shrapnel slammed into the arms and legs and faces and organs of those in front.

Then, as with the ocean, when the white wave stopped and started back, another white foamy wave came immediately behind it. The cannons continued to fire while the waves kept rolling in and getting closer, like a quickly rising tide. The Alamo had become an island with an angry white sea rising all around it.

Using the wall in front of him as a parapet, Jonathan crouched to reload his rifle. He had fired three shots and killed three men. As he quickly tried to pour powder down the gun's muzzle, he looked fifty feet to his left at Will Travis, who stood on the same level of the scaffolding.

"Keep your men firing, Jonathan!" Will boomed through the deafening roar of rifles cracks and canon explosions. He stood with a pistol in each hand, swiveling his upper body as he turned to scream commands up and down the Alamo's defenses. "Make every shot count, men!"

Will fired the pistol in his right hand and dropped a Mexican soldier who had run ahead of the others and was closest to the wall. Without taking his eyes from the advancing force, Travis shoved the spent pistol into his waist sash and transferred the other pistol into his right hand as he continued commanding, "Don't fire into the crowd! Pick out one soldier and shoot him! Make every shot coun…" Just then the back of Will's head exploded. Hair, bone, blood and brains sprayed through the air and disappeared into the darkness.

The force of the single bullet snapped the man's head back, then his body went limp. It slumped onto the edge of the scaffolding, before it slid off and flopped into the dust below. The bright young Lieutenant Colonel was one of the first to die that Sunday morning.

Jonathan bit his teeth together hard when he saw Will fall. He pounded the ramrod down his rifle barrel and turned left and right to check on his men. When Angus Cavanaugh looked back at Jonathan, they held onto one another for a moment with their eyes, each saying good-bye to an old friend. Then Jonathan rose and started moving down the line barking orders and directing the men.

Angus Cavanaugh was at the front wall's corner with a red headed son on either side of him. Initially they held back the tide. But as the bubbling flood of Mexican uniforms continued to rise and get closer, they eventually were unable to shoot and reload fast enough to stop the ladders. As the Mexican army started to lap against the outside walls, they propped up wooden ladders against them. Streams of soldiers started up the ladders, creating rivulets of men trying to erode the Alamo's adobe mud and rock dike.

The Cavanaugh men were red tigers in their corner. As one would push ladders full of men off the wall and back to the ground, the others would reload then step up to plug the hole. When they became unable to keep up with that, they began using their rifle butts to club the soldiers coming up the ladders.

In the breaking dawn, when the tide began flowing over the parapets, one of the Cavanaugh boys was shot in the throat. He fell with his back to the wall spewing red froth and sucking air through the gaping wound. Angus was still in the middle between his boys as he turned with his back to the corner. His other son stooped across in front of Angus to tend to his younger brother when the first Mexicans ran down both sides of the scaffolding toward them.

The soldier coming from Angus' left bayoneted his wounded son and the one from the right shot the older boy in the back, then ran his bayonet through the boy's heart from behind. Before the blade made it through the young man's chest, Angus grabbed each of those soldiers by the throat. Another one stepped up and unloaded his gun into the whiskey maker's stomach. Angus kept his grip on the first two and used his body as a battering ram to take the third man off the rampart with him. Before Angus Cavanaugh and the three Mexicans hit the ground, he had crushed the windpipes of the two who had killed his sons.

As the adobe and rock dam walls gave way, and Mexican soldiers flooded into the Alamo, Jonathan ordered his dwindling forces back toward the long barracks and the old roofless chapel. Through the smoke he saw Angus Cavanaugh's big black hat on the plaza's dirt floor and knew his neighbor was gone. He could tell he had six men standing, and he rallied them toward the long barracks.

Within forty yards they were swarmed by Mexican soldiers. Jonathan and his men turned back to back and started fighting and killing their opponents with the only things they had left, rifle butts and hunting knives. Through the fury Jonathan noticed Santa Anna's mounted Dragoons riding into the Alamo's main yard. He grabbed the broken stock from a dead Mexican's rifle and was using it as a short club when the two colonists behind him fell. As soon as they were down, a Mexican soldier jumped forward and plunged the long bayonet blade attached to the end of his rifle deep into the small of Jonathan's back.

Jonathan cried out in pain and anger while he instinctively swirled around and, with his rifle stock club, smashed in the left side of the Mexican's skull. The action pulled the blade from his back and Jonathan bashed his way toward the long barracks. As he stepped over the man who had stabbed him, Jonathan grabbed the arm of one of the colonists who was down on his knees and tried to help him to his feet. The mortally wounded man collapsed, and Jonathan kept going.

He fought and crippled two more of the enemy before he reached the outside wall of the barracks. Jonathan turned and put his back against it trying to stay upright. Although he was losing the feeling in his legs, he held his knife and club up defiantly at the semi-circle of Mexican soldiers who quickly surrounded him.

They each made threatening moves toward Jonathan, but it was obvious that none of them wanted to be the first one in to attack this raging frontiersman. Suddenly a mounted Dragoon, spurring his horse, burst through the arc of men. With a long pointed lance, the Dragoon took the precious life of Jonathan Michael Stevens.

After the elite fighter jerked the weapon from Jonathan's chest, he spurred his horse again and turned back into the battle. Jonathan tried to hold on, leaning against the wall for a moment before he went down on his knees.

Then somehow the grunts and screams and explosions of the battle that were almost deafening, started to magically disappear. Through the Alamo's chaos of dust and smoke, Jonathan found himself with his family on the little hill overlooking his homestead. His children were all smiling up at him. Sarah hugged him to her, then kissed him and said, "Let's go home, Mister".

Seventy yards away Jim Bowie was still in his bed in the dark musty little room. When the first soldier burst through the narrow doorway, Jim shot him in the face with a pistol. The second attacker entered the room muzzle first and got off a shot that hit Jim in the thigh just before Bowie, with his second pistol, shot that man through the heart.

The next two into the room were pushed from behind and stumbled over the bodies and furniture in the darkness. The closest one raised his rifle like a spear and started a thrust with his bayonet to spike the bedridden man. When he lunged forward, Bowie deflected the rifle with his left arm which threw the soldier off balance and exposed his underside.

As quick as a rattlesnake Bowie's fightin' knife flew from under the covers and into the Mexican's stomach just above his pelvic bone. Jim ripped the man open all the way to his sternum, as the second soldier put his bayonet completely through Jim two inches below his heart. Bowie grabbed the rifle's barrel, holding it in him, and with one last mighty slash of his fightin' knife, almost completely cut off his attacker's head.

An hour and a half after the battle started, there were only seven of the Alamo's brave defenders alive. They were in the center of the old mission plaza surrounded by well over a hundred taunting Mexicans. All the Texans were wounded, but still standing in a circle with their backs to one another holding whatever weapons were left for hand-to-hand fighting.

When Santa Anna entered the compound with his entourage, he pranced his well groomed white horse to the outer edge of the circle of men that surrounded the Texans. The bright morning sun danced sparkles off the gold braiding and medals on his immaculate uniform as he said distinctly, "No quarter! Kill them all!"

The final seven men who had stepped across Travis' line in the sand to defend the Alamo, were summarily executed where they stood.

Santa Anna stayed mounted as he walked his horse around the plaza surveying the area and waiting for the bodies he had demanded. He wanted to view for himself the dead bodies of Jim Bowie, William Barrett Travis, Davy Crockett, and the *Tejano* traitor Juan Seguin. His men had brought in the current *Alcalde* of San Antonio de Bexar to make the identifications.

While he looked around at bright red blood everywhere, and the broken dead bodies strewn about, Santa Anna took a deep breath of the smoky aftermath and savored it. In his mind this one moment was worth the tedious trek from *Ciudad Mexico*. He considered war the only truly pure and exhilarating thing in life.

By the time the requested bodies were laid beside one another in the dirt of the main courtyard, several of his officers had joined Santa Anna. The President was furious that Juan Seguin was not found among the Alamo's dead. After dismounting, he turned to General Cos and said with a gruff tone, "When we find Seguin I want him alive. He is to be hanged, not shot. That is an order!"

He sneered down at the lifeless bodies of Crockett, Bowie, and Travis. The soldiers had taken turns mutilating Bowie's body with his own knife, after they finally killed him. Santa Anna kicked Travis with his boot as he thought momentarily about hanging their bodies from the outside walls as a message for those who would defy his power.

In less than two hours he had spent over six hundred of the fathers, husbands, and sons of Mexico to take fewer than one hundred ninety fathers, husbands, and sons from Texas. Price was not an issue. The cost was insignificant. The President of Mexico didn't even notice or care about the body of Sarah's husband. It was only fifteen feet behind him, being dragged by two men to be thrown onto the pyre for burning.

26

Dearest Sarah,

I write this quickly to let you know I am all right. We have been blessed with good weather and no maladies, except for Jim Bowie who is down with some sort of consumptive pneumonia. I will leave it to Juan to give you details.

My Darling, the enemy is upon us in great number. We have made the Alamo into a solid fort and are expecting reinforcements at any moment. Our position here is strong, as is our resolve. With time and enough men, we will prevail.

You and I understand each others feelings about taking the children east for sanctuary. My Love, just know that I trust your judgment about leaving our homestead. You will do the right thing. Know also that if the time comes for you to leave, I promise I will find you when this is over.

I think of you, and our children, every moment of the day, and it gives me strength in each thing that I do. I miss you all so much and dream of our being together again. Sarah, each night when I lay down to sleep you are with me. I think back on all the happiness and joy we have shared in our life together, and that brings me such peace in these difficult times. I wish I could have provided you a better, easier time and given you more, My Darling, but I thank you so for the wonderful life you have given me. I love you more than you will ever know.

Your devoted husband,
Jonathan
29 February 1836

"I love you, Jonathan. Stay strong," Sarah said quietly after reading Jonathan's letter again. Holding the letter in both hands, she sat by herself on the front porch in the early morning light. She had stepped out there to be alone and have coffee while Mary Beth made their breakfast inside the house. Sam was down in the east pasture opening the gate so the cattle could water.

Sarah was still vexed about whether or not to leave the homestead. Luke had been gone for almost a week. He left to join Fannin's garrison in Goliad the morning after Juan came through on his mission. There had been no news of any kind since then, and she was desperate to know what was happening with the war.

Sarah reached down to the little home-made table and picked up her cup of coffee. When she raised it to her mouth and blew lightly across its steaming surface, her eyes lifted to the top of the small west hill. She froze with fear when she saw the first ten Mexican soldiers starting down from the top in a fast walk toward the homestead.

Lieutenant Denicio Bernillo had seen the breakfast fire's smoke and led his ranging squad of ten mounted Dragoons and fifteen infantry toward it. Like most of the junior officers, he had been given a small detachment to commandeer supplies and scout for the Army as it moved into the interior of Texas after leaving the Alamo. He was halfway down the hill, riding to the right side of his foot soldiers, when his Dragoons topped the hill behind him. Bernillo looked cautiously for resistance, but saw no evidence of any men. He watched the woman on the porch rise and go into the cabin.

Sam was at the far end of the east pasture. When he finished opening the gate for the cattle, he turned to walk back to the cabin anxious for some bacon and biscuits. He was daydreaming about hunting with Gabriel when movement at the top of the hill on the far side of the house caught his eye.

Sam's heart almost stopped. He saw the evil looking silhouettes of the lance bearing Dragoons atop their horses cresting the skyline of the small hill. Before his mind could react, his body was in a dead run back to the cabin. Although Sam could tell his legs were running faster than they had ever run before, his eyes and brain seemed to be watching everything from a distance at a much slower pace. He was closing the expanse between him and the house as fast as he could, but he realized the Mexicans would be there first.

Mary Beth was at the stove frying several thick slices of bacon in a black cast iron skillet when Sarah entered the cabin and closed the door. Mary Beth turned and said, "Breakfast is almost ready. Is Sam back yet?"

When she saw her Mother lean back against the heavy wooden door moving her head about frantically surveying the house, she knew something was wrong. "What is it, Momma?" She asked quickly, a little scared reacting to the look on Sarah's face. The moment her Mother replied, "Mexican soldiers are coming over the hill!" Mary Beth felt like someone had hit her hard in the stomach.

Sarah reached for the rifle hanging on the wall behind the door. It took both hands to take the long heavy piece down and she checked to make sure it was loaded. She turned and looked straight into Mary Beth's eyes as she said, "No matter what happens, do not walk out of this cabin! Do you understand me, Baby? Do not let them see you!" With that Sarah turned and went out the door with the rifle in hand.

Lieutenant Bernillo and his infantrymen stopped in front of the house. The nice looking middle-aged woman closed the cabin's door behind her and stepped onto its front porch with her big gun. The Dragoons were still riding in from behind. Sarah stood tall holding the rifle in both hands waist high with the muzzle pointed slightly downward.

"What do you want here?" She said in a strong voice while she started to cock the gun's hammer back with her right thumb.

The spring loaded steel mechanism of the rifle's large heavy hammer clicked loudly, and Sarah cast her eyes down momentarily to see what she was doing. As it made the second click, into the fully cocked position, the shaky little Lieutenant commanded, "Fire!" The surprised soldiers jerked their weapons up and twelve of them pulled their triggers simultaneously. The booms from all the rifles were so close together they sounded like one long single explosion. The great plumes of smoke from each barrel also combined to form one giant white cloud that filled the still clear air of the homestead's front yard.

A dozen half inch lead balls ripped into Sarah with a lightening power, slamming her body so that she looked like a rag doll being thrown hard against the front wall of her home. In less than a heartbeat she was gone. Sarah Stevens, the loving wife and mother, was dead before her body dropped onto the rough plank floor of the front porch.

Sam had run along the side of the house and was abeam the front porch just as the Mexican's weapons went off. He turned his head and screamed out, "MOMMA!", when he saw his mother killed and her body beat against the wall. Sam jerked the Christmas knife from his belt as he bared his teeth and raged, "NO!" He never stopped running. He screamed like a madman in a wild attack on the closest thing to him, the mounted officer.

Lieutenant Bernillo's stomach fluttered with fear and he drew his saber. The sound and smoke from the rifles to the left, and the screaming boy's attack coming from the right, made the officer's horse spook. In panic, the animal fought Bernillo's jerking on the reins as it tried to decide which way to bolt.

The last several steps, Sam raised his knife making ready to kill the thing in front of him and cut its heart out. Denicio Bernillo made a desperate round-house swing with the sword he held in his right hand and pulled hard on the reins he held in his left. The horse stumbled, which took the blade's deadly sweeping arc directly in line with Sam's head.

The boy couldn't stop himself from ducking and raising his left arm to protect his head. It all happened too fast. When the sword's blade came through, it cut a glancing blow off Sam's left hand then went up and away from his head. The angle of the sharp blade's strike, as it hit the young boy's hand, took Sam's smallest finger off at the palm. The next finger was cut off at the second joint, and the skin on the end of his middle finger was taken away down to the bone.

Sam's eyes were instinctively watching the saber when his head dodged and his hand went up. Against the background of the deep blue sky, he saw the bright red splash of blood and the digits fly away. He howled with pain and the instantaneous terror of losing his hand. As he dropped the knife from his good right hand, he grabbed his mangled left and looked down at the bloody flesh just as Denicio Bernillo made the second strike with his sword.

The young Lieutenant was still fighting his agitated horse when he gave the final blow to Sam. After his first forward swing that took the blade up and over his horse's ears, Bernillo came back with all his might, making a backhanded downward bash to the top of the sixteen year old boy's head. Had Bernillo been a more experienced swordsman, he would have rotated his hand slightly and used the blade to split the boy in half. Instead, the crushing blow that put a crack in Sam's skull was made with the flat top side of the military saber. Even the back side of the sword would probably have split the boy's head open were it not for the thick old wool hat Sam always wore. The last thing Samuel Austin Stevens saw was the blood gushing from his wounded hand.

Inside the cabin the grease had started smoking as the bacon burned in the cast iron skillet still sitting on the stove. In horror Mary Beth backed away from the front window. She was almost in shock after seeing her family destroyed so quickly. As soon as her brother fell to the officer's sword, Bernillo yelled to his troops, "Check the house!" Now they were all scrambling to the front door.

Mary Beth's body filled with strength as she desperately looked for a weapon. She dashed to the stove, and when the first soldier burst through the door she permanently blinded him with the boiling bacon grease she threw into his face. The second one in was distracted by the man's scream, and Mary Beth broke his jaw with the cast iron skillet. The third one she stopped in the doorway when she threw the skillet and hit him in the head. She spun around searching for Momma's big butcher knife.

Before she could get a good grip on the knife she was hit from behind by the rushing bodies of three other men. The force swept her to her parent's bed and the soldiers pushed her onto it. One put his knee between her shoulders, and mashed his hand onto the left side of her face, pinning her. Her knees were off the edge of the bed. Another soldier threw her skirt up and started tearing her pantaloons down.

Mary Beth's right eye was smashed into the mattress, but through her left eye she saw a Mexican pick Jonathan's gold watch from the little table at the side of the bed. "That's my father's, you bastard!" she screamed struggling against the brute force holding her down. Then suddenly she smelled the foul odor of the man who was crouching behind getting himself ready to take her.

She screamed again, closing her eyes tightly and gritting her teeth together preparing for the worst. As she did, Lieutenant Bernillo used his boot to kick the lecherous soldier away from her. The man rolled on the floor and quickly turned back ready to kill when he saw his officer standing over him. He didn't make a move, but he had the menacing look of an ill-kept hungry dog that had been slapped away from its table scraps.

"Stand her up!" Bernillo said to the two soldiers who had Mary Beth pinned to the bed. Each man held an arm tightly as they raised the young woman and turned her to their commander. Though her face was red and her hair disheveled from the mistreatment, Bernillo could see the girl was very attractive. With the back of his hand he started to brush the long black hair away from her face to get a better look. Hatred burned in her eyes as Mary Beth said, "Damn you!", and spit in his face.

The Lieutenant grabbed a hand full of Mary Beth's thick hair, and wiped his face with it, as he looked straight into her eyes. He reached for her breasts with both hands and kept looking into her eyes while he felt how full and soft she was. Through the cotton dress he rubbed her nipples with his thumbs before he squeezed both breasts hard and stepped away.

When Bernillo drew his sword, Mary Beth knew she was about to die. But instead of stabbing her, he whipped the saber forward and cast its point to the floor. Slowly he took his eyes from hers for the first time and used his long blade to lift her skirt. Her underwear was around her calves. The room full of soldiers watched as the Lieutenant raised her dress high with his sword and exposed her womanhood to them all.

He turned slowly and faced the hungry eyed soldiers. Bernillo watched them as they looked at the woman. Abruptly he dropped the skirt. "No man is to taste this woman. That is an order!" He said loudly. As he cast his eyes directly at the soldier he had kicked away from

Mary Beth, he continued, "Any man who tries to soil this one will be shot! Do I make myself clear?" He stood silently looking around the room surveying the nodding heads, and relishing the "Yes, Sir's".

"Find a horse and saddle for her. You men gather what provisions are here. Bring anything of value to me. I want this place ready for the torch by the time we leave!" the young Lieutenant commanded pompously and dismissed the men to their tasks. He turned to the two holding Mary Beth and said, "Pull her pants up and tie her on a horse. She is coming with us."

27

"You come back here now, Sam. Don't you leave me, you hear? You get yourself on back here. That's it…That's it…Com'on now."

Sam heard the gentle coaxing words somewhere in the fog. The words sounded muffled like they were being said through a cotton sack. He kept trying hard to find their source. Slowly the words became more clear, and Sam forced his eyes open as he awoke.

When he opened his eyes he immediately slammed them shut again to protect himself from the blinding prism of light that entered his head. His eyelids blinked rapidly fighting against the light and the blast of white pain that suddenly surged through his body and gorged it. He cried out with the agony it brought as his eyes watered and tears started rolling from their corners.

"Attaboy, Sam, attaboy. You're back here now. I knew you wouldn't leave ol' Gabriel. I knew you'd come back fo' me", the big black man said slowly and gently in his deep soft voice as he rocked the boy in his arms. He sat with his back against the trunk of a large live oak tree at the edge of the Stevens' front yard. Gabriel's mighty legs were on the ground straight out in front of him, and there across his lap, he held his young friend's upper body. "Everything's gonna be all right now, Sam."

Sam knew something was wrong. There was a wet cloth across his forehead. He glanced toward the pain shooting up his left arm and saw red rags tied around his hand. When he looked back to the voice, he saw tears tracking down both sides of Gabriel's familiar face. Suddenly Sam's nose filled with the powerful acrid smell of heavy smoke and his body convulsed. He felt his head being held tenderly by Gabriel's strong rough hands. Sam vomited and faded back into the fog.

When Sam woke again the picture of his mother's smiling face that had filled his head disappeared. The fog vaporized into bright light and blinding pain. Sam didn't know where he was, and his body felt hollow with sudden fear. He tried to call out, "Momma!", but a muffled croak was all that left his parched throat and cracked lips.

He heard footsteps from outside the wooden walls that surrounded him. The thing he was laying on swayed back and forth then suddenly Gabriel was kneeling beside him. His friend placed a cool cloth on his throbbing head.

"You back with me now, Sam?" Gabriel said softly looking down on the boy. "You been comin' and goin' fo' a long time. This time you stay here. You're here with Gabriel now. You're gonna be all right. Can you hear me, Sam?"

Sam recognized the kind face and whispered, "Gabriel". His eyes continued to gain their focus and he said, "Where's Momma?"

"Here, take some of this water." Gabriel said quietly as he gently put his hand under the back of the boy's head. He helped Sam take shallow sips from the dipper he pulled from a warped metal bowl sitting beside him on the bed of the wagon. Sam realized he was very thirsty. But when he drank the water he noticed its smoky taste, and was suddenly nauseous. Sam gagged and Gabriel took the dipper away.

"You just take it slow here, Sam." Gabriel said carefully laying his friend's head down. "You need to wake up a little now. Just lay easy while you get your wits about ya'. You're gonna be all right."

Suddenly Sam saw the Mexican with his shiny saber and skittish, prancing horse. When the next image, his mother falling to the floor of the porch, flew into Sam's brain he shouted, "NO!", and raised his body upright from the waist. There was a pulse of white pain in his head and the back of the wagon started to spin. Sam slipped away into the fog again.

The next time Sam came to, he knew where he was. He was hurt and laying in the back of the big wagon. When he also realized his mother was gone forever, he started crying and felt Gabriel's immense strong hand rubbing his back. The two stayed like that, silently, for a long time until Sam rolled toward the big man and said through tear-streaming eyes, "Where's my sister?"

"She's alive, Sam," Gabriel said slowly in a quandary between his responsibility to tell the young man the truth, and his need to nurture the beaten boy he loved who had just come back to the living. "Everything's gonna be all right. But first we gotta get you strong again. I caught us a chicken and made some soup fo' ya. You lay back and rest. I'm gonna go get it, an' I be right back. You just stay with me now, you hear?"

Soon Gabriel was back inside the walls of the large oak wagon gingerly feeding his friend the hearty chicken broth. Sam responded quickly to the thick warm liquid. It felt good to his dry throat and his empty stomach. Gabriel fed the boy at a slow but steady pace trying to get nourishment into his body and keep his mouth from asking questions. Progressively Sam's head continued to clear and color started into his face, but his wounded body, which wanted for healing, made him go to sleep before the soup was finished.

Many hours later the pulsing pain throbbed Sam awake. He opened his eyes and saw Gabriel perched on the sideboard of the wagon looking down at him like a huge black angel. The angel was sweaty from exertion. Sam smiled weakly and said in a meager voice, "Hi, Gabriel. I think I need some more of that chicken soup."

"Lor-dee, Sam! I knew you's gonna make it!" Gabriel said loudly into the morning air with a hallelujah in his heart. "You just stay right there. I be right back!" He bounced over the wagon's sideboard and disappeared. Within no time Sam had more nourishment.

After the second spoonful of soup, Sam swallowed and said, "You have to tell me what happened, Gabriel. I know they killed Momma." He was afraid to take his hand from under the covers. "I need to know the rest of it. Where's Mary Beth?" Sam's eyes began to tear and his quivering lower lip started to stick out. "Did they cut my hand off?"

"Just lay still, Sam, and eat some more of this bird stew. It'll make you strong. Thing's are gonna work out. You just lay easy and have another bite." Sam obeyed. He calmed down and ate the heavy soup.

"That's it." Gabriel said smiling, "You just keep eatin' and I'll tell ya' everything I know.

"First of all, they didn't cut off ya' hand. Don't know what happened, but they did take off your little finger and part of the next one. It was bleedin' real bad and I had to carterize 'em with a piece of red hot steel while you was passed out." Gabriel paused and gave a friendly, sympathetic smile to the scared young man then continued. "Sam, your hand's gonna be just fine. Nobody ever uses a little finger fo' nothin' anyway."

Sam pulled his left hand from under the tarps with which he was covered. He looked at the makeshift dressing and was relieved when he saw what looked like a full hand. It struck him that the rags weren't red. Then he realized in the pit of his stomach that he would have bled to death if Gabriel hadn't seared the wounds closed.

Sam took another spoonful of soup. "What happened, Gabriel? How'd you find me?"

Gabriel looked into Sam's eyes. He could see they were focused and he decided the boy was awake and alert. Looking up to the sky Gabriel took in a very deep breath then turned back to Sam. He figured he'd go ahead and tell the boy everything. In a hesitating voice he said, "It's bad, Sam, but if you'll keep on eatin' here, I'll tell you." Slowly, looking away occasionally to swallow hard and blink back his own tears, the kind black slave continued to spoon soup into Sam's mouth and told his story.

"Day before yesterday Missus Cavanaugh sent me to the settlement in the big wagon with the tradin' goods, just like always. I dropped off the whiskey and picked up this here flour 'n coffee 'n supplies we needed. Then I headed on back.

"I's at that little halfway hill, goin' back, when I seen the smoke. I could tell it was comin' from the plantation. It was little at first, then they's lots of it. Turned into big, black smoke! Knew somethin' bad was wrong, an' I whipped them mules hard to get 'em back home.

"By the time I got back there everything was burnin' up...the big house, the barns, the slave quarters...everything we built...everything!

"When them mules told me they wouldn't go up there, I beat 'em hard and made 'em mind! I knew somethin' was bad wrong an' people was pro'bly hurt. Wadn't 'til I pulled them mules up in the middle of it and looked around that I knew there had been a fight.

"It must a been a hard one. Everybody was dead. All the Negroes was scattered out in front of the big house like they was tryin' to protect the Missus. She was in the middle of 'em." Gabriel looked up to the sky in an effort to keep from sobbing. "Them bad ones, them Mexicans, kilt 'em all.

Gabriel slowly brought his face down, but he didn't look at Sam. There was a distant gaze in his eyes as his mind brought back the images of the story he told. "The fire was burnin' an' it was hot an' I jumped out of the wagon an' tried to find somebody that was alive. Nobody was left. They was all gone.

"I ran behind the barn to turn my dogs loose and save 'em. The barn was burnin' hot an' when I got around it, all my dogs was dead. They'd shot 'em all."

Gabriel turned to Sam. Huge tears started down the big man's cheeks. "They kilt my dogs, Sam. Why'd they do that? They didn't have to kill them poor dogs."

Gabriel paused and wiped the tears away with his sleeve. He took in a couple of deep breaths and there was more composure in his voice when he started again. "Think I walked around there fo' a little bit tryin' to figure out what was happenin'. I was screamin' an' cussin' mad! I didn't know what to do, but I knew I could'a done somethin' if I'd been there when them bad men came.

"Then all of a sudden your Momma called to me, an' I swear to God I don't know where it came from. I knew I had to get over here. There wasn't nothin' I could do fo' the folks at the plantation. They was all dead. An' I gave my word to Massah Cavanaugh, before he left, that I'd take care of your family. So I cut loose one of the mules, left the rest of 'em in they traces, and rode bareback over to your place as fast as I could!

"By the time I got here everything was burned down. Them bad men had taken away your home just like they did ours. They wasn't much left.

"I was sure proud a you, Sam." Gabriel smiled down at the boy and placed his large hand on Sam's chest. "Fo' one man you must'a put up one helluva fight. You was in the front yard with your knife layin' beside you. They whacked up your hand and beat you on the head. Looks like one of 'em stepped on you with their horse cause your leg was broke down below the knee. But by God you're still alive! An' nothin's broke bad enough that it won't heal up.

"Once I stopped the bleedin' on your hand an' got your broke leg straight again, I took the mule back to the Cavanaugh's. You was out cold and I needed to take care of the dead folk there. I brought back the big wagon 'cause I didn't know if I's gonna' need to go take you to somebody else fo' help. You was still out when I got back.

"Your poor Momma must'a been very brave with those men. She was a fine lady! I just finished buryin' her real nice up on that little hill there. When you're ready I'm gonna carry you up there so's y'all can talk.

Gabriel paused. His deep voice softened as he looked directly into the his friend's eyes and said, "Sam, I think those bad men took your sister when they left. I looked everywhere for Miss Mary Beth. All I found was her tracks next to one of your horse's tracks by the front porch. Think maybe they stole her."

Gabriel's lips started to quiver again, and he shut them together tightly. Tears were in his eyes and he looked away from Sam. Gabriel took a deep breath. He put on a smile when he turned and said sincerely, "Don't know why all this is happenin', but I'm glad you came back here, Sam. I'd sure hate to be doin' all this by myself."

"You did well, Gabriel." Sam said as the tears started from his own eyes and he looked up at his friend. "Thank you for savin' my life. We're gonna make it." Sam closed his eyes and wept.

Later that day, after Sam had rested, he asked Gabriel to take him to his mother's grave on the little hilltop overlooking the homestead. When

Gabriel started to lift the injured boy from the back of the wagon, Sam couldn't take the pain of his broken leg hanging down. Gabriel pulled charred planks from the front porch and made a splint long enough to hold the leg out straight.

Gabriel had also cut some willow tree bark for Sam to chew to help with the pain, but that just barely took the edge off it. He knew his young friend was hurting terribly from the injuries and felt helpless because there was nothing to give him for relief. Gabriel would have given anything for just one jug of his master's whiskey.

Sam gritted his teeth against the pain of being moved as Gabriel picked him up and started toward the hill. However, when they cleared the wagon and Sam saw his home for the first time, he didn't even notice the pain. He groaned in horror and disbelief at the devastation.

Except for a few leaning black charred timbers, the only thing left standing from his home was the old rock fireplace. The barn and smokehouse were burned to the ground. Some of their belongings from the house and barn were mostly broken and scattered like trash around the yard. The horses were gone. All the pigs and one cow lay dead in their pens with just their hind quarters cut off and taken.

Sam felt violated and hopeless as he said over and over in a shallow voice, "Look what they did to my home, Gabriel. Look what they did."

Gabriel never hesitated or slowed. He just kept walking. He carried Sam all the way to the top of the hill and sat him gently on the big oak stump next to the fresh grave of Sarah Stevens. As he did, Sam thought of sitting at that same spot with his Pa and wondered if the Mexican's had killed his father too.

"I already said some words over your Momma, Sam," Gabriel said. "I's just gonna leave you two alone fo' awhile. You call to me when you're done, and I'll come get you. I'm so sorry about you're Momma, Sam. She was a mighty fine lady." Gabriel wiped his eyes with his shirt sleeve and walked off the hill.

Sam stayed by his mother's grave for a long time and cried until he couldn't cry anymore. Eventually he waved his good hand to the watching Gabriel as a signal that he was ready to be carried down.

A man's determination filled the body of the sixteen year old boy who sat on the oak stump. Sam turned and looked down on what had once been the wonderful little homestead where he had grown up with his family. His eyes narrowed and his nostrils flared while he gritted his teeth and cemented the purpose in his heart.

As Gabriel's mighty arms lifted the battered young man and they started down the hill, Sam said, "Could you tell which way they went with my sister?"

Gabriel gestured his head to the right and replied, "The ones that took Miss Mary Beth headed yonder to the south. I scouted they tracks for two rises over while you was knocked out."

"Gabriel, I want you to gather up everything you can find that will provision us. We'll have to take the wagon. We're goin' to go get Mary Beth. I promised Momma I'd find her."

There was no questioning the resolve in Sam's voice. Gabriel looked straight into the eyes of the man he carried and said, "I'm with ya, Sam! I'll have us ready by mornin'."

28

The horrid stench from the massive pile of burning meat was about to make Luke throw up. He reached behind his head and tightened the rag tied across his face. As he looked around at the other men of the garrison at Goliad preparing to abandon what they had renamed Fort Defiance, he threw another double handful of dry beef jerky onto the smoking, stinking blaze. It wasn't just the burning meat, this whole situation made him sick to his stomach.

Were it not for the fact that he'd likely have been shot for a coward and a deserter, Luke would have left this irregular band of men and the pompous fool who commanded them two days after he arrived. That's when they got word that the Alamo had fallen and all inside, including his father, had been killed. Within those first two days Luke had also seen and heard enough to make up his mind that the commander of this Fort Defiance, James Walker Fannin, was a piss poor excuse for a Colonel. He hated Colonel Fannin.

Burning all this dried beef seemed a typical move for the Colonel. In talking with the volunteers who had been there awhile, Luke was told that Will Travis, as he faced the approach of Santa Anna and his Army, had sent an urgent plea for Fannin to send reinforcements to the Alamo. The next day Fannin started for San Antonio de Bexar with over three hundred men and four cannons. He stopped the expedition in less than two miles and turned back saying there wasn't enough food to make the trip. He didn't think he'd brought enough provisions to march the seventy miles to the Sequin Rancho, the next resupply point.

Upon his return, Fannin ordered hundreds of steers butchered and their meat dried in the sun to prepare his Fort Defiance for a long siege. Now the Mexican Army was approaching in overwhelming number, and the garrison was about to retreat. Before he would leave, the Colonel had ordered all the hoarded meat and grain stores burned so they wouldn't fall into enemy hands.

Luke was trying to be a good soldier and do the right thing. On the outside, that's exactly how the strong young Texan appeared. Inside, however, his emotions were ripping him apart. The brutal realities of this war were bashing Luke back and forth between being a twenty year old man facing the world, and being a twenty year old boy away from home.

It had been just over two weeks since he left his family at the homestead. He'd tried so hard to get to Goliad in time to help his Father. He had failed and would never forgive himself for that. He knew, as the oldest, it was up to him to take care of the family now. Luke wondered if they even knew about Pa yet.

Aside from the fact that he missed them terribly, there had been something else, something strong, pulling him home. It gnawed his guts day and night telling him he had to return to the homestead. Momma needed him there. He should be with his family.

Instead, he was alone with a group of men he didn't know, accomplishing nothing. There wasn't one thing about this place, or the man in charge of it, that felt right. He was afraid coming to Goliad and joining Colonel Fannin's garrison had been the wrong thing to do.

A week ago General Houston had sent direct orders for them to blow up the fort and retreat across the Guadalupe River to Victoria. But Fannin had sent out more than one hundred fifty men to punish spies and round up settlers. So instead of retreating to join the rest of the Texas Army, Fannin had split up his forces and held the entire remaining garrison waiting for those ill-thought-out sorties to return. They had been sitting for days, like goats in a pen, while one of Santa Anna's best generals thundered his well trained divisions closer to Goliad each minute.

Two days ago a scout reported the first detachment Fannin had sent out was captured. They had clashed with the Mexican forces and escaped, but the ranchero spies they were sent to punish caught them the next day. The rancheros marched the captured Goliad volunteers to Refugio and turned them over to the Mexican Army. The entire company was then executed. The scout also reported the Mexican Army with five hundred men was now camped only three miles away from Fort Defiance.

Like most of his comrades, Luke was anxious to fight the enemy. After the news about the Alamo, he burned inside to avenge his father and the other men he'd known all his life. He wanted to make the Mexicans pay for what they'd done and drive them out of Texas.

But Luke also knew that the three hundred thirty some odd men left within the walls of their makeshift fort couldn't stand against the six or eight thousand soldiers they were told Santa Anna had on the march. A third of Goliad's fighting force wore only rags for clothes and didn't even have shoes. Their poorly kept inexperienced volunteers certainly couldn't fight and kill the whole well equipped Mexican Army. They all realized retreat was at hand and that Texas would be better served if their garrison fell back to join up with the other forces General Houston had hopefully gathered.

That's why Luke couldn't believe that rather than following Sam Houston's orders and making a swift march twenty-five miles to get on the other side of the Guadalupe River, they had spent all day yesterday digging up and remounting the seven cannons they had already buried in preparation for a retreat. They also burned the little adjoining town of La Bahia and knocked down all the standing walls so Colonel Fannin could see a full sweep around Fort Defiance.

When they were ordered to hitch all the oxen to empty wagons and carts, Luke thought they would finally load and leave. But suddenly there were Mexican Cavalry units approaching the fort, and Colonel Fannin sent thirty or forty mounted men to engage them.

Their West Point educated Colonel, who wanted desperately to be a hero, thought that was the entire Mexican force. Instead of continuing to prepare for evacuation, Fannin and most of the men climbed on the walls and roofs of Fort Defiance to watch. They cheered the mounted soldiers as they chased and were chased all afternoon yesterday.

Luke had continued his job with the cannon detail. After the troop returned, Luke figured nothing was accomplished by the skirmish except jading and wearing out their garrison's precious few horses.

One of which was Luke's, that Colonel Fannin had commandeered "for the cause".

The Fort Defiance horsemen did, however, sally close enough to the San Antonio River to see that the Mexican force had now swelled to three times the original five hundred troops that had been there only a day or two before. Upon hearing that report, Colonel Fannin put the entire garrison on alert and left the oxen unfed in the corrals hitched to the empty wagons. Luke stood awake at his post all night waiting for the order to load and retreat.

The order hadn't come until after daylight in the heavy fog this morning. Now it was mid-morning and the fog that could conceal their escape was beginning to thin. Luke and four other men were burning the huge stores of meat that had been so carefully jerked in the sun while others were spiking and disabling the cannons they had just dug up and remounted. Luke wanted to scream at the stupidity!

He threw the last batch of dried meat onto the putrid blaze, basket and all, then hurried outside the small chapel building and gasped for air. Frustrated and angry, Luke ripped the soiled smoky rag from his face as he tried to get fresh air into his body and the stink out of his nostrils. He blew his nose into the rag and looked at the blackened mucus that came out.

After throwing the rag to the ground, he yanked his shirttail out and used it to wipe his stinging eyes. They were watering profusely and felt like the sockets were filled with gravel. When a small cloud of the burning meat's smoke came from the chapel door and engulfed him, he gagged and hurried out of it to keep from vomiting.

Luke walked away from the little church into the open area of the main yard. Through the fog there were sounds of chaos coming from all directions. He heard the cranky oxen bawling because they hadn't been fed or watered. Now they were protesting as men tightened the animal's harnesses and tried to load the wagons and carts to which they were still hitched.

A grizzly looking man with no front teeth came out of the fog and bumped into Luke. He carried a double armload of muskets. Luke asked gruffly, "What are you doing?"

The man replied, "Colonel wants to take these old muskets along for spares in case we need 'em. There's five hundred of 'em. Here, grab this bunch and fetch 'em to that cart yonderway." He thrust his bundle of weapons into Luke's arms as though they were sticks of firewood and wheeled around to go get another load.

Luke carried the long heavy rusting firearms through the fog toward a clicking clattering sound in the general direction the ugly man had gestured. He found two men overloading a small cart with stacks of rifles like the ones in his arms.

"That's too much weight for that little wagon." Luke said loudly when he got close enough. "Go get another cart."

"Ain't no more carts." One of the men answered as he raised himself from the pile of rifles in the back of the wooden two wheeled Mexican carry all. "Colonel said to git 'em all on here and jist tie 'em down real good. Go ahead and set 'em down on that stack there and we'll throw 'em up on top."

Luke put the heavy pieces atop the fifty or sixty others that were laying on a dirty tarp spread on the ground beside the cart. He turned away and began looking for his Captain. As he walked through the confusion created by the noise and bodies bumping into one another in the fog, he called out, "Captain Shackelford! Captain Shackelford, it's Luke Stevens. Where are you?"

When "Over here, boy!" came back through the mist, Luke recognized the voice and started toward it. He had been assigned to Captain Shackelford's Company, The Alabama Red Rovers, upon his arrival at Goliad. Luke moved briskly in the direction of his immediate commander's voice and soon found the tall thin man.

"The dried meat's burned, Sir." Luke reported.

"Very well, Luke." The Captain responded. "I want you to go get your gear and form up with the rest of our men at the front gate. The Red Rovers are leading this van. Tell the men we'll be leaving within the half hour, soon as Colonel Fannin gives the order."

With a quick "Yes, Sir!" Luke spun around and dashed off to gather his things, wondering if they really would get an order within the half hour. He'd believe it when it happened. All last night awake at his post, while Luke relived the past eleven days at Fort Defiance, his contempt for Colonel Fannin festered. Luke had convinced himself he held no faith in the man's decisions or his ability to make any.

He knew that's where he and Captain Shackelford differed. Jack Shackelford was a good man and Luke liked him. He was glad he'd been put in Jack's Company. Luke figured that was the only good thing that'd happened to him since his arrival.

Jack Shackelford was an austere looking man with a chiseled jaw and somewhat sunken eyes, when he wasn't smiling. However, like Luke's father, Shackelford had a warm friendly smile that made people feel comfortable as soon as he showed it to them. He also had a pleasant Southern manner to go along with that smile which had caused Luke to like the man right away.

Had Luke anything to do with it, Jack Shackelford would be the commander of the Goliad volunteers. When the news of the Alamo's fall reached Goliad and it was found out Luke's Pa had been among those slain, the Captain befriended the young man and comforted him in his grief. They often had long talks at night after supper where Luke was able to cry over his sorrow or scream out with his anger. Through the course of those evenings together they had each learned a lot about the other and, although they differed in their opinions about Colonel Fannin, they became friends.

Jack Shackelford was in his mid-forties. He was a physician and surgeon by training, but a patriot and adventurer by heart. He had served on Andrew Jackson's staff in the War of 1812 and had been in the State Senate of Alabama. He owned a plantation in that state, but when word of the hostilities with Santa Anna's centralist government continued, he recruited a company from the best families in Northern Alabama and came to Texas. He called his company The Alabama Red Rovers because all his men, except Luke and a few others, were outfitted in a red jean. They looked quite striking compared to the homespun clothes, rags, and buckskin worn by the balance of the volunteers.

Luke stayed with the other men of the Red Rovers for well over an hour before he heard Colonel Fannin's loud voice, "Open the gates! Prepare the garrison to march!"

29

"Put your backs into her, Boys! Ready...Ready...Heave!" Jack Shackelford commanded boldly as he, Luke, and five other Red Rovers grunted and strained pushing against the overloaded rifle cart. The cart's weakening oxen were stumbling trying to make it up the steep river bank as men pulled their leads from the front and others flogged them from behind. The carrier's two big wheels were bogged down in the mud between the river's edge and the base of the slope.

Luke's right shoulder was under the back end of the wagon and, on the Captain's command; he pushed with everything he had in his legs and back. As the cart began to move forward, Luke and the other men churned their feet in the thick, clay gumbo mud trying to keep force on the wagon and build some momentum to start up the steep bank. The thick, slick mud made gloppy sucking sounds trying to hold their feet. It seemed as though Luke couldn't get enough air into his lungs and his thighs were burning, but he still pushed with all his might. Even when the thick charcoal black goo he stood in kept his right boot, Luke never quit.

The wagon moved five feet then sank back to a complete stop.

Luke almost wanted to cry. His chest was moving like a blacksmith's big bellows as he tried to regain his wind. He pushed himself away from the back of the immobilized cart. He slopped through the heavy sludge at the water's edge, which had been made even more unstable from all the stomping feet, and tried to find his right boot.

He looked back across the river toward Fort Defiance and felt the apprehension he'd carried all morning start rolling into panic in the bottom of his stomach. His eyes searched into the woods along the shoreline for the Mexicans he knew would be attacking from their hiding places. There were only a few volunteers with loaded weapons on either side of the river guarding the column.

Twenty men with horses and ropes, all waists deep in the middle of the river, were trying to recover one of their cannons that had turned over. It was the biggest of the nine artillery pieces Colonel Fannin had decided to keep and bring along. The rest of the garrison was either unpacking the overloaded vehicles on the far side of the river, hand carrying the load piece by piece across the river, or reloading the wagons on this side.

Luke recovered his boot and filled it with water several times trying to wash out the mud. He forced his foot into the mud caked boot and hurried back to help fight the rifle cart.

Their Red Rover infantry company had easily forded the San Antonio River and taken up defensive positions to protect the rest of the column as it crossed downstream from the encampment of fifteen hundred Mexicans. Captain Shackelford had made them move quickly to take advantage of what fog was left in order to conceal their retreat. When the cannon fell over, the Red Rovers pulled back to help the column make the ford.

Luke had been jumpy and uneasy from the moment the front gates opened and they all marched out of Fort Defiance. He sensed eyes, dark Mexican eyes, watching him. He knew they could somehow see through the eerie fog that his eyes couldn't penetrate.

As they left the fort Colonel Fannin, like a rooster on horseback, had strutted up and down the column assuring the men that the Mexican Army didn't have the backbone to dare attack his command.

But Luke still felt like a little mouse being watched by a big fox. They had already spent over an hour on this crossing and Luke had no idea how much longer it would take. If the Mexicans hit them now in the middle of this debacle, defenseless and strung out in the water, they would all be slaughtered.

Captain Shackelford climbed out of the mud and up to the top of the bogged down rifle cart. He waved across the river to three mounted volunteers who were supposed to be guarding the column's rear and motioned for them to cross over. Their ponies, tired and footsore from jousting with the Mexican Cavalry yesterday, balked at the task but were forced across.

The Captain stayed atop the heavily burdened cart until he had tied a rope from each horse to the mainframe of the wagon's front end. Then he slipped back into the mud with Luke and the other infantryman. On Shackelford's direction, the brute muscle of men, oxen, and horses finally carried the five hundred spare muskets from the river's edge to the top of the steep bank.

There was no time to rest when they finally reached level ground at the top of the slope. Jack Shackelford left only one man holding the spent oxen, then turned Luke and the others back around to help finish the river crossing. For most of another hour they unloaded, carried, pushed, pulled, and reloaded until the ford was made.

Even after three hours back on the march, Luke's clothes were still clammy wet and dirty from the mud of the river crossing. He hadn't gotten all the silt out of his right boot and he could feel it raising a blister close to his heel. As he looked around at the other dirty wet men, Luke didn't say anything or stop walking. Unlike many of the volunteers trudging along on their march, he did have boots.

They started across a large prairie perhaps six miles square. The grass had been torched by the Texians, or the Mexicans, or the Indians and Luke wondered about who had done it and for what purpose. Then he put his mind to the task of trying to calculate just how far they had come from Goliad.

Although he knew they hadn't traveled far, ten or fifteen miles at the most, that wasn't the point. Luke was trying to make his head fill with something, anything, which would take him away from thinking about the eyes. He knew they were still watching him. The eyes were watching, and the fox they belonged to was waiting for the right moment to pounce.

There was a small rise two thirds of the way across the open plain. It stood out against the rest of the burned-off land because it had new spring grass that was sprouting bright green. When the Red Rovers crested that little swell, Luke squinted his eyes hard trying to look into the timber that surrounded the bare cienega. The closest finger of woods was straight ahead almost a mile away.

Luke was still looking far off to the trees while his company kept moving and started off the small rise. Suddenly, from behind, there was a horribly loud bellowing scream that immediately drew Luke's stomach into a tight ball. His throat sucked in a huge gulp of air as he cocked the big hammer on his rifle and spun around in a crouch.

In a panic Luke searched for their attackers, but when the scream came again, he realized it was one of the oxen. One of the animals pulling the heavy ammo cart had gone down on its front knees as it started into the little swell's green grass. The animal was bawling pathetically and thrashing its head about. Luke watched as the poor beast tried to eat the grass and refused to get up.

"Hold your point, Men!" Captain Shackelford ordered forcefully as he rushed past Luke in a fast walk toward the downed ox.

Luke uncocked his rifle and stood there watching as his Captain and the other officers converged on the stalled ammo cart. It was bigger than most of the other wagons, but like the others; it was so overloaded Luke was surprised the wheels hadn't come off. Soon Colonel Fannin rode up and started talking with his officers. It wasn't long before the group stepped away from the column and had a parley.

He was too far away to hear what was being said, but Luke was able to figure it out just by watching the officer's body movements. He could tell that Colonel Fannin wanted to stop and rest the teams. He watched Captain Duval, Captain Westover, and Jack Shackelford all gesturing forcefully toward the woods a mile ahead to the East. Luke knew they were trying hard to convince Fannin to keep moving to that cover before he stopped the garrison.

Eventually the officers all snapped to attention and saluted Colonel Fannin. After he returned their salutes, Captain Shackelford turned and looked toward his Company. He saw Luke watching and signaled for the young soldier and another man to come to him.

When the two reported, Shackelford sent the first man to gather a detachment of six others to go to the supply wagon and requisition food and water for the company. He told Luke to report to the Red Rover's

First Sergeant and inform him that he was to rest and feed the men. "Tell him we will stay here until the teams are grazed and rested, but I want our men vigilant still. We must maintain our guard at the front of the column."

As the other man started off with his orders, Luke looked at his friend and said, "But, Sir, wouldn't it be better to get to those woods up there before we stop? It's not that far. We can make it easy. If the Mexicans hit us here there's not even a rock to get behind. We'll have no cover at all!"

Captain Shackelford looked at Luke and said in an understanding but firm voice, "I agree with you, boy. The officers addressed that with Colonel Fannin in strong terms and he respected our opinions. However, it is considered unlikely the enemy would chance attacking a force of our capability. The Colonel has therefore ordered the animals rested and the men fed before we proceed. Now go on to the Sergeant, and tell him I will be there shortly to address our company. I need to discuss a few more things with the other officers first."

Luke sighed slightly, and mostly to himself, then said, "Yes Sir", and turned to trot to the front of the Red Rover Company.

He was still with the First Sergeant when the Captain returned from his meeting. The Company gathered up and listened to their commander.

"Gentlemen, we shall retire here until the teams are grazed and watered." Then he paused purposefully and said, "After much deliberation, the officers have decided it will be acceptable for the humans to also eat and take rations of water." The men laughed. He continued, "You men may lay down and rest, but I want our position maintained and your weapons at the ready at all times. Are there any questions?"

As the Captain finished and looked over the troop, the detail sent for rations returned empty handed. He looked at the man he'd sent in charge and said sharply, "Soldier, where is the food and water for this Company?"

"Ain't none, Captain Shackelford," was the reply he got back. "Guess somehow all the food and water supplies got left back at the fort. There's nary a speck of food nor a drop of water for this whole outfit!"

30

"What are they doing now, Sir?" Captain Lopez asked looking through the trees toward the open plain where the Goliad volunteers had stopped on the small rise.

General Jose de Urrea, the experienced Division Commander responsible for Santa Anna's southern flank and securing the Texas coastal ports, smiled as he looked through the long telescope. He took the instrument away from his right eye and kept looking at the Texans in disbelief.

Urrea was an honorable man, soft spoken and professional. His subordinates were loyal to the death because he had a way of commanding their respect, rather than demanding it. That was a trait Santa Anna mistrusted in Urrea, but used to his advantage.

Santa Anna considered General Urrea too much of a humanitarian. He preferred his General's more ruthless. On the other hand, there was no questioning Urrea's loyalty to Mexico, and the well educated career soldier was tactically brilliant in the field. Santa Anna well understood he had to secure the Texas seaports to supply his army, and Jose de Urrea was the one General he could count on to get that mission accomplished.

Without taking his eyes from the target, General Urrea handed over the spy glass to the band of officers who surrounded him. The General turned away from the Texans and looked to his group of commanders. With raised eyebrows and a jovial bobble of his head left and right he said smiling, "They're taking a siesta."

After his officers had taken turns surveying the enemy with the glass, they faced their leader. General Urrea used very clear and measured tones in giving his orders.

"Colonel Nunez, attack with your mounted dragoons from the Northeast. Pin them down where they are. Do not let the enemy escape to the timber. I want them in the open."

"*Sí, General.*"

"Colonel Salas, when the battle starts, bring forward your infantry and engage from the West."

"*Sí, General.*"

"Colonel Morales, your riflemen are to take positions along the tree line and advance as close as possible once the enemy is pinned."

"*Sí, General.*"

"Captain Lopez, ride to the artillery companies and ascertain their status and location, then bring me your report. Tell them I want every piece of artillery here, in place, tonight!"

"*Sí, General!*"

"Gentlemen, we must first take away their legs. I want every soldier in this command to know that our first priority is to kill the oxen. Once the oxen are dead the enemy will be immobile. Then concentrate on their artillery crews. Are there any questions?"

The general stopped and looked at each officer who confidently looked back at him.

"We are through stalking our prey. Are you men ready to win this battle for Mexico?!"

"*Sí, General!*"

* * * *

Luke was still searching the trees that surrounded the open plain watching for the Mexicans. The blister on his heel throbbed and he knew it would be hard to start up the march again now that he had given it over an hour to sit and get sore. Until they found out there was no food or water, he hadn't been that hungry or thirsty. Now he was both.

The fog had been gone for hours. With no shade on the broad empty field, the midday sun had slowly grown brighter, and hotter, as they waited. Luke squinted against its glare as he panned his eyes to the south.

"ATTACK! ATTACK!" The awkward high pitched holler of a startled young man's voice suddenly blasted through the hot thick afternoon air.

Luke's whole body jumped. He jerked his head around and saw the mounted dragoons coming from the northeast behind him. While he cocked his rifle, others from the garrison were already firing. Before he could get off his first round he heard Captain Shackelford's loud command, "Hold your fire! They're out of range! Save your powder, Men!"

Then came Colonel Fannin's booming voice, "Unlimber the six pounders! Blow those bastards to hell!"

There was a huge flurry of activity as cannons were unbuckled and turned toward the enemy and munitions were ripped off the ammo cart. The rest of the garrison started moving to one side of the column to face the far off enemy cavalry.

Luke looked to his right at the closest outcropping of woods. If they started a run for it now, he knew they could make that cover. He turned and without taking his eyes from the approaching dragoons, hustled himself forty feet to Captain Shackelford's side.

Just as Luke said, "Jack, we can make those trees if we get everyone moving!", the three cannons boomed simultaneously. They created a deafening roar and a concussion that Luke felt in his guts. White smoke billowed and everyone watched through it as the three rounds landed well short of the advancing horsemen.

Immediately the artillerymen began reloading. Captain Shackelford looked at Luke and said, "We'll hold for now, son."

By the time the cannons exploded again sending their deadly six pound ordinances at the enemy, the dragoons were changing their course. The Goliad cannoneers had their range now, but each shot landed well away from the maneuvering cavalry.

As the last shot missed its mark, Colonel Fannin yelled, "Load the ammunition in the wagon! Turn the cannons! We'll retreat to the timber!"

Luke wanted to bolt immediately, and would have, had Captain Shackelford and the other officers not started screaming to keep the force united. "Don't split the force! We'll move out together! Stay together, Men!"

He looked at the dragoons still advancing. Then Luke instinctively turned toward the ammo cart and cannons to see when he could start making for cover. Just then he noticed movement on the other side of the cannons behind the column to the west. At the far edge of the clearing, a couple of miles away, he saw Mexican ground troops moving on them.

Luke started to call to Captain Shackelford and show him the new threat. Before the first syllable left the young man's mouth, Luke's eyes dropped back to the ammunition wagon to a sight that made him freeze there with his mouth still open.

In disbelief and fear, Luke watched helplessly while two men swung the last heavy wooden case of cannon balls into the back of the wagon just as the driver slapped the reins and yelled wildly to the oxen. The two events simultaneously were too much for the grossly overloaded wagon. When the axle snapped and the right wheel fell off, the wagon went over on its side dumping half its precious cargo onto the new spring grass.

Luke stood in that moment, dumbfounded. The loud whiz of a round ball from a Mexican's rifle passed close to his head and jerked him back to reality. When he heard the command, "Move to the ammo wagon!" Luke obeyed.

As the garrison massed toward the broken down cart, Luke thought how strange it was to see Colonel Fannin pull a compass from his vest pocket. He watched the commander check the device and wondered what he was doing. When the men and officers drew close enough, the Colonel hastily directed them to form a hollow square and build breastworks from the wagons and baggage. For some reason he insisted the square be aligned exactly north-south and east-west.

"Shackelford, your company takes the west wall toward their infantry! Westover, I want your men on the south!" Colonel Fannin yelled as a Mexican bullet slammed with a solid thud into his horse's neck and took the animal out from under him.

Colonel Fannin went down with the horse then sprang to his feet, unhurt, barking orders to the troops. The wagons and carts were aligned with the compass headings and their cargo thrown off to the ground. The teams were cut loose and, as each wagon was hastily emptied, groups of men pushed the vehicles over to start creating a wall.

Others then extended the walls with stacks of the unloaded baggage. By the time the battle was at hand, the West Point trained Goliad Commander had recreated a textbook neat, perfectly aligned, four sided Roman Battle Square that had been used in the days before Christ was born.

Luke clutched tightly to the leads of the ox hitched to the last cart needed for the Red Rover's west wall. As he waited for the traces to be cut free, he held the bridle close to the bit because the animal was wild eyed with fear. Before the harness was cut, the approaching Mexican infantry got within range.

The strong young ox was shot several times. It folded to the ground with Luke still holding the leads. While men turned the cart on its side, Luke's body pumped itself full of adrenaline as he grabbed the dead animal's hind legs and rolled it so that the back was toward the enemy.

Men and animals began falling to the shower of whistling bullets. Luke found his rifle and possibles bag and crawled to the dead ox's belly. He lay behind the carcass between the animal's outstretched legs and used its side as a rifle rest. Luke took careful aim and killed a man with his first shot.

Luke turned on his side and reloaded. Then he killed another man. Amid the ghastly sounds of battle - men yelling and screaming, bullets whizzing, cannons booming, and rifles cracking - Luke held his concentration throughout the long, bloody afternoon.

At one point his rifle fouled from a build-up of black powder as a result of all the firing. Unable to reload, Luke looked around frantically toward the inside of the square. He started to get up from his spot behind the bullet ridden ox when Captain Shackelford yelled from somewhere.

"Stay down, Luke! Hold your position! Are you out of bullets?"

"I'm low, but my barrel's clogged. Need another gun!" Luke yelled back into the smoke unable to see Shackelford.

Soon the Captain, in a running crouch, was behind Luke. He pitched two rifles and more ammunition on the ground beside the boy then flopped down next to him.

"You alright, son?" Shackelford asked.

"Yes, Sir." Luke responded as he looked into his friends eyes, and then started to load one of the new rifles.

"You're doin' good, Luke." Jack said and patted his young friend's back. "I know your Pa would be very proud of you." Then as the Captain slipped away back into the noise and smoke Luke heard, "Stay with it, son."

About an hour before dark the Mexicans pulled away and stopped firing. Everything was quiet. Before that Luke had already noticed the noise lessening because his garrison's cannons weren't firing very much. He noticed it, but hadn't had time to think about it.

Luke propped his rifle against the dead ox's belly and slowly, stiffly, rose and looked around. Other men were doing the same. As he surveyed the four corners of their battle square where the artillery units were positioned, he realized why their cannon fire had fallen silent. All the cannoneers were lying dead at their posts.

Twenty feet away a wounded Red Rover called out lying in a small pool of his own blood, "Water. Please give me some water. I'm hurt bad."

31

From the pocket of his best uniform Lieutenant Denicio Bernillo pulled an heirloom - the gold watch that had been so cherished by Jonathan Stevens. With a look of disdain on his face he rubbed his thumb across its smooth worn surface. It was disappointing that the old timepiece was the only thing of any value he'd acquired from his efforts in this war. He wondered how much it was worth and held it toward the encampment torchlights to check the time again.

He had already been standing for half an hour in the dark outside the entryway to the President of Mexico's large ornate tent, awaiting his audience with the Supreme Commander, when the courier arrived. It angered Bernillo that the messenger was taken straight into the tent where Santa Anna was dining with his command staff, and he was left standing outside. He cursed his luck under his breath, afraid he would miss his opportunity with *El Presidente*.

As he paced in a small circle away from the two soldiers guarding the entry, he heard Captain Lopez, the courier, begin his briefing. Bernillo realized he could hear every word through the tent walls. He stepped closer to the canvass and listened to the details of General Urrea's recent battle at Goliad.

"...We retired from the battlefield an hour before sunset that day, Your Excellency. The enemy had no means of retreat as all their animals were dead. We believed we had also eliminated their cannon crews.

I personally reported to General Urrea that our artillery would be in place by the next morning, and he saw no need to further endanger our field forces. Our total casualties for the engagement were 52 dead and 121 wounded.

At daybreak the following morning we began our cannon fire on the enemy. When they returned only small arms fire, the General knew they had no cannoneers left. Once our artillery units had established their range, General Urrea ordered canisters of grapeshot.

After two direct hits from our shrapnel bombs, the Texans raised a white flag. General Urrea called a cease fire for the entire regiment.

Within an hour our command staff met with theirs to discuss the terms of surrender. I felt privileged that General Urrea asked me to participate because I have a knowledge of English. The Texans also had an interpreter from their ranks which helped greatly in the communications.

All of the rebel officers conducted themselves honorably. They were commanded by a Colonel James Fannin. Their Colonel had been shot through the thigh with a rifle ball and had to be carried to the meeting by his subordinates. Although he was wounded, he showed respect for General Urrea by standing in his presence until the General ordered a stool brought for him.

The General accepted their surrender and guaranteed their status as prisoners of war conditioned upon their entire garrison's deportation from Tejas and Your Excellency's approval, of course. The prisoners have been marched back to the fort they had occupied at Goliad. We have established a hospital there, with their doctors and ours, and are removing all the wounded from both sides to it. That task should have been finished yesterday.

Your Excellency, this document contains the terms of surrender accepted by General Urrea. It was agreed to and signed by their Commanding Officers. This envelope, Sir, is correspondence from General Urrea requesting your favorable recognition of this treaty.

With General Urrea's compliments, that is my report, Your Excellency. May I answer any questions for you, Sir?"

"How many 'Prisoners of War' do you have in custody for 'Deportation'?" Santa Anna asked in a very sarcastic loud tone.

"The total number, counting the wounded and one of their captured advance parties, is just over four hundred men, Your Excellency."

From outside the tent Lieutenant Bernillo could not see the President's face, but he heard the anger well up in the man's voice as he began to scream out.

"Captain Lopez, can you tell me why, for the love of God, you and General Urrea and all the other officers in your entire division *willfully* and *flagrantly* disobeyed my direct orders?! Every Texan under arms is to be killed! What do you not understand about that?!"

Captain Lopez, shocked and scared, responded bravely. "But, Sir, they were under a white flag. As officers we were honor bound to respect it. They surrendered their arms and agreed to deportation. They accepted status as noncombatants and agreed to leave the country. Under the rules of war…"

"Damn you, Captain! Those were not my orders!"

"Yes, Sir."

"I want you to return to that coward Urrea and tell him to follow my orders! Tell that weak kneed son-of-a-bitch to kill them all! Do you understand *that* order, Captain Lopez?!"

The bright young Captain blinked at the spit that had flown into his face from Santa Anna's mouth as he raged. Lopez remained at attention and replied, "Your Excellency, General Urrea has departed Goliad and proceeded on to the coast to secure the seaports there."

"That Bastard!" The President of Mexico railed and turned to the Generals seated at his table. "He knew what my response would be! He didn't have the stomach to follow my orders, so he left! That is treason!"

Santa Anna snapped his fiery eyes back to Captain Lopez and said through clenched teeth, "Who is in charge at Goliad?"

"Colonel Jose Nicolas de la Portilla, Your Excellency." Lopez answered still standing at a brace.

With hatred in his stare Santa Anna paused momentarily, and then continued talking through his barred teeth. "I want you to go find General Urrea. Leave tonight. Tell him how I accepted his report. You tell him his capitulation with the traitors is rejected and his personal cowardice has been noted. Tell him I will have every traitor in Goliad executed, even if I have to do it myself! Now get out of my sight!"

Lieutenant Bernillo raised himself erect quickly and stepped away from the side of the tent just before Captain Lopez rushed out of its opening. Shortly thereafter the three Generals who had been dining with the President silently left the tent. Bernillo was scared and wanted to leave as well.

He didn't know what to do. He was pacing in a small circle again when the President's secretary came from the tent and looked around in the darkness. The spit polished aide de camp saw the paling young officer and said, "I think it would be good for the President to see you now, Lieutenant Bernillo."

Bernillo's stomach flipped. He wanted to throw up, or faint. Instead, he forced himself to take in a deep breath. As the color started to return to his face, he tugged on the bottom of his jacket to straighten his uniform and raised himself tall. He knew this was his chance, and he had to take advantage of it. He cleared his throat and said, "Very well, Sir", then followed the secretary into the President of Mexico's field quarters.

The splendor of the large softly lit room put the young soldier in awe as he walked across the thick carpets. Under its tall ceiling the tent held a sitting area with comfortable looking heavily overstuffed chairs. There were elegantly framed paintings hung down on thin wires from the tent poles. Several carved wooden tables around the room also held pictures on small easels, all of which were illuminated by ornate candelabras. To the right a tapestry screen was open and behind it Bernillo saw a full sized four poster brass bed with a thick feather mattress. The brass was so highly polished the bed seemed to have gold at its head and foot.

On the other side of the tent, opposite the bed, was a large dining table made of dark hand carved wood. Around the table were eight heavy chairs carved in the same design as the table. The largest chair was at the far end of the table and there, under the full light of a beautiful silver chandelier which hung from a silver chain, sat the President of Mexico.

The secretary walked beside Lieutenant Bernillo as they both entered the sphere of light cast by the elegant chandelier. Bernillo could hear his own heart pounding when they stopped at attention just a few feet from the most powerful man in their world.

"Your Excellency," the aide began, "this is Lieutenant Denicio Bernillo of General Cos's battalion. He recently returned from the field where he demonstrated exemplary performance for Mexico in commandeering supplies for our troops. On his own initiative, he came to me seeking an audience with you."

The secretary paused and smiled at his commander. "Sir, I believe you will find Lieutenant Bernillo's report quite interesting." Without another word the man stepped back from the light, then turned and walked to the tent's door.

It was easy to tell from the leader's demeanor that Santa Anna was still fuming and thinking about the situation at Goliad. He pitched his silverware onto the plate of half-eaten food in front of him and pushed it out of the way. With his forearms still resting on the table Santa Anna looked up at the terrified junior officer.

"Bernillo is it?"

"Yes, Sir, Your Excellency."

"Lieutenant, would you like to tell me what is so important that my secretary brings you to my supper table?"

"Well, Sir, I…That is, Sir…You see I…"

"Dammit, boy! Can you speak?"

"Yes, Sir! It's a birthday present, Sir."

"What?!" *El Presidente* had lost his patience.

"Your Excellency, I know your birthday was held a few days before we reached the Alamo." Bernillo was talking very fast now. "But I remember, that night at the officer's mess table, you commented how awful it was for a man to have to sleep alone on his birthday. I remembered that, Sir, and I thought that, perhaps, a birthday present would be good. I know it is not your birthday now, but I…"

Just then the secretary walked into the light accompanied by two soldiers who held Mary Beth Stevens tightly by the arms. The aid grabbed Mary Beth by her thick black hair and raised her pretty face to the chandelier's light. He looked into her eyes then turned to Santa Anna and said, "This is the present Lieutenant Bernillo brought for you, Your Excellency."

Santa Anna smiled broadly as he leaned back in his throne-like chair and looked at the young woman.

"Well, well, Lieutenant Bernillo, I see that you are the kind of loyal officer who knows how to bring his commander good news."

"Yes, Sir, Your Excellency!" Bernillo said. He smiled himself when he saw a smile come to the President's lips while the man's eyes devoured the young girl. He knew he had pleased the great Santa Anna.

Still leaning back in his chair, Santa Anna said to the men as he looked around at each of them, "I like my presents unwrapped."

He looked directly at Mary Beth and said flippantly, "I should like to see what I'm having for dessert tonight." Then the smile left his face and with a domineering look he said slowly, "Take off your clothes."

Mary Beth stiffened. She felt the sharp point of the secretary's blade in her back as the two men at her side released their strong grip from her arms. Her eyes swept the table for a weapon. She winced, surprised by the distinct pain, as the secretary jabbed his blade into her back and drew blood.

"We can make this very, very hard on you." He whispered into her ear from behind. "Now take your clothes off for His Excellency."

Slowly Mary Beth reached for the buttons of her long cotton dress. She wanted to cry. Instead, she looked at the heartless man sitting smugly in his big chair in front of her and let her anger drive away the tears. The hatred swelled inside, and she nourished it. She made it build until it took away every other feeling she had. She felt nothing inside, nothing but hate.

Lieutenant Bernillo started breathing heavily at the excitement of watching the woman undress, and had to stop himself. He looked at the other men and saw they too were stimulated. The President reached for his wine and sat back into his throne.

Mary Beth let her dress drop to the floor, then put her arms up in front of her thin undershirt to cover her breasts. Her teeth were gritted tightly together, and her nostrils flared when she felt the sharp point in her back again.

"I want it all off, Senorita." Santa Anna said quietly savoring the moment and never taking his eyes from her firm body.

After Mary Beth had removed her undershirt, she hesitated again and started to cover her naked breasts. The President motioned with his hand and the two soldiers immediately took the girl's arms. They held them to her sides so that her bare breasts were in full view. Then from behind, while she was being held rigidly in place, the aid slowly removed her pantaloons.

With a lecherous smile on his face, the President of Mexico feasted on the young woman with his eyes. He turned to Denicio and said, "You have pleased me with your thoughtfulness, Lieutenant Denicio Bernillo. Report here with General Cos tomorrow morning and we will discuss your future. I like a young officer who knows how to get things done!"

Santa Anna looked back to the two men holding Mary Beth. Then he looked up and down her smooth body that was softly lit by the candle light of the silver chandelier. He didn't take his eyes from her as he smiled and said coldly, "Tie her to the bed!"

32

"Too bad for you, Mr. Possum. You should'a kept yourself hid up in your little hackberry tree." Gabriel said out loud as he picked the dead marsupial up by its hairless tail. He thought opossums were stupid. After he'd shaken the animal out of its tree, the varmint had sulled up and played dead.

"You got all them teeth, but you play dead possum on me thinking I'm gonna just leave you alone. That's just a good way to get yourself hit in your head with a stick. Now you're a dead possum all right."

Gabriel raised the creature at arms length, head high to himself, and studied it. It wasn't much of a possum, he thought. Wasn't quite as big as a good barn cat, but at least he had something to feed Sam. He'd caught two chickens before they left the homestead and brought them along in the wagon, but he'd already killed and used both of them trying to help the boy get his strength back.

He worried about Sam. Gabriel had made a good bed for him on the floorboards in the back of the big wagon, but he knew the boy shouldn't be out like this. Sam had gotten worse over the last several days, and Gabriel wasn't sure what to do. His young friend suffered terribly from the pain of being bounced around on the rough road, so they had to stop often to let him rest and recover. The part that scared Gabriel, however, was the fever.

Sam had some red streaks starting up his arm from where the Mexicans had cut off his fingers. Gabriel tried to keep good clean dressings wrapped around his friend's hand, but for the past couple of days Sam had gotten hot all over with fever. Gabriel knew that fever was what kept people from getting strong again. It was what caused people to die sometimes.

He wanted to take Sam to somebody for help, but the war had run everyone off. The two homesteads they'd come onto since they started looking for Miss Mary Beth were completely abandoned. Everybody was gone, or off hiding someplace.

Gabriel knew Sam wouldn't stop anyway. Every time he talked to the boy about finding a doctor or turning around to go east to a settlement, Sam wouldn't hear of it.

"We gotta keep going, Gabriel." He always insisted. "We have to find my sister. I promised Momma I'd find her! We can't stop. We've got to get to Mary Beth!"

Gabriel didn't know what to do. Maybe this old possum would help Sam get his strength back, the big man thought to himself. He had no knife, but in less than a minute using just his strong fingers Gabriel ripped open the opossum's belly, gutted the animal, and started walking back toward the shade trees where he'd left Sam in the wagon.

He didn't like leaving his sick friend for very long at a time, just in case he threw up or needed something. This was the longest he'd been gone from Sam since they left the Steven's homestead. Gabriel had left Sam in the wagon not far from the road and had gone to try and pick up the trail of the Mexicans who had stolen Mary Beth.

All the way along they had kept a line on the Mexican's trail. Occasionally, like this morning, Gabriel would have to leave the road and recheck the trail. They had expected the Mexican tracks to hit the road they were on and start traveling on it, but they hadn't yet. Gabriel was afraid the Mexicans had changed their meandering course again, and he had lost them, so he went to try and find some sign. He'd found their cold campsite and was marking their direction of travel to the west, southwest, when the opossum showed itself.

Gabriel was trying to think of something else he could put with the opossum to feed Sam as he came around a large rock outcropping on the side of the little creekbed in which he had been walking. He knew the creekbed would lead him back to the wagon. When he rounded the rock, he let the opossum slip from his fingers as shock suddenly slammed his heart and filled every inch of his huge frame.

The wagon was less than fifty yards away. It was surrounded by more than a dozen Mexican dragoons. Two of them had already dismounted and climbed into the back of the wagon where Sam was. When they jerked the sick boy from his bed and pitched him out onto the ground, Gabriel exploded. He roared like a wounded bear as he ran forward screaming, "No! You leave that boy alone!"

Gabriel had already covered half the distance to the wagon by the time the startled soldiers reacted to his yells and started turning their horses toward him. For his size Gabriel had always been agile and a very fast runner. The Sergeant in command of the squad was the only soldier with a sidearm. He jerked the pistol from his belt as his horse fought the reins and spun toward the strange creature running at them from the woods.

The big black man's wild advance spooked most of the horses. The Sergeant yanked off a shot as his horse pitched up onto its hind legs. Gabriel saw the powder flash and heard the bullet whiz high over his head, but by then he was almost to the Mexicans.

He ducked his shoulder, then rammed it up into the front end of the first skittish horse he ran past, and the animal and its rider flew back and over sideways. The soldiers were yelling to each other and their attacker in panic as Gabriel grabbed a soldier by his uniform jacket and threw him from his horse into the next nearest horse and rider. In his deep rich booming voice, Gabriel bellowed at the horses and flailed his arms menacingly at them. The closest ones scattered like a covey of flushed quail, dumping some of their riders.

The two dragoons who had thrown Sam to the ground were still in the back of the wagon. As Gabriel spun around to get the boy, one of them jumped through the air at the enraged slave. Gabriel caught the man in midair, then raised the screaming soldier high over his head and slammed him, as though he were a heavy sack of grain, onto two of the dragoons who had been thrown from their horses.

Gabriel turned again quickly to get Sam. The second dragoon from the wagon had fear bulging his eyes and panic shaking his voice as he said, "*Alto, Negro! Alto!*" He was obviously scared down to his very soul looking up at the monster that had just fiercely attacked his platoon. He held Sam's head by the hair and had a knife blade to the young man's throat.

There was nothing Gabriel could do. He didn't move. He stood still holding his mighty fists like two big mallets, breathing heavily through his nose with his teeth gritted together, as the sweat dripped from his body.

Gabriel never took his eyes from Sam while the other Mexicans swarmed over the strong slave and began to take turns beating him. They hit him hard many times and made him get down on his knees. The shaky soldier who'd stopped the ordeal didn't take the knife from Sam's throat until his comrades had Gabriel bound with his hands tied behind his back.

After he was tied, and that soldier and a few more dragoons took their turns on Gabriel, they made him sit on the ground next to the injured boy. "You all right, Sam?" Gabriel asked as he went down on his knees next to his friend. "Did they hurt you more?"

"I'm fine, Gabriel." Sam said squinting up using the big man's body to block the sun from his eyes. He smiled weakly. "Thanks for savin' me...again."

They stayed next to one another on the ground behind the wagon while the dragoons licked their wounds and gathered up scattered horses. Sam began to feel as though he was burning up as he laid shadeless in the hot sun, but that didn't matter. He knew he and Gabriel would soon be shot or hanged.

Sam turned toward his friend and said, "That was a mighty brave thing you did, comin' back for me like that. You should'a just hid out. You should'a let them take me and saved yourself."

Before Gabriel could respond, the Mexican Sergeant walked up to them. He stayed on his feet and began speaking brusquely looking down at Sam. Sam answered in kind. Gabriel wished he could speak Spanish as he listened to the two adversaries get into a lengthy, and heated, conversation. The Sergeant got the last words, then turned on his heels and walked away.

As soon as he started away Gabriel asked anxiously, "What's goin' on, Sam? What'd he say?"

"He thinks we're soldiers fightin' against his supreme Mexican Army." Sam said with disgust, still watching the platoon leader as he departed. Then he turned his head toward Gabriel. "I told him that you weren't a soldier. I told him you were an unarmed slave taking me to a doctor. I said his supreme army was a bunch of cowards who killed my mother and kidnapped my sister!"

"What're they gonna do, Sam?" Gabriel asked seriously. "You think they gonna kill us?"

Sam looked into his friends eyes and saw his anguish, then said calmly, "Naw, I don't think this fella wants to murder a sick kid and a slave, but I don't think he's real sure what to do with us either. He said he was going to take us to their prisoner camp at Goliad. He's giving the big wagon to some Colonel Portilla. He said you and I are now 'prisoners of war'."

33

Mary Beth shivered and tried to stop her teeth from chattering as she pulled her legs up closer to her body and repositioned her long skirt to block the wind. She was huddled in brush against the base of a big oak stump on the leeward side of a creek bank that had been cut steep by erosion. She knew she needed to keep walking, but when the cold wind had started in the night she had to stop and take shelter. As she arranged her skirt, the wind swirled and sent an icy hand down the back of her dress which raised more goose flesh on her bare arms. She wished she had stolen a blanket from the Mexicans.

Her back was to the west against the stump, and she was using the vertical cut of the creek bank to block the gusty March wind. She raised her eyes to the east, praying for the sun. Surely it would be up soon, she thought, trying to make her mind remember what day it was. She had to think about something other than the cold wind. Mary Beth wished she had some way to build a fire, but she had nothing. She had only the torn dress the wind was coming through and the worn shoes on her frigid feet.

She was so cold, and so tired, but she had to stop thinking about that. She couldn't let herself think about that. She had to think about other things, anything. At least the sun would be up soon. The sun would be warm, and it was on its way. She could tell where it would be rising. There wasn't yet any light. There wasn't even a glow. It was more that the stars close to the horizon were beginning to fade, but soon it would be light and warm, and she could start walking again.

Mary Beth wiggled her fingers as she worked her hands deep into the pockets of her cotton dress looking for a place to warm them. Her sore fingers ached with the cold. She felt the pecans she'd saved and wrapped her hands around them.

In the three days since her escape from the Mexicans, she had been walking day and night. The pecans, and her determination, were the things that had kept her alive. In some of the creek bottoms she crossed she had found wild pecan trees. She rooted and scrounged and shook limbs every time she found one. Although the squirrels and other animals had already gotten most of them, Mary Beth was able to find enough of the older nuts to stay alive.

She pulled some of the pecans from her pocket. In the darkness she felt around until she found two rocks and started cracking the nut's hard shells. The meat she dug out with her fingers was dry and tasted bitter, but she was so hungry she kept going until all the pecans were eaten.

As she dusted the pecan shell fragments from her dress and leaned back against the stump, she realized this would be Sunday, Palm Sunday. Mary Beth closed her eyes and allowed her mind to start wandering. It wanted to go back to the events at Santa Anna's camp, but Mary Beth forced it not to.

It felt good to have something in her stomach. Her exhausted body needed to sleep, but the night was too cold. She had to stop thinking about the cold. She would rest and think about other things. As her mind searched for pleasant things with which to fill itself, it eventually wandered to their church.

For a moment she wasn't shivering alone in the darkness. She was at Sunday mass with her family. In her mind she turned her head and there next to her was her whole family kneeling in a pew with their heads bowed. Her Momma and Pa looked at her and smiled. Mary Beth glanced around the church and saw their neighbors and all their friends from the colony.

She tried to speak to them but no words came out. When she tried to reach for her parents she couldn't move. Why couldn't she move her body? She needed to touch them. With all her might she forced her body to move. When her arm moved she slipped against the tree trunk, and awoke to another chilling blast of wind.

Mary Beth had been taken with Santa Anna's encampment as they marched southeast toward Sam Houston's army. The only peace the eighteen year old got was during the daytime when the army traveled.

During the days she was tied and put inside a covered wagon to be hauled like the rest of *El Presidente's* personal chattel. At night, after the encampment was made and Santa Anna sent for her, she was in hell.

The physical abuse was abhorrent, but even worse for Mary Beth had been finding out about the Alamo. As she listened to Santa Anna and the others boasting about slaughtering every one of the Texas defenders at Bexar, she realized that her Pa and Luke were dead. She knew then that she was completely alone. They had taken away Luke and Pa just like they had taken Sam and Momma.

Her heart and her spirit were broken. Mary Beth was ashamed thinking her parents, especially her Father, could see what she was being forced to do. The thought of her Pa having to watch her situation killed her soul, and she had resigned herself to bring an end to it. If the Mexicans didn't kill her, she'd made up her mind that she would somehow find a way to do it herself.

One hopeless morning after she had been tied and thrown into the wagon, she overheard some of the officers talking. Outside the tarp that covered her wagon, they spoke in hushed tones about Santa Anna's lack of honor and his mishandling of the prisoners at Goliad. Through the course of their conversation, Mary Beth realized that Fannin's garrison at Goliad had not gone to the Alamo. She sat upright as a small spark flashed dimly somewhere in her dead heart.

She got up on her knees and put her ear to the canvass. "The Texans raised a white flag and General Urrea issued terms of surrender." She heard one of them say. "Once they accepted those terms, they agreed to become noncombatants. They are all 'prisoners of war'. Urrea did the right thing."

Mary Beth's heart began to have something to beat for again. She realized Luke must still be alive. Her eyes started to widen with the first flickering gleam of hope. She almost held her breath in order to better hear the soldiers.

"Urrea promised to deport them all from our country. That was the honorable thing to do. That's what you do with 'prisoners of war', you either hold them until the war is over, or you deport them. What the

President wants to do is murder," the loud whisper of another officer's voice said with contempt.

A third one answered back in his whisper, "Killing an enemy on the field of battle is one thing, but executing unarmed men who have surrendered is incomprehensible. I was with Cos at the first Siege of Bexar. What if the Texans had accepted our surrender, then killed all our troops? If Santa Anna kills all the prisoners at Goliad, it will be an outrage to every civilized nation in the world. You mark my words, if he goes through with this, it will enflame everyone in the United States. They will sweep into this country like a pack of mad dogs!"

There was the sound of someone approaching. The officer's impromptu meeting broke up, but Mary Beth had heard enough. She sat back on the bundles within the wagon as her heart caught on fire. She knew Luke had to be alive, and she had to find him. She would get to him, if there was still time

Late that night, after Santa Anna and his men were finished with her, Mary Beth was tied and manhandled into the back of the covered wagon in preparation for the next morning's move. Her tormentors had been especially brutal with her that evening, and her body ached in the blackness of the wagon's inside. In the darkness she could still smell their foul breath, and she felt comtaminated as it mingled with the wet clammy odor of their bodies. Mary Beth tasted her own blood, raised from one of Santa Anna's blows, as she chewed at the ropes with her teeth trying to untie herself. The taste of it fueled the raging fire in her heart which now burned with the need to escape.

With the intensity of a hungry she-wolf, Mary Beth watched the guard at the front of the wagon while she waited for the encampment to get quiet. After the two soldiers who put her into the wagon left, the lone guard watching the wagon had put his hand up her dress and asked her how she liked being a whore. She watched him trying to figure just how she could kill him and get away.

She wanted to kill him. She wanted them all dead. Mary Beth sat in the dark wagon bed watching and thinking. Even if she had some sort of weapon, any noise would turn out the entire camp. If she were caught, she couldn't get to her brother. She didn't know how much time she had to make it to Luke. Mary Beth didn't even know what she would do when she found him, but she had to get to him before it was too late.

In the middle of the dark moonless night when the camp was still, she watched the guard lay down his long rifle. He rested it against the tongue of the wagon and looked around. Then the pig who had guarded her every night walked a few paces from his normal post, undid his pants, and started to urinate. Mary Beth used the noise he made to cover what little sound she caused slipping from the back of the wagon. She crawled from shadow to shadow, under the other wagons at the perimeter of the encampment, until she was close enough to make a dash into the treeline. When the sun came up the next morning and the camp started to move, the brave hearted girl was already miles away on her way to Goliad.

34

Jack Shackelford was cold as he lay awake on the dirt floor waiting for the sunrise. He looked around at the dark forms of the other officers and listened to some of them snore as they slept. They were crowded tightly next to one another in a small room behind the chapel in the old church at Fort Defiance. This was the first time all the Texas officers had been quartered together in the week since their surrender.

The March wind had kicked up during the night and Jack listened to it blow in erratically repeating gusts that whined outside the church walls. Just the sound of it made him colder and he thought of his mistreated men. They were huddled together outside in the main yard trying to stay warm without shelter or blankets.

At least Fannin was back now. He had returned yesterday from a five day trip to Copano Bay where he'd been taken to meet with General Urrea. They met there to secure a ship that would take the garrison of prisoners to New Orleans, and freedom.

Although the ship had already departed when they arrived at the port, General Urrea had assured Fannin that his entire command would be deported to the United States very soon. Colonel Fannin had also brought back news that the General would address their complaints about the treatment of the Texas soldiers.

"Urrea said there was no question that the terms of our surrender and the decorum of war called for humane treatment of prisoners," Fannin had told the men last night before the officers were separated and locked into the small room. "He sent that word back with us, in writing, to Colonel Portilla so there would be no question. The General promised me that every comfort in their power would be extended in the future."

Fannin's news, and his safe return, had certainly boosted the spirits of their men. As a physician, Jack had worked day and night since the battle caring for the wounded of both armies. Last night, while he made his evening rounds, he could tell that the minds of the volunteers were at ease with thoughts of going home. Jack smiled to himself as he thought of the two soldiers from Alabama who had played "Home, Sweet Home" on their hand carved wooden pocket flutes. They serenaded the quiet homesick troops outside while he went inside, from pallet to pallet, tending to the injured in their makeshift barracks hospital.

In the chill of the dark little room, Jack's own mind began drifting to thoughts of Alabama, and his home. He longed for his family and remembered beautiful Alabama springtimes they had shared. Those pleasant thoughts led to others, and humbly he began to ponder all the blessings God had given him throughout his life.

Although Jack was not an overly religious man in public, he'd received a strong Christian upbringing and held deep personal beliefs about his faith. He knew the dawn would soon bring with it Palm Sunday, the beginning of Holy Week for Christians. The Sunday before Easter marked a turn in the observance of Lent from a time of discipline and sorrow for one's sins to one of looking ahead to the Passion of Jesus and His Resurrection. Jack's heart raised the question that perhaps spending this cold pre-Easter night in the church was a sign from God.

He smiled again thinking that war is the place where many men find, or re-find, their God. On the battlefield they had faced certain defeat and had looked directly into the dark unblinking eyes of Death. Now there was hope of returning to their homes and loved ones. Was it a miracle that he and his men had been given salvation? All the thoughts from his mind were melting together with the ones from his heart as he laid quietly in the darkness on the dirt floor. Jack wondered if this experience was meant to be his own rebirth.

His meditation was broken when he heard noises coming from the chapel. Suddenly the door burst open and the small room filled with Mexican soldiers. They rousted the startled officers and commanded that they form up the Texas troops to be counted.

Jack helped the wounded Fannin out of the building into the main yard just as the first beams of Palm Sunday's light started to show in the East. The wind they stepped into had a bite to it. Its whistling added to the confusion as the cold soldiers were jostled to their feet by the armed Mexican guards and the Texas officers tried to gather their commands.

Luke had only seen Captain Shackelford and gotten a few brief words with him twice during the past week since their surrender. When he heard Jack calling for the Red Rovers to form up on him, Luke ran to the familiar voice.

"What's afoot, Captain?" Luke asked wide eyed. Although he was hopeful and comforted to see his Captain, he was also obviously apprehensive at the same time.

Jack reached with both hands for Luke's shoulders as the young man stopped in front of him. He kept the boy at arms length, but warmly squeezed his hands around Luke's upper arms and said smiling, "Hey son, are you all right?"

"Yes, Sir, I'm fine," Luke smiled back knowing his friend was sincerely glad to see him. "What's going on?"

"Don't know, Luke. You think maybe some of the boys slipped off and escaped last night? They want us to line everybody up for a head count."

"Could be, Sir, but I doubt it. I'd have probably heard something about an escape. I don't know how they'd have done it either, with all these damn Mexicans watchin' us like buzzards."

Through the confused snarl of scurrying Texans, a Mexican Colonel walked up to Luke and Shackelford. He stopped with poise, then spoke in English that was as good as or better than theirs.

"Gentlemen, I am Colonel Francisco Garay, of General Urrea's staff."

"I am Captain John Shackelford, Commander of the Red Rover Company from the state of Alabama." Jack responded as he rose himself to attention. He did not recognize this Mexican officer but continued. "This is one of my men, Luke Stevens, from the Austin Colony of Texas. Have you assumed command here, Sir?"

"No, Captain, Colonel José Nicolas de la Portilla is still in command of General Urrea's forces here in *La Bahia*," the well groomed man said as he stood with an erect posture. "I am the Adjutant for General Urrea's command staff. I am presently not a combat officer. My duties for Mexico are more administrative in nature. I returned yesterday with your Colonel Fannin after his meeting with the General in Copano and will be continuing on to headquarters." Colonel Garay hesitated slightly, then continued.

"Captain Shackelford, I understand that you are a very good doctor. I was told that you have been extremely kind in taking care of my country's wounded soldiers. I wish to thank you for your compassion, Sir."

"You are welcome, Sir." Jack responded looking straight into the Colonel's eyes. He paused, never taking his eyes from the other man's, then continued with sincere but calculated words. "As a physician, and as a military officer, I am obligated to take care of wounded men, and prisoners."

Without saying anything, Colonel Garay closed his eyes slowly and nodded his head, letting Jack know that he understood exactly what had just been said. When he opened his eyes, the Colonel spoke in a direct manner. "Captain Shackelford, it is my request that you report to the hospital. There you will find Major Miller and some men who will help you gather medical supplies. I am in need of your services at my tent. You may also bring your friend, Doctor Bernard. My men will wait for you and escort you to my quarters."

"But what about gathering my company, Sir?" Jack asked quickly.

"Others can take care of that, Captain Shackelford," Colonel Garay answered. Then in a quiet voice that was filled with a strange urgency he said, "I need for you to act quickly, Sir."

As the Mexican Colonel turned and walked away, Jack looked to Luke. Each could see from the other's eyes that they both sensed something wrong. "Stay with the men, Son," Jack said to his young friend. "And keep your wits about you. I don't know what's happening, but something's up. I'll get back with you as soon as I can."

"Yes, Sir," Luke said with a keen focus in his eyes. "You keep your own guard up, Jack." Then as his Captain went quickly to give instructions to the Company's First Sergeant, the young Luke Stevens turned and fell into formation with the rest of the Alabama Red Rovers.

35

"They're marchin' us to Copano Bay to catch a ship. We're goin' home, Cap'm!" The smiling young boy from Ward's Georgia Company responded energetically in his southern accent to Captain Shackelford's inquiry.

The happy twenty year old Georgian held the first place in a line of eighty-five Texas soldiers, from what was left of Ward's Command. They all stood outside the front wall of the fort and watched Jack Shakleford being escorted through the main gates. Every soldier who had a knap sack already had it shouldered, and all the troops were ready to march.

"Tell Uncle Sam hello for me!" Jack yelled to the group as he walked with Bernard, Miller, and the small group of others between the armed Mexican guards. "Good luck, Boys! I hope to join you soon."

Jack smiled with his own thoughts of going home while they walked the hundred yards to the southwest. The morning air was still chilled, but the biting March wind had settled itself into being just a light breeze. Outside Garay's large tent they were greeted by a very short Lieutenant who showed the two doctors to the wounded inside. Both Shackelford and Joseph Bernard went right to work examining the wounded Mexicans.

While they started moving about the cots which held the enemy's injured, the miniature Lieutenant began talking to them in English. They learned that the young officer had been educated in Bardstown, Kentucky, giving them insight into the very odd accent with which he spoke English. He was actually a cordial fellow who seemed quite pleased for the opportunity to use both his English words and his American education.

They found it entertaining to listen to the junior officer jabber in his Mexican/Kentucky accent as they attended the wounded soldiers. They began to converse openly, and for half an hour they engaged in pleasant conversation. Suddenly, from the East toward the river, there were volleys of rifle fire.

"What was that?" Jack blurted in surprise as he jerked himself upright.

"*Yo no se, Señor,*" the Lieutenant responded in Spanish inadvertently. Then he continued, "I do not know, Sir. Probably it is just the guard discharging their weapons for fresh powder."

That seemed a reasonable answer. At least once a day the guards fired off their guns to make sure the coarse black gunpowder hadn't caked from the humidity. Then they would clean their weapons and reload them with new charges so that they always had fireable rounds in their rifles.

Twenty minutes later Jack Shackelford had just finished tying a fresh bandage around the mangled leg of a scared seventeen year old Mexican soldier when he heard another sound in the distance. This time it came from the South in the direction the front opening of the tent faced. Through the open door flap Jack heard the clear distinct voice of his young friend, Luke Stevens, yell defiantly, "Hurra for Texas!"

As a few other young voices rang out, "Hurra for Texas!", there was a loud report of rifle fire, then screams. Jack Shackelford looked across the tent into the eyes of his friend, Joseph. He felt as though all the blood in his veins had stopped moving. Horror grabbed his throat, then rammed itself down through his chest and into his stomach. His eyes left Bernard's. He turned to the short Mexican officer and tried to speak. His voice cracked with a hollow sound and, "Oh, my dear God," was all that came out.

Shortly thereafter another round of rifle fire rang out from the North. More screams were heard, then sporadic gunshots. Before all the firing ceased, Colonel Garay stepped through the tent opening.

Captain Shackelford jumped to his feet and yelled out to the Mexican Colonel, "My God, Man! What is happening?! Are they killing all our boys?!"

"It is so." The Colonel replied sadly as he cast his eyes to the dirt floor.

"Oh, my Lord," Jack heard Bernard say in a hushed voice behind him.

Colonel Garay looked up into Jack's eyes and said, "I need for you to know that I did not give the order, nor did I have anything to do with carrying it out. I was told only this morning that Colonel Portilla received the order, direct from Santa Anna, in a letter delivered last night. This is a black day for the Mexican people, and I fear it will haunt us forever. I am ashamed."

The Colonel tightened his lips together to stop the tears that had begun to form in his eyes. He braced himself, and there was sincerity in his voice as he continued with his impeccable English, "I saved as many of you as I could. Had it been within my power I would have saved more. It is important to me that you know this, Sir."

Jack Shackelford stood silently, and the Colonel slowly turned and left the tent.

It was late morning before Jack and the others were taken back to the hospital within the fort. By then the Goliad Massacre was done. The Mexicans had divided the Goliad prisoners into four groups, and under the different pretenses of marching to Copano, gathering wood, or butchering cattle, had marched them away from one another in four directions. Once each group was out of sight from the others they were halted, and executed.

At the end, all the Goliad wounded from the battlefield hospital were carried into the main yard of the fort and shot on their stretchers. Colonel James Walker Fannin was the last prisoner killed.

He died bravely after being forced to witness the death of the last wounded man from his heroic band of volunteers. In accordance with formal military fashion, he handed his watch and money to the Mexican officer overseeing his execution. He then requested that he be shot in the breast, not in the face, and that he be given a decent burial. With his own hands Fannin tied the blindfold over his eyes, then opened his shirt to expose his chest.

As a doctor on the battlefield, Jack Shackelford had witnessed many gruesome sights, but the ghastly scene before him as he walked through the open yard of Fort Defiance made him sick to his stomach. The wounded men he had cared for, and served with, were being stripped naked and thrown into piles. The piles were turning red with blood. He saw Colonel Fannin's jacket being taken from a dead body. The face was unrecognizable from the gunshot wounds, but he knew from the jacket that their commander was gone.

When Jack's Alabama Red Rover Company was halted and the column ordered by the Mexicans to turn and face away from the road, the Company's First Sergeant hesitated and looked back at his men. As he suddenly realized what was about to happen, he yelled to them all courageously, "They're going to kill us boys! Turn and face 'em like men! Look the coward bastards right in the eyes!"

Luke Stevens faced the Mexican infantry as they positioned themselves along the road in front of the volunteers. In the moments it took for the mounted officer to ride up and pace his horse behind his firing squad, Luke's mind flashed to his home and family. In his heart he saw them all together walking down the little hill toward their homestead.

From the back of his horse the officer looked down directly at Luke as he started to raise his saber over his head. Luke's heart began to swell and he gritted his teeth together as his mind showed him his Pa and the other men from the Alamo. Before the Mexican could lower his saber and command the executioners to fire, the young Texan looked into the Mexican officer's eyes, then spat into the air toward him. Luke grabbed his sweat stained hat and waved it high over his head and yelled out boldly and triumphantly, "Hurra for Texas!"

36

Colonel José Nicolas de la Portilla stood alone outside the front wall of Fort Defiance while the last execution column was dismissed by their commanding officer. He watched his soldiers solemnly leave ranks and quietly split into small groups walking away to their tents. He wondered what thoughts were in their minds.

Portilla's eyes lost their focus as his own mind wrestled with the gravity of what he had just done. He had forced his good soldiers to kill over four hundred unarmed men.

He told himself he had no choice; he was following his orders. The orders had come directly from the President of Mexico specifically to him. There was no alternative; he had to follow orders. Portilla was trying so hard to make his heavy soul believe those things; he didn't even notice Colonel Garay approaching.

Garay saw the blank stare and knew the other officer's mind was somewhere else. His own heart was numb, and he felt sorry for Portilla. The two men had served together occasionally over the years at different duty stations throughout Mexico. They were not close, but Garay considered the preoccupied man standing all alone thirty feet in front of him to be a good soldier, and a friend. He wondered how either of them would be able to carry the memory of this dark day they had somehow been put into by fate.

He walked quietly up to Portilla then stopped and said, "José, I know you may want to be alone right now, but I've just been told that a company of your dragoons is coming in. They apparently have prisoners. I thought you should know."

With a troubled face Colonel Portilla focused his sad eyes on Francisco Garay. He said quietly, "Walk with me, Francisco," as he nodded his head slightly in a gesture to the north.

The two men walked up the road away from the fort to wait for the platoon. As they stopped in the shade of several old cedar trees which grew beside the dusty road, they could see the dragoons coming in the distance escorting a very large wagon.

"Do you think he knew, Francisco?" Colonel Portilla asked without looking at Garay when they stopped walking. "Do you think Urrea knew that Santa Anna would order the prisoners killed?"

"I'm not sure what you mean, José."

"Do you think that the reason General Urrea left here, and went to the coast was because he knew the President would order us to execute all the prisoners?!" José burst out with a desperate anxiety pushing his words. "Do you think he left because *he* wouldn't have done it?! Or maybe he knew he would *have* to carry out the President's orders, like I did, and didn't want all their dead souls on his conscience!"

"I don't know, José." Garay said pensively. "I honestly don't know."

"Well damn him if he did!" José blurted through his teeth, and clenching his fists he turned his back to Garay as he swore. "Damn his soul to hell! Damn him for leaving me here to do this!"

José turned back to Colonel Garay and looked directly into his eyes. In a forceful voice that almost begged for concurrence he said, "I had to do it. You know I was given no choice. I had to follow my orders! You would have had to do the same thing if Urrea had left you in command."

Francisco Garay looked away from Portilla's pain-filled eyes. He knew his friend was right. He looked up into the tops of the old cedar trees and said sadly, "I know."

Each man stood silently with his own thoughts as they waited together on the side of the dirt road while the dragoons and their prisoners slowly plodded toward them.

Gabriel was in the back of the big wagon on his knees next to Sam while one of the dragoons drove. His hands were tied together at the wrists, but they were in front of him so he could care for the feverish boy whose condition had worsened by the day. Gabriel used his body and an old scrap of tarp to make shade for Sam.

From the half full bucket of water beside Sam's bed, Gabriel took a wet rag and mopped his friend's head and the bare part of his chest where his shirt was open. This morning Sam had become delirious from the fever that torched his body, and he had been drifting in and out of consciousness. The kind black man looked down at Sam's face. He knew he was losing the boy, and there was nothing he could do about it.

Deep down inside, Gabriel was scared. Although he'd never had much in his life before, everything he did have and almost everything he cared about, was gone. The only part of his world that hadn't been taken away was Sam. Gabriel would do anything to hold onto that last piece of his life. He'd do anything to take care of the boy. But now these bad men had them both, and Gabriel was powerless. He knew that if the bad men didn't kill his friend, the fever would soon take him away.

As Gabriel put the rag back into the bucket, he straightened his back and looked over the side boards of the wagon. Twenty feet away from him in the grass next to the road were the dead bodies of a hundred men. They were loosely scattered next to one another in a long line that paralleled the road. Most of them laid face up with their eyes open.

The shock of seeing the grim sight made Gabriel stop breathing. He sat still with his mouth open while the blood left his head and legs and arms. His feet and hands started to tingle, and he said in his low deep voice, "Oh, Sweet Jesus".

Gabriel's body started to shake slightly as he began breathing again and looked down to Sam. With his wrists tied and his thumbs sticking up together, Gabriel's hands looked like a worn dark brown mahogany bird as he spread his callused palms and placed them protectively over the boy's fevered head. He looked back over the side boards while the wagon continued to pass the dreadful massacre site.

"Oh, Dear Lord", Gabriel said quietly as his mind began to absorb the magnitude of a hundred dead bodies strewn like discarded rubbish so far along the side of the little road. He sat back onto the bottom of the wagon's floor and looked at Sam. He could feel the cold lips of Fear sucking all the strength from his arms as he realized this had to be the prisoner camp they were being taken to. He was glad Sam was passed out. Gabriel closed his eyes and asked Jesus to let the boy just slip away in his sleep. He didn't want his friend murdered like those other poor men.

When the column reached the shade of the cedar trees where the two Colonels stood waiting Sergeant Delgado, the squad leader, raised his right arm to signal for a halt. He dismounted and handed his horse's reins to another soldier, then smartly snapped to attention and saluted Colonel Portilla. After the Colonel returned his salute, the Sergeant stayed at attention and gave his report.

"Sir, Second Ranging Squad has completed patrol of the roadways as ordered. The roads are clear and passable. We captured two prisoners and commandeered this large wagon. We observed no other enemy activity."

"Very well, Sergeant Delgado," Portilla responded, and as he started to walk around to the side of the big wagon he continued, "Where are the prisoners? In the wagon?"

"Yes, Sir," Delgado answered stiffly and started to walk behind his commander. "The wounded man laying down has a fever. I'm sure he is a combatant. The Negro is his slave. He is a combatant too. He attacked our platoon."

Gabriel still had his hands spread guardingly over Sam's forehead when the two Colonels and the Sergeant walked around to the back of the wagon and looked in. He looked back and forth at the two commanders as they spoke. Although he had no idea what they were saying, Gabriel never took his eyes from the men as they spoke to one another in Spanish.

"This one is just a boy, Sergeant. What makes you think he's an enemy soldier, and how did you capture these men?"

"Sir, the boy has been wounded." Delgado answered defensively. "I'm sure he was in a battle. As for their capture, we found the wagon and thought it was abandoned. When we started to investigate, the Negro attacked us. We were able to subdue him, but he hurt three of our men. One has a broken arm!"

José Portilla stood silent for a moment. Francisco Garay, sensing his friend obviously in a quandary about the prisoners, spoke in English to the black prisoner.

"Are you and the boy rebel soldiers?"

Gabriel didn't answer.

Garay tried again. "Do you understand me? How did the boy get hurt?"

Gabriel looked down at Sam, and then took his eyes back to Colonel Garay. He answered slowly but clearly. "Mexican soldiers attacked Sam's home. They kilt his Momma and took his sister. Then they burned the whole place down. Sam tried to stop 'em, but they hurt him real bad. Me and him was tryin' to find his sister when these men took us."

Colonel Garay nodded his head while he slowly blinked his eyelids and said, "I see." He turned to Portilla and said in Spanish, "These men are not soldiers."

Garay looked into the back of the wagon which was empty except for the prisoners and the sick young man's bed. He turned to Delgado and asked, "Where are their weapons? Were these men armed when you captured them, Sergeant?"

"The boy had a knife." The soldier answered trying to make it sound significant.

"Did these men carry firearms, Sergeant?!" Garay asked curtly.

"No, Sir!" Delgado answered as he straightened his back upright.

Garay turned toward José Portilla and held the commander's eyes with his own as he hesitated, then continued talking, "Then these were not Texans under arms when you caught them. Is that correct, Sergeant?"

"Well, they did not carry firearms, Sir. That is correct."

Colonel Portilla took command of the situation saying, "Sergeant, you and your men did a good job on your patrol. You did exactly the right thing bringing these people along to determine their status. As you know our orders are specific with regard to dealing with rebels under arms. Colonel Garay and I commend you for your performance. Now that we have determined they were not armed rebels, these men are to be released."

"But, Sir," Sergeant Delgado started to protest.

Colonel Portilla looked squarely at the subordinate and cut him off with, "Yes, Sergeant Delgado. Is there a question about my decision?"

As soon as the Sergeant answered, "No, Sir," very meekly, Portilla said, "Very well. You are dismissed. You may quarter your troops and tend to your animals." Delgado saluted and turned to walk to his horse. As he did Portilla looked at Francisco Garay and said, "Would you tell the Negro what is going on? I will send some men to take this boy to the hospital."

Garay nodded.

Colonel Portilla turned to walk away then stopped and turned the upper part of his body back toward his friend. With sincerity in his eyes and in his voice he said slowly, "Francisco, thank you."

37

Gabriel stood quietly not far from the cot in the Fort Defiance hospital where Joseph Bernard and Jack Shackelford crouched over Sam. The two doctors were trying to gently remove the boy's clothes so they could examine him. When they undid the bandages from Sam's left hand they both reeled back from the foul smell of the oozing wound.

Joseph Bernard turned to Gabriel and ordered, "Get two buckets of water. They're by the door over there."

Joseph looked up at Jack Shackelford. From the blank look on his face and the disconnected way Shackelford had rotely undressed the patient, Bernard knew his friend was still in some sort of shock over the massacre. Bernard compensated for his colleague, letting him deal with his own trauma, while they continued to undress the feverish boy.

Slowly, by continuing to ask Jack for his opinions about the patient's condition, Joseph was able to bring Shackelford back into the reality of the moment. From wherever he had gone, into whatever recesses of his mind, Jack gradually rejoined his friend. By the time Bernard had cleaned the decomposition and puss from the wound on the patient's left hand, they both were able to concentrate on the sick boy they were treating.

"Do you think we'll have to take off his arm?" Jack asked as he examined the red streaks emanating from the wound and traveling up Sam's left arm.

"I don't think it's blood poisoning yet," Joseph answered. "He's burning up with fever though. I'm afraid if we take the arm it's liable to kill him."

"I understand that, Joseph, but if we're going to remove the arm don't you think we should do it while he's unconscious? Of course, we don't know how much strength he has."

Bernard turned to Gabriel who was standing close behind them and listening to every word. "How long has he had the fever? And how long has he been unconscious?"

"Fever started five or six days ago, Sir." Gabriel told him respectfully. "When them red lines started comin' up from down by his poor hand. Wadn't 'till this mornin' that he started comin' and goin' passin' out like that. When he's awake he was saying things like he didn't know where he was or was dreamin' or somethin'."

"Did you put this splint on his leg?" Jack asked the big man.

"Yes, Sir. I think the Mexicans stepped on him with a horse, an' that leg was real crooked. I tried to get it back straight."

"You did a good job." Jack said with a comforting smile. "Has the boy taken any liquids? Have you given him any soup, or has he taken any water the last couple of days?"

"A little water, Sir, not much." Gabriel replied.

Gabriel's lower lip began to tremble as he thought of the things the doctors had said to one another. He knew why they were asking him these questions. Big tears filled his dark tired eyes and Gabriel said earnestly, "Sam's a strong young man. He's a good young man. You're not goin' to cut off his arm are you, Sir?"

Joseph Bernard answered. "It may come to that. We'll just have to see. But right now you're going to help me get some fluids into this boy. He's very dehydrated, and we've got to get his fever down. You say his name is Sam?"

"Yes, Sir, Sam is his name."

Bernard started to pat Sam's good hand trying to wake him. "Sam, Sam, you have to wake up, Sam."

The doctor stuck his hand into what remained of the fresh water in one of the buckets and, with the ends of his fingers, flipped water into Sam's face. When the boy's eyes started to flutter and open, Bernard said in a loud but compassionate voice, "Sam, you have to wake up. I'm Doctor Bernard. You are in a hospital now. You are going to be all right. I need for you to wake up now. You have to help me make you better. You have to wake up and help us, Sam."

Joseph looked up at Jack while the boy was starting to awaken. Jack's head was turned away slightly, and Bernard could see that his friend's eyes were again looking at something else, either far away or very deep down in his soul. He tried to bring Jack back saying, "You want to help with this, Jack?"

Hearing his name, Shackelford came back into the hospital room long enough to look around and say absently, "No, Joseph, I think I'll just sit for a while. Do you mind?"

Joseph smiled sympathetically sensing his distraught friend's need to be alone with his pain. "The black and I can handle it. Why don't you rest for a bit," he said quietly patting the sick boy's hand.

A few hours later, in the afternoon, Colonel Garay quietly entered the long barracks room that served as the hospital. He saw Doctor Bernard and the Negro slave from the wagon each sitting at the bedside of the sick youngster spoon-feeding liquids into him. Jack Shackelford was sitting by himself on the side of an empty cot at the far end of the room. He was slumped forward with his head deep in his hands and didn't look up when the Mexican approached.

"Captain Shackelford, may I have a word with you?" Colonel Garay asked softly.

With red bloodshot eyes Shackelford looked up, but didn't say anything. Jack's body and his soul were hollow. His feelings seemed to have all bled out like the blood of his murdered men. He was empty.

"Captain Shackelford," Garay began, looking as though he wasn't sure how to continue, "is the boy going to be all right?" Jack did not respond. Francisco Garay looked away trying to compose another question. He pursed his lips, hesitated, then went on obviously unsure of himself, "Captain Shackelford, there is a women out in the field with the dead. I believe she is a white woman. I am not sure what to do, but there has already been enough tragedy on this day. Perhaps it would be a good idea if you were the one to approach her." Garay paused again, then asked, "Will you come with me?"

Jack rose, emotionless, and without saying a word followed the Mexican officer toward the front gates. In the yard they passed soldiers beginning to load the piles of bodies onto carts to be transported for burning outside the fort. Jack thought briefly that this walk might be a ploy to take him to his own execution, but as he passed his fallen comrades, he didn't care.

They left the compound and never talked as they walked side by side for three quarters of a mile. Fifteen feet behind them two armed Mexican soldiers followed in silence. When they topped a small rise Jack quit walking, overcome with anguish as he saw the evil spectacle laid out before him in an open field.

The red jean of his valiant Alabama Company was the first thing visible. The dead bodies of his Red Rovers and others were sprawled loosely together in a broken line that approximated the formation they were in when the executioners fired. Most of the brave lads had died next to the road in their place within ranks, but a few had obviously been able to escape the assassins for at least a short distance.

Jack Shackelford was shocked and repulsed by the devastating sight. His face began to tingle and his legs suddenly felt limp. Colonel Garay saw Jack begin to falter and grabbed his left arm. He held Shackelford upright and said firmly but compassionately, "Steady yourself, Sir."

After a moment they began to walk slowly toward the atrocity. Jack wasn't sure he could stand getting close enough to see the faces of the boys. He knew their families, and he had told the mothers he'd take good care of their sons. Jack's heart flooded with guilt as he thought about bringing those bright young men all the way from Alabama to be slaughtered.

Jack wanted to avert his eyes from the heartbreaking sight as if that would somehow take the guilt and the pain away, but he forced himself to look ahead. He set his jaw against the pain he felt inside. He made his body keep going and fought against the almost overwhelming need to cry.

The Mexican Colonel slowly started taking smaller paces and eventually came to a stop. Colonel Garay looked at Jack then pointed ahead and said. "There she is. Our men saw her search for a long time as though she were looking for someone. See if you can help her."

Jack's eyes found the kneeling woman. She was slightly left of the woeful formation's center and even at this distance, he realized he could hear her crying. As they slowly walked toward her, Jack saw that she held a dead soldier in her arms.

The woman never looked up as he walked to her from behind. When he was a few feet away Jack noticed the bruises and human teeth marks showing on the woman's shoulders and back through the openings where her soiled dress was torn. The sight caused Jack to clench his own teeth together hard to fight off the quick pang that suddenly hit his stomach.

Jack Shackelford made his legs take two more steps, and he looked at the dead soldier she held in her arms. His soul collapsed. There in the crying young woman's arms, being rocked gently back and forth, was the lifeless pale body of his friend, Luke Stevens. In the dead boy's right hand, still clutched tightly, was the well used hat he always wore.

Tears again began to flow from Jack's eyes, and he felt as though he couldn't breath. Involuntary quick sobs drew short breaths of air into his lungs. He stopped himself and swallowed hard. Jack looked down at the poor grieving woman who cried hard as she rocked his young friend's body. As he kept fighting back his own tears, he spoke slowly and softly to the woman.

"Are you Mary Beth?" he asked.

Still holding Luke, the battered young woman turned her head. She looked up to the tall man standing behind her. Her eyes began to focus on him through their tears, and she said still crying, "How'd you know my name?"

When the girl answered Jack was overcome with sorrow. He felt as though his heart was being ripped out, and he winced at the pain. He couldn't speak, but he reached his hand out to the girl as his diaphragm spasmed into several short silent sobs. He briefly caught his breath and forced out the words, "I am Jack Shackelford. Your brother, Luke, was my friend."

Mary Beth kept looking up at him. "You knew Luke?" She asked and the semblance of a smile came with more of her tears.

His voice began to quake and Jack was crying, but continued. "He talked of you and your parents and his brother, Sam, all the time." Then Jack fell to his knees and put his arms around the girl. Mary Beth's head went to his shoulder, and Jack put his hand behind it and held her tightly as he looked up toward the clouds trying to stop crying. "He loved you all very much."

Mary Beth sobbed violently into the man's shoulder. She had no feeling left in her exhausted body as she sobbed in the sanctuary of the strong stranger's arms. Jack held her and patted her back tenderly trying to give comfort to the sister of his friend.

Jack wanted to be strong. He wanted to take away the girl's pain and tell her everything would be all right, but he couldn't. Holding her tightly he turned his head and looked at the lifeless bodies of his brave men and boys, scattered pitifully in the dirt on either side of him, and he couldn't stop crying himself. All he could do was hold her.

"I tried to get here in time." Mary Beth sobbed into Jack's shoulder as she let herself trust the first kind, gentle human touch she'd known since the Mexican's raided her homestead. "I tried to get to Luke before it was too late!"

She pulled away from Jack's embrace slightly and looked down at her brother. Mary Beth kept her right arm around Jack and put her left hand to Luke's cheek. She didn't take her eyes from the pale still boy laying across her lap as she said through her tears, "He was all I had left in this world. I was too late. Now they've taken him, too."

She took her arm from around Jack and reached for her brother. "I'm so sorry, Luke." Mary Beth said as she began to sob heavily and put her arms around the dead boy.

Jack reached for the girl and gently pulled her away from Luke. He had found his strength, and as he stopped crying he said tenderly, "You could not have stopped this, Mary Beth. It's all right. There was nothing you could have done." He started to put his arms around the young girl again when he heard voices behind him.

As Shackelford turned his head toward Garay, who had stayed back to let him have time with the girl, he saw the Colonel rushing to the two armed guards. The guards were farther back up the small rise than Garay, and they were facing up the hill with their rifles shouldered. "Hold your fire!" He heard Garay command. "Put your weapons down!"

The soldiers did as they were told, and Jack looked to the top of the rise to see what was causing the disturbance. He saw the large slave from the hospital cresting the rise carrying the wounded boy, Sam, in his arms. Beside Jack, Mary Beth said in a small voice as she, too, saw Gabriel, "I know that man."

Forty yards down from the top of the rise Gabriel smiled broadly as he looked into Sam's face. "I told you we found Miss Mary Beth. See there she is, Sam. When I heard them men say there was a white woman out here, I followed 'em, and sure enough it was Miss Mary Beth. That's why I came back and got you. We found your sister, Sam!"

Mary Beth never took her eyes from the big man walking toward her as she rose to her feet. "Gabriel? Gabriel!" She called out. Then, suddenly, she recognized Sam and realized he was alive. "Gabriel, is that Sam!? Sam you're alive! Oh, God, Sam!" She screamed out as she started running toward her little brother.

From the cradle of Gabriel's two strong arms Sam raised his head and saw his sister running toward them. With tears in his eyes he looked up at Gabriel's beaming face, then turned and smiled at Mary Beth.

38

LUKE MOSES STEVENS
1815 - 1836
B E L O V

Sam looked at his work then started to carve an "E" into the rough, partially burned plank board that had been part of their homestead's front porch. Although his left hand was healing, he still couldn't use it for much of anything. He steadied the board with his left forearm while he held his Christmas knife in his right hand and carved his brother's grave marker. With just one hand he worked very slowly, but at least it was something he could do.

He stretched his spine, then leaned back against the base of one of the smaller live oak trees on top of the little hill overlooking the burned out ruin that had once been his home. Sam sat by himself on a tarp spread on the ground not far from where his Momma and Luke lay side by side in their graves. He had already finished his Mother's marker, and it was in place. Sam wanted to do a nice one for his brother, too.

Mary Beth was with Gabriel at the bottom of the hill in the charred rubble of the house. Sam watched as the big man moved the few blackened timbers that were leaning against the standing rock fireplace. When the burned beams were out of the way, he saw Gabriel help Mary Beth remove some of the stones from the front by the heavy mantle above the hearth. The stones concealed their Pa's hiding place where he had kept their family money, important papers, and other valuables. His sister reached into the secret hole, and Sam smiled as he recognized the dark colored box she retrieved.

The young man was glad that he hadn't thought of checking Pa's hiding place before he and Gabriel left to find his sister. He didn't know why he hadn't thought of it, he just hadn't. He was glad now because he knew that the Mexicans would have stolen whatever was in the box when he and Gabriel were captured.

Mary Beth opened the heavy little box and looked inside. She closed its lid and waved to Sam. With Jim Bowie's working knife still in Sam's right hand high over his head, he waved back, and Mary Beth started up the hill with Gabriel at her side.

Sam kept working on Luke's marker until his sister and Gabriel made it up the hill, and both sat in front of him on his tarp. Mary Beth put the box from Jonathan's secret place in the middle between them saying, "It was still there. Pa was right. He always said his hidin' place would be safe, even if the whole place burned down."

The two young people smiled both feeling a little pain, and pride, at the use of their Father's familiar name. It had been over a month since the Goliad Massacre, and they were slowly beginning to heal, physically and emotionally. Although they had no idea how they would survive or what they would do, they hadn't lost everything. They had one another. For the time being that was all that mattered, and they each knew inside they could do whatever it took to carry on.

Doctors Shackelford and Bernard had saved Sam's arm and nursed him until he was strong enough to travel. They had also helped Mary Beth deal with the wounds her body and spirit had suffered. Although they were against the idea, Jack Shackelford and his friend Joseph prepared Luke's body for the long slow journey home before the two doctors were sent to San Antonio de Bexar to perform amputations on the Mexican wounded still suffering from the Battle of the Alamo.

"Pa was sure proud of that box," Sam said looking down at the twelve inch wide, twelve inch long, seven inch deep dark grayish black container on the canvas in front of him.

"He had it for a long time," Mary Beth smiled as she responded and touched the old piece with her fingertips.

The box was made of solid lead, and it was heavy. It had been given to Jonathan by the English smelterers who worked with him at the Potosi lead mine when he and Moses Austin left the operation. The initials JMS, for Jonathan Michael Stevens, were engraved in large fancy letters on the lid.

"What's in it?" Sam asked as he stuck his knife into its scabbard and, with his left forearm, let Luke's marker down gently to the ground.

There was almost nothing left from the homestead because everything was either stolen or burned by the Mexicans. They still didn't even have a gun. Both Sam and his sister had hoped there would be enough money in the hiding place to at least buy a rifle and some powder.

Mary Beth turned the heavy piece so Sam couldn't see as she removed the top. She reached inside and methodically started removing its contents. "This is the deed for our land grant from Stephen Austin," she said. "These are church papers. One is from the preacher saying he married Momma and Pa, and this one is from the priest saying we became Catholic so we could settle here." Mary Beth smiled and looked up at Sam. She reached inside, and as she lifted out some paper and coins, she said enthusiastically, "And this is seven hundred dollars, American!"

Sam let out a whoop and shook his clenched good hand into the air. He turned to Gabriel who was smiling broadly back at him. As he looked back into his sister's face, Sam said, "We may not have anything else, but by God, at least we're not broke!"

There wasn't much more inside the lead container, just a small amount of Mexican currency and a couple of letters. After they had looked through those, Mary Beth started to replace everything back into the box. Gabriel stood up and stretched.

As he pulled both his muscular arms behind his head to work his shoulders, he looked off into the distance and said, "Y'all hungry? Think I'll go check them snares and see if I got us a rabbit or somethin'. Miss Mary Beth, you think you feel like eatin' some…" Gabriel stopped in mid-sentence and focused his eyes to the South.

Mary Beth jumped to her feet and felt fear in her stomach as she said, "What is it, Gabriel?! What do you see?!"

"Riders comin'," he answered, keeping his eyes squinted toward the South. "Must be twelve or fifteen of 'em. They ridin' like Mexicans."

She jerked her head and gave a quick look at her brother, then Mary Beth searched for the riders. As Sam reached for the crutch Gabriel had made for him and got to his feet, he heard his sister say, "We'll have to hide up here. Gabriel, can you take the mules and hide them out as far away as you can on the other side of the creek?"

Gabriel started off the hilltop in a run then stopped. He turned around and said, "Don't be scared. I be back up here with you before them men get here." He spun around and dashed down the hill.

As Gabriel passed the midway point running down the slope, Sam reached his sister's side. His keen eyes soon found the Mexicans, and he stood for a moment watching their approach. Sam leaned on the crutch with his armpit and took his hand from the wide spot that served as the device's handle. With the index finger of his good right hand, Sam pointed to something within the oncoming column of men and said to Mary Beth, "What do you make of that?"

The brother and sister stood together on the highest point of the little hill straining their eyes to see the advancing horsemen. They could make out individual bodies and see that the men definitely sat their horses like Mexicans. There were two riders side by side leading the trotting formation that followed single file behind them. The third man in line carried a pole in his right hand with the bottom of it stuck into his stirrup. Attached to the pole was a large flag with one lone star on it.

39

Juan Seguin was heartsick as he and his cousin, Maximilian, led their Company of fifteen *Tejanos* toward the Stevens' homestead and saw only the rock fire hearth standing amid the blackened waste pile of burned wood. Juan was shocked at the devastation as he slowed his horse to a walk, still a long way from what had been his friend's front yard. He turned his face toward Max, and when their tired eyes met he said solemnly, "*Ay Dios Mio.*"

He turned back remembering his friends with their warm hospitality and clenched his jaw muscles to fight against his sorrow. Juan had just ridden his men a long thirty miles out of their way to check on Sarah and had prayed every step that he wouldn't find something like this. Of course he knew about his friend Jonathan's fate, and he had wondered if Luke made it to Fannin's Garrison before the massacre, but he was unprepared for the sight before him. Juan's stomach began to churn with the fear of what he might find when he reached the house.

Slowly they rode on toward the Stevens' home place. Juan hung his head and tried to stop his brain from imagining what horrible things must have happened to Jonathan's family. Every time he looked up, the vision before him slammed his heart, and he had to avert his eyes. He became uneasy, afraid for the safety of his own family. The thought of his wife and children in the path of this war made him burn inside and want to race back to his *hacienda*.

As they rounded a stand of brush and approached the cabin's yard, Juan wondered how many more wretched sights of suffering and anguish this war would bring to his eyes. Images of some of the horrors he'd seen mixed together with the faces of lost friends and comrades in Juan's mind, and he felt hate begin to rise up within him. He saw the smug face of Santa Anna, and Juan's jaw tightened even more as he wished he'd killed the evil bastard with his own hands.

"Juan, look. Over there." Maximilian said to his cousin.

Seguin instantly snapped back from his thoughts and instinctively reached for his pistol. His eyes followed Max's direction, and he saw movement at the bottom of the hill. The pistol was already out of his sash and cocked when Juan recognized Mary Beth and the slave Gabriel coming toward him.

Juan spurred his horse hard and ran him across the small field. Joy exploded from his mouth as he shoved the pistol back in place and yelled out, "Mary Beth!"

When he was thirty yards from the two survivors, he set the bit back in the horse's mouth with a fierce yank and jumped out of his saddle while the animal was still trying to stop. Juan landed in a run and quickly had Mary Beth in his arms.

The young girl cried while she and Juan hugged tightly, and Max rode up with the detachment of soldiers. Mary Beth sobbed into their old friend's shoulder, "Oh, Juan, I can't believe you're here. I'm so glad to see you."

Seguin pulled himself back and looked into Mary Beth's face while he kept his arms around her waist. With concern and apprehension in his voice he asked, "Where is Sarah? Where is your mother, Mary Beth?"

Mary Beth held back her tears and looked into the handsome man's eyes. "They shot her, Juan," she answered, then she continued between jerky breaths with tears flowing down her cheeks. "The Mexican soldiers came and killed Momma on our front porch! They hurt Sam, but he's alive. He's up on the hill there."

Juan raised his eyes to the hilltop and saw the boy leaning on a crutch waving down at him. He turned his eyes back to Mary Beth, and she went on.

"Juan, they murdered Luke at Goliad. Pa's dead, too. What are we going to do?!" In the security of having her parent's strong friend and his men there, Mary Beth found herself releasing all the fears she'd been keeping inside. She couldn't stop herself as she unloaded her burdens, "I don't know what's going to happen to us. I've got to take care of Sam. They destroyed everything we had. What am I going to do, Juan?"

He pulled her to his chest and hugged her tightly. Juan patted the girl's back gently and said in a quiet comforting tone, "Max and I are here now, Mary Beth. Everything's going to be all right. We are here to help you with anything you need."

Juan pulled back from her again and looked into her eyes. "The war is over," he said, and a kind smile started across his face. "We won. Now we can all get on with our lives. We will take care of you. Everything will be all right."

Mary Beth said weakly, "It's over? The war is over?"

Juan hugged her back to his chest and said into the side of her head, "Yes, Little One, it's over. You won't have to worry about the soldiers anymore. It is done."

Mary Beth stayed in the harbor of Juan's strong arms feeling truly safe for the first time since her Pa had left the homestead on his way to the Alamo. She held tightly to him until Juan motioned behind her back for Gabriel to come take her. As he pulled himself back from the girl he said, "Give me a moment with Max and the men, then I will go with you to see your brother."

Gabriel stepped forward and took Mary Beth's arm with his right hand and put his strong left arm around her shoulders while Seguin turned away and walked to Maximilian. The two cousins talked alone for a few minutes, then Juan turned and walked back to Mary Beth while Max went to the troop and told them to dismount.

"Did Mrs. Cavanaugh send you over here to take care of Mary Beth and Sam?" Juan asked when he approached Gabriel, and the black man released his arm from around the girl.

"No, Sir," Gabriel answered sadly as Juan took Mary Beth's arm, and they all started to walk up the hill. "Missus Cavanaugh was kilt, just like Miss Mary Beth's Momma. Them bad men came while I was gone to the settlement, and they burned down the whole plantation and kilt everyone there, even my dogs. Just like here, they's nothin' left of the Cavanaugh's place."

"If it weren't for Gabriel, Sam and I would both be dead." Mary Beth told Juan with sincerity as she walked beside him, and he held her left forearm in his right hand. They continued walking slowly up the easy slope while Mary Beth explained to Seguin the tragic events that had changed all their lives. Juan's soul went hollow when she spoke of her kidnapping. She gave no details about her time as Santa Anna's prisoner, but from the difficulty with which she spoke, Juan knew what had happened. When she finished her story, three quarters of the way up the hill, Juan stopped and turned to Gabriel.

"You are a very brave man," he said looking directly into the big slave's sorrowful eyes. "You did well." Juan reached to Gabriel's shoulder and grasp it with a firm, warm grip. "Thank you for taking care of our friends."

Something to the right moved in Juan's peripheral vision. He turned to see Sam coming down from the top toward them hobbling on one crutch. Leaving the others to follow, Juan hurried toward the injured boy.

"Juan, I can't believe you're here. Thank God you came!" Sam said enthusiastically when they closed on each other. "Oh, it's good to see you!"

Seguin smiled broadly as he reached Sam and put his arm lovingly around the boy, thinking again suddenly about his own family. He squeezed Sam's shoulders tightly and looked down at his bandages and splinted leg. "You don't know how good it is to see you, Sam. I'm glad we made it here, too."

Juan choked back a tear, surprised somewhat that he felt overcome by emotion. His mind was trying to make him see the horrors these two children had been through. He made it stop and raised himself tall, taking in a deep breath. He stepped back and turned to Sam saying with all the calmness and confidence he could fake, "Let me look at you. Are you going to be all right, son? Heard the whole Mexican Army tried to kill you."

"Yes, Sir," Sam smiled back to their longtime friend. "They gave it their best shot, but I'm still here."

Mary Beth and Gabriel walked up, and Sam looked at them as he continued, "We're all still here. Guess they should'a brought a bigger Army."

Juan smiled and hugged the boy tightly around the shoulders again. "You're Jonathan's son all right!" he said proudly.

While he held the boy, Juan looked over his shoulder to the graves of Sarah and Luke. He squeezed Sam tighter and said, "Mary Beth told me about your mother and Luke. She and your brother were wonderful people. Your father was one of the best men I've ever known, and one of the best friends I shall ever have in my life."

He felt Sam sob and Juan stepped back and looked at the young man. "I am so sorry for your loss, Sam. We will all miss them terribly, but they are together now in a better place. We must remember that, and we must always remember what they died for."

Juan reached out and put his hands on both of Sam's shoulders and looked deeply into the watery young eyes. "They died for a free Texas, Sam. The war is over. We won. Now we have the freedom your mother and father and brother wanted for all of us. It won't bring them back and it won't ease the pain we feel, but we can always be proud that we knew these extraordinary people who gave their lives for our freedom."

In the small field at the bottom of the hill, Maximilian dealt with the soldiers. He put some of the men to watering and feeding the horses and had the remainder start building a fire and preparing food. Once the soldiers were lined out and started performing their tasks, Max walked up the little hill to join his cousin and the others. The first things Max saw when he reached the crest were the two fresh graves of Sarah and her son. He removed his hat and made a sign of the cross in front of his chest. Max stood and silently prayed for their souls, wishing he had known those two good people better, then turned to join Juan. As he approached the ground-cloth where they were all sitting, he heard his cousin giving them the news about the war. Maximilian quietly sat on the tarp next to the big slave and listened to Juan explain what had happened.

"The Alamo fell shortly after Max and I saw you last. He and I were unable to get back there to your Father and the rest of those brave men before it was taken. We formed our own Company of *Tejanos* from the men we had recruited for the Alamo and joined General Houston's Army.

"The Texas Army of the People had left Gonzales and retreated to the East. They had just crossed the Colorado River when we caught up to them. A few days later we learned about Fannin's defeat and capture at Goliad.

"I don't know why Fannin didn't join Travis at the Alamo, but he was trying to retreat and join our army when they were captured. It wasn't until later, after we had gone on and camped at the Brazos River, that I found out about the savage massacre of all the unarmed prisoners."

Juan paused and then said with a sad tone as he looked at Sam and Mary Beth, "I am so sorry about Luke. I did not know until now whether he made it to Goliad or not, but the thought that I was the one who told him to go there has weighed heavily upon me. I wish I had never come this way when I left the Alamo, but I had promised Jonathan that I would. It is a burden I shall carry the rest of my life."

After another short pause Juan continued with more force in his voice. "When the news of Goliad reached us, our whole Army went into rage. The men were anxious to fight already after the fall of the Alamo, but the news of Fannin's entire garrison being killed in cold blood steeled the purpose of our struggle in every soldier's heart. It became very difficult for General Houston to continue our retreat. Many of the men thought him a coward because we did not stand and fight right away.

"However, General Houston had a purpose in the retreat that the men couldn't see. By retreating farther and farther into Texas, he baited Santa Anna to follow, which strung out the Mexican Army and their supply lines. By the time we reached a place called Buffalo Bayou down by Harrisburg, Santa Anna had only about seven hundred men with him.

"We crossed the bayou and camped on rising ground waiting for Santa Anna's Army. They crossed the same bridge and made an encampment only three quarters of a mile away below us. As we prepared for battle, some of the officers wanted to attack immediately and others thought it better to wait for Santa Anna to come to us on the high ground. Houston let us all talk, but gave us no indication of his battle plan.

"The next morning General Martin Perfecto de Cos crossed the bridge over the bayou with five hundred and fifty men to reinforce Santa Anna. General Houston sent your father's old friend, Deaf Smith, to blow up the bridge behind them. His plan was to stop any further reinforcements and cut off Santa Anna's only means of escape, but some of the officers objected because the bridge was also our only way out.

"Once the bridge was destroyed, we all knew a battle to the death was at hand.

"General Houston waited and watched. That afternoon several of the other officers and I were with him when the General himself climbed a big tree to observe the Mexican camp. He came down saying Santa Anna was with a concubine and the rest of the camp was quiet. He laughed saying he believed they were taking their *siesta*.

"As he sent us to our companies to await the signal to attack, he said to us, 'We attack together on my command. You tell every man jack under you that when we attack they are to remember the Alamo and remember Goliad!'"

Juan rose to his feet and clenched his fists in his passion. "When the attack began, those were our battle cries. We hit them hard and fast with every man screaming out, 'Remember the Alamo!' and 'Remember Goliad!'

"The arrogant fool, Santa Anna, didn't even have perimeter guards posted, and we overran the camp while they were still trying to react. Our soldiers held nothing back in their fury. They fought to avenge the atrocities of the Alamo and Goliad and the mistreatment of our country and her citizens. Our volunteers killed over six hundred of Santa Anna's men and captured the rest. In less than half an hour we defeated the wicked son-of-a-bitch and destroyed his army in that one battle!"

Sam, Mary Beth, and Gabriel sat in silence absorbing the news and dealing with the different thoughts and images rolling through each of their minds. Mary Beth lifted her face to Juan and Max. All softness left the young woman's features and her dark eyes narrowed with hatred. There was a menacing, cold tone in her voice as she said with her bottom teeth showing, "Did you kill that bastard? Did you kill Santa Anna?"

"He is still alive," Juan answered. "He ran from the battle when it started and escaped. The next day he was found hiding in grass, lying on his belly like a snake. He had stolen the uniform of a common soldier, and might have gotten away with the disguise, had one of the other prisoners not snapped to attention and addressed him as '*El Presidente*'."

Juan could see the anguish in Mary Beth's eyes, which were still narrowed, as he looked into them and continued, "Had I the chance I would have gladly killed him myself. Most of the volunteers wanted to hang him immediately, but General Houston stopped the effort. He said he did not want to make the despicable creature into a martyr, and he was probably right.

"Houston forced Santa Anna to sign a treaty for the independence of Texas. We are a sovereign nation now. When I left there was talk of sending Santa Anna to Washington and turning him over to the Americans."

"You should have killed him," Mary Beth said in a hollow voice. "I wish he had been hanged."

"I know, but it is done now, child," Juan said like a father. "The war is over.

"Maximilian and I were sent with the forces that are overseeing the Mexican retreat. Their soldiers have no more will to fight. The armies are passing thirty miles south of here, so Max and I left them to check on your family."

Juan stopped and looked at Max. When his cousin smiled and nodded back to him, Juan sat down again next to the Stevens children and said, "Max and I have talked it over, and we think it would be a good idea for you to come with us to San Antonio de Bexar. You can live with our families. There is nothing for you here, and the frontier is a hard place, especially with Sam's injuries to deal with." He smiled, and then said,

"Besides, your father and I promised each other last fall at the Siege of Bexar that we would each take care of the other's family if anything happened. You have to let me be a man of my word."

Sam and Mary Beth sat back surprised at the idea, but each pondering it. They looked to one another and Mary Beth said, "I don't know. This place has always been our home. What do you think, Sam?"

Sam's eyes left hers, and he looked at Gabriel. He turned to the two *Tejanos* and asked, "What about Gabriel?"

Maximilian answered for them without hesitation, "Gabriel is welcome to come as well, if that is what you would like."

"May we have some time to talk it over?" Mary Beth asked as she looked from Juan and Max to her little brother.

"Of course, Max and I will go check on our men," Juan said, and with that the two men rose and started off the hilltop leaving the other three sitting together on the ground.

"I think we should go with them," Mary Beth said after she had thought for a while. "Everything here has been destroyed. We don't even have a shelter. I'm not sure we can make it here alone without Momma and Pa."

"Without them, and Luke, I'm not sure I want to," Sam answered. He pulled in a deep breath to fight the ache in his heart and said, "What do you want to do, Gabriel?"

The big man cleared his throat and looked up to them saying, "I do whatever y'all tell me to do, Sam."

"Gabriel, you're a free man now," Sam said earnestly looking straight into Gabriel's dark eyes. "You can do anything you want. Nobody owns you anymore, and nobody can tell you what you have to do anymore."

"Sam's right, Gabriel," Mary Beth followed in. "You're a free man now. The Cavanaugh's are all gone. Nobody owns you. You have been so good to Sam and me, and I thank you for that. You saved both our lives, and we could never repay your kindness, but you can honestly do whatever you want now."

Gabriel sat quietly listening as Mary Beth continued, "Gabriel, we both love you. I hope you know you will always have a home with us.

If we go to Bexar, Sam and I would both want you to go with us, but that would have to be your decision - not ours."

The thought of being a free man during his time on earth had never come into Gabriel's thinking process. He had been a slave all his life. Gabriel sat back and thought hard about what his two friends had just said to him.

Mary Beth looked at her brother and asked, "What do *you* want to do, Sam?"

The boy looked down at his bandaged hand, then lifted it up to Mary Beth and said smiling, "I think we should go with Juan."

Gabriel spoke up. His voice was soft and unsure at first, then gained strength and volume as he continued. "I never been a free man before. Not real sure how to do it. But if you two go with them, I'll be goin', too. If it's all right for me to go, I be goin' with y'all!"

"It's settled then," Mary Beth said. "I'll go tell Juan and Max."

His sister got to her feet and walked down the hill while Sam sat with Gabriel. The boy looked down at the remnants of the only home he could remember. Sadness came over him as he thought about their life at the warm little homestead coming to an end. He was afraid that if they left he might not ever make it back to see this special place again.

Sam thought about his Momma and Pa. He remembered things he'd done around there growing up with his brother. As he thought about how badly he missed them, he felt a knot start in his throat. Suddenly he was scared about moving to San Antonio de Bexar and being all alone in a place they didn't know.

Sam's mind went back to his Pa, and he thought of their last time together. He turned and looked at the old oak stump that had been struck by lightning, where he'd sat with his Pa on their last afternoon together three and a half months before. He smiled and said to Gabriel, "You know, I thought that thing was dead."

Gabriel smiled, too, as he looked at the stump of the strong old oak which stood alone on the other side of Sarah and Luke's graves. Long white beams from the bright midday sun of early May were shining down through the other trees casting a brilliant light on the bold green leaves of new spring shoots, sprouting from the heavy trunk.

PART
THREE

40

"There's a yellow rose of Texas that I am goin' to see…" Gabriel sang out loudly into the clear crisp air of the sunny February morning. The sudden blast from his solid deep voice, as he began happily into his song, startled the mules pulling the Cavanaugh's big wagon and caused the animals to momentarily quicken their pace.

Gabriel continued singing as he turned and smiled at Sam on the seat beside him. It tickled Gabriel that his sudden musical interlude had also spooked Sam awake from his daydream and caught the young man off balance. The surge from the surprised mules flipped Sam backwards, and he grabbed wildly for the front of the wagon seat to keep from flying into the back with their cargo.

Sam caught his balance and scooted himself up to the front of the big hardwood plank that served as the wagon's seat as he shoved his dislodged hat back onto his head. He cranked up the corners of his mouth into a playful smile and said to his big partner, "Very funny, Gabriel. You 'bout scared the shit out of me!"

With his eyes on Sam, Gabriel just smiled a bigger smile and added a little more enthusiasm to the song. "She cried so when I left her it like to broke my heart, and if I ever find her, we never more will part. Oh, she's the sweetest…"

Sam readjusted his hat and sat back into position on the smooth-worn seat. He poked Gabriel on the arm and said grinning, "Sure hope that singing of yours doesn't give those mules the damn colic. It'd be a long walk to San Antonio from here."

The twenty two year old settled himself into a comfortable posture with his feet resting up on the front of the wagon and thought about how he really did enjoy Gabriel's singing. It made the miles go easier. He liked that song, too. Sam guessed the two of them had probably

231

sung that song at least a million times in the five years since they had started their business hauling freight to and from San Antonio de Bexar in the big wagon that had belonged to Gabriel's owners.

While Gabriel drove and continued singing, Sam looked off into the distance to the northwest toward the homestead. He found it hard to believe they had been gone from there for almost six years now. Sam's mind began falling back through the years and Gabriel's song made him think of Emily Morgan, the Yellow Rose of Texas.

Of all the people around the country who sang the popular song, Gabriel and Sam were among the few who knew what, and who, the song was about. They had listened to Juan Seguin tell the story many times, and it was Gabriel's favorite because Emily was a slave girl. She was the woman General Houston had seen with Santa Anna the afternoon of the battle at Buffalo Bayou when Texas won her independence.

Everyone now called it the Battle of San Jacinto because of the big open area close by where Santa Anna camped and most of the fighting took place. Houston had thought the woman was one of Santa Anna's concubines. It turned out that she was as loyal to the Texas cause, and as much a hero, as any of the volunteers who fought against the Mexicans.

Emily Morgan was a "high yellar" Negro, a mulatto, who was indentured to Colonel James Morgan. Colonel Morgan had been assigned to guard the Port of Galveston and protect the Texas government officials in hiding there. He was the Texas patriot also responsible for General Houston's supply lines and loaded flatboats with provisions from his own plantation on San Jacinto Bay to feed Houston's Army.

When Colonel Morgan departed for Galveston, he left his servant, Emily West Morgan, in charge of loading the flatboats as most of the local population had fled before Santa Anna's army advanced into the area. Emily and a young slave boy named Turner were loading supplies into a boat destined for General Houston's men when they were both captured by Santa Anna's scouts. Because of Emily's exceptional beauty, the two prisoners were taken directly to *El Presidente*.

Santa Anna was so struck by the attractiveness of the twenty year old slave girl he ordered his encampment to be made there immediately on the plains of San Jacinto. His officers protested the poor strategic location, but Emily used her comeliness to beguile the lecherous commander, and he stayed with his decision. Santa Anna ordered his officers to have the boy, Turner, show them to Houston's exact location.

As the soldiers departed, Emily convinced her friend to escape from Santa Anna's men and warn the Texans of the enemy's approach. She then catered to *El Presidente*. The young mulatto slave used all her charms to keep Santa Anna well occupied, and distracted, until the very moment the Texas Army attacked.

Although Juan had never met Miss Emily Morgan, he professed that she was a true heroine of the Texas War for Independence. Juan himself had been made a Lt. Colonel at San Jacinto because of his bravery in battle with his *Tejano* Company. Several days after the war had ended, General Houston, still suffering from an ankle shattered during the battle by a Mexican roundball, commended Juan at a dinner held in the command tent for the victorious officers. At that dinner Juan met Colonel James Morgan, and learned about The Yellow Rose of Texas.

As Gabriel finished booming out the last stanza, "And the Yellow Rose of Texas shall be mine forevermore", he turned to the quiet Sam. He said, "See, them mules ain't sick. I think they likes my singin'."

"Well, if their ears fall off and they start pukin', don't say I didn't warn ya," Sam smirked. "And by the way, I ain't pushin' this wagon all the way to San Antonio."

Gabriel smiled as he looked down the road and popped the reins on the mule's backs. He always enjoyed being out on the road with Sam. It gave him a sense of freedom he didn't feel in town with all the people around. He kept looking straight ahead and said, "Sho' is a pretty mornin' out here for you to be so quiet. Not that I ain't enjoyin' that part, it just don't happen very often. You alright, Sam?"

"Yeah, I'm fine, Gabriel. Just thinkin' about stuff. You know how your head gets to rollin' around sometimes, and you start thinkin' about things and rememberin' things and wonderin' about things. Once you get started they just keep rollin' around and rollin' around in your head."

"So what you thinkin' about, Sam?"

"I don't know, Gabriel. Just things. Like, what do you think ever happened to the 'Yellow Rose'? I heard Colonel Morgan freed her for what she did at San Jacinto and sent her back to New York."

"Naw, I don't think so, Sam," Gabriel said seriously and his eyebrows knitted down low on his forehead. "I do believe she heard they's a mighty handsome black man ridin' around this country in a big wagon huntin' for her." He burst open his big smile and laughed out, "She's pro'bly still here in Texas waitin' for me to come find her!"

Sam laughed.

"You're sure saucy this mornin', I'll give you that," Sam said stretching his body and extending both his arms high over his head, then out to the sides clenching and releasing his fists. "But I think mostly you're just full of prunes."

"Well, I just ain't used to seein' you so still and quiet. You ain't gettin' sick on me, are you, Sam?"

"No, I ain't sick, Gabriel. Just thinkin'. Rememberin' things, you know. Do you realize it's been purt'near six years since we buried my Momma and Luke and left the homestead with Juan and Max?"

"That's a long time, ain't it, Sam? Don't seem like it's been that long, but then, sometimes, seems like all that happened a real long time ago."

"It's been almost a third of my life. That's kinda what I's thinkin' about."

"Well, things sure have changed, ain't they, Sam? They's changed a bunch for all of us. Everything's mighty different now, mighty different."

Sam and Gabriel both got quiet while the mules drew the heavy wagon another mile or two down the dirt road. The eyes deep inside each of their hearts followed the events and images their brains had recorded over the last six years. The time seemed to have gone quickly, but so much had happened. So much had changed.

They had said good-bye to the homestead from the gravesides of Sarah and Luke, and then traveled to San Antonio de Bexar with their *Tejano* friends. Upon their arrival, Juan accepted the surrender of the Mexican forces still there and held a burial ceremony honoring the ashes of their father, Jonathan, and the other brave men who had defended the Alamo.

Stephen Austin made it back from Washington and came to see them in San Antonio. He was devastated over the news of Jonathan and Sarah's deaths. Since he was still a bachelor, and the Seguin's had a large family to care for, Austin offered to take Sam, Mary Beth, and Gabriel to live with him. When the three decided they would rather stay in San Antonio, Stephen helped Juan secure a house close by for the three refugees.

Sam remembered how pale and delicate Stephen Austin had seemed, compared to the days before the war when he and Jonathan worked so hard together establishing the colony. They all assumed that Austin's tireless efforts in the United States generating support and money for the Texas cause, and the difficult trip home, had fatigued him. They didn't realize Stephen's health was failing.

Two and a half months later, during the new country's first election in September, Sam Houston defeated Stephen to become the Republic's first president. Houston said he would only serve if Stephen Austin accepted the appointment as Secretary of State. Stephen agreed to serve, but died in office three months later, two days after Christmas, at the age of forty three.

Inside Sam flinched, recalling the pain he and Mary Beth felt when Stephen passed away. The Christmas before they had been together with their whole family, and in one year everything was gone, even their family's oldest friend. Sam's hand went to his belt, and he touched the knife his father had given him on that last Christmas morning. Sam still wore it at his side every day.

As he continued thinking about Stephen Austin, a small peaceful smile settled across Sam's lips. He and Gabriel were on their way back to San Antonio from a little town that had been established four years before on terraced bluffs overlooking the Colorado River. Because of the place's extraordinary natural beauty, the Republic's officials had picked the spot as the capital for their new nation. Sam was glad, and thought it fitting, that they had named the town - Austin.

"Sure wish the Senator was ridin' back with us on this trip," Gabriel said breaking the clear morning's silence by verbalizing his thoughts.

Sam came back from his own thoughts and said, "I do, too, Gabriel. Hope he's doin' all right."

41

"We have to make this the best *fiesta* ever! Now you little raccoons go help your mother hang those *luminarias*," Mary Beth said enthusiastically to the Seguin children. Her mouth broke into a big smile while she raised her index finger to her lips. Light twinkled from her eyes and her nose squinched up as she settled into a loud whisper, "I'm going to rock your baby sister to sleep."

In the shade of the plank board front porch overlooking the open area their homes faced, she sat in a wooden chair rocking and patting the back of her friend's ten month old baby. She watched the small herd of children scatter out across the plaza toward their mother, the other women, and a few old men who were setting decorations for the upcoming pre-Lenten celebration. Mary Beth began humming softly and gently kissed the baby's head. In her arms was the youngest of Maria and Juan Seguin's eight children, the one they all called "Little Sarah".

Mary Beth was ready to have her own children and she longed for the day when she might. She and the other women talked about it sometimes, but Mary Beth usually tried to stay away from the subject. Some of the biddies made her feel awkward to be twenty four years old and unmarried.

Maria Seguin, however, was not one of those women. Juan's wife had treated Mary Beth like a sister since the day she, Sam, and Gabriel were brought to San Antonio de Bexar. Through her kindness, taking Mary Beth into her home and into her heart, Maria had helped the young girl recover from the tragedy and sorrow she carried from the war. Now Mary Elizabeth Stevens and Maria Gertrudis Flores de Abrego Seguin were best friends and did almost everything together, especially when the men were gone.

Mary Beth watched the children, who were playing more than helping, as they swarmed around Maria and the other adults hanging brightly colored decorations for the fiesta. The scene reminded her of the way she, Luke and Sam had played around the homestead when they were small. Mary Beth smiled looking down at the baby now sleeping soundly in her arms, and thought of the pleasure she got from these children and their mother.

Other than her Momma, Mary Beth had never had a friend who was a girl. Growing up on the frontier, the young woman's only companions had been her two brothers. Now she had Maria, and also Rosa, Max's wife. Rosa was her friend, too. The three of them laughed and talked and shared chores together all the time. They were one another's mutual support system, looking after and taking care of each other, because the men were away so much.

After the war when they first came to San Antonio, Mary Beth and her brother had stayed with Juan and Maria while Gabriel slept in Max's tack room. The house they were given by Juan and Stephen Austin was nearby, but it was small and had been damaged during the fighting. Mary Beth, Gabriel, and the Seguin's had worked on the dwelling almost everyday, making the place livable and adding a room onto the back for Gabriel, while Sam's wounds healed.

Mary Beth had dedicated herself to taking care of her little brother and making a home for them. By the time Sam's body was mended and ready, so was their house. The two Stevens' children and their black companion then had a real home in which to begin their new lives. Shortly thereafter they came up with the idea of starting a business hauling freight in the big wagon.

The idea presented itself after Juan was elected Senator to the Second Congress of Texas, the first one after the war. As Senator, traveling in the performance of his duties, Juan witnessed the explosive growth independence from Mexico brought to the new Republic. While immigrants, primarily from the United States, flooded into Texas both through the ports and over land, the existing towns swelled and new ones sprouted seemingly overnight. The growth had brought opportunities for them all, and one of the opportunities was carrying goods from one town to the other.

However, as these masses of people created new opportunities for Texas, they also brought Her new problems. The infant nation had no controls, no floodgates. So while the enormous inflow carried in good families of hard-working settlers anxious to own land and start new lives, it also washed in the debris of mankind. Money-hungry land speculators, unscrupulous lawyers, vagabonds, and fugitives streamed into Texas looking for fast fortune and power in a new place that didn't yet have laws or law enforcement to get in their way.

These newcomers had heard many stories about the valiant Texas War for Independence. They had been told, and retold, accounts of the atrocities and cruelty perpetrated by Santa Anna and the Mexicans. As they grew, these stories gave the new immigrants a black and white definition of good and evil with which to align themselves. The immigrant's own diverse ethnic backgrounds could then be dissolved in the common good of opposing the evil Mexicans.

To many among the poorly educated growing mobs, any dark skinned person speaking Spanish was a Mexican and therefore responsible for the massacres at Goliad and the Alamo. In the same way vicious animals prey on the weak, some of the newcomers exploited these anti-Mexican feelings as the number of settlers swelled. Certain ones, the debris, used it as an opportunity to oppress the native *Tejanos* who were trying to recover their lives after a devastating war. Conflicts developed.

Mary Beth hummed softly onto the top of Little Sarah's head as she gently rocked the limp little body already asleep in her arms. She unconsciencely drew in a deep breath, then marveled at the wonderful smell that only comes from clean little babies. The smile that brought to her lips was suddenly stopped by burly noises that abruptly overshadowed the giggles of the children playing around the open yard in front of her. Stormy clamor began to roar, and Mary Beth knew it came from the *cantina* two buildings behind their small plaza.

42

Cardinal Bustamante sat by himself at a spartan wooden table in the center of the room and raised his tired eyes to the fading late afternoon light. The high ceiling was the only part of the room still directly lit by the setting sun as its rays came through small windows high on the walls above the numerous cabinets and wardrobes. The Sacristy, a chamber where sacred vessels, robes, and other property used in ceremonies for the church were kept, was off a small dark hallway to the side and behind the altar of the grand National Cathedral.

It was the only place in *Ciudad Mexico* where Eduardo Bustamante could be alone with his thoughts, safe and undisturbed. For a moment the priest wished God would transform him into a bird and grant him wings. Then he could escape up high and away into the dimming light, before this evening came. Before he had to perform again - for the chameleon.

Knowing that wouldn't happen, he rose from his chair and lit several candles that were on the table and in wall sconces around the room. Soft light from the small flames brightened his hideout, and the Cardinal poured himself another chalice of hearty red wine. He took two large gulps of courage, and then turned to the opulent white robe that had been pristinely laid out for him.

The color of the garment was supposed to symbolize purity. It represented the purity of God and the clergy of the church serving Him. Those thoughts made Eduardo's heart ache for he knew that in his efforts to preserve the Church, he was far from pure.

Yes, he had kept the Church alive and viable through the changes and turmoil Mexico had endured in the years since the devastating war with the Tejas rebels. He had done things he had to do in order to keep the Catholic Ministry strong and maintain his position, but at what cost?

As he looked into the stark whiteness of the heavy material spread out before him, he wondered if performing his duty to the Church would cost him his own soul. Never taking his eyes from the ceremonial robe, he sat back into his chair, took another ample drink from the goblet, and thought back across the events leading to this night he dreaded.

Alone in his sanctuary, Eduardo remembered the morning when the first news of Santa Anna's defeat and capture in the Tejas Rebellion had been delivered. His initial reaction and emotions were mixed. The government courier's information was brief, and Eduardo knew it was incomplete. There was much uncertainty about everything except the facts that their country had lost the war, and Santa Anna had been captured.

That morning, shortly after the news arrived, Eduardo personally led the Cathedral's normally scheduled mass. It was an event that had marked his soul with an experience he would never forget.

As he delivered his sermon and looked out onto the congregation, he began seeing faces, but they did not belong to the people at the mass who were lined up behind one another in the long rows of pews. They were bruised and bloodied faces of young Mexican boys and older men who had been driven off to war. They looked up at him with dark sunken eyes filled with anguish.

Eduardo's strong voice echoed through the vast open Cathedral when he cried out trying to push away God's vision. He started to raise his hands to his own face in order to shield his eyes, but his hands were covered with blood. "No!" he screamed, terrified as he lifted his head to the ornate ceiling and slammed his eyes shut to drive away the horrible apparition. Behind his eyelids, and inside his soul, all he could see then was the sinister gloat of Santa Anna. In his torment, Eduardo never finished the sermon.

More days passed and brought with them more news of cruelty and horror from the war. When the soldiers returned, many seeking forgiveness in their confessions, the Cardinal realized God's Will had been done. His country was rid of Santa Anna. Their sacrifice was heavy, but the cold one, with nothing behind his dark eyes, was gone.

The defeated tyrant had been taken away to the United States. Mexico's new President and the legislature rejected the Treaty of Independence Santa Anna had signed with the rebel's General Houston. Although their rejection of the Treaty discredited Santa Anna, Mexico took no direct action toward Texas. The new leadership was well occupied trying to recover the nation after the costly war, then trouble with France soon dominated the government's attention.

The King of France, Louis Phillippe, sent envoys demanding that Mexico pay the French Government 600,000 pesos. The money was for compensation to French citizens who had lost property during Mexico's own War for Independence. As they tried to rebuild the country after the war and Santa Anna's dictatorship, the Mexican government was in no position to meet the French demands. The communications became more heated, and France threatened war.

While the nation struggled and tensions with France grew, Cardinal Bustamante worked tirelessly strengthening the Church. Because the people needed the stability and hope religious faith brought to their lives, he was able to increase the Church's wealth and power. It was almost a year after his country had lost the Battle of San Jacinto that Eduardo heard of Santa Anna's return to Mexico.

When he began receiving accounts of the past leader's arrival, Eduardo pieced together, in his own mind, exactly what had happened. Santa Anna had learned of Mexico's internal strife and trouble with France. He then booked passage back from the United States and stayed aboard ship while he sent infiltrators ashore to verify the political situation and orchestrate his landing. When the fallen leader, who had lost Tejas to the rebels, stepped onto his native soil that spring day in the port city of Veracruz, the streets were lined with cheering crowds.

The Cardinal had hurriedly braced the Church, and himself, for an immediate insurrection. However, rather than inciting a rebellion, Santa Anna simply nourished, with his well wishes, the throngs who were set to meet him in each city he visited. He played out the part of the returning prodigal son with dramatic gusto then, with much ceremonial humility, quietly retired to the country.

During his presidency Santa Anna had acquired three estates, which combined, totaled over 450,000 acres. The quarter of a million acre, *Manga de Clava*, was his favorite. He went there to wait and watch, while Cardinal Eduardo Bustamante waited and watched from *Ciudad Mexico*. In the different ways a hungry coyote waits to pounce and a fearful shepherd watches his flock, time passed slowly for the two men.

A year later France blockaded the port of Veracruz. The following December, rather than pay the French demands, Mexico declared war on France. Santa Anna seized his opportunity. The flamboyant politician stepped forward with assurances he was the only experienced general who could lead an effective defense against a French invasion. He then rushed to the port.

Santa Anna drew upon all his skills in channeling his bold inspirational performance and rallied the Mexican Army. When the French Admiral Charles Baudin landed 3,000 troops in Veracruz, Santa Anna was ruthless in pushing his own forces to defeat the enemy. As the battle was won and the Mexican Army forced the French back to their boats in retreat, a wounded French soldier torched off a final round from his cannon before he abandoned his post.

In his peripheral vision, Santa Anna saw the open barrel of the Frenchman's dangerous black cylinder when it spit up its flame and sparks and smoke. That same instant the crude device sent a four pound solid lead ball flying, at a velocity that made it invisible, straight past scores of his Mexican foot soldiers and officers. Reflex and terror caused the General to snap his eyes toward the cannon just as his body took the blow. Santa Anna was still conscious when he felt his own leg smash into his back from behind and knock him forward to the ground.

In the telling of Mexico's victory and Santa Anna's fall, as news was rushed to *Ciudad Mexico*, Cardinal Bustamante found himself wondering which was perceived as the more important event. The General was cast as the bleeding Savior of Mexico giving his life to drive away the murdering French invaders. Bustamante hastily sent his own spies to the battlefront in order to get accurate information. Secretly he hoped for a report that Santa Anna had died from his injuries.

When his agents returned, Eduardo learned that Santa Anna had indeed been hit by cannon fire during the French retreat in the battle at Veracruz. The lead ball had completely destroyed the man's left leg. Although the limb was clumsily amputated the following morning, Santa Anna had not yet died from his wounds. He was removed from Veracruz and taken to his estate at *Manga de Clava* to recover.

Through the following year Santa Anna's body healed while he, and the Cardinal, separately watched the political situation in Mexico deteriorate. Federalist rebel uprisings increased. When the government proved unable to deal with the insurrections, Santa Anna sent out his own private mercenaries and virtually destroyed the rebel army and its leaders. Once he had accomplished that, Santa Anna knew the Presidency of Mexico was his for the taking - and he did.

Shortly after swearing his oath of office, Santa Anna once again began transforming the Presidency into a military dictatorship. He seized all power and authority, then governed Mexico with his federal soldiers and fear. With his boot on the throats of the Legislature and the Mexican states, Santa Anna turned his attentions to filling his administration's empty pockets.

The treasury was virtually bankrupt when Santa Anna assumed the Presidency. With the same unrestrained drive he used in battle, the new Dictator was relentless in raising money. He burdened his country's struggling economy with ever increasing taxes and raised all import duties by twenty percent. He personally sold mining concessions to the British. As his power grew, Santa Anna extracted "voluntary" contributions from all homeowners in *Ciudad Mexico*.

Once his complete power was established and undefiable, Santa Anna approached the Church. He summoned Cardinal Bustamante and the three senior Bishops to a meeting at the Presidential Palace. At that short meeting, *El Presidente's* message had been simple and clear. He informed the clergy that if the Church, and they, were to continue to exist in the Mexico he had created, then the Catholic Ministry would be required to "loan" money to the government. There were no other options.

Eduardo had paid the extortion money.

However, as money from the Church and the other sources flowed into the government, the country continued to decline. The people began to see that the huge amount of capital with which the government was gorging itself was not being used for the common welfare of the citizens. It was being spent instead for the greater glory of the President and his disciples.

Over time the general populace had started to buckle under the heavy burden of their taxes. Signs of discontent with the administration became more conspicuous. Bustamante could see that Santa Anna sensed the need to reestablish himself in the people's hearts as their beloved leader.

A pulsing noise created by the chanted exaltations from the distant crowds approaching the *Zocalo* brought Cardinal Eduardo Bustamante away from his remembrances and back into the reality of the evening. Dressed in his great white robe of purity, Bustamante hesitated slightly before he left the Sacristy. He stepped into the small dark hallway which led to the altar, and then walked solemnly past it to the far end of the Cathedral.

When their elder approached, the awaiting clergy swung open the majestic temple's imposing massive wooden front doors. Bustamante stepped out onto the wide top steps of the National Cathedral and looked across the almost empty ceremonial plaza below.

43

Within a minute the parade arrived. At its head was the Presidential coach polished to a shine glossy enough to reflect back to the crowds the light from every street lamp and the countless number of hand-held torches. In the vehicle, on a special platform built for the occasion, the President of Mexico stood elevated above the crowds. With both arms extended high over his head, Santa Anna held in his hands a personal offering to the Mexican citizens who mobbed the streets behind him.

Eduardo drew in a deep breath and raised his eyes to the dark sky while the cheering rabble flooded from the narrow streets into the *Zocalo's* open area as they followed the Presidential coach. At the base of the stairs, which made the grand entry up to the National Cathedral, the coach stopped and Santa Anna dismounted. Soldiers held the masses back while *El Presidente* slowly climbed the steps toward the Cardinal.

The leader feigned the effort it took to hold the special package he carried while maneuvering his artificial cork leg up the stairs on his long quest to reach the Church. At the top Santa Anna hesitated, then turned to the crowd and raised his offering in triumph. A deafening cheer rose from the plaza. Eduardo was almost overcome by the putrid smell. The President of Mexico turned deliberately and slowly, from one side to the other, so that every person in the *Zocalo* could see the decomposed remains of his freshly excavated, amputated leg.

Eduardo swallowed hard and turned his eyes away from the rotten travesty as another roaring ovation spread across the mob before him. Santa Anna kept his eyes on the oozing clump of bone and flesh as he lowered it from above his head and held it out in front of his chest at half an arms length. He raised his eyes dramatically to the mass of people who had been whipped into frenzy by the elaborate parade through the streets of the city. The entire plaza fell suddenly quiet. In his solid convincing voice, Santa Anna addressed them boldly and loudly.

"Dear people of Mexico, just as all of you have been called upon to serve our beloved country, I too was called upon to serve. I tried to be brave for Mexico in our battles against evil foreigners who would destroy our nation. I fought side by side with your fathers, sons, and brothers in our efforts to keep Mexico a free and prosperous land! I gave this leg for Mexico when we drove away the French invaders at the Battle of Veracruz!

"But, good citizens of Mexico, this leg was nothing! I would gladly have given my life to save Mexico! So many of our brave countrymen did give their lives fighting our battles. They made the ultimate sacrifice for Mexico. Compared to those soldiers, my sacrifices, all of our sacrifices, are nothing!" Santa Anna paused hoping for a cheer, and it came.

He waited for the crowd to quiet and then began again in a slow serious tone. "Today Mexico faces another enemy. This enemy is more sinister and dangerous than any of the foreign nations who have tried to steal our land. It threatens our very way of life, and if not defeated, this new enemy will destroy Mexico!

"The evil force I speak of is like a vile sickness that gradually weakens a strong body, then ultimately, kills it. This adversary is sinister and dangerous, because it attacks Mexico from within! It is a foe that does not fight honorably with cannons and bayonets. This new enemy of Mexico fights only with slander and lies! It sulks in the darkness and infects the unpartiotic souls who have no dedication to our great country!

"My fellow citizens, God called upon the strong people of Mexico to create a righteous and sovereign homeland. Through your selflessness you answered God, and built His nation!

"Many in your families gave their lives so that we could have a free and independent Mexico. However, as we all sacrifice daily to repair the damages inflicted by foreigners upon our country and our economy, there are those within our own society who defile our work.

"They do not believe that Mexico is worth all that we have given for her. They think each of you are fools because you work so hard to give your country the resources to recover. They proclaim that I do not care about you and my beloved Mexico!

"These lying cowards are the new enemy of Mexico! Together we will defeat them and their treachery! I ask that you each shine the light of truth on them. The truth about our love for Mexico will send them slithering back into the darkness like the vermin they are!"

El Presidente looked deliberately at the decomposing mass he held in front of him and waited. Slowly he raised his face back to the crowd and said, "To you brave believers, to those who believe in the truth of our sacrifices for our homeland, I offer you this!"

Santa Anna heroically thrust the remnants of his amputated limb high above his head. He again slowly and deliberately turned his upper body so that all in the *Zocalo* could see what he held. The passion in his loud measured voice elevated as he spoke with conviction, "My body has been broken in the defense of our country! My spirit, and my love for Mexico, will never be broken!"

He paused to let the crowd cheer. He waited for the roar to subside, and then continued with sincerity in his voice as he looked across the expanse of people packed into the plaza. "I give you this part of me as a symbol of the sacrifices we make for Mexico! May it give you the strength to remember the truth about my dedication to you and our sacred Republic!"

The plaza exploded with loud and triumphant praise for *El Presidente*. Santa Anna's chest swelled, and he started breathing very heavily in his excitement while he waited for his finale. As the emotional undulating masses began to settle, he lowered the leg and spoke with loud reverence. "I call upon the Church to bless this which I suffered for Mexico, as a symbol of our sacrifice and our unity!"

The President bowed his head when he turned to Cardinal Bustamante. Awkwardly he settled himself onto his good knee, and he showed pain in his face when he stuck his artificial left leg straight out to the side. One of the altar boys rushed to help, but the President sent him away by shaking his head with a sad and humble gesture.

The crowded masses watched in awe and silence as above them, at the top of the torch-lit steps, there appeared to be the Savior of Mexico kneeling before God with a holy offering. Santa Anna raised his face to the light, and the white clad priest, while he received the Church's blessing.

44

"I think we should have a *Fiesta* everyday!" the seven year old Sonia Seguin sputtered through the space that was left where her Father had helped her pull her two front baby teeth. She held onto the right side of Mary Beth's flowing skirt, looking up at her idol, as they entered the Stevens' home. "They're the most fun of anything, Mary Beth, aren't they?"

"Yes, *novialita*, they're the most fun of anything!" Mary Beth said, as she maneuvered herself and the three little girls into her house in the darkness. Over her right shoulder she carried a sleeping four year old, and she held the hand of Sonia's five year old sister, Elaina, with her left hand. "Tell Sam to get in here and get us some light."

"We're coming, we're coming," Sam said from several yards behind his sister as he and Gabriel heard what she was saying. He made his way past the little girls, who were all stuck to Mary Beth in the doorway, and started lighting lamps and candles. When Gabriel walked in, he smiled and gently took the sleeping one from Mary Beth's arms.

"Well, you two were sure a lot of help getting back here," Mary Beth said sarcastically to her brother as she dangled and flopped her right arm, trying to get circulation and feeling back into it.

"Hey, don't talk to us about that," Sam grinned. "You were the one who told Sonia that she and the girls could spend the night. Gabriel and I had nothing to do with it. We'd pro'bly still be there enjoyin' the *Fiesta*."

"Now, aren't you the one who said, 'Don't let us stay out too late tonight. We have got to get an early start in the morning!'" Mary Beth mimicked her little brother as she bounced her head from side to side. Sonia giggled and let it be known that she was on Mary Beth's side by saying, "Yeah, Sam."

"Yeah, Sam." Mary Beth stood tall and put her arms around her two miniature reinforcements. "Now help me get these little *señoritas* to bed."

Sonia jabbered, as usual, while Sam and his sister got the girls ready to tuck into her bed. Just outside the doorway to Mary Beth's room Gabriel slowly swayed back and forth holding the smallest one, trying to keep her asleep, until the other two were in bed. The precocious little Sonia did not want the evening to end.

"I'll bet you like fiestas, don't you, Sam?"

"Yes, Sonia, I like fiestas a lot."

"I love fiestas. Fiestas are my favorite thing in the whole world! Are they your favorite thing in the whole world, Sam?"

"Yes, Sonia, I think they're just about my favorite thing in the whole world."

"What's your favorite thing about the *Fiesta*, Sam?"

"I don't know, the music, I guess."

"Oh, yeah, I like the music, too, Sam. What's your favorite thing, Mary Beth?"

"My favorite thing? Well, Sonia, my favorite thing about the *Fiesta* is the dancing!"

"I love the dancing, too. You danced a lot. You danced with everybody, didn't you, Mary Beth?"

"I don't think I danced with everybody."

"I'll bet you did. You danced a lot. Did you see my Mother and Father dance? They're really good dancers, aren't they?"

"Yes, Sonia, your parents are wonderful dancers! Now you get in bed. It's time to go to sleep," Mary Beth smiled pulling back the covers and showing the girls to their spots. She motioned to Gabriel, and he carefully placed his sleeping little charge onto the bedsheets. "You have to be quiet. I'll get in bed next to you in a little bit. I want to talk to Sam and Gabriel for a minute."

"But, Mary Beth…"

"What is it, honey?"

"You didn't ask me what my favorite thing is."

Mary Beth held back a laugh and looked up at her brother and Gabriel who were both standing at the foot of the bed. Sam opened his mouth and threw his head back rolling his eyes making believe he would pass out from exhaustion. His sister put her hand softly onto Sonia's forehead and gently brushed the child's thick black hair up with her hand. In a voice that made it sound as though it were the most important thing in the world, Mary Beth said, "What is your most favorite thing about the *Fiesta*, Sonia?"

Seriously, and with no concern whatsoever about how funny she looked saying the word with no front teeth, Sonia smiled and sputtered, "*Piñatas*! The *piñatas* and the *candy*!"

45

From a small open courtyard in front of the well-kept country homestead, Erasmo Seguin watched as his son and Maximillian rode in from the southwest accompanied by four of Erasmo's *vaqueros*. The modest white *hacienda*, known as *Casa Blanca* to the unnumbered tired travelers who had enjoyed its hospitality over many years, was on the Seguin *Rancho* thirty miles east of San Antonio de Bexar.

Erasmo squinted into the late afternoon sun angling its light over the approaching rider's shoulders. Well before he could make out details on the other men, the sixty year old man could sense the angst on Juan's face and feel the burden his son bore heavily in his good heart.

"They joined the three herds together about eight miles past the *Arroyo Azul*," Juan reported as he and the others stopped their horses at the low wall that enclosed the inviting little entry yard of his parent's home. "Looks like they stole over four hundred head and moved out fast to the southwest. Amelio says they were all *Anglos*. From the tracks they made, I'm sure he's right."

Erasmo tried not to show the impact of the devastating news he had expected. After the war he left his life of public service and turned to living out his days on his ranch rebuilding his own life. The Seguin family interests had suffered greatly through the course of Texas winning Her independence, and it wasn't only the material destruction at the hands of the Mexican Army. Erasmo had given most of the *Casa Blanca* resources to supply the Texas volunteers with beef cattle, horses, mules, and corn during their struggle to defeat Santa Anna.

Many considered it a miracle the elder statesman of San Antonio de Bexar had survived the war. The fortress everyone now called The Alamo was the *Mission San Antonio de Valero*, then already six and a half decades old, when Erasmo was born in its shadow in 1782. A true native son of San Antonio, he had spent his adult life working for a civilized society and a better Mexico. Because of his politics before the war, helping to draft the Democratic Constitution of 1824 and supporting states rights, Erasmo had symbolized the *Tejano* movement against Santa Anna's autocratic dictatorship.

As a result, the politically active town postmaster had been elected *Alcalde* of San Antonio de Bexar shortly before General Martin Perfecto de Cos occupied the town, which had led to the Siege of Bexar. During the occupation Erasmo was arrested and held for execution. However, partially because Cos personally considered Erasmo Seguin an honorable man, and partially because he was afraid that the town's people loyal to Seguin would riot, Cos spared the Mayor's life. The General banished Seguin from the city and forced him to walk the thirty miles to his Casa Blanca Rancho.

Four years after the war ended, the Texas Congress had voted to compensate Juan's father $3,004 for all the supplies he'd provided to the Texas cause. Although the value was far short of reimbursing him, the elder Seguin used the money to help restore *Casa Blanca*. Now most of what he had accomplished for his family in six years of long hard work, rebuilding their holdings, had just been taken away by cattle thieves.

"Amelio, you men put away the horses and get some rest," Erasmo said in a mild tone with a small reassuring smile on his lips. "You've worked hard these last few days, and I thank you. You men did well. Now go clean yourselves and get something to eat."

"*Sí, Patron,*" the tired, down-hearted foreman said in a soft voice that reflected his own discouragement.

Erasmo looked to his son. "You and Max come into the house, Juan. I think a wash basin would do you both some good, as well. Your mother will make a hot supper for us. We'll sit together at the table tonight and talk."

Juan stretched his aching back while he hesitated in his saddle and pursed his lips together in frustration. He swiveled his upper body turning to look over his right shoulder back to the southwest and twitched with a grimace as the move caused a sudden stab of pain through his lower spine. Quietly Juan dismounted, then handed his horse's reins up to Amelio.

"*Tia*, this looks delicious!" Max said to his aunt in an effort to take the tension out of the air that evening after Juan's mother had served the table and they all sat down to eat. "Juan has been making us eat cold tortillas and parched corn. My stomach thought I was in the army again!"

"I hope you like it, Maximillian," she answered smiling. "I knew you two would be starving. There is plenty. It is so good to have you boys at our table again." Then tilting her head slightly downward, she looked from under her eyebrows as only mother's do when making a point to their children. She looked at Juan while she kept speaking to Max. "I miss having you and my Senator here."

"If I were still your Senator, Mother, I would come more often," Juan said, in a tone that told her he understood her message, and not to continue with it.

Juan Seguin had been the only Texan of Hispanic descent elected to serve as Senator in the second, third, and fourth Congresses of Texas. During those years he often stopped at Casa Blanca on his way either to or from Austin. He usually traveled with Sam and Gabriel, for companionship and mutual defense, as they hauled their freight between the cities. Although Juan rarely went to Austin now, Sam and Gabriel still stayed with their friends, Erasmo and Maria Josefa, on a regular basis.

Juan's father bowed his head, and they all followed his lead. "Father, thank you for this day and the food you have provided for us," Erasmo began. "Thank you for bringing my son and his cousin safely to our home once again." Juan's mother reached for her son's hand, and they both drew comfort from the caress while the old gentleman continued from the head of the table. "Oh, Lord, please give us strength, and courage, and wisdom, in all the things that we do. Help us to be mindful that we are so much more richly blessed than most, as we face the trials of this day. We thank you, Father, for always being with us, and standing by us, and helping us. In the Name of the Father, the Son, and the Holy Spirit, we pray. Amen."

The four *Tejanos* crossed themselves, and the elder Seguin spoke again. "Thank you both for coming so quickly. I hated to send for you, but I didn't know what else to do. I wasn't expecting this." He paused and sighed, then looked into the thick flame of the table candle closest to his plate. In a voice that had some distance to it, as though he were talking more to himself and the candle than to the others at the table, he said, "I didn't have enough men to fight with, even if we had caught them. They would've just killed everyone, like they did those two poor boys I sent to check the water. I guess I'm getting too old. I wasn't expecting to fight thieves in the night."

"I wish we had been here, *Tio*," Max said to his uncle. "But you are right. There were too many of them. There are too many bad men all over this country now. They would have killed you all and taken the cattle anyway. Those animals were not worth wasting people's lives. You did the right thing."

Juan's stomach churned and knotted as he listened to Max's words. His guts were being pulled apart by the dichotomy of emotions welling up inside. Half of him was filled with sympathy and sorrow for his father and wanted to hold and comfort the old man. The other half was pure rage and anger over the violation of his family, and it wanted to punish and kill the low-life anglo thieves.

Erasmo slowly shook his head while he looked at the candle's flame and said once again, speaking through a shallow sigh, "I just wasn't expecting it."

"None of us expected to live like this!" Juan burst out in frustration as the anger side of him gained majority and took control. "This whole country is turning into a dung pile of thieves and murderers! They rape us and get away with it, because they know there is nothing to stop them!"

Max quit eating. They all looked at Juan, surprised at his emotional outburst. Juan stared directly into his father's eyes and said, "This is not what we fought for, is it?"

"No," Erasmo quietly answered holding his son's stare for a moment. He turned his eyes back to the candle and said to the flame, "We fought for a land better than this. Civilized. Where people live free and equal under laws. Laws that are made by the people, not tyrants or kings. And, I will always believe, that was worth fighting for."

"Well, that's not what we have," Juan snapped. "Father, you know there is not a goddamn thing I can do about these thieves. Even if we could raise enough men, the bastards will have the cattle scattered and sold before we could even catch up to them. The Texas Rangers would help, if there were enough of them to do any good. But there aren't!"

"I know, son," the old man said calmly.

"What will you do now, Father?" Juan said with a pained expression, his face still heated with his rage. "They have stolen everything you've built back! Those thieving white bastards have wiped you out. They are destroying this whole country!"

Erasmo reached for his wine glass, and his eyes looked from Maria Josefa to Maximillian, then back to his son. When he had regained his father's focus, Juan continued, "I deal with this pillage everyday, Father. These people take, and take, and take. They are like a cloud of locust swarming on the *Tejanos*. They consume everything we have, and even then - they want more!"

Juan looked at his cousin, then back to Erasmo. "Max knows this is true. He stays in Bexar most of the time now, just to protect our families, while I am out trying to settle disputes between the people who were born here, and the interlopers who want to move in and take everything. I am not the *Alcalde* of San Antonio de Bexar anymore, I am the *arbitrator*!" The old man's eyes shifted to his nephew and Max nodded with a solemn face to confirm Juan's loud allegations.

"These people despise us!" Juan started again, and all at the table watched the frustration and anger showing on his drawn face. "They can't speak Spanish, but there are so many of them here now they think English is this country's language. They treat our native born people like we are immigrants too stupid to learn *their* native tongue. It is ridiculous! Before I quit the Senate, I tried to pass a bill that would print laws in both Spanish and English, so our people could at *least read* the laws that were being passed. I was almost laughed out of the chamber!"

The articulate younger Seguin paused. The older one sensed his son's need to vent the demons that were clawing at his compassionate heart and the anxiety that shadowed his honest spirit. Erasmo nodded to Juan giving him enough endorsement to continue.

"All of these people, still wet from the boats that brought them here, truly believe that every *Tejano*, every person of Mexican descent, was part of Santa Anna's Army. They think that we are the dregs of a beaten enemy. They treat the people born on this land like lower class slaves who were conquered by some noble white man's army!"

Juan's lips pulled back, and his clenched front teeth showed his pent-up anger. The lines that the years and the sun had put on his face tightened together compressing the fire in his eyes, and he slammed his fist hard on the table. "Damn them to hell!"

Maria Josefa's body jerked, startled by the force with which Juan hit the table. Their glass goblets all turned over, spilling red liquid across the table in several directions. Juan's glass broke as it fell on its side.

"Juan!" his Mother said sternly.

"I am sorry, Mother," Juan apologized, as they all jumped into action trying to control the mess. The men used their napkins while Maria Josefa ran to get towels. They mopped up the wine with the rags she brought, and Juan shook his down-turned head saying, "That was so foolish of me."

"Son," Erasmo said calmly. Juan looked up into his father's kind face as the old man smiled and said, "We have more wine."

Juan burst open his big smile and with a sheepish tilt of his head, like an embarrassed little boy in trouble, said to Maria Josefa, "I'm very sorry, Mother."

She frowned, "It's been a long time since I spanked you, young man." The lines on her forehead softened, and the corners of her mouth turned up. She wadded the soiled towels into a ball in her hands and nodded toward the table saying with aggravation, "I didn't make all that food to be eaten cold. You men sit down and eat. I'll be right back." She turned and started toward the kitchen, then twisted her head and said over her shoulder, "Juan, behave yourself, or I'll also bring back a switch to spank you with."

Juan was calm, and somehow felt better after his ravings, by the time his mother returned with a fresh carafe. He sprang to his feet and helped his Mother into her chair when she was ready to be seated. He bent forward and, from behind, kissed her on the cheek as she sat. He said, "This supper is outstanding. Thank you." Then he looked behind her back and said teasingly, "You didn't bring that switch, did you?"

She pushed him away from her chair and said in a smart voice that made Max chuckle, "No, but I know where it is, if you don't mind your manners, young man."

They began again their dinner and the men all complimented Maria Josefa, several times, on how good the food tasted. As they worked their way through the generous helpings, Juan looked around the table and said, "I don't know what we should do. I'm not sure how I can help you, Father." He looked to his cousin and continued, "Do you have any ideas, Max?"

"No, Juan," Max answered wiping his lips with his new napkin. He slowly reached for his wine glass while he kept talking. "I think you're right about going after the cattle though. By the time we gathered enough men, there wouldn't be anything to catch up to. They're probably already splitting and selling the herd."

Erasmo turned from Max and looked at Juan. The anger he had heard earlier in Juan's voice, and the frustration he now saw in his son's eyes, troubled Erasmo much more than the loss of the cattle. His own heart suffered from the pain that he knew filled his son.

"Juan, don't worry about the cattle." The old man said as he held his son's eyes with his own. "And don't worry about your Mother and me. We still have enough to live on, and we still have enough to rebuild this ranch."

With both strength and reassurance in his voice, he went on. "The men who did this are contemptible, wretched scum who will someday meet the end they deserve. They're the things my dog licks off his backside. They can't stop me. I won't let them stop me. I'm going to carry on, the way I should." He pointed the index finger of his right hand, which was worn and cracked from ranch work, at his son as he finished his statement. "And so are you."

"You're much too good a man," Erasmo said, letting the pride in his son show through into his voice, "to let the trash that has blown into this country stop you from doing what you know is right. Thank God our people have a man like you. They need a leader who knows right from wrong, and cares about the difference!"

The elder Seguin was now the one with passion and anger building in his voice. His eyes narrowed slightly as his volume rose with his words, "And I don't mean just *Tejanos*. You sound like you think all Anglos are bad people. Is that any different than what you accuse them of saying about us? You know that's wrong, Juan."

Juan nodded his head and slowly closed then opened his eyes. "I know," he spoke quietly thinking about what he'd said earlier and relating those words to the decent white men he'd known and served with.

Erasmo calmed his tone and said, "Son, I can only imagine the things you deal with now as *Alcalde* in San Antonio de Bexar. I wish there were some way I could make it easier for you, or could do something that would help." He paused. "What that would be, I don't know, with these times as they are."

"You always help me, Father." Juan smiled back looking into the character time and experience had put on the older man's face. "I guess in every generation we each get our own trials. You dealt with yours, now Max and I will have to deal with ours."

"And you will do it well, son." Erasmo began, and tears of pride blurred his eyes. He looked to Max, "You will both do it well." He smiled to Maria Josefa who sat across the table opposite his place. Erasmo looked back to Juan and said, "Your mother and I are very proud of you, Juan. If you were a lesser man, the wrong things wouldn't trouble you so. You have the right way in your heart. Listen to what it tells you, and you will always do the proper thing."

The old man straightened himself into his chair at the head of the table. He knew it was time to bring closure. He took in a deep breath and said, "Raise your wine glasses. I should like to propose a toast." They all took their glasses and lifted them. Erasmo pronounced boldly, "To the future, and the men who lead us into it! May their…" He stopped suddenly as they all heard noises from outside and the dogs within the *vaqueros'* quarters started to bark.

Juan and Max jumped up from their places. By the time Juan reached the front window, Max had gotten their pistols and swords. "Juan!" Max yelled, and when Juan turned to the call, Max pitched a pistol to his cousin.

Juan deftly caught the weapon and quickly looked through the front window's pane into the moonlit night. Max closed the distance between them as he strapped on his sword belt. He held the other sword belt out to Juan as he finished notching his own into place saying, "Can you see anything, Juan!?"

Juan turned from the window and said wide-eyed, "Yes, I can see them coming!" He broke into a laugh that made him feel good. "It appears we have company." He grinned, "There's a young fellow, with a big black man sitting beside him, coming in a huge wagon! Looks like Sam and Gabriel are on their way back from Austin."

46

"I'll tell you one goddamn thing. I'm gettin' tired of that pepper belly son-of-a-bitch tellin' us what to do!"

Ross Michaels listened to the affirmative grunts and watched the nodding heads of the small crowd of ne'er-do-wells agreeing with him in the stuffy, dirt floored cantina. Michaels chucked a shot of stout mescal into his mouth, and grimaced at the taste, before he swallowed the room warm liquid. He started to reload his small reddish brown clay cup with another shot of the amber colored Mexican liquor while he continued, "Juan Seguin sure as hell ain't God! Son-of-a-bitch acts like he is, but he ain't!"

Ross Micheals had been in Texas for almost a year and a half. He had blown around from settlement to town, looking for easy marks and easy money, wherever he could find a card game or a gullible soul. He'd adapted himself to the culture, in order to blend in, but he hated Texas and everything about it.

Had he any choice he would never have left New York City. He had been somebody in New York. He lived well there, by his standards, trading in stolen property. He had connections, on the waterfront and in town, which allowed him and a small band of thugs to move plundered or pirated items both in and out of the city. He had no education, but he ate well and he drank well, and people in the waterfront taverns knew who he was. Now he was exiled to a dirty, poor Hell filled with backwards, stupid people. His whole life had changed because of one whore.

He'd only ever had one real need for women. As he saw it, that was the only reason the bitches even existed. But always, the minute he'd finished using one, he suddenly couldn't stand the dirty slut. Once he'd satisfied himself, everything about the woman, her hair, her smell, her face, repulsed him - until the next time he needed to use her.

A stupid, worthless little whore had ruined his life and caused him to be in Texas. He would never forget, or forgive, the bitches for that. Over the past year and a half he'd made some of the Mexican *putas* pay for what had happened to him. They were no different from the slut who almost got him killed in New York.

That one had been just a regular tavern prostitute in one of the dark waterfront places where he went in the evenings to find out what needed to be stolen or smuggled. One day in New York, Ross Michaels had just fenced the silver serving pieces and some jewelry stolen from a wealthy family in the north part of town, and he wanted to celebrate. As he kept buying drinks for the small crowd of regulars, the young sweet breasted serving wench caught his eye and he took her upstairs.

When he'd finished with the little harlot, she began fawning over him in hopes of getting more money for her performance. Her actions revolted Michaels, and he started to beat the woman. The fact that the slut fought back infuriated him. Ross drew the knife from his boot and cut her, several times.

He hadn't intended to kill her. The whore was still alive when he left. However, she was laying dead in a huge mass of blood when the tavern's big raw boned owner found her and went into a rage. Although Ross knew the authorities would quickly find out about the girl, he feared the coarse rough bastard who owned the bar would kill him before the police even started an investigation. By noon the next day, Ross Michaels had used his contacts to be on board a ship leaving the port of New York City for Galveston, Texas.

"I'll tell you one goddamn thing." Michaels said loudly, looking around at the others. He often started his statements the same way, especially when he was drinking, which was also often. "That's the biggest thing wrong with this country! They still got Mexicans running it!

"Hell, the way it is livin' around here, you'd think those son-of-a-bitches won the war! Well, by God, they didn't!" Ross slammed his hand on the dirty rough wooden table, then continued. "Santie Annie was whipped, and run out'a here!

"If *I'd* been here when all that fightin' was goin' on, I'd a run every goddamn one of those jabberin' pepper bellies out of this country!" He smirked at the small semicircle of faces nodding back at him, "Especially that jay-bird Mayor we got. That smart talkin' son-of-a-bitch thinks he's the hookin' bull around here. Well, I'll tell you one goddamn thing; he ain't!"

Ross threw down another cup-full of the mescal and continued his brash ravings, "Somebody needs to turn that son-of-a-bitch into a steer." He laughed out at his own impromptu joke. "Hell, they're all steers. None of them Mexicans have any balls! We ought'a herd all them steers back to Mexico where they belong!"

The others laughed out their grunts of concurrence with the idea.

47

"*El Presidente's* special envoy has just arrived, General. He is being shown to his quarters." The spit polished young aide reported smartly, excited after receiving permission to speak. "He says he brings orders directly from Santa Anna and wants an audience with you immediately."

General Rafael Vasquez, commander of one of the northern battalions responsible for defending against the Indians and crushing Federalist uprisings, remained seated at his desk. He took two puffs on the half-smoked black cigar he'd been working on before he removed it from his mouth, placed it into the crude ashtray, and said, "Very well, Lieutenant. Bring him to me. Have the other officers alerted, and tell them to stand at the ready. I may be needing them after we find out what the great Santa Anna has on his mind."

"*Sí, General.*" The young soldier snapped a smart salute to his forehead and held it. The salute General Vasquez returned was far less than crisp. He finished it by reaching for his cigar. As the aide left the airless unventilated room, Rafael sent a few more plumes of heavy white smoke toward the low ceiling as he wondered just what the pompous bastard in *Ciudad Mexico* would order him to do this time.

Whatever it was, Rafael Vasquez knew he wouldn't like it. He had been safe for a while at this post because it was far from *Ciudad Mexico* - and Santa Anna. As long as he kept his area quiet, with regard to Indians and political unrest, he was left alone.

Rafael suddenly got a bad taste in his mouth when he thought about the last time *El Presidente* had sent for him. It had been three years ago. He was summoned to join with Santa Anna's regulars in order to crush a Federalist uprising in *Acajete*. Although he had obeyed his orders, it had been a horrible experience. He had been forced to fight against his old friend, General Jose de Urrea, who led the uprising against Santa Anna.

Vasquez respected José de Urrea, as a military officer and as a man. The two of them had soldiered together, in various places through different times, since the springs when they were both young cadets with their minds filled with nothing but girls and glory. José was a good man, and a friend. It wasn't hard for Rafael to see through the accounts of what had happened with the rebel's Colonel Fannin at Goliad. He figured José de Urrea had been responsible for winning the battle, and Santa Anna was responsible for the massacre.

There had been many times, before and after that uprising, when Rafael Vasquez wondered why he hadn't joined Urrea and the others against Santa Anna's dictatorship. Perhaps if enough of them had banded together then, or could do so now, Mexico would be a free nation with a just government.

But Rafael knew Santa Anna's fist was too strong. The pockets of men willing to speak out against the oppression were scattered so far apart in this vast land, and the consequences were so severe, that opposing the President was impossible. Vasquez spit on the floor trying to get the acid taste from his mouth and crushed his cigar out into the clay ashtray on his desk. He rose and walked across the compacted dirt floor of his office. He took his uniform jacket from its peg on the wall, put it on, and began buttoning the polished brass buttons.

"The Supreme Commander, *El Salvador de Mexico, El Presidente Antonio Lopez de Santa Anna Perez de Lebron*, extends his compliments to you, General Vasquez!" The messenger began, standing at a stiff brace, after the initial salutes were exchanged. "I am Captain Denicio Bernillo, from *El Presidente's* Personal Command Staff. His Excellency has entrusted me with these very important orders for you, Sir." Bernillo handed forth a leather satchel and sat it on the desk in front of the seated General Vasquez.

Rafael Vasquez slowly opened the pouch and removed the documents. In a glance Vasques could tell the several pages were filled with much convoluted verbiage of the type he'd seen before. He recognized the President's elaborate signature at the end of it.

Without taking time to read the lengthly piece, the General looked up at the fancy young officer standing before him. He wondered what kind of political or family connections the Captain had in order to be on *El Presidente's* personal staff. Simply because of his position, regardless of his connections, Rafael knew the boy could not be trusted.

"Tell me what this says, Captain Denicio Bernillo. I'm sure *El Presidente* has made you familiar with all of it." Vasquez said, wanting a chance to evaluate Bernillo by listening to him respond.

"*Sí, General,*" Denicio said, and then broke from standing at attention as though he were talking to a peer.

Vasquez let it go.

"As you know, Sir, the Treaty of Independance for Tejas was signed by His Excellency while the rebels held a gun to his head. It is therefore null and void, and was never accepted by our government.

"We have been monitoring the situation in Tejas with the rag-tag government the rebels have tried to establish. They have no control over the people, no money, and no standing army. Tejas is being filled with Yankees from the United States and many of them believe the only hope they have of survival is to join the Union of American States. We cannot let that happen, General. Tejas is still part of our sovereign Mexico.

"*El Presidente* wants you to lead a surprise expedition into Tejas and secure the Camino Real. In order to accomplish that, the key is capturing San Antonio de Bexar. You are to take the city and hold it, before the rebels can react. If you can successfully do that, His Excellency will send our forces to blockade their ports and cut them off from the United States.

"By making the attack swiftly, you should meet no significant opposition. There is, however, one man from San Antonio de Bexar who may be able to mount a response. His name is Juan Seguin. He is a member of their government and was influential in the *Tejano* movement during the war. We know he has been supporting some of the Federalist uprisings within our country. *El Presidente* wants Seguin captured, alive if possible."

General Rafael Vasquez had listened to every word and had not taken his eyes from Bernillo. He reached into a bowl on his desk and retrieved a fresh cigar. As he began rolling it between the fingers of both hands, he put his elbows onto the desktop. Captain Bernillo quickly produced a match from his uniform pocket, struck it on the front edge of the desk, and bent forward to light the General's cigar.

48

The midmorning sun cowered somewhere behind the thick blanket of low gray clouds. Gabriel pulled the left reins tight and slapped the outside mule's backs with their loose right leads, guiding the animals onto the main road leading back to San Antonio de Bexar. He and Sam sat in their usual places on the smooth plank seat. Maximillian and Juan sat horseback riding abeam them on either side of the big wagon. There had been very little conversation since they all said *adiós* to Erasmo and Maria Josefa and left *Casa Blanca* for their journey home.

"You know Gabriel and I will go with you, Juan." Sam said sincerely as the loaded wagon settled into the worn ruts of the well used road that wound its way through the hilly country between Austin and San Antonio. Sam was heartsick thinking about Juan's elderly parents and the wrong that had been done to them. He wondered how there could be such stone hearted cruelty to hurt two old people like that.

"We'll help you get your father's cattle, and we'll catch the rotten bastards who stole 'em." The young man's blood was rising and he finished in anger, "The sons-a-bitches need to be hanged!"

Gabriel looked up at Seguin who was on the other side of the wagon riding next to Sam. When Juan smiled at Sam but didn't say anything, Gabriel spoke up, "Sam's right, Senator." Gabriel always addressed Juan as "Senator", ever since the first time Juan had been elected to the Texas Congress. That title gave the big Negro a way to be familiar with the man he was with so much, and still show respect.

"You know we're with ya'. All you need is to tell us what you want us to do. We'll jump in anywhere you say." Gabriel turned and smiled at Maximillian who was riding along beside him, then looked back to Juan. "Me and Sam and Mister Max'll get them bad men. We ain't gonna let them do that to your folks an' git away with it."

Juan smiled at the genuine honesty in Gabriel's voice. He knew the three men he traveled the dirt road with on this overcast morning were as good and true as the words the black man spoke. Those words made his mind flash to Sam's parents and the first members of the Austin Colony, remembering the trials and hope they had all shared in settling this wild land. He also thought of the hateful words he'd spit forth at his parent's supper table, when he broke his mother's wine glass.

"Thank you, Gabriel. I thank you both." Juan said, straightening himself in his saddle. "If I thought there was a chance of catching those miserable dogs, I'd take you up on your offer. There are no men I would rather have with me in a fight like that either. You are sound men, like Sam's father, and I know I could count on you anywhere - for anything.

"But, I'm afraid it would be fruitless, and we have other battles to fight. For every good man and his family who move to Texas now, there is a thief or a murderer who follows them in. This country is becoming a haven for cut-throats and criminals. If we can't pick our enemies, we need to at least try to pick our battles. We need to fight the ones we can win, if we're going to have a place to raise our children."

"It's getting bad here isn't it, Juan?" Sam said, stating the obvious and nodding his head. He turned to Juan but spoke loud enough for Max to hear, too. "A few days ago in Austin, in the afternoon right in the middle of the main street by the Capitol, Gabriel and I saw a man shot dead. Some of the people said it was over a card game, and some of 'em said the man had moved in on some other fella's land. But two men shot this man and just walked off. Left him layin' dead in the street."

"The man who got killed, was he white or *Tejano*?" Juan asked.

"He was a *Tejano*, Juan. I don't know who he was."

Juan looked over at Max. "This land of ours gets more crowded and more dangerous everyday. It is dangerous for everyone, but it seems to be more so for *Tejanos*."

Sam watched Max's eyes when he nodded back to his cousin. There was something else from Austin that Sam and Gabriel had heard, and it remained lodged in Sam's throat. It was something that both Juan and Max needed to know, but given the situation he and Gabriel had walked into at *Casa Blanca*, Sam had kept quiet. Now this bit of information, this awful thing, was wedged inside Sam, and it felt too heavy to get out.

"Juan," the younger man began slowly, "There's something you need to know." He swiveled his head toward Max, "Both of you."

Max pulled his horse up short, then maneuvered it around the back of the slow moving wagon, and went forward. When Max was next to him on the outside, Juan asked solemnly, "What is it, Sam?"

"While we were in Austin, we heard there are folks in some towns, I guess there are a lot of 'em, that are running out the *Tejanos*. They're makin' every one of 'em leave their towns. They're either running the *Tejanos* out, or burning 'em out. Sounds like there has already been lots of people hurt, or killed."

"*Ay, Dios Mio*," Max said quietly, and a pained expression drew up the lines on his face.

"Do you think it is true, Sam?" Juan asked, not wanting to hear the answer.

"Yes, Sir, I'm sure it's true. Everyone was talkin' about it. A bunch of 'em were talkin' like they thought it was the right thing to do. Like they thought it was something every town ought to do."

"Where are the towns?" Max wanted to know.

"They're all over Texas, Max. Not just one spot, but everywhere."

Juan looked at Max, then faced down the road and took in a very deep breath. He rode quietly for a short time, his eyes focused somewhere ahead, while he digested the tragic news he'd been afraid might come someday. Eventually he sat up straight in his saddle again and nodded to Max, then turned to his two other companions and said, "What would you think of moving North?"

"What?" Sam exclaimed.

"Moving our families north, out of Texas," Juan answered seriously. "Max and I have been talking about it for awhile."

Sam was shocked. He turned in the seat and looked at Gabriel. From the look he got back from his friend, Sam could tell Gabriel was as surprised as he was. Juan was the mayor of San Antonio de Bexar. He had fought for Texas. He was born here and loved this land more than anyone. The thought of Juan Seguin leaving San Antonio de Bexar was inconceivable to Sam.

"What do you mean, Juan?" Both surprise and sadness showed through in Sam's question. "You couldn't leave San Antonio, or Texas."

"They may have left me, Sam," the *Tejano* said with sadness in his own voice.

"We have all talked about what has happened here since the war. So many of the people coming here now are keeping Texas from becoming the country we fought for. We have few laws and even fewer people to enforce them. Look at what is happening to the *Tejanos*. They are being run out of towns probably built by their forefathers because people either associate them with Santa Anna's atrocities, or want their land."

Sam knew his friend's words were true. He felt his stomach draw up, the same way it had when he was a boy on the little hilltop talking to his Father about the changes that were being caused by Santa Anna. Sam realized he was scared. Scared about his whole life changing again.

"Are you talking about all of us moving, Juan? I don't understand," Sam said.

"That is what we have talked about, Sam," Juan answered sincerely. "Maria and I have small children, and God willing, we would like to have more. But we fear for the children's safety all the time now. We have to."

Juan looked to his cousin, then turned back to Sam and continued, "Maria and Rosa are more terrified everyday. They are afraid they will be alone, living without husbands, in a place where they and the children cannot be Mexicans or Texans." Juan paused, "I can't blame them, because I share their fears."

Juan gently pulled the reins on his horse as he said, "Let's stop for a moment, Gabriel."

"Whoa mules, whoa!" Gabriel commanded with a firm deep voice as he began a slow pull on the heavy leather leads held between the thick fingers of each of his large strong hands. The stopping mules and Gabriel braked the loaded wagon to a wallowing slow stop, and the two *Tejanos* turned their horses so that the four men were facing one another.

When the animals settled and all was quiet, Juan leaned slightly forward in his saddle and spoke with directness in his tone. Seguin nodded his head toward his cousin as he began talking about Max's wife. "Rosa's family has one of the old Spanish land grants far to the north in Mexico. Her father's people have a vast amount of land beside the *Rio Bravo*, above *El Paso del Norte*, in what's called the Mesilla Valley. Her uncle has sent word that it is safe, and we are welcome there."

Gabriel and Sam sat, fixed on every word their friend spoke. Sam felt himself going numb inside as Juan continued.

"Max and I, and our families, love this land. We were all born here and we will continue to do all that we can to help make this a decent place to live. I still believe in the things we fought for; that Jonathan and Sarah gave their lives for. But I do not believe in, nor will I let my family be brutalized by, what this country is becoming. If the course Texas is taking now doesn't change, we will leave Her."

Juan stopped and looked to Max. His cousin spoke up, "Sam, we want to stay here. This is our home. We will not leave unless we are forced to, but Juan and I have talked much about this, especially since his Father sent for us. There may come a time when we will have to go.

"If that time comes," Max continued, "you two and Mary Beth are part of our family that will be coming with us, if that is your choice. But, that is something you will have to decide. You may want to remain with…You may want to stay in Texas and we want you to know that we will understand and respect your decision. It will not affect our feelings for one another."

The numbness subsided within Sam as he realized what Max was saying. "Are you saying that we might want to stay here because we're not *Tejanos*, Max?" Sam asked somewhat insulted at the idea.

Juan interceded, "Sam, you are adults now. All we are saying is that you and your sister and Gabriel are not bound by our decisions. You are free to make your own decisions. We just want you to know that."

Sam took in his friends' words and realized they were trying to get their point across delicately, without being insulting. He put on his Father's big grin. "Gabriel," he said loudly and looked at his partner, then continued talking as he turned toward Juan and Max, "Could you tell me how it would be possible for these two poor worn out ol' Mexican *hombres* to get along without you and me to take care of 'em? Hell, just missin' all our clever conversation would pro'bly cause *both* of 'em to just shrivel up and waste away like *two old horse turds*."

They all laughed, and Sam was satisfied with his response.

"You are right, Sam." Juan said smiling. The smile left his face and he turned serious as he looked over at his cousin. Max nodded and Juan faced Sam and Gabriel. He said earnestly, "Now there is one other thing, my friends. You are the only men we could ask this of. Should something happen to Max and me, will you make sure our families get to safety with Rosa's people?"

49

"She's getting a fever, too," Mary Beth said with the back of her hand touching the small hot forehead of Sonia Seguin. She looked across the room to the little girl's mother who sat at the bedside of Sonia's sister, Elaina, wiping that child's face with a wet rag. "They're all going to get it, Maria. You and Rosa take care of the children. I'm going to find the doctor."

"No, Mary Beth, you stay here with us." Maria said quickly. "It's dark outside now. I don't want you out by yourself. It's not safe."

Maria looked toward Rosa, and then said to them both, "We'll all take care of the children. We'll do what we have to 'til the morning. I think we should all stay here together, and we will be fine." As she finished, the anxiety of a woman fatigued from dealing with decisions and sick children suddenly burst out from somewhere below the surface, and Maria said angrily through her teeth, "Sweet Jesus, I wish the men were home!"

"They're bound to be home soon, Maria." Rosa said trying to give comfort. "We'll get through this all right, and so will the children." She smiled warmly looking into Maria's cloudy face and said with upbeat sarcasm, "You know, this isn't the first time the children have all decided to get sick together…while the men were *conveniently* away somewhere."

Maria closed her eyes and nodded her head while she brought her lips together in a tight, half-smile. She was still in the process of reclaiming her strength and composure when Mary Beth said, "Ladies, I'm going after the doctor. You two are being old ninnies. I don't care what you say, I'm not going to just stand here and watch all these babies get sick. What if it's something serious? I'll find that doctor and bring him here." She intentionally didn't give the other two women a chance to interrupt her and was almost at the front door by the time she finished talking. Mary Beth opened the door and went out quickly saying, "I won't be gone long."

* * * *

"Well, lookie there," the foul smelling newcomer said in his Tennessee accent through the greasy whiskers of his beard. From the shadows between the buildings he watched Mary Beth as she walked quickly along the opposite side of the street. He looked past Ross Michaels who continued to urinate in the darkness on the outside wall of the cantina.

Michaels was already hawking the young woman by the time the man spoke. He watched her breasts bounce with every fast step. Ross never took his eyes from her body while he finished urinating. He stroked himself a couple of times as he marked her direction up the street and said in a raw, graveled voice, "I think I'd like a piece of that pie. Go inside and fetch the other two."

* * * *

Dr. Cyrus Oxford was in his mid-fifties and had doctored for the people of Texas for almost two decades. Born in England, he migrated to Boston as a young man seeking fame and fortune in the new world. He had found neither. He had, however, found a woman to love him and more work than he could handle caring for indigents at a church sponsored hospital.

When Cyrus was thirty, his wife died while giving birth to their first child. The child, his son, only stayed in this world for a few hours, and then followed his mother. Although Oxford had used everything he knew, he couldn't prevent either of them from leaving. Shortly thereafter Cyrus also left. He left Boston, the practice of medicine, and for five years, his mind and soul.

One day Oxford found himself in the streets of New Orleans listening to Stephen Austin tell a crowd of people about the American Colony settling in the Texas wilderness. The young man's voice stirred something within the dark empty void inside Cyrus. As he saw hope in the faces of those around him while they listened to the promise of a new life, the lonely man decided he was tired of having nothing to live for and nothing to lose. That afternoon he signed on to join the next group leaving for the Austin Colony.

The new land was more spectacular than he had dreamed, and he fell in love with it immediately. He also fell in love with the brave hearted people, both pioneers and natives, who worked to master the vast wilderness. Because of the starving lack of medical attention, Cyrus soon became Dr. Oxford again.

Within three years Juanita Peralas de Luntas, a strikingly beautiful twenty eight year old widow, became Mrs. Oxford. They settled in Victoria, with her two children, on land owned by her family. They lived happily there until the Texas War for Independence when the home was destroyed by Santa Anna's passing Army.

It happened while Cyrus was at the Brazos River with Sam Houston's Army, shortly before he served at San Jacinto. Juanita joined with two other families and escaped to the Northeast with her children ahead of the Mexican soldiers. After the war, Cyrus searched for two months desperately trying to find his family. When they were together again, and found their home was gone, Cyrus moved them all to San Antonio de Bexar.

"Cyrus isn't here, Mary Beth." Juanita Oxford said from the doorway of her home. She raised the oil lamp she carried and looked behind the young woman standing before her at the edge of the street. "You didn't come here by yourself, did you, dear? You shouldn't be out alone in the dark. Where are your men?"

"They're out of town, Juanita. The children are sick. They're all getting a fever, and I had to come get your husband. Where is he?"

"Some men came an hour ago, and Cyrus left with them. There is something serious going on. All the town elders are meeting at the Church." Juanita's voice was apprehensive as she spoke. She focused past Mary Beth again and turned her head looking up and down the dark street. "I don't know when Cyrus will be back, but you wait here with me until he comes home."

"Thank you, Juanita, but I can't," Mary Beth said with determination. "Maria and Rosa are alone with the children, and I need to get Cyrus over there. Besides, they'll be worried if I'm gone too long. The Church isn't far. I'll find Cyrus, and at least tell him, so he can go to Maria's when he can. There will be someone there who can walk me home."

"No, I think you should stay here, honey," the older woman said firmly. "Besides, I told you, something's wrong. They didn't tell me what it was, but Cyrus left with them in a big hurry."

"Thank you so much, Juanita," Mary Beth said almost over her shoulder as she quickly backed away and started to turn up the street leaving the Doctor's wife standing in the doorway. "But I have got to go."

Mary Beth's eyes had adjusted to the light of the lamp Juanita held in front of her as they talked, so the street seemed even darker than before as she started off in the direction of the old San Fernando Church. Because she couldn't see well, she began walking more slowly, looking down to see where she was stepping. While her eyes were working hard to pick up more light, her sense of hearing seemed keener, and she heard something from behind and across the street.

The young woman involuntarily sucked in a deep breath as she whipped around to look. There was only the dark street with even darker shadows between the buildings. She began walking forward again while she continued to keep her body twisted and watched the street behind her. As she turned her upper body back toward the church, she heard another noise behind her, but didn't look back. She quickened her pace - faster and faster and faster. Suddenly she could hear several footsteps behind her.

Mary Beth was running when she turned the corner in front of the Church, and the footsteps stopped. She ran to the entrance of the Chapel and fumbled with the door latch. As it clicked and the door opened, she turned to the street behind her and saw - nothing.

Several men were standing in the front of the church, and the ones who were seated in the pews stood up when Mary Beth entered the back of the open room panting for breath. "What is it child?" One of the older men asked as they all stared at the woman who had burst in upon their meeting.

"I need to speak with Dr. Oxford," Mary Beth answered through her heavy gasps for air.

Cyrus appeared from within the group and started to the back toward the girl. "Mary Beth? I'm here. What is it? What's wrong, Mary Beth?" He asked while he walked.

As he approached, obviously concerned about her, Mary Beth smiled and said, "I'm fine, Cyrus, I just got a little scared of the dark coming over here." She took in a deep breath and told him about the children, then asked if he would come to the Seguin house when they were finished.

"We're through here," he said. "I'll come with you now and walk you back to Juan and Maria's house." Cyrus had a serious look on his face as he spoke. "Do you have any idea when Juan and Max will be back?"

"No," she answered looking into the man's eyes anxious to know what was happening. "Soon, I hope. What's going on here, Cyrus?"

Cyrus took in a slow deep breath and used it to carry his solemn words. "We have just received word that the Mexican Army has a large force moving to attack San Antonio de Bexar. They will be here very soon."

50

"I think I can smell them tortillas and beans from here!" Gabriel pronounced loudly, raising his face high and taking in a deep breath through his nose, as the big wagon crested the last small hill on the road leading to San Antonio de Bexar. Over the trees in front of them, they could see from the town the warm glow of lights that told them they were almost home. "You know, I'll bet Miss Mary Beth even has some bacon we can have. I think I can smell that, too!"

Sam turned his head to either side of the wagon and gave a sly smile to Juan and Max. Juan spoke up through a grin, "Gabriel, you sound as though you haven't eaten in a month. Is Sam's cooking so bad that you can't eat it when you two are on the road?"

"Naw, Senator, it ain't that...exactly. I mean, if a fella's out on the road miles and miles from nothin', 'bout to starve to death, and has to eat somethin' just to stay alive, well, you know, he can force hisself to choke down just about anything. And I guess, sometimes, that even includes Sam's cookin'...if a fella's starvin' bad enough!"

The *Tejanos* laughed and Sam pushed Gabriel's arm. Sam raised his hands to his hips imitating a woman and said in a high prissy voice, "Well, you notice he only complains about my cooking when he thinks he can find someone else to feed him. I think you are fickle, Gabriel, and I shall remember how I have been treated." Sam kept his right hand in position on his hip, as a girl would do, and lifted his left hand up to the front of his friend's face high enough for the others to see as well. He wiggled the nub of what had once been his third finger at Gabriel. Sam rocked his shoulders back and forth while he bobbled his head and said in a wounded female's huff, "Just see if I work my fingers to the bone anymore fixin' nice suppers for you, Mister Two-timer."

While the heavily loaded wagon creeped and creaked along toward the outskirts of town, the mules began to sense that they too were almost home and quickened their step. "See what you did now," Gabriel said to Sam, pretending to be serious. "All that talk about your cookin' has done scared my poor mules." The big black man smiled broadly up at Juan and continued, "These mules are very sensitive, you know. I think they has weak stomachs."

"I think they're just ready for the barn, Gabriel," Maximillian laughed and stretched his back as he stood up in his stirrups. "And so am I."

"I know what you mean, Mistah Max. I don't expect any of y'all are gonna have to rock me to sleep tonight," Gabriel answered, and then said emphatically looking at Sam, "Especially after I get to eat some *real* cookin'!"

The mules were fussy as Gabriel maneuvered them past the outlying buildings and turned them onto one of the dirt streets leading toward their homes. The animals had everyone's attention while Gabriel worked the fidgety team trying to make them behave. As they finished the turn, Max looked ahead up the street and said, "What is that? What's going on up there?"

In the dim light they all saw a small group of people gathered to one side of the street. Advancing, they could make out two men standing close to the street side wall of one of the buildings. In front of them, more into the street, stood a woman with three men circling her like a rangy pack of hungry coyotes ready to attack a small doe. At almost the same instant that the woman looked up and yelled, "Sam!" Gabriel whipped the mule's backs hard with their reins and boomed out, "Yha, Mules!"

Mary Beth's brother flew out of the wagon and ran ahead of the mules toward his sister. Juan and Max spurred their surprised horses and charged behind Sam, each drawing their pistols. Gabriel continued to beat his mules and thunder, "Yha, Yha!"

The stranger who had worked his way between Cyrus Oxford and Mary Beth, then maneuvered Cyrus toward the front of the building, jerked his body and ducked his head as he turned to see the onrush of men and mules come out of the darkness. Like a cockroach fleeing a sudden light, he disappeared around the building's corner into the black shadows. The three who encircled Mary Beth also flinched with surprise as they spun around to see what was coming.

Sam was several strides ahead of the *Tejanos'* horses and yanked the knife from his belt as he closed the distance to get to his sister. Mary Beth dashed out from between the three vagrants and ran to him. Ross Michaels saw the flash of Sam's blade and started to reach for the knife sheathed in the side of his boot.

As Michaels bent forward, Mary Beth and Sam reached one another. The young man stopped and moved the girl to one side so he could face the strangers. Before Ross Michaels' hand started to close around his knife's shank, Juan and Max had blasted past Sam and set their horses to a hard stop throwing dirt forward onto the three dark men.

The two scruffy accomplices were between Michaels and the row of buildings on the south side of the street. Their heads bobbed up and down and side to side, like two pullets cornered in a chicken yard, both too stupid to decide what to do or which way to run. The open barrels of the two *Tejano's* pistols were complicating their thought process, when the ground they were standing on suddenly shook and the big wagon with its six mules tore up the street creating a minor earthquake as they stopped.

Above the dust and noise created by the earthquake, a giant black monster rose and pulled out a musket. He held it in one hand like a pistol and the big hammer clicked loudly when he cocked it with his thumb. The pullets looked into the large black circle at the end of Gabriel's barrel, and their heads quit bobbing. Their decision was made. Ross Michaels stayed in his position, bent forward slightly at the waist, during the few moments it took for Mary Beth's rescuers to get into place. He pretended to brush the dirt thrown up by the commotion off his pants leg then slowly rose, smiling up at Juan Sequin.

"Well, good evenin' Mayor," he said as he straightened himself. "You just about scared the devil out of us, comin' in like that."

"What's going on here?" Juan demanded sternly. He turned and looked over his shoulder quickly toward Mary Beth and Sam, then right back to the three men in the street. He kept his gaze, and his pistol, on the men and said loudly, "Mary Beth, are you all right?"

Mary Beth and Sam walked up from behind to the right of the two mounted *Tejanos*, between them and the line of buildings. Cyrus had already started walking toward them and took Mary Beth from Sam when they all came even with the horsemen. As the doctor put his arm around the young girl's shoulder she said, "I'm fine, Juan. I'm not hurt, I was just scared."

Ross saw Juan Seguin's nostrils flair and the look of rage in his eyes. Sensing he was about to be shot, Michaels quickly cowered and raised his hands in front of his chest with his palms toward Seguin in a gesture to stop. "Now hold on there," he squirmed. "Remember, you're the Mayor. We wasn't doin' nothin'. I swear. I think there's a misunderstanding here."

Juan pushed his pistol forward and his elbow locked into position so that he could look down the barrel at the mad dog who would dare to assault Jonathan's daughter. His eyes narrowed while he took in a slow full breath and cocked the weapon. Ross Michael's voice took on a higher pitch and a faster pace as he whined, "You're the Mayor. You can't just gun somebody down in the street. There's laws, you know. You're the Mayor; you have to mind the laws. We wasn't doin' nothin'. I swear! Don't kill me."

Michaels turned to Mary Beth and pleaded, "Ma'am, please, tell him we didn't do nothin' to you. We was just playin' around. I swear to God."

The steel cold expression on Juan's face didn't change, and he kept his pistol pointed dead center on the begging man's chest. Juan cast his eyes to Mary Beth without turning his head. Mary Beth spoke slowly, "They just scared me, Juan."

In the moment that Juan hesitated Michaels started talking again, running his sentences together. "I'm Ross Michaels. I'm kinda new here. I…I didn't know that young lady was…"

"I know who you are." Max broke in gruffly.

Ross turned, looking up at the other *Tejano*, and found no compassion in that man's eyes either. Max broke away from the man's stare to look back at the two he held his pistol on. Juan's cousin never stopped guarding the other men as he spoke slowly with obvious disgust, occasionally glancing at Ross Michaels.

"You're the windy, bar-fly who hates Mexicans. People say you're a real whiskey warrior…with a very loud mouth. I heard that you could have beaten Santa Anna's Army single handed…and run all of us "pepper bellies" out of Texas."

"Oh, no, sir," Michaels responded quickly, his eyes widening with sincerity as his voice took on a lower tone and his words came out more slowly. "No, sir, that could not have been me. Someone has given you some bad information there. I mean, sure, these boys here and me wish we could have been here to help out in that Great War for Texas. We really do. I mean, we'd a been glad to do our part."

Ross turned his sincerity and his wide eyes toward Juan as he continued, "Your Honor, that is a fact. We'd a sure pitched in, but that's just 'cause we like the people here so much. Somebody might'a confused me sayin' somethin' bad about Santie Annie and his Army, but I swear, I ain't never said nothin' bad about the people here. I really like it here. I do."

Juan turned his head and looked at Mary Beth and Cyrus. Ross Michaels followed his look and kept talking, "And as far as your daughter there, Sir, well she and that man was out by theirselves on this dark street. That pro'bly wasn't real safe, and me and these boys was just…"

"*Que paso aqui*, Cyrus?" Juan interrupted firmly, as though Ross Micheals was not even there; asking the doctor what was going on.

Cyrus answered in Spanish. "Your children are sick with a fever, Juan. Several other people in town have it, too. I'm sure they will be fine, but Mary Beth came to get me and take me to your house."

As Juan started to turn back to the three itinerants, Cyrus said, "There's something else, Juan. We just left a meeting of the town elders at the Church. Some men came into town this afternoon with word that the Mexican Army is moving to attack San Antonio de Bexar. They've got a column of soldiers only five, maybe six days out. We're sending out riders tonight to the outlying areas to try to raise some men."

The bottom of Sam's stomach seemed to fall away and the hair on his arms felt bristly as he turned away from Cyrus and looked at Juan. Juan's eyes met his, then they both looked to Max and Gabriel. Not understanding a word of the language Cyrus spoke, Ross Michaels was spooked by the sudden silence and the looks his captors were exchanging.

"What'd he say?!" Ross asked anxiously, panning the people in front of him almost begging for an answer.

Juan looked straight into the man he should have already killed. The *Tejano's* cold stare made Michaels' body involuntarily lean back. Barely opening his mouth, Seguin spoke loudly, in a threatening low voice that left neither doubt nor option.

"He said you three men have just joined - 'The Army of the People'."

51

"Surprise attack, my ass!" Rafael Vasquez said to himself under his breath, and then spit a large blob of stringy, brown stained saliva to the ground beside his trail weary horse. He stuck the smoldering black cigar back into his mouth and puffed. His tongue burned. The whole inside of his mouth burned because of all the cigars he'd smoked since Santa Anna's lap dog, Captain Denicio Bernillo, had brought orders for this suicide mission.

He thought about that as he pulled the soggy end of the dark strong smelling cylinder from his lips and looked at it. The smoke from its other end wiffed into his nose and caused him to bark two short coughs. He moved it to the side, away from his face. Rafael smacked his mouth twice, and then rubbed his burned tongue against the raw skin on the roof of his mouth. It felt as though all the tissue was rubbing off.

The General pulled his right arm back, like he was throwing a rock, and flung the cigar to the ground hard, then spat again saying angrily, "Son-of-a-bitch is a madman!" The words came out louder than he wanted, and Vasquez turned left and right to see if any of his men had heard him. He looked for a moment at the expedition of Mexican soldiers to either side and behind him, then looked ahead to the small ridges above the little valley they were starting into.

They had stayed low, moving only in the valleys and draws, to keep from being seen. He had also moved the men extremely fast for a whole column of soldiers. The men and animals were worn out from the pace, and Vasquez knew he had to balance speed against strength. If his force was too spent from the march, they would be useless in battle.

In Rafael's mind the whole concept of a secret attack on Tejas was absurd anyway. Only a madman would think that an overland expedition of Mexican soldiers could slip into Tejas without being seen and execute a surprise assault on her biggest city. He was obeying his orders, but in his soldier's mind he was sure the Texans already had reports he was on the march. By now they would be armed and waiting for his arrival.

Even if he could take San Antonio de Bexar, in his heart Vasquez was afraid the consequences for Mexico would be devastating. The population in Tejas was at least double what it had been during their last war, and Mexico had lost. If the Texans mobilized an Army before Santa Anna could attack by sea, they would defeat Mexico again and perhaps counter attack and take his entire country.

On the other hand, as a strategist, Rafael Vasquez feared even more that this ill-conceived mission he led would bring his country to war with the United States. The people of Tejas and the Americans were already closely aligned. Santa Anna was right about that point. An unprovoked attack on Tejas might be enough to join the allies together in a war against Mexico - a war that his country could not possibly survive.

General Cos couldn't hold San Antonio de Bexar six years ago with twelve hundred soldiers, and the entire Mexican Army under Santa Anna had been defeated by the Texans. Rafael Vasquez knew that he and a few hundred tired soldiers didn't have a chance in hell of taking and holding San Antonio, and he didn't care what the great *El Presidente* said, or the cretins on his *Personal Command Staff.*

Vasquez looked to the Regiment's right flank and saw Captain Denicio Bernillo riding ahead of the company of foot soldiers he'd been assigned. Bernillo was in a pout over the fact that Rafael had made him come on this campaign. For a moment the General wished he'd killed the arrogant little bastard and denied he ever received Santa Anna's orders.

The pompous young Captain had insisted his instructions were to wait at the General's Headquarters for word about the outcome of the expedition, then personally transport his report directly back to *El Presidente.* As he watched Bernillo, Rafael was glad he had given the Captain no alternative but to serve as an officer on this mission. He said under his breath, "You whiny little prick, so proud of bringing me orders from Santa Anna's Inner Circle. Well, by God, now you can either die with me and my men, or you can watch first hand the death of our country."

Vasquez didn't take his eyes from Denicio Bernillo as he pulled a cigar from his breast pocket, and lit it.

52

"Sho' is a lot a men down there, Sam." Gabriel said in a hushed voice to his friend. They lay fifteen feet from one another just below the skyline of a ridge where the cedars, mesquites, rocks, and prickly pear cactus all mixed together. Sam hid behind the base of a mesquite tree with his rifle resting in the fork of its rough barked trunk, and Gabriel was on his belly in the shadows of an old cedar's boughs. The two men were watching General Vasquez's expedition of Mexican soldiers continue up the little valley toward them.

"I see 'em, Gabriel." Sam responded, watching the troops advance. He turned his head and looked at Gabriel saying, "What do you think?"

"I think they sho' is a lot a men down there." Gabriel answered, raising his eyebrows and nodding his head slightly.

"We'll do just fine," Sam said with resolve in his voice trying to reassure his partner. "All we have to do is wait for Juan's signal. Can you see where he is over there?"

They both looked across to the ridge opposite theirs and Gabriel said, "Naw, I don't see him, Sam, but I saw where they went. I think the Senator's in that bunch a cedar trees down yonder below them big rocks."

Sam couldn't see anyone on the other side, but that was good. It meant they were hidden well. Juan had split the force of a hundred and twenty some odd volunteers they had raised. He took half the men across and left Max in command of Sam and Gabriel's side. They were all hiding now on the high ground at the narrowest point where the little valley the Mexican Army traveled turned into more of a canyon. The volunteers were waiting for Colonel Seguin's signal.

"We have to catch them by surprise," Juan had told his men three hours before. The Texan's were all standing together when Juan and Max rode in after scouting the ambush spot. Juan stayed mounted so all the men could see and hear him.

"We are outnumbered," Juan said, and then continued boldly showing the men confidence with his broad smile. "But I think, as Texans, we are somewhat used to that by now!" Some of the men smiled and there were a few chuckles. However, many of the volunteers, the newcomers, were too concerned about the upcoming fight to change their worried expressions.

"We must even the odds and make the Mexican's think that our force is much larger than it actually is. Their column is marching on low ground in a small valley a half mile from here. I'm sure they are doing it in an effort to keep from being seen. We will take positions on either side of the valley where the canyon walls narrow.

"I want you men to spread out and make yourselves well hidden just below the ridgelines. We will hold until they are directly between our two sides, then catch them in a cross fire. Aim for the mounted cavalry and officers first, not the footsoldiers. Do not fire into the crowd. Pick one target and shoot him. Reload as quickly as you can, pick another target, and shoot him. It is very important that we make every shot count. If we each take out a man on the first volley, they will think they are under attack by a whole regiment, and it will substantially lessen their number."

Juan stopped and surveyed the group. When he was sure he had the eyes of every man he continued, "We must catch the enemy by surprise. Surprise and high ground are the two things we have in our favor." He paused again and said sternly, "No man is to fire on the enemy until my signal. However, once I give the command, "Fire", do not stop shooting until it is over. Is that understood?" He looked across the nodding heads.

"Very well then," Juan nodded back to the group. "When we get there, tie your horses securely out of sight behind the ridgelines. Leave the saddle cinches tight. If we route the Mexicans, we may need to charge down to the battle. If they route us, escape as you can, and we will rendezvous at Three Forks. Does everyone know where that is?" After the affirmative nods and "Yes, Sirs" Juan asked, "Are there any questions?"

Hearing none, Juan finished with, "Men, we have faced Santa Anna's armies before and beaten them. We must stand up now and show Santa Anna that free Texans are still men of courage and determination. We do not know why the Mexicans are moving to attack San Antonio de Bexar, but we will stop them here before they can reach our homes and families!"

53

"This is bullshit! This ain't our fight."The Tennessee born thug said turning left to the two men squatting beside him. The three were crouched behind a large craggy boulder that was forty yards below the top of the ridgeline and four hundred yards down from Sam and Gabriel. He turned right and looked at Ross Michaels, who was only a short distance away, standing next to a splotchy gray and white stone outcropping.

Somewhere behind the perpetually dirty whiskers of the man's beard, a mouth kept moving as he continued, "I didn't come down here to git my ass shot by a bunch a damn Meskins! What in the hell are we doin' here, Ross? I ain't kiddin', this is bullshit!"

Ross Michaels didn't say anything as he looked at the man, then let his eyes pan down to the Mexican Army moving up the small valley toward them. He turned his head as far as he could to the left and moved the upper part of his body peering around the brush and rocks trying to see the rest of the Texas volunteers. They were all strung out up the canyon above Michaels and his companions.

When Max dispersed the group to take up their ambush positions, Ross had purposefully moved himself and his three men to the far south end of the line. He looked back down the ridge to his right to make sure none of the Texans had moved past them to the south. He could see no one down the line below them.

Michaels turned his focus to the three men still crouched behind the large rock and said, "I'll tell you one goddamn thing, *I* ain't gonna get shot. I ain't gonna get shot today. An' I damn sure ain't gonna get shot *here*, by some stinkin' pepper belly half-ass soldiers!"

Ross looked quickly toward the Texans again, then back to his three. He spoke in a loud whisper, exaggerating the movement of his lips as though the men were going to see what he was saying instead of hearing it. "Once this thing starts, everybody'll be watching the Mexicans. Soon as nobody's lookin', we're gettin' the hell outa here."

He closed the fingers of his left hand and jerked his thumb pointing south. "We'll head that away, then turn east and make for the coast. Ain't nothin' to stay around here for, thanks to that dark haired bitch that like to got us all killed the other night." Michaels hesitated. His head moved up and down slightly while the corners of his mouth turned down as he seemed to be pondering something, and then agreeing with himself. "Maybe we oughta swing back and pay her a little visit 'for we leave."

When the others nodded back enthusiastically, Ross Michaels smiled.

"All right then," he said with the smile still on his lips. "I guess we can make one little stop before we leave." With that he lifted his rifle and cocked its hammer as he put the stock to his shoulder. He pointed the end of the barrel toward the middle of the column of Mexican soldiers and fired.

* * * *

Juan Seguin sucked a short gulp of air into his throat, in the blink that it took for his eyes to leave their solid fixation on the advancing Mexican column. "What the hell!?" He exclaimed as his body came out of its sudden reflex jerk. Shocked, Juan quickly looked around toward the positions where the Texas volunteers were scattered up and down the canyon walls. "Where'd that shot come from!?"

"'Cross the canyon." The closest man to Juan's left said, and pointed with the end of his rifle's barrel.

"Dammit!" Juan spit through his bared front teeth. Only the first third of the Mexican force was even within range. There was now no way to get their army in a cross fire. A wave of anxiety came over Juan trying to tell him that his side had just lost the battle. He drew in a deep breath and blew it hard through his closing lips causing his cheeks to puff out. Juan drew in another deep breath, and then bellowed, "Fire!" His command echoed back and forth across the canyon.

54

Captain Denicio Bernillo and his horse both lifted their heads in curiosity as the loud whizzing noise passed above them. An instant later the distinct report of Ross Michaels' rifle reached their ears. Only a few of the Mexicans even noticed the handful of dirt kicked up by Michaels' roundball when it harmlessly hit the ground in the middle of the advancing column. However, every soldier in the command heard the weapon's boom and realized they were under attack.

"Up there!" One of the front row infantry soldiers called out, pointing to the top of the canyon's west wall. Denicio snapped his eyes toward the spot and saw the gray smoke of a discharged rifle lifting from the rocks. His stomach convulsed and Denicio raised his left hand quickly to his mouth. He nearly threw up as panic took over his body and pulled the blood from his face, and arms, and legs.

Bernillo swallowed hard to hold his stomach down and grimaced at the taste. His eyelids fluttered as the acid heave from his belly filled his eyes with watery tears. By the time he finished the swallow and started panting trying to recover, more whizzing noises filled the air. They were all around him.

With the back of his hand, Denicio wiped at his watering eyes and through them saw miniature clouds of gray smoke puffing from both sides of the canyon. Men began falling and crying out in pain, as he heard the first cracks from a hundred rifles. Fear pulled Denicio's body back in his saddle, which made it look like he was reacting to a sudden blast of heat.

Except for the quick quartering glances he made at the men falling to his left and right, Bernillo could not move his body. A short high pitched whimper left his throat as he recoiled and froze, leaning back awkwardly in the saddle. Suddenly his body moved by itself, jerking instinctively as it reacted to the sudden loud smack he heard, or felt, directly in front of him.

Between Denicio's legs a shudder went through his horse's body. A .50 caliber lead ball had ripped straight through the animal's brisket; tore the top out of one lung, then destroyed its heart in less than half a second. His mount's front legs crumpled and Denicio Bernillo felt himself flying forward out of the saddle.

He hit the ground hard. Dirt went in his eyes and up his nose. He couldn't get a breath and was terrified thinking he'd been shot. Denicio cringed for a moment, not wanting to die, when he felt and heard the slamming hooves of hard running horses.

Still trying to get his burning lungs to take in air, Denicio rolled himself toward the thundering. The column's mounted cavalry was charging forward toward their attackers. They were bearing straight at him. Without thinking, Denicio was suddenly on his hands and knees scurrying toward the carcass of his dead horse. As he curled his body into a ball next to the bleeding animal, he slammed his eyes shut fearing he'd be trampled by the onrush.

The sound of the cavalry stampeding over and around him was almost deafening, but short-lived. The thunder passed quickly and rolled up the canyon toward the fight. Denicio's eyes were still closed when he heard another volley of at least a hundred rifles banging from the canyon's upper walls. It took big exagerated blinks to blow open his watering, dirt-filled eyes. Through the resulting mud, he saw the expedition's cavalry abruptly stopped when it ran into an invisible wall of well-aimed deadly lead balls.

Three quarters of the cavalry company's men and half its horses crashed into the ground throwing dark brown dirt clods and billowing light brown dust high into the air. Denicio saw a second bank of the little gray gunsmoke clouds strung out up the canyon just below the ridgelines. Beyond the large uneven dust plumes and squealing horses, Denicio could also see some of the soldiers who were still mounted. One by one, they were being knocked off their horses by the enemy sharpshooters.

Individual cavalrymen started wheeling their horses about and riding back toward the column. Horsemen riding fast toward Denicio began, sporatically, blasting out through the dust clouds. As the soldiers raced past their fallen comrades, a dozen confused riderless horses fell in behind them and followed.

Bernillo jumped to his feet before the riders reached his position. His sense of survival had overcome his fear and panic. After the few retreating cavalry passed, Denicio stopped one of the loose horses that came behind them. Once he grabbed the animal's reins, Denicio swung himself into the saddle and rode away from the ambush. He didn't even notice that he was riding through the wounded remnants of the infantry company he commanded. Only a handfull of brave men were still functional. They continued to reload and fire their weapons while their Captain rode past them and away toward the southwest. Denicio heard the loud turbulence of two more bullets that tore up the air close to his left ear. Abruptly, he and his new horse cut right into the first off-shoot draw that led away from the small valley.

55

"Sounds like a helluva fight. Sure do hate we're missin' it," the dark bearded man laughed through his Tennessee accent. He turned, looking off to the east toward the sounds of constant gunfire.

"Yeah, ain't you though?" Ross Michaels cackled back to him. "I feel the same way. I sure wish I's over there gittin' my ass shot by some damn Meskin."

He paused, slightly, then went on, "But ya' know, it is liable to be the shits if the damn Mexicans win this thing. Don't know about you, but I've had about all them jabberin' son-of-a-bitches I can stand. They start takin' over this country again an', well, I don't know, but it'll be the shits. An I'll tell you one goddamn thing, I'm gettin' my sweet ass outa' here if they do."

"Yeah, mine too!" Whiskers grunted in an emphatic reply.

They rode north in silence a while longer. Cresting the top of a rise, Ross Michaels stopped his horse and stood up in his stirrups. He looked back to the northeast wondering to himself if it was about time to turn and make their way to San Antonio de Bexar. He had been thinking about the dark haired girl.

"What the hell is that?" Michaels heard one of his companions say. He turned and saw the other three men all looking at something coming up the little draw below them at the bottom of the rise.

"That's a goddamn Meskin soldier," the bearded one responded. "What in the hell is he doin' here?" He turned and looked at Michaels. "We gonna kill him, Ross?"

Ross spotted the soldier trotting his horse up the little arroyo toward them. As he got closer one of the others said, "Shit, Ross, that's a goddamned officer. That's a goddamn Meskin army officer!"

"We gonna kill him, Ross?" Whiskers asked again in a lower tone. There was a little more urgency, and desire, in his voice.

"Just a minute!" Ross snapped, trying to think. He looked past the oncoming rider and didn't see anyone behind him.

"What's he doin' by hisself?" Michaels asked himself out loud.

He turned to the others and said, "If we start shootin', we're liable to bring a bunch more of 'em right in here on top of us." He began talking more slowly, speaking his thoughts in the order and pace at which they came into his head. "Don't think we oughta let him get on the other side of us though. What if we rushed him and cut him off? The four of us ought'a be able to take him."

The Mexican was fast approaching as Michaels got back a couple of head nods. "Don't shoot him 'less ya' have to." He said firmly, then barked, "Let's go!" and spurred his horse hard in the ribs.

When Denicio Bernillo saw the two horsemen closing in on him rapidly from the left, his immediate reaction was to turn his horse and run. He jerked the reins and set the horse to a rough stop. When he yanked the horse's head left to start the turn and spurred the animal into it, he saw the other two riders pressing down to cut him off from behind. They had the angle. He'd never make it past them.

He dug his heels into the animal's sides as hard as he could and continued the turn to go back up the arroyo. When he came around, the first two men he'd seen were dropping into the bottom in front of him with their pistols drawn and cocked. He spun the horse around again to see the second pair closing in on him from behind.

Denicio almost started crying. He knew he was about to die.

With the four riders closing on him in the bottom of the small draw, Denicio stopped spinning his horse and faced the two who had cut him off from the front. He dropped his horse's reins and raised his hands high over his head. He held them palms open to show he was unarmed and pleaded loudly, "Do not shoot! I hold no gun! Do not shoot!"

"Don't make a move, you son-of-a-bitch!" Michaels growled, pointing his cocked pistol at the Mexican's chest while he closed the distance between them.

"Do not shoot, please. I hold no gun." Bernillo continued.

"You speak more English than that!?"

"Yes," Bernillo answered. "I speak English. You do not have to kill me, please."

"Who the hell are you? An' what are you doin' here!?"

"I am Captain Denicio Bernillo," he answered with slightly less fear in his voice. "I was forced to come on this expedition by General Rafael Vasquez. I am not supposed to be here. I bare you and your country no harm. I did not want to come and I protested, but he, General Vasquez, made me be here."

"Why aren't you with the others?" Michaels said gruffly, demanding to know.

"I was almost killed!" Denicio burst out. "The battle was lost anyway. They destroyed our cavalry." He turned his head listening to the gunfire coming from the east. "I think General Vasquez is in the retreat now."

"So you're a goddamn deserter!" The black beard blurted from behind their captive.

Denicio turned his body with his hands still held above his head, trying to look back at the voice with the strange accent. He caught the man's eye and the two from behind nudged their horses to bring them more toward the direction the Mexican had been facing. While they moved Denicio answered politely, "No, sir, I was just in the retreat. As I told you, I bare your country no harm, and I am not supposed to be here."

The black beard hissed, "Let's kill him, Ross. We're waistin' time messin' with this piece a shit."

"Shut-up!" Michaels growled.

His face was still drawn up in a scowl and his eyes squinted when he turned to the Mexican and said, "You say the Texans got your cavalry?"

"Yes, Sir. Almost the whole company. They made a charge. It was a bad thing to do."

"So you think the Texan's might win the fight?"

"*Si.* Yes. Listen to the guns." Denicio paused and raised his chin while slightly turning an ear towards the battle. The amount of shooting had lessened and seemed to be coming from a more southerly direction.

"I think General Vasquez is in the retreat now," he said lowering his chin and turning his face back to Michaels.

Ross pulled himself upright in his saddle and raised the corners of his mouth up into a smirk. His head wobbled left and right as he looked around at his three companions and sighed sarcastically, "Now ain't that gonna be a hell of a fine deal! We'll be the goats and the jaybird Seguin'll be a goddamn *hero*.

"Well, piss on it! We's plannin' on gittin' outa this part a the country anyway."

"So, you were in the retreat also…like me?" Denicio asked slowly and carefully.

"Yeah, somethin' like that," Ross Michaels answered, grinning around at the others. "Guess you could say, we weren't supposed to be here neither."

Bernillo's eyes panned the group of ruffians he faced. Although he looked at them all as he spoke, his primary focus was on Ross Michaels when he said, "I told you about our General Vasquez."

He paused.

"You mentioned the one who made you be here. Is that *Juan Seguin*? Did he lead your forces?"

"Yeah," Ross responded with surprise. "You know that high talkin' bastard?"

"I know who he is. I take it, you are not loyal to him?"

The gang laughed and one of them said, "Shit, Ross'd cut that pepper-belly's heart out, an' eat it!"

They all laughed more.

Denicio Bernillo surveyed the group until they got quiet again. He spoke slowly and deliberately, again paying most of his attention to Ross Michaels. "Perhaps we should make this an opportunity to talk," he said. Denicio could see he was getting Michaels attention. "As I told you, I bare you and your country no harm. You have no need to kill me. There may be a way I can help you with your problem." Denicio continued to look directly at his captors and slowly began lowering his hands from their surrender position. "With your Juan Seguin situation."

"What?" Michaels said flatly, letting the Mexican continue to lower his hands.

"I think there is a way we could help each other. A trade, if you are willing."

"Go on," Ross nodded that he was listening.

"In exchange for my freedom, I would be very willing to help you against *Señor* Juan Seguin. If you will guarantee my release, I will give you much in return."

56

"Mary Beth! Mary Beth! Gabriel's coming!" Little Sonia Seguin shouted as she ran along the front wall of the Stevens' house making for the front door. When she reached it, she lifted the latch and popped her head inside.

"Gabriel's riding down the street! He doesn't have anybody with him!" As she saw Mary Beth turn from the wash basin and look at her, Sonia continued, "Gabriel's coming, Mary Beth, but I don't see my Papa. Where's everybody else?"

Mary Beth hurried through the doorway and stepped outside, wiping soap suds from her hands onto her long apron. She saw the big black man on horseback trotting the animal up the street toward their home. Without taking her eyes from Gabriel, Mary Beth patted Sonia's back and said, "Good job, honey. You did a real good job. Now go get your mother and Rosa. Tell them to come on over here. Now, honey, go on."

All the Seguin children had broken their fevers and were in various stages of recovery. As usual, Sonia Seguin was the perkiest and far too frisky to stay in bed. Mary Beth had offered to take care of Sonia in order for Maria Seguin to get some rest.

After being sick and confined indoors, Sonia's energy level had definitely rebounded, so much so, that even the patient Mary Beth had finally given Sonia the "outdoor job" of watching for the men to return. It seemed the only way that at least some of the Stevens' chores would get done.

It was difficult for Mary Beth not to run down the street toward Gabriel. She waited anxiously by her front door for the other two women. By the time Maria and Rosa hurried out of their houses to join her, Gabriel was almost to them.

Gabriel stopped his horse with a deep throated, "Whoa", and the three women swarmed up beside him. "What is it, Gabriel?" Mary Beth asked, afraid almost to the point of tears. "Where are the men? What has happened, Gabriel?"

Gabriel held his huge, almost pink, light colored palm open toward the women in a gesture for them to be calm as he nodded his head slightly up and down. With his rich soothing voice he spoke gently, "All the men're just fine. Don't you ladies worry none. Everybody's all right. None of your men are hurt."

Maria and Rosa started crying. They grabbed onto one another and Maria said, "Thank God!" as she pulled her apron up to her eyes.

Mary Beth continued to look up at Gabriel and said, "Where are they, Gabriel? Tell us what happened."

"Well, we whupped the Mexicans. Guess that'd be the most important thing. Three days ago, they's a big fight. We took 'em by surprise. They had a lot mo' men than we did, but we whupped 'em." Gabriel stopped talking momentarily, then shook his head and said sadly, "They's a lot a poor men died that day."

"Gabriel, where's Sam? Are you sure he's all right?" Mary Beth asked quickly. "And what about Juan and Max? Why aren't they with you?"

"They sent me on ahead, Mary Beth. But, they's all fine. I promise ya, they ain't hurt none."

Gabriel stretched his tired back. As the big man raised himself up in the saddle and filled his muscled chest with air, the horse he was on seemed to get smaller. Gabriel looked over his shoulder, then turned back to the women and said, "I has'ta get back to 'em though. We got fo' men that are hurt bad and can't ride. The Senator and Dr. Cyrus sent me in ta' fetch the big wagon, so we can bring them men home in it."

"So our men are all waiting for you to get back, Gabriel?" Maria said, as almost more of a statement than a question. She had stopped crying, as had Rosa, but they were still holding onto one another.

"No, ma'am, Mister Max may already be headin' back this way by now."

Maria's face slid into a puzzled expression with her head tilting itself slightly sideways. Her mouth opened, but when it hesitated as though uncertain about which words to bring out, Gabriel responded to her body's vernacular.

"Well, ya' see," he started off, "when all that shootin' was done, we all got back together on the west side a this big canyon we was fightin' in. Dr. Cyrus was runnin' around tryin' to find out who all was shot or hurt. An' the Senator was helpin' him out, an' tellin' everybody they did good an' such.

"Turned out none of our fella's was kilt, thank goodness, but we was missin' fo' men - that bunch that was botherin' Miss Mary Beth the other night. We looked and looked fo' 'em to see if they's hurt, but never found none of 'em. Sam says, he bets they took off runnin' when the shootin' started.

"Anyway, the Mexican's left to the southwest, an' we let 'em go on. The Senator took Sam and a few men with him to follow the Mexican's Army. He said he wanted to make sure they kept on goin' and didn't turn back around again.

"He told Mister Max to take charge a' the rest of the men. Before the Senator and Sam left, they all decided that the boys what needed to go home could go ahead an' take off, 'long as they's ready if the Mexican's decided to come back. That's when they sent me after the wagon.

"The Senator and Sam took off after the Mexicans to follow 'em. Mister Max stayed there to help Dr. Cyrus, then he was gonna bring the men from here back home. I's supposed to run ahead an' git the big wagon an' some of Dr. Cyrus's things. He made me this here note."

Gabriel reached his thick fingers awkwardly into a small pocket and produced a wrinkled piece of paper. He handed the message to Mary Beth saying, "He said you's to read this Mary Beth. He asked if you'd all help Missus Oxford gather up these things here he needed."

Mary Beth took the paper and read its words. When she looked back to Gabriel, his dark brown eyes were waiting for hers. He didn't know exactly what the communication said, but he held her eyes with his while he said, "Dr. Cyrus said that, if you was able, he'd sure be obliged if you'd come back with me in the wagon to help him git those men back to San Antonio. They's a couple of 'em that's hurt real bad. He says he's gonna need some good help, to git 'em back alive."

"Of course I'll go with you, Gabriel," Mary Beth said solidly. Then she turned to the other two women.

Gabriel listened to the young woman sound very much like her mother when she said smartly, "I'll help Gabriel with the mules and the wagon.

"Rosa, will you make him something to eat - and fix some fresh things to take to the men?

"Maria, here is the list. Juanita Oxford will know where these medicines are. We need to make bandages. I have some cloth whole-goods at my house. Have the children gather anything we have that will carry water. Cyrus says we'll need a lot of it for the men coming home."

Mary Beth stopped talking and looked at Gabriel. The kind black man gave an approving nod to support her. He smiled to himself, and thought of Sarah Stevens.

The strong young woman turned her eyes back to Maria and Rosa, who were standing together, still holding one another by the arms. Mary Beth straightened her back and sharply bobbed her head down emphasizing the words, "Quickly girls, let's go!"

57

"Well, lookie there," the black bearded wretch from Tennessee drew out the words and the syllables. Before the last word escaped past the long dirty hair on his face, he jabbed his thumb into the ribs of another member of Ross Michaels' band of thugs. They both turned their upper bodies to watch Mary Beth Stevens pass by.

"Think we oughta' tell Ross his girlfrind came back to town to see him?"

Mary Beth saw the two men watching her. She was in the back of the big wagon sitting on a wooden box that was tall enough for her to see over the sideboards. Almost all the way back to San Antonio de Bexar, Mary Beth had ridden in the back of the wagon to care for the four men who had been wounded in the battle. Now she, Gabriel, and Cyrus were driving through town, and Mary Beth sat up straight so that she could see what was causing all the commotion.

In the long shadows cast by the late afternoon sun, Mary Beth saw the backs of a large group of men. They were crowding themselves forward in a mob that seemed to overflow out of the cantina onto the west side of the dirt street. The outer edges of the mass pulsed in and out, pushing and craning toward the doorways and windows. They were obviously all trying to see, and or hear, whatever was happening inside. While Gabriel guided the wagon slowly up the street and past the bar, there were occasional unintelligible roars from the throng.

Mary Beth watched the two dark men watching her, and the wagon, pass. The cold figures were both wading in the stagnant back eddies of the crowd. The sight of them made her mouth go dry, and she unconsciously pressed her knees tightly together. Then Ross Michaels' face came into her mind.

Upon seeing the face, she remembered Gabriel's words when he told that Michaels and his bunch were missing from the battle with the Mexicans. Mary Beth twisted her body on the cargo box and turned her face up to Cyrus and Gabriel.

"Gabriel," she started.

"I see 'em, Mary Beth," he answered with his eyes locked on the two ruffians in the outer part of the mob.

"Aren't those the men…?"

"Yeah, they's a couple a the one's disappeared when we fought the Mexicans. One of em' was with that bad man bothered you that night with Dr. Cyrus."

"They were both there that night, Gabriel," Cyrus broke in. "The one on the right ran off when you all came in. Wonder what they're doin' here?"

"I wonder what's goin' on in that saloon." Gabriel answered cautiously. "Don't know what'd be causin' such a fuss."

"You think maybe there's news about Santa Anna?" Mary Beth asked of the two men.

Suddenly, above the clamor of the restless crowd, through one of the open windows, the three travelers heard the slightly slurred words of a loud, unmistakable voice.

"I'll tell you one goddamn thing. That lyin' Santie Annie lovin' son-of-a-bitch has played every one of us for a fool!"

The crowd roared.

Gabriel popped the reins against the mules' backs and kept the big wagon moving toward Cyrus Oxford's home.

Juanita Oxford had already prepared the extra room in her home for the wounded men. There were two beds made and two pallets on the floor. Cyrus had occasionally used the room before as a small makeshift hospital for the sick or injured.

While Cyrus and Mary Beth stabilized wounded limbs and held bandages in place, Gabriel carried the four men, one by one, through the dark hallways and small doors into the little hospital. As he started to lay the last man down, they heard a voice from outside.

"Cyrus! Cyrus, where are you?" It was Maximillian.

"Back here, Max," the Doctor answered and started toward the front of the house.

By the time Cyrus and the others reached the front room, Max had already let himself in. Mary Beth smiled as she started around Gabriel's wide frame to greet the *Tejano*. She stopped short. There was a stern look on Max's face as he surveyed the room and then focused on Cyrus.

"What is it, Max? What's wrong?" Cyrus asked apprehensively.

"There's trouble, Cyrus. Bad trouble. We need to get together as many of the town elders as we can."

Mary Beth immediately knew the mob at the cantina had something to do with whatever this was. She felt like an ice cold steel blade was entering the bottom of her stomach, and cutting its way up through her insides.

"Max?" was all she could get out.

"That bastard Ross Michaels, and the scum he runs with, somehow captured a Mexican commander during our battle. At least that's what they claim. Michaels and his men have the Anglos whipped into a rage because the Mexican captain has sworn that *Juan Seguin* is a loyal Mexican citizen. He swears Juan has always been loyal to the Mexican cause and claims to have documents to prove it!"

"No, Max," Cyrus said, shocked at the absurd thought. "Nobody would believe that."

"Cyrus, there's already vigilante talk - about burning out all the *Tejanos*. We've got to get the elders together and stop this!"

"Where do we start?"

"You get as many as you can, from here south, and I'll go north. Tell everyone to meet at the San Fernando Church as quickly as they can get there." Maximillian paused, and then looked directly into Gabriel's wide eyes.

"Gabriel, I want you to take Mary Beth and Rosa to Juan's house, and stay there with them. No matter what happens, don't leave the children and women alone. They may need protection, and I know I can trust you with that."

"I'll take care of 'em, Mister Max. I promise ya', I won't let nothin' happen to 'em."

58

"Gabriel, it's Cyrus, open the door! Now!" the Doctor said sternly, disturbing the quiet night air, while he rapped the knuckles of his clenched fist on the thick dark timbers of Juan and Maria Seguin's front door. "I've got Juanita and some men with me. Hurry!"

The low thunks of heavy metal on thick wood, from unseen bolts being moved on the inside of the door, answered Cyrus. The door swung open slightly and Gabriel's head appeared around its edge. Oxford, his wife Juanita, and two of the town elders pushed against it and scrambled into the house.

"What is it, Cyrus?" Maria asked, scared.

"Where is Maximillian?" Rosa burst out at almost the same time.

Doctor Oxford looked at the two women as he started speaking to Gabriel. When the sounds started out of his mouth, his eyes quickly followed them to their target. He fired the words off like rifle shots, quick and to the mark.

"We've got to get the women and children out of here, Gabriel. Get the wagon, mules, and horses. We'll help Maria and Rosa get what things the wagon will carry. Mary Beth, you and Juanita get the children ready to travel. We have no time to waste!"

"What about Mister Max?" Gabriel asked seriously, standing stiff and tall.

"Max said to tell you…'It is time for you to take the family to Rosa's people'."

Cyrus watched Gabriel's eyes widen and his nostrils flare out. The big man stood still, but the muscles of his jaw bulged out, and he took in a deep breath when Cyrus continued solemnly, "He said you'd know what he meant."

* * * *

Mary Beth lifted Sonia Seguin into the back of the wagon, then climbed in herself. She moved the little girl up to the front with the other children. As she made a place for the child on the wagon's floorboards, she wrapped Sonia in a handmade quilt. Mary Beth looked at the piece's patchwork designs as she tucked it around her small innocent friend. She caught herself thinking about the evenings she, Rosa, and Maria had spent together sewing this little quilt and several others.

The young woman stood up in the back of the Cavanaugh's oak wagon and looked around the small plaza in front of their houses. The open area was lit only from the light of a nearly full moon. She didn't understand what was happening, or why. She wanted Sam here with her. Mary Beth thought about her little brother trying to find her during the war. She looked over at the house they had rebuilt, that she had tried so hard to make into a home for them.

Tears filled her eyes as those thoughts brought more remembrances of Sam and their life at the homestead with the rest of their family. While Gabriel and the others continued the evacuation at a quickening pace, Mary Beth slipped from the back of the wagon. She hurried to her small house and opened the door.

The open doorway let in enough of the moon's soft light for her to walk straight to the fireplace without lighting a lamp. As she passed through the indefinite shadows that disguised the familiar room, her hands reached out. They seemed to lead her body to the hearth stone they had touched many times in the years this place had been the Stevens' home. Even in the darkness the hands knew exactly what to do, and quickly had the hiding stone removed. Her right one reached inside the uncovered hole where the stone had been. The sad young woman felt comfort when her hand touched Jonathan's lead box.

She carefully pulled the heavy piece from its sanctuary. Quietly in the darkness she held it, and then turned toward the door light. She looked for the engravings on its top. The ornately cut letters, JMS, showed themselves on the top of the lead box, in both reflected light and shadows. Mary Beth swallowed hard, and smiled.

Her heart jumped, and her eyelids slammed together hard in reflex, when the box suddenly flew out of her hands. Something powerful had grabbed her from behind and quickly pinned both her arms against her ribs. A hand slammed itself onto her mouth so hard she grunted out in pain. There was a horrible musty taste, and smell, that engulfed her.

"Well, lookie here," a sour Tennessee accent said into her right ear. "I knew our girlfriend was back in town, but I didn't know she'd be bringin' me a present. Let's see what ya' got in the box here, Bitch."

Whiskers kicked Jonathan's box, and it tilted onto its side. "Heavy," he said and kicked it again. When the lid came off, letters, coins, and paper money spilled out - half in the darkness of the room and half in the light of the doorway.

The foul smell got even worse as he leaned against the side of Mary Beth's face and spoke slowly. "My, my. Ain't that a nice little present you got for me?"

She felt his hips push against her from behind. His hand released its tight grip from around the upper part of her left arm and went to her breast. He squeezed it hard as the rotten hot breath came off the right side of her face again saying, "I got a little present for you too, Bitch. The others ain't here yet, so it's just you and me. Ain't that real cozy?

"Ya' see, Ross's kinda' busy right now, but I knew he wouldn't mind me cuttin' off the first piece a your little pie. They'll still be enough of it left for the rest of 'em."

He turned his face and pressed the prickly beard against her cheek. Mary Beth felt a tongue come out of the whiskers. As he started to lick, she heard a loud gagging so close to her face that she recoiled from the sound. Its volume made her right ear ring as though someone had fired a pistol next to her head.

As suddenly as the stinking lout had grabbed her, he released her.

Mary Beth spun with clenched fists, and her teeth gritted together. Her eyes teared with fury as she came around. In her rage, panting fast and heavy out of her mouth through the closed teeth, spit flew from her lips. She squinted and blinked into the darkness trying to focus on the smelly bastard, who'd have to kill her now, before she'd let him touch her again.

Almost immediately the focus came, and she was shocked. Silhouetted by the moonlight from the doorway behind him, Mary Beth saw her dark attacker in an unnatural position, bending backwards pulling at his throat. He was frantically trying to keep Gabriel's huge left hand from crushing it.

The man flogged and resisted, like a large mean rooster, surprised to find itself in the first stage of having its neck wrung. Gabriel kept forcing the fighting creature to the ground, where the darkness and shadows were more dense. It became harder to tell what was happening. The two men sank from Mary Beth's sight taking their combat from the moon's soft illumination into the lightless space closer to the floor.

As they vanished into the shadows, the young woman's primary sensory faculty transitioned from sight - to sound. The short blasts of air emitted from the throats of each man, as he strained with all his might against the force of the other, came out of the darkness in muffled grunts and quick hard pants. The noises they made seemed intensified by the darkness. Audibly, it was impossible to distinguish one man from the other.

As the time interval between each low gutteral sound progressively lengthened, Mary Beth's eyes strained at the blackness while the loud fury of the mortal struggle began to lessen.

Slowly, rising from that dark shadowy shroud, in silhouette against the open door's moonlight, there appeared the outline of a Tennessee skinning knife's long curved blade. Mary Beth screamed, "Gabriel, look out!", as her body lunged into the darkness toward the two men. She grabbed wildly for the knife.

When he sensed Mary Beth coming through the shadows into the fight, Gabriel's right arm was already drawn back making ready for the blow. He knew the dark creature he fought had a knife loose somewhere. Against his taught muscles, flexed full and hard in the struggle, Gabriel felt the young woman's body as she scrambled headlong into their deadly brawl. Her light frame was insignificant against the weight and power of the two strong men.

The instinct to protect his family exploded within Gabriel and his right fist tightened into a dark brown sledgehammer.

As a Negro who grew up in slavery, there were solid dams Gabriel held within himself. The strong checks created in his childhood, and reinforced as he grew, suddenly burst forth with a flood. The dams released all the rage and adreniline they were built to hold back. He yanked forward the neck being collapsed with the new surge of anger flowing into his left fist, and turned the man away from Mary Beth.

"No!" Gabriel's deep voice boomed, sounding like the huge deafening blast of a cannon being fired off inside the small house.

His left hand had now become a blacksmith's vice, the jaws of which were tightly screwing together. The vice gripped an ugly hair covered surface securely in place, so that it could receive a piledriving blow from Gabriel's mighty sledge.

When the big hammer landed, the black bearded face was crushed. The back part of it mashed, some few inches behind, into a spinal cord that led from the base of a breaking skull. The sound that came loudly from out of the darkness was distinctly that of a dropped ripe melon - as it hit the floor.

Limply, off Mary Beth's arm and across Gabriel's chest, the Tennessee skinning knife made a lame try before it fell away and clanked onto the wooden floor boards. The vile man with the thick black whiskers, never took another breath.

59

"What does he look like, Juan?" Sam asked, continuing their long trail-ride conversation as the two men rode side by side in the moonlight.

"Who? Santa Anna?"

"Yeah."

Juan smiled and he looked at the young man. Although they rode alone in the middle of the night, he could see Sam clearly. Over the last few days the moon had become full and bright in the clear April night's sky. The big white ball reflected back to earth enough of the sun's light to cast vivid shadows of the two men and their mounts as they traveled the empty dirt road approaching San Antonio de Bexar.

They had elected to travel on by moonlight, rather than spend another night sleeping on the ground away from home. Their scouting force had dwindled on the way back as men split off from the group and headed for their own homes. It had been a long journey, but Juan felt sure the Mexican expedition would not return. Now, although they knew their arrival would be quite late, both Juan and Sam were determined to sleep in their own beds.

In the tones of light the moon threw off, the *Tejano* thought it uncanny just how much Sam looked like Jonathan. He had noticed for some time that the more the young man matured, the more like his father he became. Juan had often mentioned his observations to Sam and the others, of course, but under this moon's light, on this solitary evening, the likeness was remarkable.

For a moment, in the quiet peace of the lonesome moonlit road, Juan almost felt Jonathan was riding slowly next to him on the way home. Juan paused, in that moment, and thought of Jonathan - and Sarah - and

Stephen Austin. He remembered back to the beginnings of the Austin Colony and the times before the war when they were all together.

A flurry of images and feelings from those days suddenly flew around inside Juan. He smiled with memories of laughter, and his chest swelled as thoughts of their dreams and plans rolled over him. He remembered the hope they all had, and the promise the future had held.

But as quickly as they took flight, those images and feelings fluttered down and landed back on the roost of reality. His friends were gone now, and things were different - some things.

Texas had won her independence from Mexico, but it was not the same place it was before. Most of the people here now had no idea who Jonathan Stevens, Jim Bowie, or Stephen Austin really were. The stories about those men didn't tell of their settling this wild land, or what they had done to make this country civilized.

Juan was saddened when he realized that, for the most part, the newcomers also knew little about the war and its sacrifices, much less why it was fought. The only thing many of them knew about the war was that Mexico, and anyone of Mexican descent, was the enemy who would slaughter and butcher if given the chance.

Few of the immigrants spoke Spanish, and most of the *Tejanos* spoke no English. Juan saw again in his heart that the simple inability to communicate had not only kept the two cultures from accepting one another, but it had also created a wall of distrust. That wall divided native Mexican born *Tejanos* to one side, and Anglo born immigrants from many different nations, on the other.

And now, the one horrid man who was the initiator, and the reason for all these things - was somehow back in power.

Santa Anna! The hair on Juan's neck tingled against his collar as he sat taller in his saddle, and thoughts of the rotten bastard filled his mind. His hatred swelled, as it did every time he considered how one man was responsible for the death of so much, and so many.

Santa Anna had extinguished the flame of democracy in Juan's Mexico. His friends the Stevens, Bowie, Austin and many more were gone now, and countless numbers had suffered, because of that one man.

As he focused on the image that looked like Jonathan riding by his side, Juan wondered if his dead friends could see all that had happened since they left. He wondered what they would think if they were here now. What would they do if they were here?

Unconsciously, Juan said out loud to his friends, "We should have killed the son-of-a-bitch."

"Yeah, well, what does he look like?" The image of Jonathan next to him responded.

"Sam," Juan said quickly, half startled, then hesitated as he returned to the bright midnight on the dirt road approaching their hometown. "He looks like a man. That's all he is, son. He's just a man."

Seguin wanted to leave the uncomfortable thoughts of Santa Anna, and return to the pleasant images of better times with his friends. He turned his face up to the full moon. It seemed so close. The darker spots against the bright surface seemed to give the image a soft texture. He felt as though he could reach up and touch the moon's delicate face. Juan's thoughts began to rise as his left hand also lifted.

"Juan?"

Seguin stopped, and kept himself in the saddle.

"I want to know what he looks like."

Juan looked back to his young friend and kept his gaze there while he spoke. "He seems - dark." Juan started off slowly, and then continued, "But, when you look at his features, he really isn't. He actually has a sallow complexion. Although his hair is black, as you would expect, it is his eyes. His eyes are deeply penetrating, and *sombrío*, so that they make it seem like he is a dark soul.

"I don't think he's what people would say is either ugly or handsome. Other than his eyes, the look of his face, to me, is rather nondescript.

"He *is* nearly six feet tall, so he can make himself an imposing figure to some, I suppose. But physically, he's not anything special, Sam. He's just a man. I promise you, you know many men bigger, stronger, and certainly better looking than Santa Anna."

Sam looked ahead as he rode silently for the next fifty yards. He turned to his friend in the moonlight and said quietly, "Guess I had him pictured as something more than that."

Juan smiled at the boy. "Before I met him, I did, too. Oh, he's a great politician. And, he's an orator who can move a crowd, without question. He tells people whatever they want to hear.

"He has convinced some that he's a god. Others think he is the Savior who was sent to protect and provide for them. To many of the lost downtrodden souls in Mexico, Santa Anna is the chosen divine leader who will bring order to their troubled lives."

The *Tejano* jerked himself upright, taking in a deep breath, which he used to spit out in anger, "But he is none of those things! He is just a wretched, greedy man who would betray his mother for his own advancement!

"Santa Anna is a bad man with power, and he'll do anything to keep his power. He's a man with no morals and no principles."

Juan took a breath and the anger in his tone changed slightly, "But make no mistake, Sam, he *is* just a man."

Seguin caught himself, somewhat surprised that his teeth were gritted together, and his face was warm with anger as he stopped talking.

Sam looked straight at Juan. The young man felt something strange moving inside, and he said softly, "My Pa said that. He said Santa Anna was a 'bad man with power'. Said that made him the worst kind. Said we couldn't let him have his way."

Sam tried to stop the tears, which caught him off guard, when they welled up in his eyes. His throat tightened. In a long time he hadn't spoken, or thought, about the conversation the last time he saw his father.

"When he left for the war, Pa promised me...y'all wouldn't let Santa Anna win."

Juan saw the pain the young man carried with the words he spoke about his father. Seguin's own throat tightened as those words brought his friend, Jonathan, back across his mind. They each rode for a short time in silence with their own thoughts as they entered the outskirts of San Antonio de Bexar. The bright moon caused the scattered outlying buildings to cast thick distinct shadows.

"We should have killed him." Juan said, at first to himself, as they turned onto an empty street.

He twisted his upper body toward Sam and spoke directly to Jonathan's son. "Everyone was afraid of making him into a martyr. We should have killed him. People forget martyrs, especially ones that are murderers."

They began passing more buildings. Juan turned his face up, and the moon lit it with her reflected rays. "We won the war with sacrifices and the blood of good men like your father. But we didn't finish it - and so now you and I, and my children, are still dealing with that tyrant pig!"

Sam looked ahead at the dull colored buildings on either side of the street. On one side, the building facades were brightly lit by the moon. Across the street, the opposite storefronts to the other side, were veiled in gloomy lightless shadows. The normally active street was completely empty because of the late hour. To the tired young man trying to get home, the stark silence created an eerie void that made it seem as though everyone in the town had disappeared.

"But we are home now, Sam." Juan said changing to an upbeat tone. "We should be talking about good, happy things - like sleeping in a real bed!"

He laughed and turned toward his young friend as they rounded a corner. Ahead they could see the little plaza their houses faced.

Sam smiled back and said, "Now you're talkin'!"

"And eating some real food!" Juan exclaimed. He tilted his head down. The *Tejano* lifted his eyes up and looked at Sam from underneath the brim of his hat as he continued sarcastically, "Prepared by a woman - who actually knows how to cook!"

"Bitch, bitch, bitch…" Sam answered in a playful defense. "You sound like Gabriel. You two wouldn't know good cookin'…"

"Sam!" Juan interrupted suddenly. "Look!"

Sam immediately jacked his eyes in the direction Juan pointed. A horrible twinge sucked at his stomach and groin as he focused on his small house. The roof had burned and caved in. Charred black smudges rose from the glassless window openings.

"Oh, my God!" left his lips. Sam grabbed a tighter grip on the reins he had been holding loosely with his fingertips. When his body lunged forward in the saddle as he started to prod his horse into a run toward the house, Juan grabbed his arm firmly.

"Sam, Max's house!"

The boy pulled himself up and yanked the reins tight to steady his horse. He looked over the neck of Juan's mount to see Maximillian's house was also burned.

"What's happened, Juan?"

Seguin looked into Sam's eyes. In the instant they held one another no words were spoken, but each told the other about his fear for their families. The next second Juan spurred his horse toward his house, and Sam raced to his own blackened rubble.

His horse was still jamming its hooves into the dirt trying to stop when Sam flew out of his saddle and landed in a dead run. He sprinted into the black hole that had been his home. Suddenly he was engulfed by an acrid smell.

His soul ached as he recognized the distinct musty odor given off from a home burned with all its belongings inside.

The young man jumped quickly around the burned black debris and the fallen timbers that were criss-crossed at odd angles. Nothing was left.

Sam exited through the front opening where their stout wooden door had been. He gasped for fresh air, trying to free himself of the foul smell and taste. After a couple of fast deep breaths, he left his horse standing in the street and ran to Juan's house.

Juan's house wasn't burned. As Sam approached, and his fear started into panic, the boy could see that most of the front windows were broken. He neared the front of the house and heard doors slamming. There were also noises that sounded like furniture being thrown around. Sam drew the Christmas knife from his belt and started into the front door.

The soft light from the full moon shining through the open doorway and windows was the only illumination inside the *Tejano's* home. Sam was in a crouch, coiled and ready to fight, as he moved away from the doorway. He stalked quietly toward the noises coming from the back of the house.

Suddenly, a door to one of the back rooms flew open. Sam's body tensed and he instinctively tightened the grip on his knife handle. Juan burst out of the room with his pistol in one hand, and the remnants of a child's broken toy stick horse in the other.

"Juan." Sam said. "Are you all right?"

Fire raged in Juan's eyes as he spun toward the sound. His pistol made a loud clicking noise and was cocked before he realized the voice came from his friend. Even in the poor light, Sam saw Juan's pistol pointed dead center at him when the *Tejano* came out of his turn.

"Juan, it's me!" Sam blurted out as he plunged into the shadows diving onto the floor.

"Sam? I almost killed you!" Juan panted.

"Juan, are you all right? What's happened here!?"

Sam got up off the floor and both men moved into the moonlight shining through a broken window.

"I don't know, son. Something terrible and, whatever it was, it happened fast." Juan quickly uncocked his pistol and shoved it into his waist sash. He looked at the broken toy he held, and then threw it violently across the room. Juan didn't look at Sam as he started briskly toward the door saying, "We've got to find Cyrus!"

The two men easily caught their tired horses in the plaza and bounded into the saddles. Sam fell in behind Juan as they raced the empty streets to Cyrus Oxford's home.

Juan was already out of his saddle and on the ground running by the time Sam stopped his horse. "Tie the horses!" Juan yelled over his shoulder as Sam jumped to the ground. In a flash, Sam wrapped the animal's leads around the hitching post and started for the house. His friend was still pounding on the door as Sam caught up.

When there was no answer, Juan tried to open the door. It was bolted shut. Even when he rammed it hard with his shoulder, the heavy door didn't budge. They both yelled the doctor's name, and kept rapping on the thick brown oak.

"Quiet! Just a minute!" They both heard Juanita Oxford's voice say cautiously. "Please be quiet!"

Both the men stepped back as Juanita undid the stiff bolts behind the big door. She pulled, and the hinges squeaked when it opened. Juanita Oxford jumped into the doorway in front of Juan, and before he could say anything, she burst out in a loud panicky whisper, "Juan, what are you doing here!? You know it's not safe!"

She moved forward more and looked behind Juan and Sam as she kept speaking rapidly, "Where is Cyrus? Where is Cyrus, Juan? What's happened to Cyrus?"

Juan grabbed the woman's shoulders gently but firmly. He looked directly into her scared eyes and said, "Juanita, we came here to find Cyrus. We just got to town. What terrible thing has happened here?"

Tears filled the woman's eyes. "Oh, Juan, Cyrus didn't find you? You haven't seen Cyrus?"

"No, Juanita. What?" Juan said with panic now in his voice.

"*Ay Dios mio*, Juan." Her eyes closed and her chin crumpled as she began to cry. "Come out of the doorway. You have to get inside. It is not safe for you out here."

Juanita looked quickly around the street before she closed the door behind Sam and Juan after they stepped into the house. While she fumbled with the dead bolts, Juan said with exasperation, "For God's sake, woman, what is going on?! What has happened here?"

When she turned to them, Juanita Oxford's hands were trembling. She started to speak and her voice shook so that Sam drew up a chair for her, in fear that she might pass out. Although she began to sob, she spoke slowly and distinctly.

"Juan, I'm so sorry. I can't tell you how sorry we all are. Cyrus tried to stop it. All the elders tried…

Cyrus went to find you. He left four days ago. He wanted to stop you before you got to San Antonio. He obviously didn't find you. It is very dangerous for you here, Juan.

While you were gone, some men brought in a captured Mexican officer. He swore that you were a Mexican citizen who had always been loyal to their cause. They supposedly produced papers to prove it. They kept spreading the lies and getting people together in groups while they yelled about it.

The town elders tried to stop it. There were vigilantes. Their crowds started turning into drunken mobs around town. It was horrible.

We got Maria, Mary Beth, Rosa, and the children out of town in the middle of the night. Gabriel is taking them away from here, to Rosa's family. They left for Laredo.

The night they left, Gabriel killed one of the vigilantes - with his bare hands. When they found the man the next day, they burned Sam's house - then Max's.

Oh Juan…That night, while we were getting the children out of town, the vigilantes, they…Juan, they hanged Max!"

Juanita Oxford's head fell forward, into her hands, and she wept.

Sam's head tingled, and he thought he was going to throw up. His body was suddenly so heavy that it wouldn't move, but his eyes still worked. They looked up from Mrs. Oxford, and across to Juan.

The *Tejano* stood motionless, except for barely discernible movement of his chest, as he took in and released shallow breaths. When his eyes moved, and looked across to Sam, all the lines on Juan's face compressed. His lips squeezed tightly together, and huge clear droplets fell from his dark brown eyes.

Each man stood empty, looking at the other, and neither knowing how to react to the shocking news. Cyrus' wife was suddenly there next to them, standing upright, and speaking with newfound strength in her voice.

"You have got to leave San Antonio de Bexar - now - both of you. If they find you here, they will hang you, too. We can't let them get you."

Juanita took Juan's hand and squeezed it. "Juan, you have got to get to the women and children. You have to keep them safe. That's the only thing you can do now, Juan. You understand that, don't you?"

"*Sí.*" Juan replied faintly, while he closed his eyes and nodded his head. When his eyes opened, he looked at the woman. The whisper, "Oh, Juanita," jumped from his lips. They hugged onto one another tightly, while Juan wept.

Soon the doctor's wife walked into the street to make sure it was clear, then motioned for Juan and Sam. She embraced each of them before they mounted their saddles.

"*Buenas suerte*, my friends," she said. Tears again filled her eyes, as the two men rode quietly into the darkness on the shadowy side of the street.

They slipped out of town undetected. On the first small rise they came to, the *Tejano* stopped and turned to look back at the town where he was born. Juan Seguin, the only man alive who fought for the freedom of Texas in battle at both The Alamo and San Jacinto, then turned away to go find his family - and take them to Mexico.

60

"I brought you some supper, Gabriel," Mary Beth called out to her friend as she approached the spindly corrals and weathered little barn on the north end of Laredo. The sun still had an hour's work to do so it caused long odd shadows to stretch out from the gaunt structures. "Figured you were 'bout to starve."

"Naw, I ain't that hungry," Gabriel answered and surprised Mary Beth with the very uncharacteristic response. He was looking toward the northeast as he spoke and walked through the powdered dust within the corral. "Sho' wish Mister Max would git on in here. Sam and the Senator ought'a be here by now, too."

As he approached the thin twisted poles that were made into the fence around the corral he turned to the young woman. Gabriel lifted both his muscled forearms, rested them on the top of the posts, and leaned forward toward Mary Beth. As he did the smell from the food she carried engulfed him. He looked from the plate, which was loaded full with beans, tortillas, and bacon, up to the girl's friendly face.

"Well," Gabriel's big bright smile burst open. "You know, maybe I ought'a eat a little somethin'. Just ta keep my strength up an' all. I thank ya' fo' this food, Mary Beth."

"You're welcome, Gabriel. Are you going to be all right out here again tonight?"

"Oh yeah, I kept pretty warm last night." He answered as he opened the gate and they both started to move toward the back of the big wagon, which was parked several yards from the animal pen. "I sho' don't like being this far from y'all women and the children though."

"I know. I don't like it either."

Mary Beth sat the supper plate onto the tailgate of the wagon. She turned to Gabriel and reached up to his shoulders with her hands.

Knowing exactly what she wanted, Gabriel put his big hands around her waist and effortlessly lifted Mary Beth up to sit on the back of the wagon. He then hopped up himself, twisting in mid-air, to sit down on the tailgate next to his supper.

"It's probably best that you're here watching our things anyway though," Mary Beth continued while Gabriel started his supper. "Besides, if anything happened, I'll bet us three women could yell loud enough for you to hear us in Galveston."

Gabriel swallowed and nodded his head while he tore a tortilla in half. "I 'magine y'all could. But y'all still keep them guns loaded, you hear?"

· "We will, Gabriel. Don't worry. Now go on and eat your supper."

Mary Beth looked to the northeast toward San Antonio as Gabriel had done. Although she couldn't show it around the other women and the children, she was desperately worried about the men. It had been a slow trip to Laredo in the wagon with the children. There was no doubt that Max should have caught up with them by now.

It had taken six days to reach Laredo. This would be their second night in the town. The man who owned the town's cantina had three rooms he rented to them for the women and children, but not Gabriel.

"The Negro will have to stay with the other animals," he had told them in a distinctly nasal voice. "I'll charge you the same as for one extra mule."

Other than going back into the desert to live out of a camp, as they had been doing on their journey, there was no choice. These were the only quarters available for rent and the tavern-keeper made sure they understood that.

Mary Beth knew three women in the desert would not be safe without more men to defend them. Still, if the long days and cold nights of their trip hadn't been so hard on the children, she would have preferred taking their chances in the desert.

She'd felt an immediate dislike for the seedy cantina owner who seemed to relish taking advantage of them. To Mary Beth he looked and acted more like a rat than a man. He had little black eyes that would never look straight at her. His long sharp nose twitched above a scraggly uneven mustache when he spoke, and his front paws constantly fidgeted in just below his chin. The repugnant little creature also asked too many probing questions.

He prodded constantly at the women, and even the children, trying to find out details about who they were and what business they had being in Laredo. It seemed much more than casual curiosity. When the platoon of Mexican soldiers arrived in Laredo just before noon today, Mary Beth knew the rat had something to do with it.

The troop had come directly to the cantina, but didn't dismount to go in and eat. Instead, the owner came out and spoke briefly with the officer. The soldiers then rode away to the other end of town. Later in the afternoon Mary Beth watched the tavern-keeper leave the cantina and walk away in the direction the soldiers had gone. Not long after he returned to the bar, the platoon of Mexican soldiers rode out of town to the west.

"You think the soldiers will be back, Gabriel?" Mary Beth asked then looked off to the west where she had watched the armed horsemen disappear into the mesquite trees.

"Don't know. I'd sho' like ta know what that bartender told 'em though. They didn't stay in town here very long."

"Yeah, I know." She answered and brought her eyes back to the wagon's tailgate. She looked into Gabriel's face and said, "I don't trust that little man. I wish we hadn't stayed here."

"He ain't a good man." Gabriel shook his head as he spoke. He sat his empty supper plate between them on the wagon's bed and turned to raise his focus back to the northeast toward San Antonio. "I ain't too sho' what we ought'a do now with…"

Gabriel stopped in mid-sentence. Mary Beth's heart stopped too. Her head snapped toward the direction of Gabriel's stare and she strained her eyes to see what he saw.

"Lordee!" Gabriel exclaimed as Mary Beth's eyes searched the distance. "Yonder comes Sam and the Senator! They comin', Mary Beth! See 'em?" He put his left hand on the top of the girl's shoulder and pointed with his whole right hand toward Sam and Juan who

326

were riding toward them from just over a quarter of a mile away to the northeast.

"Hallelujah! They here, Mary Beth!"

Mary Beth squinted her eyes. Just as the young woman picked up the image of her brother and Juan Seguin on horseback, the feeling of joy in her heart was slapped out of the way by stark terror.

"Oh my God!" She gasped as Mexican soldiers raced from the mesquite trees on either side of Sam and Juan and surrounded them.

61

"I can get you in to see them," the beady eyed rodent said in his nasal tone. He stood looking down at Mary Beth, Maria, and Rosa who were all sitting at a table in the rear of the empty cantina. Outside the mid-afternoon had become warm and still, which made the air within the dark tavern seem even more stagnant than normal.

Gabriel had taken all the children outdoors, so the women could talk. It had been two days since Sam and Juan were arrested by the soldiers and the three women had heard nothing. The only thing they knew for certain was that the two men were imprisoned in the stockade at the far end of Laredo.

"What are you talking about?" Mary Beth eyes squinted together slightly with disgust as she responded to the creature.

"I said, I can get you in to see your men." A smile spread across his lips and stretched out the rangy whiskers on his upper lip. "But, it will cost you money."

The three women looked quickly at each other then Maria raised a cold stare to the tavern owner.

"How much do you want?" She said.

"Twenty dollars. Gold."

"I'll pay it. Take me to my husband, now!"

"No, not you." The man responded quickly. "The young one. Her." He pointed to Mary Beth as he continued. "Only the daughter can come."

"I'm not *Señor* Seguin's daughter." Mary Beth said forcefully.

The bartender smiled again and said, "I know, but I told them you were."

He looked away from the girl and up to the ceiling saying in a manner that made it sound as though it didn't matter one way or the other. "Now, if you want to see them, pay me the money. If not, I honestly don't care."

The skinny little man paused then looked straight down to the three women to drive home the words, "And, you should put some food together for them. The prisoners haven't been fed for two days."

An hour later Mary Beth stood with the cantina owner as he knocked on the front door of the stockade building. She carried two covered plates of food and a bundle of tortillas tied up in a scarf. As she waited for the heavy door to be unbolted from the inside, she wished Gabriel was standing there beside her.

They had called Gabriel into the cantina after its owner had made his proposal. Gabriel wouldn't even consider letting Mary Beth go alone with the bar man. He insisted that he go along with them.

"Only the girl. I can only take the girl with me." The bartender had said. "I will take care of the young lady. You can trust me."

Gabriel knew he'd be much more likely to trust a water moccasin and refused to let Mary Beth go. Eventually, however, the women asked the cantina owner to excuse himself and give them a moment to discuss the situation in private.

When he was out of earshot Mary Beth said to Gabriel, "Listen, we've got to know what's going on with Sam and Juan. I'm not afraid to go with that little scavenger. I'll be all right. But Gabriel, we've got to think this through. What if you went with me and they arrested you, too?"

With that Rosa spoke up also. "That might be just what they want. Who'd take care of us and the children? We need you here so we'll be able to do whatever we have to when Max gets in."

Maria looked at him and said sincerely, "Gabriel, you're the only man we have right now. We can't afford to lose you, too."

Reluctantly, Gabriel had agreed.

There was a loud "*whack*", then another, from behind the stockade building's thick front door as bolts slammed back out of the way. The door swung wide open and the cantina owner led Mary Beth inside. As she entered the room she smelled the strong, distinct odor of dirty men.

"*Buenas tardes, Señorita.* I am Sergeant Gomez." A medium built soldier standing in the middle of the room greeted her. His smiling face was shiny with perspiration.

"*Buenas tardes.*" Mary Beth said quietly realizing the soldier was looking at her body rather than her face when she returned the greeting. Another soldier closed the door behind her and the solid loud thud made Mary Beth jump.

"This is *Señor* Seguin's daughter." The tavern owner said as he fidgeted his fingers under his chin. "I brought her to see her father, and to bring the prisoners some food. I told her it should be possible for you to let her back into the prisoners' cell. Could you do that for us, Sergeant Gomez?"

Gomez turned to the man and said slowly, "Well, I suppose I could."

He continued as he turned his gaze to Mary Beth and smiled, "Assuming she is willing to cooperate."

The Sergeant stepped toward Mary Beth, then started to pace a slow circle around her as he said, "As the one person with sole authority over her father and the other young man, I have to be very careful. You see, it appears those two men have committed grave crimes against the Republic of Mexico. I may have to execute them."

With those words, a chill went from the bottom of Mary Beth's stomach up through her spine to the back of her neck. She had been looking straight ahead while the soldier circled behind her. Now her face turned to the right to see him as he started to come around to that side. Her eyes followed his cautious deliberate movement until he came to a stop facing her.

"Until my Lieutenant returns, I am in charge of the prisoners." Gomez slowly extended his right hand. He turned it palm up and looked into it as though he were examining something there. "I suppose you could say that I hold their lives in the palm of my hand."

The Sergeant raised his eyes to Mary Beth and said, "That is a considerable responsibility, isn't it, *Señorita*?"

"*Sí.*"

"And we wouldn't want anything bad to happen to them, would we, *Señorita*?

"*No.*"

"That is why I must be very careful. For example, what if someone tried to hide a weapon and sneak it into those desperate men. People could get hurt, or killed, *no*?

Mary Beth looked straight ahead and nodded her head slightly.

Gomez gingerly lifted the white sack cloth that covered one of the plates of food Mary Beth held. As he peered under it he said, "You are not hiding any weapons from me, are you, *Señorita*?"

"Of course not."

"Well, you understand my position. I must check for myself. We wouldn't want any harm to come to anyone, would we, *Señorita*?"

Sergeant Gomez lifted the covers from the two plates one at a time. Then he took a wooden spoon from one of the dishes and stirred it around in the food.

"Nothing here." He said and reached for the scarf full of tortillas. He bounced the bottom of the rounded bundle in his hand then peered into the top without untying the knot.

"Nothing here." He handed the tortillas back to Mary Beth. She held the scarf at the top, like a small sack, under one of the plates of food.

"What about here?" Gomez said and smiled as he reached his hands out to Mary Beth's sides and started to pat them up and down. "Are you hiding anything from me under here, *Señorita*?"

"No." Her body muscles tensed as Mary Beth gritted her teeth together and stood still.

The Sergeant stepped closer and hooked his index finger down the top of the girl's dress bodice just below her neck. He pulled it out, bent forward, and looked down inside. He maneuvered the opening, and his head, making sure he got a complete view of Mary Beth's smooth full breasts. Then he stepped back and put a hand under each breast and bounced them in her dress material, as he had done the tortillas in the scarf, saying slyly, "Nothing in here."

"What about here?" He grinned as moved his hands to her hips. Gomez reached around behind and squeezed her hard. Then he slowly moved his hands back around her hips to the front.

Mary Beth jerked back, bending at the waist to get his hands off of her. "That's enough!" she spit. She stared at the jailer with her teeth barred and pure hatred in her eyes. Her flint-hard eyes never moved and her voice didn't falter as she repeated very slowly with anger and resolve, "That is enough!"

The shine of perspiration on the Sergeant's red flushed face had turned into droplets of sweat. He raised himself upright and looked at the two other men in the room. He saw both their faces were also flushed.

Gomez took in a deep breath and exhaled it through his mouth, which caused his red cheeks to puff out. He looked at Mary Beth then turned and smiled at the bartender. "I don't think she is hiding anything from us."

He turned back to Mary Beth saying with a smirk, "Thank you for your cooperation, *Señorita*." He kept his eyes on her and barked, "Corporal, I think we are in no danger from this lady. Please escort the *Señorita* to the cells."

There was a low heavy jingle of thick metal keys from behind her. Mary Beth looked away from Sergeant Gomez when the Corporal walked passed. The younger man went to a large door in the back of the room and unlocked it. He pushed it open and motioned for her to enter in front of him.

When Mary Beth passed through the door into the cell area, Gomez smiled at the cantina owner. The Sergeant dug into his pocket, then handed the rat two silver coins.

62

When Mary Beth walked through the doorway into the cell area of the small military stockade, she winced and stepped back from the gagging smell of human sweat and body waste. "Agh", was the sound that escaped from her throat as her eyelids batted themselves together involuntarily protesting the acid in the air. She forced herself not to drop the plates of food, because her body desperately wanted to jerk both hands to her face and protect her mouth and nose from the putrid assault.

While her body was still recoiling from the shock of the horrible smell, she heard her brother's voice.

"Mary Beth, what are you doing here!?"

She opened her eyes and tried to focus toward the sound. Mary Beth stood at the head of a wide hallway that separated rows of steel bars on either side of her. The area was even darker than the still hot room where she'd left Sergeant Gomez. As her eyes adjusted trying to find Sam, she could tell there were three cells on each side of the center walkway. They were all the same size, about eight feet square.

"Sam?"

Just then she saw the young man's face press against the bars of the last cage on the right. Juan Seguin's face appeared through the bars of the next one closer to Mary Beth.

"Juan, Sam, are you all right!?" She rushed toward the bars.

"Stay back!" The jailer shouted. His surprising command seemed to explode in the confined dark space.

Mary Beth stopped, trying to keep the food from sliding off the plates, and turned her head back to the Corporal.

"Stay away from the prisoners!" He snarled.

The twenty five year old soldier walked slowly up to Mary Beth.

"The Sergeant said I could see them!" Mary Beth spat at the man.

"Stay away from the prisoners. You can pass the food through there." He pointed to a small horizontal opening in the otherwise vertical steel bars of Juan's cell.

Mary Beth looked up and saw Juan's face looking at the guard with an intense stare filled with hate. His left eye was closest to her. She saw that it was swollen almost shut and the area between it and his temple was caked with dried blood. The sight sent a sharp hollow twinge through the deepest part of her belly.

"Oh, Juan," She grimaced. Then, gaining composure, Mary Beth said in a stronger voice, "Here, I've brought you some food." She shoved a plate through the opening in the black bars.

"Here, take it! Take it!" The girl said as Juan turned and looked into her eyes. There was a sudden mad impulse inside her. The impulse told her that she had to get the food inside the bars. She had to get the food to Juan and Sam before something bad happened.

As soon as Juan had the plate, Mary Beth side-stepped to her brother and shoved the second plate through the opening to his unit.

"Here, Sam! This one's for you!"

She quickly stuffed the bundle of tortillas in behind the plate.

Sam took the food and immediately placed it on the floor. He popped upright again and grabbed for the girl's arm through the bars.

"Are you all right?! What are you doing in here?! You shouldn't be here!"

Mary Beth reached for her brother and as she started to say, "Sam, tell me...", she felt the pain caused by the strong fingers of the guard when he seized her shoulder like a hawk clutching a small rabbit in its talons trying to crush the life out of it.

She winced and sunk her shoulder toward the man while he pulled her away from the prisoner. Sam flung his hand, making a wild swing trying to grab the Corporal's throat, but missed.

"Let go of her, you son-of-a-bitch!"

"I told you to stay away from the prisoners." The guard said sadistically continuing to pull Mary Beth away from Sam, as she was forced to her knees by his grip. He peeled his lips back into an evil smile, enjoying his control over the woman, and kept his teeth showing while he spoke in the slow domineering tone of a coward who liked to bully women. "You're not supposed to touch them. You don't listen very well, do you? I guess you think you're better than everyone else. Is that what you think? You think you don't have to listen to me?"

"Oh, please, you're hurting me!" Mary Beth grimaced while her body continued to be forced down to the dirt floor from the pain of the guard's grip. She reached for his wrist with her hands. He squeezed her shoulder even more tightly until she had to let go.

"Take your hands off that woman!" Juan Seguin demanded in a booming voice that rebounded off the dark walls. He stood with his back straight and both hands clenched into tight fists around the bars of his cell. "Now!"

The soldier started to obey, then looked up to Juan and tightened his grip on the girl's shoulder again. Mary Beth winced and cried out with the pain.

"Corporal! What are you doing?" Sergeant Gomez barked from the open doorway. "Let the girl go!"

Mary Beth felt the tight grip on her right shoulder go limp. She immediately jerked herself away from it. Her left hand tried to massage away the pain while she got up off the thick grimy dirt of the floor.

"She was getting too close to the prisoners." The guard said, in a lame try to justify his actions to the Sergeant. "She's not supposed to touch them."

The cantina owner stood behind Sergeant Gomez. He took one step to his left and his face appeared next to Gomez's shoulder as he tried to look into the cell area. The bartender reacted as though someone had slapped him in the face when the smell from the dark room reached him.

Mary Beth straightened herself upright. She continued to rub her throbbing shoulder and glared at the two men in the doorway. She told them with her face the betrayal she felt in her heart.

"I'll take care of this, Corporal." Gomez said in a solemn voice as he watched the girl's face. "You go to the well. Take two buckets. The prisoners need fresh water."

The guard left the room without looking at Mary Beth. The two men in the doorway didn't speak, just stepped aside so he could pass. Sergeant Gomez turned into the front room briefly, and then walked into the cell area carrying a simple wooden chair.

"I apologize, *Señorita*." He said. "We have treated you badly. I will leave you alone with your father now, but please, sit here."

He placed the small chair two feet away from the front of Juan's cell, on the side closest to Sam's. He gestured for her to be seated and said, "I will wait at the door. You may have ten minutes. Then you must leave."

Mary Beth sat in the chair and reached for Juan and Sam. They each stuck a hand through their cell bars and took one of hers.

"*Señorita, no.*" Gomez said firmly. She looked up and saw the Sergeant shaking his head and gesturing with his hands that she was not to touch the prisoners. Mary Beth slowly moved her hands back to her lap. Gomez walked to the doorway, pulled a watch from his uniform pocket, and nodded to Mary Beth as he checked the time.

"Mary Beth, you shouldn't be here." Sam was the first to speak.

Immediately Juan also spoke and said, "How are the children and Maria? Are they all right?"

"Everyone is fine." She said quickly. "We are staying in some rooms behind the cantina. Gabriel is there watching over them."

"*Gracias a Dios!*" Juan gasped with relief, raising his eyes upward.

"What is going on?" The anxiety in Mary Beth's voice clawed out for an answer. Her eyes teared from a mix of passion and fear as she continued, "We had to literally escape from the mobs in San Antonio in the middle of the night! Gabriel killed a man. We didn't know where you were. Max isn't even here yet!" She took several quick pants of breath while searching their faces for some reassurance, and unable to hide the growing panic in her own. "Why did they arrest you? What is happening!?"

Juan and Sam exchanged a solemn look through the steel bars separating them. They turned to Mary Beth at the same time and each started to speak. They both stopped talking immediately. Sam waited and Juan spoke up.

He said gently. "Mary Beth, you must be calm. We only have a few minutes. It's important that we use them wisely."

The young woman sat back in the chair. She closed her eyes and took in a deep breath to compose herself, while she nodded her head that she understood and agreed. When she opened her eyes she was calm, and focused. She leaned toward the two men, rested her elbows on her knees, and steeled her emotions while she nodded again for Juan to continue.

"Mary Beth, we cannot return to San Antonio de Bexar. Our homes there were destroyed."

Juan stopped. Tears filled his dark eyes and his lower lip began to quiver. He spoke slowly. "And Maximilian will not be joining us. They killed him." He swallowed hard and pressed his lips tightly together.

Mary Beth didn't change her expression or body position. She shifted her eyes to look at her little brother's face, and held them there. When she looked back to Juan, big tears were running down each of her cheeks.

"We must get to Rosa's family above *El Paso del Norte*. We will be safe there." Juan continued regaining strength in his voice.

"These people here know who I am. I am a great political prize for the commander of this region. However, they don't yet know who you two are. We can't let them find out who your father was.

"The lieutenant in charge of this detachment has gone to get a Major Esparza, who is over him. He may be the one who decides what will happen to us. I need to know how much money and jewelry you and Maria were able to bring. I will need something to bargain with."

63

"I don't want your money, Colonel Seguin." Major Ricardo Esparza said with a taunting superiority in his tone, as he moved his face to within inches of Juan's. "And I don't want your wife's jewelry, either."

Juan sat in a rough hewn wooden chair, his back rigid, with both hands tied behind him. Esparza, in his youth muscular and raw boned, was now at forty, fleshy and developing a sizable paunch to his belly. With hot breath, he spoke through chipped yellowing teeth. The foul smell coming from the officer's mouth made Juan want to stop breathing and spit, lest he be contaminated by whatever had rotted inside the other man.

The Major paused, then raised himself tall and moved his face back from the *Tejano's*. Each man's eyes were fixed intently on the other's as Esparza's voice deepened and changed to the consistency of coarse gravel.

"I want…*your soul!*"

* * * * *

Mary Beth sat on the open tailgate of the big wagon. It had remained parked next to the meager corrals across from the cantina. The vehicle's bed was still filled with the few remnants of household belongings they had quickly gathered that last night in San Antonio de Bexar. Gabriel stood beside her, bent forward at his waist, with both of his heavy forearms also resting on the tailgate.

"Just can't believe they killed Mister Max like that." He said.

Gabriel looked from the young woman out to the open area in front of them where the children meandered, rather than played. Their normal energetic activities, and associated noise, were sadly missing.

In their own ways the children were beginning the process of dealing with Maximillian's death.

In one of their rented rooms behind the cantina, Rosa was in bed. She had exhausted herself with three days of mourning and had finally drifted off to an uneasy sleep. Maria Seguin sat quietly rocking herself back and forth in an uncomfortable straight backed chair at the end of Rosa's bed.

Maria sobbed quietly. She tried to control herself, in order not to wake Rosa, but she was having little success. Maria's heart was heavy, and haunted. The news of Max's death had been devastating for them all. Her poor Rosa had emotionally fallen apart. The children, who were already tenuous from being taken from their homes, were now all the more fragile and scared.

However, Maria's tears were not only those of a refugee mourning the horrible death of a close family member. Her heart was also haunted by the fear of uncertainty - uncertainty over a new family member. Maria knew that she was at least three months pregnant.

"Gabriel, I don't know what we're going to do." Mary Beth said, as she sat on the back of the wagon and kept her gaze fixed on the little ones. "We can't just stay here from now on. With Max gone...and God knows what's going to happen with Sam and Juan...I just don't know what to do."

Her face turned away from the children and she looked at her big friend. Tears began to well up in her soft brown eyes as her chin started to tremble and wrinkle up.

The big black man kept his forearms resting on the open tailgate of the wagon while he looked straight into Mary Beth's watery eyes. "You and me got to stay real strong, Mary Beth." He said. "Everybody needs us to be strong. Sam and the Senator is liable to be...well, it's liable to be a while before they can get out and help us. The children and they mother's are mighty helpless right now. You and me's all they got."

Gabriel paused, and then gave Mary Beth his big soft smile. "Now, don't you start cryin' on me, Gal. We ain't got time fo' that. Besides, if you start cryin', then I'll start cryin'. Then we really will be in a fine mess."

His words made the girl sputter out a chuckle. Mary Beth sat up straight and reached into the front pocket of her dress for a handkerchief. She blew her nose and wiped the tears from her eyes. "Alright", she said.

"Now that's better." Gabriel smiled. "Listen, you think they's gonna' let you take some food to Sam and the Senator today?"

Mary Beth acted as though she were taking her anger out on the handkerchief as she shoved it back into her pocket. "They'd better! I'll bet Sam and Juan are starving, since they wouldn't let me in yesterday. I guarantee you those jailers didn't feed them anything."

"Yeah, well that Major fella' worries me." Gabriel said. "He's a bad man. He's the one's liable to make it hard on them boys. Don't know if you shoulda' told the Senator 'bout Miss Maria gonin' to have a baby, an all. That might just make it rougher on him."

"Dammit, Gabriel!" Mary Beth bristled. "We all talked about that before I went. Juan had a right to know. He should know about the baby. It wasn't right to keep it from him."

"Don't get mad." Gabriel said. "I know what everybody decided. Just don't want that to make it harder on the Senator while he's in they jail. That's all."

"I know, Gabriel. But don't you think…" Mary Beth's words stopped in mid- sentence when she heard a squeal from one of the children. She snapped her head toward the open area where the children were. The unmistakable voice of Sonia Seguin sounded out again in a piercing high pitched screech, "Papa! Papa!"

Instantly both Gabriel and Mary Beth saw the little girl running toward the street. Their eyes instinctively looked out in front of the fast moving child. Mary Beth jumped down from the wagon's tailgate and Gabriel stood up straight as they each saw what Sonia was running toward.

In the middle of the dusty street, Sam and Juan were walking slowly toward the cantina. Three armed soldiers followed immediately behind them.

64

"We're not leaving you here, Juan." Mary Beth said with determination. "I don't care what you say. We won't go without you."

In the warm still afternoon, all of the adults – Juan, Maria, Rosa, Mary Beth, Sam and Gabriel – sat around a worn and scarred wooden table in the back of the empty cantina. Mary Beth sat next to her brother. They were both across the table from Juan. Outside the doorway of the dingy bar the three armed Mexican soldiers stood quietly at their post.

"There is no choice, Mary Beth." Juan responded. "You must be gone by tomorrow morning. It's the only way."

"Juan, this is ridiculous. I don't understand." She said.

The *Tejano* looked at Maria, seated in the chair next to him, then reached for her hand. He took his wife's hand and pulled it toward him. Juan stared into Maria's eyes for a moment, as if seeking reassurance and support, then he looked around the table at the others.

His eyes stopped at Sam. The young man sat in filthy, torn clothes. He looked haggard and exhausted. Juan's mind flashed to the image of Sam leaning on his crutch, hobbling down the hillside from Sarah's grave, the day he and Max found them at the end of the war.

Juan changed his attention back to Mary Beth. He then spoke slowly and deliberately not only to her, but to the others also. "There is no other option." He said. "Unless I do this, they will take me to prison in Mexico City. The sentence will be indefinite.

"Then, they will certainly execute Sam. Everything we have left will be confiscated, and all of you turned out into the streets as beggars, or worse. I have no choice but to do what they want."

Juan paused. His eyes surveyed the others. He saw only hopelessness and defeat on their faces.

"In the morning you must all leave for sanctuary with Rosa's family. Sam, you and Gabriel will take the women and children to El Paso del Norte. The Mexican's have agreed to let you pass. I will follow, when I can. It is the only way."

When Gabriel spoke next, in his deep voice, everyone turned to him somewhat surprised, because Gabriel was normally a listener, rather than a talker.

"We'll do whatever you say, Senator." He said. "But Miss Maria's gonna' have a baby. You sure she can make a trip like that? I don't know where it is, exactly, but I know it's a long ways from here. This is mighty hard, dry country, too."

Gabriel's right, Juan." Rosa said. "I think we should stay here, at least until Maria has the baby."

"That isn't possible." Juan said. "I made a deal with them. It's the only way I can get all of you away from here."

"Juan," Maria spoke up, as she squeezed her husband's hand and brought her other hand over to hold both of his. "The children and I will not leave. Our place is here with you.

"If you have to do this, the children and I will stay here with you. When the time is right, we will join the others. We, the children and both of us, will go together then - together like we always have.

"Juan, I will not have it any other way."

"Then my children and I will stay with you." Rosa said. "Besides, you'll need help having the baby."

Maria turned to the other woman. "Rosa, we've all talked about taking the families to the North for a long time. You have to go. You are the only one who can get the others to safety.

"Take your children, Sam, Mary Beth and Gabriel to your people. When you are there safe, we will follow as soon as we can." She paused, then smiled a sad smile and said, "I think it's what Max would want you to do, don't you?"

A distant cloud bank softened the eastern horizon the next morning. When the sun began to rise, it shot colors of bright orange, pink and red up through the clouds. Wherever there were gaps in the cloud bank, radiant white rays streaked up toward the heavens.

"C'mon mules!" broke the dawn's early silence when Gabriel slapped the harness reins against the animals' backs and the big wagon slowly lumbered forward. Rosa sat on the wagon seat beside the big black man. In the wagon's bed, her children sat crowded between household goods and trail supplies.

Mary Beth and Sam were on horseback and rode next to one another on Gabriel's side of the wagon.

After the little band passed the outskirts of Laredo, and started to look smaller as they made their way to the northwest, Juan turned to his wife. He reached for Maria and put his arms around her.

They held one another and she sobbed quietly with her face buried against his chest.

"I wanted a better, easier life for you, Maria - and for the children." He said. Juan closed his eyes and held Maria more tightly. "Someday..."

After a moment Juan cleared his throat. He released from their embrace and kissed his wife. Juan then turned and walked toward the stockade building on the other end of Laredo in order to fulfill his bargain.

At the top of the first small rise on the road out of Laredo, Sam and Mary Beth stopped their horses. They turned them back toward the little town and started to wave goodbye again. Both Sam and his sister could see the silhouette of Juan walking in the direction of town, away from Maria.

"Think we'll ever see Juan and Maria again?" Mary Beth asked.

"Think we'll ever see Texas again?" Sam responded.

Jonathan and Sarah's children turned their horses around and started the seven hundred mile trek to the Mesilla Valley.

Later that same day, in the early spring of 1842, Juan Seguin was inducted as an officer in the Mexican Army.

PART FOUR

65

December 9, 1852

"Sho' don't seem like it's fixin' to be Christmas, does it, Sam?" Gabriel said. He patted the mule on its side as he reached under its belly for a loose end of the wagon's leather harness.

Santa Fe's cold December air condensed the moisture from Gabriel's warm breath. The big black man's words created small white clouds as they left his mouth.

"Feels like it comes around faster every year," Gabriel continued, "but it just don't seem like it ought to be comin' around so quick again."

"Yeah, Gabriel, I know what you mean." Sam answered while he backed another mule into its place on the other side of the one Gabriel buckled into the traces. "But it'll be here in a couple of weeks, an' we gotta' get our tails all the way back down to Mesilla before then. You know how Mary Beth is about Christmas."

* * * *

At arm's length Mary Beth held up the dark blue material she had been piecing together. She turned it toward the morning light streaming through the small window that was recessed into the thick adobe wall of her home's small front room. She smiled at what was beginning to look like a new shirt and said softly to herself, "Merry Christmas, Gabriel."

She turned back to the table where she and the other two women had been working and flipped the material in order to spread it out. The big shirt looked like a tablecloth as it settled down over the flat workspace. Mary Beth retrieved the threaded needle she had jabbed into a small pin cushion and began to sew.

"Gabriel will be very proud of his Christmas present." Rosa said.

She looked back to her own sewing and started once again trying to thread her needle. With the small silver needle between the fingers of one hand and the black thread between the fingers of her other, Rosa reached as far as she could out in front of herself to try to bring the tiny items together. Her forty-five year old eyes strained to bring them into focus.

"Are your arms too short, *Tia?*" Katrina asked with a big smile that threatened to turn into a giggle. "Would you like me to hold them out here for you?"

Mary Beth chuckled.

Rosa looked up from her task and gave a sidelong stare to her twenty-three year old relative. "Just wait, Little Lady. You'll get old one day, and then *your* arms will be too short."

"Oh, *Tia*, you know I'm just teasing you. You're not old." Katrina said. She looked at Mary Beth and winked. "I'm sure there are many young women…who have such short arms."

Rosa pursed her lips and gave a quick look down her nose as the two younger women laughed. She stabbed the thread through the needle's small eye, and smiled, before she held her accomplishment up for the others to see.

Mary Beth nodded her congratulations to Rosa and looked at Katrina's smiling face as she went back to her sewing. Katrina's happy, soft laugh made Mary Beth smile. Katrina had always had a wonderful laugh, even back when she was a gangly, awkward thirteen year old.

Mary Beth often thought about how much Katrina had changed in the past ten years. When Mary Beth, Sam, and Gabriel first arrived with Rosa and her children at the Melendres Land Grant in the hot summer of 1842, Katrina was just an adolescent girl who had not quite started the budding process of becoming a woman.

Over the decade that they had lived in the Mesilla Valley, Katrina had blossomed. She was now the full flower of a beautiful young lady.

"I wonder when Sam, and Gabriel, will be back?" Katrina asked. She didn't take her eyes from her sewing as she spoke.

Mary Beth and Rosa looked up at one another and exchanged small grins.

"Oh, I don't know. By Christmas I should think." Mary Beth said.

"Sam better be back before then. I mean, they've been gone a long time. He said they'd be back in plenty of time to have Christmas, didn't he?" Katrina asked. She never looked up from her sewing to make eye contact with the other women.

Sam and Gabriel had been gone for three weeks on a trip up the Camino Real to Santa Fe. They took trade goods from the area, especially the Mesilla Valley wines that had become so popular. The two men were back in the freight hauling business.

When they first arrived in the Mesilla Valley from Texas, Rosa's relatives, the Melendres family, had graciously welcomed them all into their large *hacienda*. Sam and Gabriel worked on the family's land grant for six years. They helped with the farming in the valley, and worked cattle on the open rangeland beyond the plowed fields.

After the United States war with Mexico over the annexation of Texas, more people began to move into the Mesilla Valley area. A large number were veterans who held land script vouchers for serving in the war. Texas claimed the land on the east side of the Rio Bravo, across the river from the Melendres Land Grant.

Many of the newcomers tried to homestead land that had been settled and owned for years by the local Mexican citizens. Their claims were always rejected by the courts, but nothing ever happened to the interlopers. As a result, many of the established local families had moved to the west side of the river and started the town of Mesilla in order to be on uncontested Mexican soil.

As the population grew, so did the commerce. It seemed natural for Sam and Gabriel to think about taking goods from one place to the other.

The Cavanaugh's big wagon that they had used for so long, had barely made the trip from Laredo up the Camino Real through Mexico to the Melendres Land Grant in the Mesilla Valley. Its carcass was now under a big cottonwood tree beside the Rio Bravo.

Gabriel and Sam bought and outfitted another wagon in the spring of 1849. It wasn't as well made as the old Cavanaugh wagon, but it was sound. It was also big enough to carry a good load.

"Sam will be back in plenty of time to have Christmas with us," Mary Beth said. "You miss him, don't you, Katrina?" She was happy when her younger friend looked up, and nodded.

* * * *

"I admire your knife, Mister."

Sam stopped running the reins through the top rings of the mule's harness and turned his head toward the man's voice.

"I said, I admire your knife, Mister. That there's a dandy. Been around awhile, hadn't it?"

Sam turned to face the stranger while his hand touched the handle of the knife that had been at his side since the Christmas he was sixteen years old.

"Yeah, I've had it a long time."

Sam eyed the tall man in front of him. From the way the stranger was dressed it was obvious he was one of the mountain men people talked about. They lived high in the mountains and usually trapped and traded for a living.

The fellow, who didn't look much older than Sam, had a friendly smile behind a thick blond beard. His deep blue eyes were a stark contrast to the white animal fur of his hat that also wrapped around his face and framed it. He wore a long, thick buffalo skin coat that hung down to his knees. Heavy, brown leather leggings went from there to the thick Indian moccasins on his feet.

"Well, if a fella' takes care of a good knife; she'll take care of him." The mountain man grinned at Sam as he began to pull his right hand out of a coarse sewn fur mitten. "My name is Walker. Richard Jackson Walker."

He extended his right hand to Sam.

"Stevens. Samuel Austin Stevens, and this is my partner, Gabriel."

"I'm pleased to meet you." Walker said. He shook Sam's hand, then turned and reached his hand out to Gabriel. "I'm pleased to meet both you fellas. Don't see very many Negroes out in this country. Bet you're the first one some of these folks have ever seen."

Gabriel shook the man's hand and said cautiously, "Yes, sir."

"Oh hell, Gabriel. Hope I didn't give you no offense. 'Pologize if I did."

"No, sir. No offense taken." Gabriel said.

Walker began putting his hand back into the big fur mitten. "I understand you boys have put together a bunch to head down to the Mesilla Valley."

"Yeah, we're takin' this wagon load." Sam said. "There's some more traders coming along with us to share the lookout and protection."

"Well, I got a pretty good string of horses I need to take down that way. Got a rendezvous set in Socorro to give some of them to a couple of fellas I know. Rest of 'em I intend to sell to the army at that new Fort Fillmore." Walker said. "Y'all know where that is?"

"Yeah, it's not very far from where we live down there." Sam said.

"Was wonderin' if we could throw in and make the trip down with your group?" Walker said. "I got four good men who are watchin' the horses. They know how to handle themselves in a tough spot, if you know what I mean."

"Well, Mr. Walker, we're leaving as soon as we finish getting these mules hitched." Sam said. "Where are your horses?"

"I wouldn't want to hold you up. The ponies are several miles back, between here and Taos. Y'all go ahead on. If it's all right for us to ride with you, my men and I'll catch up with you by tomorrow sometime."

Sam looked at his partner. Gabriel nodded an approval back to him.

"We'll see you on the road south, Mr. Walker, sometime tomorrow."

66

December 10, 1852

"You still see 'em back there, Gabriel?" Sam dipped his head back gesturing over his right shoulder while he held the wagon leads in each hand. He didn't look back, but kept his eyes straight ahead as he drove the slow moving wagon.

Gabriel put his hand on Sam's right shoulder to steady himself. He stood up on the wagon's floorboards and turned to look behind them to the north for the mountain man and his horses.

To the west the sun was still above the flat topped mesa on the far side of the valley. However, the straight-lined shadow it threw was approaching the Rio Bravo in the valley floor. The Sandia Mountains rising to the east were beginning to change colors indicating the first phase of the sun's daily retreat.

"Yeah, they still a good ways back there, Sam." Gabriel said. With the angle of the afternoon sun's light it was easier to see the approaching horses and men in the distance.

"Can you tell how many horses they have?" Sam asked.

"Can't really see how many, but a bunch. Seventy-five or a hundred head maybe. Still too far out to tell."

"Think we oughta' find a spot and go ahead and make camp, Gabriel, so they can catch up to us before dark?"

"That's 'probly a good idea." Gabriel said. He turned and faced forward. "How 'bout right up yonder in that big flat spot?"

Sam pulled the leads in his left hand and steered the wagon toward the open area where Gabriel had pointed. Still standing, Gabriel raised his right arm high over his head and made a large circular signal then pointed to the camp site. The drivers in the three wagons following them all nodded and trailed behind Sam's lead.

It was still an hour before dark when Richard Jackson Walker rode his big paint horse into camp. His men kept the horse herd going on down to the river to water them.

"Wasn't sure we's gonna' catch up to you boys. Y'all move along pretty good with them wagons."

"Glad you made it in before dark." Sam said. The dried beans he'd put in the big dutch oven pot were beginning to soften as the water heated. He stirred them one more time before he rose from beside the campfire.

"Sure 'preciate y'all waitin' on us tonight." Richard Walker said. He reached down his hand and Sam shook it.

"Oh, that wasn't a problem." Sam said. "These mules were so tired of Gabriel's singin' they were about to quit on me anyway."

Walker flashed a big smile as he gave Sam a warm handshake. He turned to Gabriel, who was standing by their wagon, and continued, "Well, I thank you both for letting us throw in with you and make the trip down."

Gabriel smiled back at the tall mountain man and said, "Now, don't be thankin' us too much. You ain't tasted Sam's cookin' yet, Mr. Walker.

White teeth burst into view from behind the man's thick blonde beard as he laughed full and deep at Gabriel's comment.

"So, you think Sam's cookin' is liable to be the most dangerous part of this trip, huh?"

"Mr. Walker, they ain't no doubt about that!" Gabriel laughed, too.

"Tell you what, Boys." The mounted man said still smiling as he looked from Gabriel to Sam. "*Mr. Walker* is in the graveyard back in Missouri. We buried my daddy when I was fourteen years old. My friends just call *me* Walker."

67

December 10, 1852

Walker tilted his metal plate toward the camp fire in order to catch some of its light. The bean's thick liquid residue reflected yellow firelight against the plate's dark surface. With small circular motions he used the last piece of his tortilla to mop the final remnants of bean juice. He quickly stuffed the sopping roll of day-old flat bread into his mouth, and then sat the plate by the fire as he leaned back.

"Well, Gabriel, I'll give you the fact that you're much more experienced with Sam's cookin' than I am." Walker said. "But, after lookin' at the politician end of a hundred horses since daylight this mornin', I'd say those were some damn good *frijoles*! I's about to starve to death."

"Yessir," Gabriel replied grinning, "Guess a starvin' man can usually tolerate just about anything."

Gabriel smiled proudly over his joke when Walker and the other men who encircled the warm mesquite fire laughed. He looked around at the group and continued, "But I sure hope we don't wind up havin' to eat all those horses y'all brought along. Sam never has learned how to cook a horse proper." He paused. "Usually gets 'em too salty!"

When the new round of laughter died down, Sam responded "Sure is picky, ain't he?"

"Sam, I am mighty grateful for the supper, but if it's all the same with you, I just as soon you stick to cookin' these damn fine beans." Walker said. "Horse meat gives me the colic!"

All the men laughed again.

"Well, guess we'll just have to survive on beans and bacon then." Sam said. "We've done it before, haven't we, Gabriel?"

"Yeah, seems like we've done it a time or two, Sam." Gabriel smiled. He looked at Walker and said in a serious tone, "I's just teasin' about Sam's cookin'." He paused again before his big grin burst open, "Don't think it actually has kill't nobody - yet!"

From underneath the brim of his hat Sam looked at the mountain man. "Once you get to know my partner a little, you'll notice that he only gets this feisty *after* his belly's full."

"Kinda' figured that, Sam." Walker said. "Strong as Gabriel is, don't look like your cookin' has stunted his growth too much. How long y'all been pards?"

"Oh, since I's a kid. Close to twenty years, maybe. Long time."

Walker reached for a leather bundle that was on the ground behind him. He started to unwrap it and said, "Think I could use a little dessert after that fine mess of beans." He pulled a bottle from a fur pouch and uncorked it before he held it out. "You boys like a little snort?"

"Think I would, thank you." Sam replied. He reached for the bottle, put it to his mouth and took a short pull.

"Whew! Jesus, is that stuff for drinkin', or tannin' hides?" Sam sputtered handing the whiskey back to its owner.

Walker offered the bottle to Gabriel. The big black man shook his head and waved it off with his hand. "'Preciate it. Believe I'll hold off though. Sam's liable to need me to shoot a bandit or an Indian for him tonight."

"Suit yourself." Walker said. He raised the container to his lips and took a big swig. He swallowed, and then pulled in a deep breath. "Hot damn!" Smiling at Sam, Walker said hoarsely, "It is smooth, ain't it?" He stuffed the cork back into the neck of the bottle and popped it with the palm of his hand.

"So, you're from Missouri?" Sam asked.

Walker sat the whiskey on the ground next to the small wooden crate on which he sat. "Yep, originally. My folks had a little homestead there. Wasn't much to brag about, but we got by alright. You?"

"Well, I was actually born in Missouri, too. My family moved to Texas when I was still just a baby. Grew up east of San Antonio de

Bexar." Sam said. "Lived in San Antonio for awhile before we came to the Mesilla Valley 'bout ten years ago."

The mountain man reached for the bottle and removed its cork. "Want another hit? Tastes much better after the first jolt."

Sam took another drink, just to be friendly. The liquid didn't burn his throat this time, but it felt hot as it made its way down to his stomach. He handed the whiskey back and watched Walker take his turn.

"So, you lived out here long?" Sam asked.

"Yeah, left home when I was sixteen and joined a trader's wagon train that was passin' through headin' west on the Santa Fe Trail. Thought I needed to see more country than the little drink-water towns in Missouri. Wanted a little more adventure. Couldn't take the idea of my life bein' nothin' but scratchin' dirt and sloppin' hogs on some little farm somewhere."

"Then you been out here ever since?" Gabriel asked.

"Well, Gabriel, mostly." Walker chuckled. "Taos, up towards the high country, has sorta' been our headquarters for the past ten years, or so. Done a lot of travelin' though.

"Not long after I got out here I met an older kid from Missouri named Christopher Carson. We were camp swampers and skinners together, then gradually worked our way up to meat hunters and trappers for different outfits. Guess he's the closest thing I ever had to a real partner. Anyway, we wound up coverin' a lot a ground together."

"You're not talkin' about Kit Carson, are you?" Sam asked seriously.

"Well, yeah, you know Kit?" Walker answered.

"No, I don't." Sam said. "But he's getting' to be a pretty famous man out in this part of the world. War hero and all. Is it true he's blazed a trail out to California before?"

"Shit." Walker said. "Is that true? Hell, I been cross country with him from here out to the Pacific Ocean - twice!"

"You've crossed all the way to California from here?" Sam was impressed.

"Yep, I was on the first two mapping expeditions with Kit and Fremont. John Fremont was just a Lieutenant the first time we met him. I missed the third trip 'cause I had a broken leg. That's when the war with Mexico broke out.

"Kit was still gone to California when General Kearney came up the Santa Fe Trail from Fort Leavenworth to take this part of the country for the Union. My leg was healed up by the time they came through, and Kearney hired me on to guide 'em.

"He took Santa Fe pretty easy, left some troops there, and then we headed south. When we got to Socorro, where I need to be tomorrow or the next day, we met Kit on his way back from California with dispatches for President Polk in Washington.

"Ol' General Kearney got pissed off when he found out the war in California was about over. He made Kit turn around and take him and some of the troops back out there. They sent me on south with Colonel Alexander Doniphan and the rest of the outfit to capture Chihuahua."

"So you fought in the war?" Gabriel asked.

"Had our first fight down where y'all live in the Mesilla Valley, at *Brazito*." Walker answered. "I wound up gettin' traded to different outfits as we kept movin' deeper into Mexico. Made it all the way down to Mexico City when the war ended."

"Guess you have done some travelin'." Sam said.

"Yep, 'bout got it out of my system, I think." Walker said. "That's just what I told Kit. Dumb son-of-a-bitch is getting ready to drive six or eight thousand head of sheep from here to California."

"What?" Sam asked, shocked.

"Yeah," Walker said shaking his head and pulling the cork from his bottle. He held the whiskey up to Sam momentarily. When Sam declined, the mountain man took a big drink and swallowed hard before he continued. "With all the gold fever out in California, he thinks he's gonna' drive six or eight thousand head of sheep out there and sell 'em for a fortune. Told him I didn't want any part of it."

"Eight thousand sheep…from here to California?" Sam was dumb founded.

"Oh, he'll do it." Walker said. "Once that tough little bastard sets his mind to somethin'; he'll get her done."

Walker shook his head, took a short pull from the bottle, and smiled. "Don't get me wrong, fellas. Money's not a bad thing. Hell, I like it just as much as the next man. There just ain't enough of it to get me to jack with eight thousand sheep from here to California!"

Sam laughed. "I don't blame you. That sounds crazy."

"Yep, that's exactly what I told Kit.

"He told me I was getting' like an old woman. No spirit for adventure. Think that's when I told him he could stick every one of those sheep up his ass!

"Anyway," Walker took another quick nip from the whiskey bottle. "Kit's hell bent on taken them sheep to California. I took my part of our poke and put it in these horses.

"I'm gonna' spend the winter down south where it's warm. I swear I'm gettin' mighty tired of freezin' my ass off up in them lonely mountains every winter, too."

The tall mountain man paused as if digesting the words he'd just spoken. He stuffed the cork back into the whiskey bottle and looked up.

"Shit. Don't think that maybe I am turnin' into an old woman, do ya'?"

68

December 11, 1852

"Y'all got any water on this wagon?" Walker asked as he rode his big spotted horse up to Sam's side of the wagon. The sun was high. The large horse herd and the small band of traders had been moving since shortly after daylight.

Sam looked at Gabriel, and grinned. "Little thirsty today, Walker?"

"Aw shit." Walker stuck out his tongue and rolled his eyes. "I feel like a stepped on buffalo chip. Think I'd trade this horse for a bucket of water and a shady spot."

"Well, if we needed a tall paint horse, Gabriel and I might give you some of this cool water we have in this great big canteen here." Sam pulled the large canteen from under the wagon's seat. "But, I'm not sure what we'd do with an extra horse. What do you think, Gabriel?"

Gabriel just looked at Sam and grinned, then popped the reins on the mule's backs.

"If my head didn't hurt so bad, that'd almost be funny enough to laugh at, Sam. Now, give me a drink of that ga'damn water." Walker said as he reached out for the canteen.

While they kept moving, Walker took the large tin container from Sam. He put it to his lips, tilted his head back, and took deep swallows. After the last huge gulp, Walker let out a deep throated "Aghhhhh".

With one continuous motion of his left hand the sweating frontiersman swept the white fur hat from his head and stuck it on the front pommel of his coarse-made saddle. With his right hand he lifted the burlap covered canteen high over his head and turned it up. Water flowed down over his thickly matted, long blonde hair. Walker looked up, and momentarily took the water flow directly into his face.

"Phaaa…son-of-a-bitch." Water flew through the air from the front part of the mountain man's thick beard as he brought the canteen down from over his head. He put the canteen back to his lips and sucked down several more large gulps. He stopped and burped loudly, then took a few more big swallows.

"Never know what you're gonna' get in a bottle of homemade whiskey." Walker said. "Guess that sum'bitch last night was a little green."

Sam laughed looking at his new friend. "You must be right. Guess maybe that's why you're lookin' a little green around the edges today."

"You oughta' see how spoiled it looks from this side." Walker said, rubbing his head. He stuffed the furry cover back onto his head and handed the canteen to Sam.

"Next time we stop, I'll ride down to the river and fill your water jug." Walker smiled. "If I don't founder on all this water, I might just make it now. Thanks for takin' pity on me."

Sam raised himself up on the wagon's floorboards to take the canteen back. He smiled as he shook his head. He turned to Gabriel. From the big grin on his old friend's face, Sam could tell that Gabriel liked the cut of this rough man they'd just met.

"Socorro's not far up yonder. It's between those buttes where the valley gets narrow." Walker said.

"Yeah, we been through there. Lots a times." Sam said. He was suddenly annoyed that Walker apparently didn't understand that he and Gabriel had been up and down the *Camino Real* many times before.

"Oh hell, Sam, I know that. But there's something I gotta' tell you before we get there." Walker said. "I need to explain…"

"Indians!" A high pitched voice screamed from the next wagon twenty feet behind Sam. "There's Indians up there! Get your guns out!"

"Don't shoot, gadamit!" Walker boomed as he jerked his horse short and wheeled it around.

His spirited horse was high stepping and ready to bolt when Walker turned over his shoulder and looked back to Sam and Gabriel. They each already had a long gun in their hands.

"Don't shoot!" Walker pushed the palm of his left hand towards them. "Shit! That's what I was startin' to tell you. This is who I'm supposed to meet here!"

Walker turned back to the other wagons behind them. He screamed. "For God's sakes, don't shoot!"

69

December 11, 1852

"God dammit, Stevens, what the shit's goin' on here?!" The craggy faced trader said as he pulled his wagon even with Sam and Gabriel's rig.

The two other wagons pulled forward and tucked in closely behind them. The animal teams fidgeted at the maneuver while brakes were set and men piled out of the wagons. The whole group, armed with an impressive conglomeration of shotguns, rifles and pistols, moved on foot to the front of Sam's wagon.

"What's that son-of-a-bitch doin'?" One of the men asked as he approached.

"It's only three Indians, let's shoot 'em!" said another.

"Just hold up 'till we find out what's goin' on." Sam said loudly. "Not sure what this is, but Walker said to sit tight 'til he gets back. I don't want to start somethin', but everybody keep your guns out... and ready."

A couple of hundred yards to the east, even with the wagons, the horse herd had stopped and the animals were beginning to graze. Walker's men remained at their spots, positioned around the horses. Like every one of the traders, the mountain men all watched Walker ride his large paint up to the three Apache braves who sat horseback on a small rise less than a quarter mile to the west.

Walker and the Indians remained mounted while they spoke and gestured with their hands and arms. To those who watched it seemed like a long time before Walker turned his horse and rode it slowly back toward the wagons. When he was halfway back, the three Apache turned and disappeared over their small hill.

The man still seated in his wagon next to Sam and Gabriel's was middle-aged and leather skinned. The desert sun and wind had worn deep vertical grooves into his darkly tanned face. The tops of those creases met with other horizontal fissures in the skin's surface that had been caused by years of squinting against bright cloudless desert skies.

"Explain yourself, God dammit!" The leather faced freight hauler demanded as Walker approached the crowd of traders. "What the hell you got goin' on here! You drag us into a ga'damn bushwhack, or what?"

"Take it easy, Mister." Walker raised his right hand towards the man. "An' don't do nothin' rash. I told everybody I had a rendezvous set down here before we left Santa Fe."

"You're tradin' with them damn Indians?" The wagon driver questioned coarsely.

"Shit." Walker said. "I been tradin' with 'em since before any of you ever got out to this country.

"I'm gonna' give 'em a few of these ponies, then be on my way. Doesn't have to concern any of you. Y'all can just keep movin' on south with your wagons if you want to."

A voice from the crowd said, "It was only three Indians. We shoulda' shot 'em when we first saw 'em. That's what I say."

Walker looked sternly toward the voice. "Now that'd a been a mighty stupid move." He said slowly. "Them three were just a small scoutin' party, checkin' to see where we were with these horses.

"There's two different Apache Chiefs, with braves from each of their tribes, camped up yonder by Socorro waitin' on me. If you dumb bastards had killed those three young boys for no reason, you'd be fightin' like hell to keep your hair right now."

"If there's Indians around here, I say we turn around and get the hell back to Santa Fe!" One of the traders said as he jerked the barrel of his shotgun toward their back trail.

"I'm with you! They can pay some other dumb sumbitch to get scalped for this load." Another wagon's mule tender said. "They ain't payin' me enough for this shit."

More scared men chimed into the rough chorus.

Sam and Walker looked at each other. Sam said, "What is this, Walker? These Apache raid and murder our people all the time."

"Sam, there's different Apache. I can pretty much tell you this bunch doesn't make war on the whites. Not down where y'all live." Walker said.

"Indians is Indians. Murderin' bastards are all the same. They can all go to hell, and you can too, Mister! Yaaah, mules!" The rough faced wagon driver yelled and whipped his animals into a turn away from Sam and Gabriel. "I ain't getting' my ass killed on this trip. I'm goin' back. To hell with all of you!"

There was another rough grumbling chorus of "I'm goin' with you.", "Me, too.", and "This is bullshit!" from the men gathered around the front of Sam and Gabriel's wagon as they all turned and started toward their rigs. Gabriel's mules tried to move when the other wagons began turning around and he pulled the reins tight to hold his team steady.

Walker looked at Gabriel, and then at Sam. "I'm goin' on to Fort Fillmore when I'm done up here." He said. "You boys are welcome to come along. You won't have no trouble from these Apache here. You can trust me on that, but I understand if you want to turn around and head back to Santa Fe with these others."

70

December 15, 1852

"See the two out in front? The one on the right is named *Mangas Coloradas*, 'cause of the red sleeves on his shirt. You'll see 'em when they get in here close enough." Walker said to Sam while they stood by their morning campfire, each with a cup of coffee. They watched with Gabriel as a mounted group of twenty-five or thirty Apache men rode toward them from three quarters of a mile away to the west.

"*Mangas Coloradas* is the Chief of the *Membres* Apache. They range in the *Gila*, all that country back behind them there to the west.

"The one on the left is *Cochise*, his son-in-law. *Cochise* is the Chief of the *Chiricahua* Apache tribe. They run farther south mostly, due west a ways from where y'all live down in Mesilla. They go from there way over towards California. Both tribes use the *Gila* as their hunting grounds though.

"Their two tribes are part of a bigger bunch all called the White Mountain Apache, after some big mountains way farther on west of here. Like I tried to explain before, the ones who give y'all so much hell down in the Mesilla Valley are mostly the *Mescalero* Apache. They range to the east of the *Rio Bravo*, out of those pine mountains on past the big white sands.

"Although they don't have no set boundaries or anything, the *Rio Bravo* is kinda' the dividing line between the different tribes of the White Mountain Apache and the *Mescalero* Apache. *Mescalero* just seem to be a meaner bunch, probably 'cause they've had more problems with the whites movin' into their territory.

"I've known ol' *Mangus Coloradas* for a long time. Don't know his son-in-law that well, though." Walker paused and sipped his coffee. He never took his eyes from the approaching Indians.

"What's gonna' happen when they get here, Walker?" Sam asked.

"Well, we're gonna' talk…and be real friendly. When I introduce you and Gabriel, I want y'all to give the two Chiefs each a bag of that tobacco and a bag of that sugar I laid out this mornin'. Make damn sure you give *Mangus Coloradas* the biggest bags." Walker said grinning.

"They're all just regular men, so treat 'em that way. But be sure to show respect to *Cochise* and *Mangus Coloradas.*

"They'll probably want to sit for a while and smoke some of that tobacco, so we can visit and catch up on the news. I gotta' tell 'em about Kit comin' through some of their country with all them ga'damn sheep."

Sam and Walker finished their coffee while they watched the approaching Indians. When the group was within a hundred yards, Walker raised his right hand high and called out a greeting.

"Raise your right hands high, boys, and smile." Walker said. "It's kinda' like a courtesy to welcome 'em into our camp, and show that we ain't holdin' no weapons."

Walker turned his head and looked at Sam and Gabriel. When he saw the apprehension and anxiety showing on both their faces he grinned real big and said, "Now, just be friendly like some of your momma's strange kin folk just showed up for a visit."

He walked a few paces toward the two Chiefs as they pulled their ponies to a stop. *Mangas Coloradas* and *Cochise* dismounted and came on foot toward Walker. The rest of the Indians stayed on their horses.

Sam watched the mountain man extend his right hand to *Mangus Coloradas*. He'd never thought about Indians shaking hands, and watched curiously as the two men grabbed each other's wrists. Although he couldn't understand the words they were saying, the tone was that of two old friends who hadn't seen one another for a long time. They held each other by the wrist with their right hands, and each clasped the other's shoulder with their left.

After Walker exchanged the same type greeting with *Cochise*, he turned and gestured for them to come meet his friends. He spoke several words in Apache then said, "Sam Stevens."

Sam extended his hand and *Mangus Coloradas* grabbed his wrist firmly. Sam took the Apache Chief's wrist while looking him in the eyes, then smiled and said, "Pleased to meet you."

When the Chief released his grip, Sam looked at Walker. "That's the way to do it, Sam." His friend said. He turned and spoke out boldly. "Now, this is the great Chief of the *Chiricahua Apache, Cochise*."

Cochise was a tall handsome man with features much finer than the other Chief. *Cochise* smiled as he reached to take Sam's wrist and mimicked, "Pleased meet you." His hand was large and his grip was strong.

Sam returned his smile and said, "Pleased to meet you, *Cochise*."

When Walker introduced Gabriel, *Mangus Coloradas* hesitated as the big black man stuck out his right hand. He reached tentatively and took hold of Gabriel's thick wrist. Gabriel wrapped his hand almost completely around the Indian's wrist, and then smiled.

The Chief looked down at Gabriel's hand as they held one another. *Mangus Coloradas* brought his left hand up and rubbed the skin on the back of Gabriel's hand. The Indian then turned his palm up and looked to see if any of Gabriel's skin color had rubbed off on his fingertips.

Mangus Coloradas looked up into Gabriel's face and studied its features with obvious curiosity. Gabriel was nervous but kept eye contact with the Indian and smiled again slowly, showing his bright white teeth. When *Mangus Coloradas* gingerly turned up the corners of his mouth into a smile, Gabriel realized the Indian Chief was also nervous.

The Chief kept his firm grip on Gabriel's wrist and reached with his left hand and touched his own hair. He turned his head to Walker and said something in Apache, and then pointed to the top of Gabriel's head.

"He'd like to see your hair, Gabriel. Would you mind takin' off your hat?" Walker said.

With his left hand Gabriel slowly removed his hat and held it down to his side. When the Indian saw the coarse, tightly curled hair under the dark man's hat, the smile left his face. He reached up to touch it then stopped. He looked at Gabriel as if asking permission.

Gabriel, still smiling, nodded his head then tilted it slightly forward toward *Mangus Coloradas*. The Chief touched Gabriel's hair, and then ran his fingers through it. He turned and said something to *Cochise*. Then he turned and spoke loudly to his braves who were behind him still sitting on their horses. Finally, he turned and spoke to Gabriel while he looked directly into the black man's eyes, then squeezed his wrist before he released his grip.

Walker came over to Gabriel and patted him solidly on the shoulder as he said with a good hearted chuckle, "Well, Gabriel, guess you're the new hero here. *Mangus Coloradas* thinks you're part buffalo. He says you are blessed by the Great Spirits…a man of honor."

When Gabriel looked awkward and turned to Sam, his friend smiled and winked. He turned back and was introduced to the other Apache Chief.

"Go get the tobacco and sugar, Sam." Walker said while *Cochise* was taking his turn touching Gabriel's hair.

Sam wound up making two big pots of coffee that morning while they sat around the fire with the band of Apache. The Indians enjoyed putting their new sugar into the cups of hot liquid and passing them around. They also passed around the tobacco pipes that Walker and *Mangus Coloradas* produced from their bags. The biggest entertainment of the morning, however, was touching Gabriel's hair. Every brave had to do it, at least once.

Walker gave the Apache Chiefs twenty horses. Ten were from Kit Carson, as a token of respect so that he could bring his eight thousand sheep through their homelands. Walker laughed when they discussed Kit's venture.

"They think the 'Little Chief' is crazy, too." He said.

"'Little Chief'?" Sam asked.

"Yeah, '*Vi-hui-nis*', that's what they call Kit." Walker said. "Oh, they show him great respect. He's a straight talker and a tough son-of-a-bitch. But, shit, he ain't barely five and a half feet tall."

Sam was shocked. From the stories he'd heard, Sam pictured Kit Carson much differently.

Walker let the two Chiefs pick the twenty horses they wanted. He, Sam, and Gabriel stayed by the campfire while the Indians rode out and cut the animals from the herd. When they were done, *Mangas Coloradas* and *Cochise* rode back to say their good-byes, and thanks, while the braves started to herd the horses west toward the Gila.

As the two Apache Chiefs turned their horses and started to ride away, Sam asked Walker, "I can understand Kit Carson's deal, but why'd you give them ten horses?"

"Well, Sam, some of it was pay-back. They were mighty nice to me the last time I stayed with 'em a couple of winters ago.

"Guess respect was part of it. Most people think of 'em as godless savages, but they're damn honorable men...when you get to know 'em a little. And, we're all trespassin' on their land, if you really want to know the truth.

"Some of it was insurance, too, I guess. I kinda' like to come and go as I please." He turned to Sam and smiled. "Never does hurt a fella' to have a friend or two in a pinch, does it?"

Walker stretched and raised both arms over his head. He turned to Gabriel and said boldly," Well, Mister Buffalo Spirit Man, quite a mornin', wadn't it? Did those heathens rub you bald headed?"

"Don't think so." Gabriel laughed. "But they sho' tried, didn't they?"

"Yeah, this was a hell of a morning!" Walker exclaimed. "Think I'll pull the cork outa' that bottle of green whiskey and we'll have ourselves a little "reward"! Then let's go see who's doin' what down in the Mesilla Valley. That suit you two all right?"

71

December 22, 1852

"The only other place with a bottom rocky enough to cross with this big wagon is down below Mesilla." Sam said loudly to Walker as Gabriel spanked the reins on the mule's backs. The loaded wagon lumbered up the far side riverbank following the ruts worn from the trips many other wagon's had made in and out of the *Rio Bravo*.

Once on top, Sam and Gabriel halted the wagon and waited for the horse herd to cross. The riders let the animals stop and drink deeply from the river before they pushed them across to the west side. As the herd started up the bank, Walker rode his large spotted horse up to the wagon.

"That's the *Melendres Hacienda* over there." Sam said pointing to the west. "We'll go by and say "hello". I'm sure they will let you graze the horses on their land 'til in the morning. Tomorrow I'll take you down to Fort Fillmore and introduce you to the Colonel in charge."

Some of the horses had gotten into the deeper water on the crossing. The whole group had to wait while the wet ones rolled and dusted themselves in the dry desert sand above the river bottom. Once the horses were through wallowing, it took another half an hour to reach the large Melendres compound.

"Sam! Sam, you're back." Katrina Melendres called from the front doorway of the main house when the freight wagon pulled up. She ran toward the wagon. Along the way she started wiping her hands on her long apron, then switched tasks and began primping her hair as she kept advancing.

Sam jumped out of the wagon and moved quickly toward Katrina. Walker turned and looked at Gabriel. The big black man smiled broadly back at Walker and said, "That'd be the main reason we stopped by here. Miss Katrina."

"Yep, I can understand that. She's a nice lookin' girl." Walker said.

"Yeah, they pretty sweet on each other." Gabriel said, and set the wagon brake.

"Sam, I'm so glad you're back." Katrina said. She reached both her hands out and Sam took one in each of his. "You've been gone a long time. We missed you. Mary Beth and I have been together almost everyday since you left."

"Well, Mary Beth said that if we didn't make it back before Christmas, we might as well just stay gone." Sam said. "I missed you, Katrina. Is everyone all right?"

"Yes, everyone is fine. And, now that you and Gabriel are home, we can all enjoy Christmas. I was worried about you this time, Sam."

"You know better than to worry about me and Gabriel." Sam said. He turned, releasing Katrina's right hand. "Come here, I want you to meet someone." Sam kept her left hand in his and led her toward the wagon.

As they approached Walker dismounted. Katrina smiled at Gabriel. "Welcome home, Gabriel. How was the trip?"

Gabriel remained seated in the wagon, but politely removed his hat. "It was a fine trip." He said smiling. "Mighty fine trip. How you doin', Miss Katrina?"

"I'm just grand." She said. "I'm so glad y'all are back."

Sam stopped in front of his new friend. "Walker, may I present *Señorita* Katrina Melendres. Katrina this is Richard Walker. He made the trip down with us from Santa Fe."

Katrina extended her right hand and said, "I'm very pleased to meet you, Mr. Walker. Welcome to our *hacienda*."

Walker removed his fur hat. He gently took Katrina's small hand in his and his deep blue eyes looked directly into her dark brown ones. "The pleasure is surely mine, Miss Melendres." Walker said in Spanish with a gallant tone that surprised Sam. "You are very gracious."

Katrina was struck by the fact that the tall man was dressed more like an Indian than a white man. His leather clothes weren't shabby, but he looked un-kept and wild. His very thick blonde beard and his deep blue eyes didn't seem to fit at all with his costume. However, she did see that behind all the hair on his face he had a nice friendly smile.

"Katrina, Walker lives in the mountains north of Santa Fe. He runs with Kit Carson." Sam said. "He's brought some horses down here to sell to the Army. Wait 'til I tell you about the Indians we met on the way down here."

"You ran into Indians?" Katrina gasped.

"They weren't hostile." Sam said. "Friends of Walker's, actually. Anyway, we'll tell you all about it later.

"I need to talk to your father now. Is he around? Need to ask him if Walker can bed down his horse herd on your land tonight.

"Then we gotta' get this wagon to town and unload it. Have to let Mary Beth know we're back and tell her Walker is spendin' the night with us."

* * * *

"I don't want that smelly mountain goat staying in this house!" Mary Beth whispered loudly, and emphatically, to Sam. They were behind the closed door of her bedroom in the modest adobe home they had built not far from the Mesilla Plaza.

"He's my friend, Mary Beth. He's a good man. I like him." Sam whispered back angrily.

"Well, he may be a good man, and I'm glad you like him, but he's dirty and he smells bad! He's so hairy he probably has fleas and lice, too. I'll never get the smell of that man out of this house now. If he slept here I'd have to burn the sheets!"

"Mary Beth, you're bein' ridiculous! Me and Gabriel are dirty and smelly from the trip, too." Sam said.

"Yes, you are." Mary Beth shot back. "But not like him. You two are going to take a bath and clean up tonight. I don't think there's enough soap in this whole town to get that man clean!"

"You're embarrassing me. I've invited him to spend the night with us and that's all there is to it!" Sam's loud whisper hissed and sputtered. "He's gonna' be our guest."

Sam walked out of the bedroom by himself.

Before he could say anything, Walker said, "You know, Sam, I been worryin' about those horses out there this close to town with only four men watchin' 'em. I sure appreciate your hospitality, an' all, but I think I better run back out there and help watch 'em tonight.

"I'd feel like a real sorry ass to get those ponies all the way down here and have somethin' happen to 'em. Maybe I can take you up on your offer of a bed after I get them horses sold off. I'll come by an' get you in the mornin', and we'll ride down to that Army Fort.

"Tell your sister I'm real sorry about her flower pot, an' all." Walker said shyly, then turned and walked out the door.

Walker had not gotten off to a good start with Mary Beth. When they arrived in Mesilla, Sam had burst into their house boldly declaring that he and Gabriel were home as he led Walker into the front room. Mary Beth was sitting at the table putting the finishing touches on the shirt she'd been sewing as a Christmas present for Gabriel.

Although it was still before sundown, the evening temperature was starting to drop so Walker had donned his big buffalo skin coat when they rode into town. With the coat on Walker looked like a grizzly bear when he entered the adobe home's small doorway. Their unannounced entry surprised Mary Beth and she scrambled to hide the shirt before Gabriel could see it.

Gabriel came into the room behind Sam and Walker. When she saw him enter Mary Beth said, "Gabriel, stop! Don't come in here!"

Surprised, Walker turned toward Gabriel. When he turned, his buffalo coat knocked from the table the cup of tea Mary Beth had been drinking. Walker heard the china tea cup shatter as it hit the floor, and he turned back toward Mary Beth. With that movement, his big coat tipped the table's flower vase that Mary Beth had filled with aromatic sage and creosote sprigs.

Walker grabbed wildly for the flower vase as it started to fall. The water it held began to spill across the table. Mary Beth pulled the big shirt up quickly with both hands to keep it from getting wet.

With the fingertips of his large hands the mountain man got the flower pot up off the table as he tried valiantly to control the spinning glass container. He bobbled the vase back and forth between the fast moving digits of each hand like a man who'd just been thrown a hot biscuit.

The urn was still dancing through the air, as if trying to escape the grizzly bear, when all its contents came out and landed on Mary Beth's bosom. Sage and creosote stayed atop her full breasts while the water quickly ran down to her lap, and onto Gabriel's present. The vase continued its getaway and Walker lunged after it as Mary Beth reacted to the cold water with, "Aghhhh!"

Off balance when the nice flower holder finally crashed loudly onto the floor, the mountain man and his big coat bumped into the pantry shelf hanging on the wall. The end they hit came loose from the adobe mud bricks. The shelf sagged to one side and fifteen jars of the peaches, that Mary Beth and Katrina had pickled during the summer, slid off and burst on the floor in rapid-fire succession.

Walker stood looking at the beautiful woman sitting wet and wide-eyed behind the table, her mouth open in shock at the sudden destruction of her home.

"Sure is a mighty pretty shirt you're makin' there, Lady." He said.

72

December 23, 1852

Father Carlos Ropa walked to the doorway to check on his superior. The bright young priest had been assigned to serve as secretary to Mexico's aging Cardinal. The astute twenty-four year old knew that it was an important position politically. He was privilege to all the Cardinal's responsibilities both within and outside the Church and he knew that would be helpful in securing his future within the clergy.

Some, however, viewed his work as no more than that of a glorified *mayordomo*, a butler, because he also saw to all the old Cardinal's personal needs as well. That didn't bother Father Carlos. He actually enjoyed making sure the Cardinal was properly cared for. He truly liked the old man. He had become his elder's confidant, and friend.

Ropa stood silently in the doorway that led from the Cardinal's personal quarters into the small outside courtyard. The Cardinal often took his breakfast or evening meals out there because he liked the smell of the flowers and the quiet of the peaceful setting. Ropa's superior sat alone at a small round table. He was leaning back in his chair with his eyes closed and his face turned upward, as if absorbing the morning sun.

It appeared the breakfast on the table in front of the aged man was untouched. The young priest started into the courtyard to encourage the elder to eat something, but stopped himself. He suddenly suspected the Cardinal might be contemplating the large Christmas Mass he had been preparing. For a moment Carlos Ropa watched the front of his elderly friend's robe to make sure he was breathing, and then slipped back out of the courtyard.

Cardinal Eduardo Bustamante had not slept all night. After his dinner conversation with Lucas Alaman, he couldn't. Alaman was the leader of Mexico's conservative party that would soon take over control of the legislature in January. At the elegant state dinner the Cardinal learned of Alaman's plans for their country. Eduardo had felt physically sick ever since.

This morning Eduardo sought the sanctuary of his little garden patio in an attempt to give his worried soul some rest. He tried to take his thoughts to the Christmas sermon he'd looked forward to giving. As he thought through the words, his mind looked out over the imaginary congregation in front of him. There in the special pew, listening to his Christmas message, he saw the battered Ines, Santa Anna's wife.

His mind left the Christmas service and wandered to the funeral mass he'd conducted for Ines. He remembered how heartsick he felt over her early death. Eduardo's blood began to rise over thoughts of the woman's life made dreadful by her vile husband. His mind flooded with the memories of Santa Anna.

Less than a month after Ines was buried, *El Presidente* married again. The tyrant knew that Cardinal Eduardo Bustamante would condemn the marriage and not perform the ceremony so he forced another priest to do the service. At the wedding another man even stood in his place representing the almost fifty year old Santa Anna when he was married to Dolores de Tosta. The bride was fifteen years old.

Santa Anna had again been a corrupt abomination as the country's leader. He liked the celebrity and trappings of the Presidency, but not the work. He periodically took leaves of absence or simply turned the Presidency over to others, then always came back to resume his dictatorial rule.

A year after Ines' death, while Santa Anna was on a leave of absence from the Presidency, *Mariano Parades y Arrillagra* led a rebellion in *Guadalajara* against the government. Without the consent of the Congress, Santa Anna gathered an army to lead against *Parades.* However, disillusioned and unpaid, Santa Anna's army deserted.

Santa Anna fled to the rugged mountains of his native state and hid. *Parades* assumed the Presidency. When government troops apprehended Santa Anna in 1845, he was exiled to Cuba and forbidden to return to Mexico.

That same year the United States annexed Texas. *Parades* raised an army of thirty-two thousand men, which was four to six times larger than the U.S. Army, and declared war on the United States. When the fighting began along the Rio Bravo, Mexico lost the first three engagements.

Santa Anna monitored Mexico's situation from his exile in Havana. As the hostilities increased he corresponded with the President of the United States, James K. Polk. Santa Anna convinced the American President to allow him through the U.S. warship blockade at the port of *Veracruz* by promising to produce a truce and a peaceful settlement with Mexico.

Upon his arrival in *Veracruz*, Santa Anna proclaimed the reestablishment of the Democratic Constitution of 1824. *Parades* was removed from office and Santa Anna assumed the Presidency of Mexico. He also took command of the Mexican Army and led it against the United States.

It had been another horribly devastating war for Mexico. Santa Anna turned the office of President over to his Vice-President and marched his army north to Buena Vista to attack the American forces under General Zachary Taylor. When they engaged, for two days, the armies fought to a standstill.

At the end of the second day of battle, Santa Anna's officers informed him that his soldiers were exhausted and virtually out of food and water. Santa Anna also learned that the American's General Winfield Scott had landed in *Veracruz* and would likely move on Mexico City. In his arrogance Santa Anna became concerned that another Mexican General would have the glory of repulsing an American invasion of Mexico's capitol.

That evening Santa Anna withdrew his army from the field of battle and turned toward Mexico City. While his army marched back, Santa Anna raced to Mexico City ahead of them. He carried two captured American flags into the capitol and proclaimed a great victory over General Zachary Taylor's army.

About a month later Santa Anna faced General Winfield Scott's forces at *Cerro Gordo*. The Mexican Army was devastated. Over a thousand Mexican soldiers were killed or wounded and three thousand taken prisoner. Santa Anna barely escaped, leaving behind his extra artificial leg and a war chest of fifty thousand pesos.

There were many more bloody battles as the Americans marched toward the capitol, but within only a few months, Mexico City fell. As a result of the defeat, the United States took Mexico's northern territories. The U.S. paid Mexico fifteen million dollars in compensation for taking half of her sovereign land – over half a million square miles. Santa Anna escaped into exile.

"Your Grace, are you all right?" Father Carlos Ropa asked in a gentle tone. He bent forward at the waist and placed his hand on the Cardinal's shoulder.

The elderly clergyman looked up into the younger man's face. Tears were streaming down Eduardo's cheeks. He reached for the napkin by his breakfast plate and wiped his tears.

"No, son, I'm not." He said slowly. "My heart is filled with sickness…and hatred."

"What's the matter, Father?"

"I spoke with *Señor Alaman* last night at dinner. He will lead the Conservatives when they take over our Congress next month. We discussed the course of Mexico's future." He stopped.

"What is it, Father? What happened?" Father Carlos asked softly.

"He believes Mexico should be governed by a European Prince. Until that can be accomplished, he has arranged for Santa Anna to return from exile and rule Mexico again as a military dictator." Cardinal Bustamante looked away from his young friend. He took in a soft, deep breath. "After five years, the evil one is returning."

73

Christmas, 1852

"This is the handsomest thing I ever had." Gabriel said, as he walked back into the living area of their adobe home on Christmas morning. He raised his thick arms almost shoulder high and turned around to show-off the new shirt Mary Beth had just given him. "I'm mighty proud a this, Mary Beth, mighty proud."

"Oh, I'm so glad you like it, Gabriel. Merry Christmas!" She beamed.

"I know it took a lot a work. You shouldn't a did this." Gabriel said as he looked down and admired his new garment. He raised his face and grinned broadly. "But, it sho' is nice. Thank you."

He walked over to Mary Beth and she stood up from her chair. Gabriel wrapped his arms around her and they hugged as she said, "You're welcome, Gabriel. I'm glad it fits."

"Well, I think, to celebrate this fine shirt and this fine Christmas mornin', I'll let us all have a piece of my Christmas cake!" Gabriel said enthusiastically.

Mary Beth still made a cake for Gabriel every Christmas. It had become a family tradition. The cake was just for him and he wasn't obliged to share with anyone.

Sam folded away the leather gloves Mary Beth had given him and said, "Now you're talkin'. Think you can eat that cake without gettin' it all over your fancy new shirt?"

Gabriel answered through his big smile. "I'll be careful, Sam. Besides, I'm just gonna' give everybody a *little* piece this mornin'. I just wanna' taste how good it is. I gotta' make the rest of it last fo' awhile."

"Yeah, a small piece would be good." Mary Beth said. "We don't want to ruin our dinner. Let's have a quick bite, then we need to load the rest of the cakes and pies and go pick up Rosa and her family. I told Katrina we'd be at the *Malendres' Hacienda* by one o'clock for the Christmas Feast."

"Wait a minute." Sam said. "There's one more present."

As Gabriel walked to the table to cut his Christmas cake he looked back at Sam and winked.

Sam reached behind his chair and produced a package which was slightly larger than a loaf of bread. What appeared to be a box was wrapped in brown paper and tied with red ribbon. There was a small folded white paper note under the ribbon on one side. He handed the gift to his sister.

Mary Beth took the package and sat down in her chair. She put the package on her lap and pulled the note from under the ribbon.

"What did you boys do?" She asked as she started to read the note. "You didn't need to give me anything else. You've already done..."

The note read: *"For Miss Mary Beth Stevens with my deep apology and sincere wish for your merry Christmas. Richard Jackson Walker"*

Mary Beth's head drew back slightly in surprise as her forehead wrinkled and the corners of mouth turned down. "What is this?" She looked at Sam. "It's from that big smelly friend of yours."

"Well, open it."

Mary Beth removed the ribbons and wrapping paper, and then carefully opened the box. She lifted away a layer of straw packing inside and found a white flower vase that was trimmed in gold.

Her eyes widened. She pulled the vase from the box, removed more straw from around it, and held it up.

"Mmmm, that's mighty pretty, Mary Beth." Gabriel said. He laid a small piece of his Christmas cake onto one of the plates on the table.

"It's *real china*." Sam said. "Walker took me to see it before they packed it."

"You knew about this? Mary Beth asked.

"Well, yeah. He asked me if I thought you'd like it. Do you like it?"

Mary Beth sat all the way back in her chair. She examined the china vase as she held it in both hands. Her eyes stayed on the piece while she said slowly, "It's very beautiful. Yes, I like it."

"Good. I knew you would." Sam said.

"Now, here's y'all's cake." Gabriel said. He sat Mary Beth's plate on the small table next to her chair and handed the other plate to Sam. "Y'all need some mo' coffee to go with it?"

"Yeah, Gabriel. I need a little freshen up with mine. Thanks." Sam answered.

"No, I'm fine." Mary Beth said, absently. She was still absorbing the stranger's gift.

Gabriel walked to the stove and used a rag to wrap the hot handle of the coffee pot. He carried the pot in one hand and the plate that held his piece of the cake in the other as he walked back to where Sam was seated. Sam raised his coffee cup and, just as Gabriel started to pour, there was a knock on the door.

Mary Beth was startled. She looked up and said, "Who could that be?"

"Don't know." Sam answered while he nodded for Gabriel to add more of the steaming black liquid to his cup. "You better answer the door."

Mary Beth carefully replaced the flower vase into the straw inside the gift box and sat it on the table next to her cake plate. She walked to the front door and started to open it. As she reached for the handle her little brother spoke again.

"Mary Beth, it's probably Walker. I asked him to go out to the Christmas Dinner at the *Melendres' Hacienda* with us. Katrina said it was all right. I figured you'd pitch a shoe if I told you ahead of time."

"Sam!" Mary Beth gritted her teeth and scowled at her brother.

"Answer the door." He said.

Her teeth were still clenched when Mary Beth opened the heavy wooden door. The instant she saw what was waiting on the other side, her jaw muscles relaxed and her eyes, which were squinted in anger, flew open with surprise.

Before her stood a tall, clean shaven man with neatly cut and combed blond hair. He wore a tailored dark grey suit coat over a heavily starched white shirt. In his left hand was a wide brimmed black felt hat. His black wool pants were freshly pressed and tucked into the tops of polished black riding boots.

As Mary Beth looked the person over her gaze went to his face. It was a very smooth, handsome face with high cheekbones. The man had a strong pronounced jaw line which terminated in a square chin that had a distinctive dimple in the middle of it. He had blue, penetrating eyes.

Mary Beth stood in the doorway and suddenly realized she was being held there by the man's deep blue eyes.

"Miss Stevens, I'm Richard Walker." She heard the man say. "We met the other night under circumstances I regret. Please accept these, and my apology."

The man put forward his right hand that held a mixed bouquet of sage and creosote sprigs. Also arranged in the bouquet were long white feathers with black tips.

"As you know, it's difficult for one to find flowers in the dessert this time of year. I hope you like the color of the feathers. The Indians believe that these eagle feathers have special powers."

Mary Beth took the bundle and looked at the large white eagle feathers next to the tiny yellow blossoms of the dark green creosote sprigs.

"This is very nice. Thank you." She found herself saying.

"Walker, glad you made it." Sam announced from behind his sister. He opened the door wide. "Welcome. Come on in the house."

As Walker entered the home walking in behind Mary Beth, Gabriel said, "Hey Walker, just in time. I cut a piece of my special Christmas cake here for you."

74

Christmas, 1852

The Christmas Feast at the *Melendres Hacienda* was more like a full blown *fiesta*. Families from throughout the Mesilla Valley were already there when the Stevens' group arrived. Lively music played from inside the large adobe home as Katrina waded through a giggling crowd of children playing in the front courtyard in order to come out to greet Sam and the others.

"Merry Christmas! Welcome." She started to call, when she was distracted by two small running children who bumped into her legs. She kept walking toward the new arrivals while Gabriel stopped the wagon and set the brake. Sam and Walker were each on horseback on either side of the large freight wagon. They dismounted as Katrina approached.

The young woman walked straight to Sam's side of the wagon and reached for his free hand. "Merry Christmas, Sam. I didn't think you'd ever get here."

Walker led his horse around the back of the wagon and walked up behind Sam. "Here, Sam, I'll take your horse." He said.

"Mr. Walker? Is that you?" Katrina asked. Her surprise was quite evident.

"*Si, Señorita. Buenas tardes y feliz Navidad.*" Walker smiled, giving his Christmas greeting and removing his hat.

"Oh my word! Forgive me, but you look so different." She said.

"Hope that's not a bad thing." Walker grinned. He put his hat back on his head and reached for the reins in Sam's hand. "Here, Sam, let me take him."

"It's not a bad thing at all. You look very nice. I'm very happy that you could join us." Katrina said trying to be gracious.

As Walker led the two saddle horses away toward the nearby hitching post, Katrina looked up to Mary Beth who sat next to Gabriel and Rosa on the wagon's seat. Katrina gestured toward Walker with quick sideways bobs of her head. Her large brown eyes were open wide and she mouthed the words, "He's handsome."

"So what are you goin' to do now that you've sold those horses, and have all that money in your pocket?" Sam asked. The two men sat next to one another at the Melendres' large dining table. A few other men also remained scattered around the table, nursing their coffee and finishing the last of their cake or pie desserts.

Most of the other men had gone outside for some air or a smoke. Everyone was stuffed from the huge meal that had lasted almost two hours. The women were all busy washing dishes and putting things away.

Walker sipped from his coffee cup then put it on the table next to his half empty dessert plate. "Well, Sam, like I told you, I'm stayin' down here for the winter anyway. Think I'll see what it feels like to stay warm for a change.

"I do have some other business though. I'm glad to tell you about it, but I need you to keep it like a poker hand. It's not somethin' you can tell other people about."

"I don't keep any secrets from Gabriel and Mary Beth." Sam said.

"Oh, that's fine. I didn't mean you couldn't tell them. I think y'all can keep a trust, can't you?" Walker asked.

"Sure."

"Well, I got a couple of letters in my saddle bag." Walker said. "There from a fella' I served with down in Mexico. I'll go get 'em and let you read 'em. I'll be right back."

Walker stood and started for the door then stopped short. "You can read, can't you, Sam?"

"Yeah, Walker. I can read."

"Good." He said turning to leave.

When Walker returned he handed Sam a worn envelope and sat back down saying, "I got this letter a little over a year ago. He was one of my commanding officers during the war in Mexico. Good son-of-a-bitch. His first wife was General Zachary Taylor's daughter. Guess she died of the fever. Anyway, when the war broke out he went to Mexico to help his ex-father-in-law."

Sam opened the letter and read:

25 July 1851

Dear Walker,
I hope this letter finds you in both good health and good spirits. Despite the austere circumstances of that war, I do think often and fondly of you and the other brave men we served with in the Mexican engagements.

It has been my good fortune to serve in my present capacity with an old friend of yours. You have been the subject of many stories shared over a dram or two of good whiskey ever since he and I discovered we shared you as a mutual acquaintance. The Honorable John Fremont is now serving as the first United States Senator from the state of California. He has asked me to extend his warmest regards to you and Mr. Christopher Carson.

Although the good Senator Fremont and I differ on certain issues, we are both committed to the preservation and strength of the Union. In that regard, we are convinced that a railroad connecting the Eastern and Western United States is vital to the future of our nation. With his extensive knowledge of the frontiers, Senator Fremont believes a southern route to California is certainly the most feasible.

As he was born in Georgia, he also understands the significance, both commercially and politically, of connecting the West with our nation's Southern States. I'm sure you have heard about the growing tensions between the Northern and Southern States as debates over states rights, slavery, annexation of Western Territories and economic policies continue to become more heated. I believe it is of paramount importance to the balance of our Union that the Western States be connected to the South by rail rather than to the North.

Senator Fremont and I are exploring options for a southern railroad route to his state of California. He and I agree that you and Mr. Carson are the two honorable and trustworthy men capable of overseeing that effort west of Missouri. Will you and Mr. Christopher Carson consider leading our representatives in surveying our needs through the frontiers with which you two are so familiar?

We are financing this operation privately. Both you and Mr. Carson will be well compensated, I assure you, but I must ask that you hold this entire matter very confidential. Please reply as soon as possible with your decision and your financial requirements.

Walker, the significance of this endeavor is beyond my ability to communicate. I urge you to accept this most sincere request.

Respectfully,

Jefferson Davis
United States Senator
State of Mississippi

"Jesus, Walker," Sam said. He looked up from the letter. "You really think they could build a railroad all the way to California?"

"Hell of an idea, ain't it?" his friend replied then took a sip of his coffee.

"So this is what you're really doin' down here," Sam said.

"Well, sort of. I talked it over with Kit. He wasn't too keen on the idea, besides, he'd already started getting wound up on his stupid plan to get rich with those damn sheep." Walker said.

"I wrote Colonel Davis back and told him that Kit couldn't do it, but I'd be happy to help out. Jeff Davis is a good man. Figured it was important, and since he asked me, an' all."

"So what's the deal?" Sam asked.

"Don't really know. Kind'a strange." Walker handed Sam a second envelope. "I got this letter about six weeks ago. Glad you can read."

"What do you mean?" Sam asked.

Walker chuckled. "Well, I got to thinkin'. That's probably why Fremont and Davis sent these letters to me instead of Kit. Kit can't read."

Sam opened the heavy paper of the envelope that was not nearly as worn as the previous one. He read:

12 September 1852

Dear Walker,

Much has transpired since I received your letter with regard to your offer to serve our country by assisting with the railroad plan. Although I have been heavily involved in the growing political controversies surrounding the Presidential election, I remain steadfastly committed to the concept of connecting California and the Western Territories with the Southern United States. It is a matter on extreme importance to the welfare of our Union.

We have received information that a route with the highest probability for success may lie to the south of the existing United States territory. I have discussed this matter at length with Mr. Franklin Pierce, whom I trust will shortly become the next President of our nation. He and I believe that if this is indeed the situation, there are options that can be employed.

I have asked my friend, Mr. James Gadsden, to personally explore the area in question. He has much experience with railroads and is staunchly committed to the concept of connecting California to the Southern States. He has my utmost confidence in this matter.

James Gadsden will arrive in the town of Mesilla in Mexico on or about the first week of the new year. Will you meet him there and make your services available to him? I have told him of our relationship and my high degree of confidence in your abilities. I assured him that you will serve his needs as you would my own.

Walker, again I must emphasize the need for confidentiality as to the nature of this matter. In order for you to identify his person, James Gadsden will deliver to you a letter of introduction from me.

With my lasting gratitude,

Jefferson Davis

Sam folded the handwritten letter and replaced it into the heavy envelope. He looked up to Walker as he handed it to his new friend.

"Guess that's what I'll be doin' now that I sold those ponies." Walker said.

"Wonder who this man Gadsden is?" Sam asked.

"I'm sorta' curious about that myself, Sam." Walker said sincerely.

Sam cocked his left eye and said, "Now I know why you gave those horses to the Indians."

"Well, actually, I'd a done that anyway, Sam." Walker said. He finished the last swallow of his coffee.

75

December 28, 1852

"Is Sam already gone?" Katrina asked as soon as Mary Beth opened the door to the Stevens' home.

"Yes, he and Gabriel left an hour ago." Mary Beth replied. "He was hoping you'd come by, but they decided they'd better get on the road."

"Oh...! I tried to get here, but I couldn't get away. Mother needed help with the house chores. She makes me so crazy sometimes. I really wanted to see Sam before they left."

"Don't worry, it's a short trip." Mary Beth said. "They're taking a load to *El Paso del Norte* then bringing some supplies and mail back to Fort Fillmore. He'll be back late tomorrow, or the next day. Want some coffee?"

Katrina huffed, exasperated, and then said, "Yeah, some coffee would be good, thanks. I swear, seems like all we ever do is wait on Sam to get back from some trip." She walked into the living room and sat down.

"I know. It would be nice if they were around here closer all the time, but they've been doing real well with the freight business." Mary Beth said as she walked to the stove. "They're getting so many good loads now; it's hard to complain about all the work." She used the end of her apron as a pot-holder and lifted the coffee pot. It was almost empty.

She dumped the dregs into the metal slop jar on the floor and started pouring fresh water into the coffee pot from the pail Sam had filled before he left. As she reached for the small sack of coffee beans, Katrina said, "Mary Beth, don't make a fresh pot just for me."

Mary Beth took a handful of the hard little dark pods and placed them into the coffee grinder. "It's alright." She said starting to crank the handle. "I need some more coffee this morning anyway. The boys got most of it before they loaded up." She pulled the small drawer from the bottom of the device and lifted it to her nose to smell the aroma of the freshly ground beans. "Ummm, I love that smell." She said, and then dumped the coarse granules into the water in the coffee pot.

She centered the pot on the top of the cast iron stove and used her apron to protect her fingers again when she opened the stove's small door handle. Mary Beth took two short mesquite limbs from the wood box on the floor and stirred the coals inside the stove with one of them before she added the new pieces of wood.

"There," she said, "it'll be ready in a minute. Now, we've got to talk about the New Year's Day Fiesta. I need to find out what you're wearing."

"My long pleated skirt, of course, for the dancing!" Katrina's face lit up as she answered. "I got those new red and blue ribbons for Christmas. I'm going to dress my short brim grey hat with them. I'll leave the ends long so they can fly out behind when Sam twirls me."

"Don't know what I'm going to wear." Mary Beth said. She walked across the room and flopped into her chair. "I may have to go in a tow sack. I don't have anything to dress up in."

"Oh, you always look so pretty, Mary Beth. You've got lots of nice dresses. Wouldn't be worried about impressing Mr. Walker, now would you?" Katrina asked slyly.

Mary Beth gave a coy look to her young friend. "Maybe." She said. "You do think he will be there, don't you?"

"I think we should have Sam make sure of it!" Katrina answered playfully. "I wonder if he can dance?"

"Will you promise me another dance, Miss Stevens?" Walker asked. Mary Beth took his arm and he led her toward the edge of the Mesilla Plaza after the music stopped playing.

"I might." She answered, breathing a little rapidly after being twirled to the fast rhythmed dance. "If you'll do two things for me."

Walker stopped. He turned and fixed his deep blue eyes on her face. "Yes."

"First," she panted, "let me catch my breath from this dance!"

He smiled.

"Then, please call me Mary Beth."

"If you'll dance with me some more, and call me Walker, then we'll have a deal."

Mary Beth smiled, too. "Deal…Walker."

Sam walked over with Katrina on his arm. They were both out of breath from dancing, too.

"Hey, you dance pretty well, for a smelly old mountain goat!" Sam said.

"Sam!" Mary Beth bristled at her little brother.

"Well, he does." Sam said. "Where'd you learn to dance like that, Walker?"

"Didn't spend all my time up in the mountains with the other mountain goats." Walker laughed and looked at Mary Beth. "Used to make it down to civilization, occasionally. Even made it to the Palace of the Governors in Santa Fe for some pretty good parties every now and then. Hell, I like dancin'…with a pretty girl."

Mary Beth blushed and looked away.

"Can I get you ladies somethin' to drink?" Walker asked. "I could sure use a beer. How 'bout you, Sam?"

The four of them walked to a wagon at the south end of the plaza. It was loaded with three large casks of beer turned on their sides with black tap valves plugged into the end of each barrel. There was a smaller cask that held sweet cider. It sat upright at the end of the wagon with a small tap coming out of its side.

After the ladies got cider, Sam and Walker each drew a beer. They strolled the outside of the Plaza and watched the dancers in the middle of it. The small area, surrounded by its storefronts and homes, was bustling with the activities of the annual New Year's Day Fiesta.

"Let's go down to the river and find some shade." Sam said. "I need to get away from all this noise for a little while."

Walker looked at Mary Beth and she nodded. "Suits me." Walker said and slugged down the last few swallows of his beer.

The two couples took a short, pleasant walk to the edge of the *Rio Bravo*. The afternoon sun was warm and bright in the clear blue January sky. The jagged tops of the Organ Mountains rose up in front of them across the river and the sun's light sparkled off the dusting of stark white snow on the very tops of the tallest peaks.

They found a fallen cottonwood tree whose trunk made a perfect bench for the two women to sit with their long skirts. Salt cedars, which often choked the river and created the thickly grown areas of the valley known as the *Bosque*, were on the bank that rose above them. The salt cedars were just high enough to filter the sunlight and provide the secluded site with shade.

"What a nice spot," Mary Beth said. "We should have a picnic here sometime. What do you think, Katrina?

"Oh, yes, let's do," Katrina said.

Sam piped in. "Long as y'all fix somethin' besides bacon and beans, I'm all for it. Gabriel and I have *picnics* with that every damn day!"

"No bacon and beans, Sam. I promise," Katrina said. She reached out her hand to Sam. "This is so pretty down here. Why don't you take me for a walk?"

"Sure." He took her hand and said over his shoulder as Katrina led him upstream, "Guess we'll be back, Walker."

Katrina looked back at Mary Beth, and winked.

Mary Beth was shocked at the suddenness with which they had left. She wanted to stop them. She found herself fidgeting on the tree bench and put her hands down on the coarse bark in order to stop herself.

"A picnic would be very nice," Walker said. "I've eaten outside a lot, but I don't think I've been on an actual picnic since I was a kid. We used to picnic after church. My mother had a place she liked down by a river close to where we lived. She'd pack a bunch of food before we left for church, and we'd have a picnic every Sunday on the way home. Hadn't thought about that in a long time."

"We'll do it then. Sometime soon," Mary Beth said.

"I'd like that," Walker said.

He looked up at the rich blue sky, then away to the Organ Mountains. "Sure is nice down here," he said. "Don't guess I ever thought about the desert being this pretty."

"It's much different than where we were raised," Mary Beth said. "But I love it. This desert has a beauty all its own. I'm glad you like it here."

"I do. And I like the people I've met here…very much."

Mary Beth looked into Walker's blue eyes and he stepped closer to her. She opened her mouth to speak, just as something moved in her peripheral vision. She startled as her eyes shot to a large dark figure behind the salt cedars.

Walker reacted and spun toward the direction she looked. While he turned his right leg came up and his hand went to the top of his new long black boot. In the instant it took for him to turn, he already had a large knife in his hand as his inside foot came back down and hit the ground. "Show yourself, and do it slow and easy!" he growled.

"Walker, it's me, Gabriel! Folks said they saw you and Sam walkin' down this way. I needed to find you."

"Damn, Gabriel. Don't go sneakin' up on people. You scared the hell out of us." Walker called as he stuck the long knife back into the scabbard between his tucked in pant leg and the side of his boot.

"Are you alright, Mary Beth?" Walker turned and asked.

She was amazed how quickly and instinctively the man had defended them. "I'm fine," she said. "It just surprised me when I looked up."

"What is it, Gabriel?" Walker asked. He watched the big black man start down the bank around the salt cedars.

"Brought somebody with me," Gabriel answered as he kept walking.

A second man followed Gabriel out of the brush. He looked fit and well kept, but had the grey hair and drawn face of a man in his mid-sixties. The fellow wore a suit with a starched white shirt and neck tie. He sported a small brimmed, black felt hat.

The stranger came straight to Walker and extended his right hand. He had sharp, piercing eyes but a friendly open smile. He said, "Richard Walker? I'm extremely pleased to meet you. My name is Gadsden. James Gadsden."

76

January 6, 1853

"Miss Stevens, it is very kind of you to go to all this trouble and have an old traveler to your table." James Gadsden said, as Mary Beth sat a large plate piled high with hot biscuits in front of her guest. "Thank you so much for your hospitality."

"We're glad to have you, Mr. Gadsden. It's not often we get to share a meal with someone from back east. You'll have to tell us all the latest news," Mary Beth answered smiling.

"I shouldn't know where to begin, madam. Everything seems to move so rapidly nowadays. I swear, it's hard for one to keep up with all the changes," he said.

"Well, just give us one more minute before you start and we'll be ready." Mary Beth said as she looked over the table checking to make sure everything was right. Before she turned and walked back to the kitchen she said, "I hope you'll like our local wine. Sam, go ahead and fill the glasses."

"The gravy's ready." Katrina said, without looking up and still stirring the contents of a large black skillet. She wrapped a cup towel around its cast iron handle and used both hands to lift the heavy device in order to pour the steaming gravy into a waiting bowl.

As the two ladies approached the table, Walker stood and pulled out the chair at the end of the rectangular table for Mary Beth. James Gadsden also stood. Sam reacted and rose from his seat opposite Mary Beth's and pulled out the chair to his right for Katrina.

Gabriel remained seated watching everyone. When he looked at Sam, his friend winked and discretely motioned for him to stand up. The big black man quickly jumped to his feet.

"Thank you, gentlemen. How nice." Mary Beth said. She placed the gravy next to the plate of biscuits and took her spot but remained standing. "Sam, would you say the blessing?"

Their supper began with various compliments from all the men about the food. Then there was a brief lull as everyone started eating.

"Now that you've been here a few days, Mr. Gadsden, what's your impression of our Mesilla Valley?" Katrina asked.

"Breathtaking, my dear. This country is completely remarkable. I shall be unable to describe it adequately to the people back in Washington, I'm sure," he answered.

"And this trip has already been quite fruitful. Walker has pointed out many errors on the maps we have compiled. I am very anxious to go a-field tomorrow and see what lies to the west of here."

"How long do you think you'll be gone?" Mary Beth asked initially looking at Gadsden then turning to Walker as she realized the question was really for him.

"Well, that depends on James and how much he thinks he needs to see. The maps the army made him really are pretty good. I think we can get on some mountain tops in the southern part of the *Gila* and see far enough across the dessert that we won't have to travel all the way out west. Just have to see how things match up. Guess we'll be out a month, maybe a little longer."

"Oh, that's a long time," Katrina said, and reached under the table for Sam's hand.

"Well, we'll be covering a lot of ground." Walker gestured around the table to the other men. "But since it's only the four of us, we'll be able to move pretty fast. We're travelin' light, just one pack mule and us."

"Don't you think you should take more men?" Mary Beth asked.

"Well, no," Walker answered. "I know James and Colonel Davis are concerned about keeping this enterprise confidential. We don't need to get anybody else involved or attract any attention."

"But what about the Indians?" Katrina asked seriously.

"Don't think we'll have any trouble with the Apache," Walker said. "If you're worried about getting' through Indian country, you either take a whole lot of men - or just a few. I think we'll be alright."

He smiled reassuringly at Katrina. "Besides, we've got the "*Buffalo Spirit Man*" ridin' with us. Any Indians we see will probably spend all their time pettin' him." Walker raised his hand and rubbed Gabriel's head.

Gabriel smiled, pulling his head away from Walker. "Hey, I'm special, watch out."

They all laughed.

"Are you sure you ladies will be alright with these men gone for awhile?" James Gadsden asked.

Katrina looked at Sam and responded smartly, "Oh yes, we're quite used to them being *gone all the time*."

"I'm sure we'll be fine, Mr. Gadsden." Mary Beth said. "Now, please tell us the latest news, and tell us about these two friends of Walker's who have gotten us all into this."

"My, where to begin?" Gadsden took a large sip from his wine glass. "I'm sure you're all familiar with John Fremont from the accounts of his mapping explorations of the West. He was in California when the war started and he served with distinction against the Mexican Army. After the war he and his wife acquired quite a bit of land that many thought fairly worthless.

"As it turned out, when gold was discovered in California, John became a multi-millionaire. Once all the haggling finished in Congress over admitting California into the Union as a free state rather than a slave state, John was elected to go to Washington as one of the new state's first two senators.

"That's where he met our other friend, Jefferson Davis, who was serving as senator from the state of Mississippi. Although Fremont and Davis disagree on the question of slavery, both men are committed to the preservation of the Union. I'm sure you've heard that there has been much talk of the Southern states seceding from the United States because the North has an upper hand politically now that there are two more free states than slave states.

"Senator Fremont wants desperately to connect by railroad his state to the rest of the Union. Jefferson Davis wants the western territories connected by railroad to the South instead of the Northern states. I believe that both men also see this as a way to help preserve the Union by putting a balance back in the political power between the North and the South.

"At any rate, as often happens in politics, these two senators with opposing viewpoints on the core issue of slavery, have become strong allies on this matter of a southern route for a transcontinental railroad."

James Gadsden stopped talking. He looked to Mary Beth and said, "My word, Miss Stevens, I hope I'm not being a bore at your supper table with all this talk."

"Oh no, Mr. Gadsden, not at all. Just the opposite. I think we all find this current news quite interesting." Mary Beth said smiling. "Please continue."

"You are kind." Gadsden said and took another drink from his wine glass. "Let's see now, where was I? Jefferson Davis resigned his seat as senator in September of 1851, a little over a year ago, in order to run for the office of Governor in the state of Mississippi at the request of his state's convention. He lost, unfortunately, by less than a thousand votes.

"He was quite active in the past presidential election. The new President, Franklin Pierce, has offered Jefferson a Cabinet position, which he turned down. I trust that by the time I return he will have been convinced to accept it and become the nation's Secretary of War.

"Davis is perfectly suited for the post. He graduated from West Point at the age of twenty, has not only served the Republic as a military officer, but also was the Chairman of the powerful Senate Committee on Military Affairs. As Secretary of War he would be very influential, especially with regard to advancing the proposition of a transcontinental railroad."

James Gadsden paused again and looked around the table. After a brief silence Sam asked, "What brought you into this, James?"

"Well, Sam, in another life I was President of the South Carolina Railroad Company." James replied. "I've been promoting railroads for a long time. I believe they are the economic future of our country.

"As Southerners, Jefferson Davis and I have also been friends for a long time. Over the years I have often shared with him my dream of connecting all the Southern railroads into one system and tying them into a Southern transcontinental railroad to the Pacific. I know with all my heart that it is possible."

"This land you're lookin' at is in Mexico." Walker said. "How you gonna' talk the Mexicans into lettin' you cross it with a railroad? You're not gonna' start another damn war for it, are you?"

"Good Lord no," Gadsden answered. "The people in the States would never stand for that. Besides, war is too expensive. I believe that for the amount of land we may be talking about, we can probably purchase it from Mexico."

James Gadsden watched the curious look that Sam and Walker exchanged with one another. Gadsden said, "You see, there are actually many in the United States who feel that Mexico was treated badly at the end of the war when we only gave them fifteen million dollars for taking half of their country. Also, Mexico has never recovered financially from Santa Anna's dictatorships. Their treasury needs money desperately.

"Jefferson Davis and I have discussed this with the new President, and he is not opposed to the idea. Depending on what I discover on this trip, I believe it is possible to convince President Pierce to pursue this plan."

Shortly before daylight the next morning Sam, Gabriel and Mary Beth sat at the table eating their breakfast. Mary Beth had made the boys a hardy breakfast of leftovers from the night before, along with some fresh eggs and coffee. She wanted to send them on the trail with full stomachs and preparing their meal had given her a way to take her mind off her apprehensions about them leaving. She had hardly slept all night.

"You're not eating much, Mary Beth," Sam said.

"Oh, I'm still full from last night."

"That sho' was a mighty fine supper," Gabriel said. "Mighty fine." Just as he finished saying, "Pretty good this mornin', too," they all turned when they heard a tapping on the front door.

"That couldn't be Walker." Sam said. "We're not supposed to leave for another hour. Can't even see how to saddle the horses. It's still dark outside."

Sam went to the door cautiously and said, "Who is it?"

"It's me, Walker. You up? Can I come in?"

Sam opened the rough wooden door saying, "Damn, Walker, a little early aren't you. You want some breakfast?"

"Naw, Sam, thank ya'. Guess I ate enough last night to hold me."

Walker moved past Sam into the Stevens' home. His new starched shirt and grey jacket had been replaced by his buckskins and big buffalo coat. Instead of the long black riding boots, leather leggings and thick moccasins covered his legs and feet. He removed the white fur hat from his head as he entered.

"Mornin', Walker," Gabriel said, still seated at the table.

Mary Beth remained seated also. She smiled at the unexpected visitor and said, "My, you look different."

"What is it, Walker?" Sam asked after he'd closed the door and walked back to the table next to the others.

"Well, I'm sorry to come by this early, an' all. But I saw the light and figured y'all were up. Anyway, I's kinda' wantin' to speak with you, Mary Beth...for a little while...alone." Walker swallowed.

Mary Beth's eyes stayed on the mountain man while Gabriel and Sam looked at each other and then at Mary Beth. After a short, uncomfortable silence Mary Beth said, "Sure, Walker, let's step outside and let the boys finish their breakfast."

Mary Beth grabbed her shawl from the wall peg by the front door on her way out. She and Walker stepped outside as the sky behind the Organ Mountains was turning a bright rose pink with white vertical sprays of light fanning through it. The early dawn air was chilled and still.

"Oh, it's cold out here," Mary Beth said and dug her arms into the soft wool of her shawl.

"Here, put this on." Walker said, removing his big buffalo skin coat. He wrapped it around her shoulders.

Mary Beth was surprised by the weight of the coat and nearly staggered when he placed it around her. Instantly she was very warm. The big garment engulfed her and hung down almost to her feet. She felt like a little girl who had crawled down deep under her parent's heavy quilts on a cold winter night.

"Mmmm, this feels good, thank you. Won't you get cold?"

"No, I'm fine," Walker said. He looked at her face in the soft predawn light for a moment.

"Listen, Mary Beth, I's hopin' to talk to you last night, but that just didn't work out after the supper with everybody around. I've been wantin' to talk to you, but...I'm sorry to come by so early like this, but it's all the time we've got. I've been thinkin' about this all night."

"What is it?"

"Well, I know that you're scared and worried about Sam and Gabriel goin' on this trip. Just want you to know that it was their decision to go. It's somethin' they decided they wanted to do. I didn't push 'em into it, at all."

Mary Beth smiled and said, "Actually, Walker, it was *our* decision. The three of us talked it over before they told you they would go."

From the look on his face Mary Beth could tell that Walker was surprised, and relieved.

She continued, "Listen, the three of us in our little family have been through a lot together. Just because we decided this was something they should do, doesn't mean that I can't get worried about them. Besides, I'm the only woman. Someone has to do that part."

Walker grinned. "I feel better." He stepped closer to Mary Beth. "Just didn't want you thinkin' I was forcin' Sam and Gabriel into somethin' you didn't want them to do. Don't think I could stand you havin' hard feelings about me."

Mary Beth's heart was beating faster. She looked into Walker's deep blue eyes and said, "I'm glad you came by so early this morning, Mister."

Walker slid his hands inside the big warm coat and put them around Mary Beth's waist. He pulled her toward him and she responded by stepping close to him and reaching up to his muscled shoulders. Walker wrapped his long arms around her and ran his hands slowly up the length of her warm back. As he felt the fullness of her breasts against his chest, the muscles below his stomach tightened. He kissed her soft waiting lips…long and gently.

77

June 28, 1853

1 June 1853

Dear Walker,

Once again, I extend my heartfelt gratitude for your exemplary service. James Gadsden's exploration mission was quite successful. He has assured me that he prevailed solely because of your efforts and your skills in the frontier.

Since his return we have been able to use the information gathered from your weeks in the desert to convince President Pierce to pursue the idea of a southern route for a transcontinental railroad. He has agreed that James Gadsden will be appointed as the United States Minister to Mexico in order to establish a dialog with that nation.

Our government recently received word that Santa Anna returned to Mexico City in April to assume the Presidency. He was apparently placed there by a man named Lucas Alaman. This Mr. Alaman now holds their country's highest cabinet position and is the person actually directing the country. Our sources have confirmed an agreement that Santa Anna is to serve for only one year, as a figurehead for Alaman, while different leadership from Europe is arranged.

The President's office has sent correspondence to Mr. Alaman requesting an audience. It is our intention to confirm James Gadsden's new position and send him to Mexico City with all haste. If we prevail with negotiations prior to a new regime change and European involvements, I hope I can call upon your services again should the need arise.

With this dispatch I have also enclosed additional compensation for you and the other men who accompanied James. He has spoken very highly about the quality of support and the character of Mr. Stevens and Mr. Gabriel. Please extend to those men our sincere gratitude for their service, along with this remunerative gesture of appreciation.

Walker, when I asked for your help I knew you would perform with distinction, as I have seen you do in the past. I am extremely grateful for what you have done.

Sincerely,

Jefferson Davis
Secretary of War

Walker folded the letter and placed it on the Stevens' table. He removed the second envelope from the leather courier satchel, opened it, and looked at the money inside. He smiled.

The spit-polished Lieutenant standing at attention in front of him said, "Sir, will you be sending a reply to the Secretary? I am to personally see to your dispatch, Sir."

Walker straightened his back feigning an important air then grinned at Mary Beth who sat next to him. He looked at Gabriel and Sam as he handed the leather pouch with an official *U.S. Army* stamped on its side back to the young officer.

"Yes, Lieutenant, I will be responding. I'll bring a letter to you at Fort Fillmore in a day or two."

"Sir, I am to personally see to your dispatch to the Secretary of War. I will be pleased to come fetch your letter, I mean your response… Sir. I will…"

"That will be all, Lieutenant," Walker said.

"Very good, Sir."

The young man snapped a brisk salute, then wheeled about, and marched out of the small adobe home.

As he closed the door Walker laughed and said, "Damn, I always wanted to do that to an officer!"

"What does the letter say, Walker?" Mary Beth asked as she leaned toward him.

"Yeah, what is it? Sam asked, too.

"Well…" Walker leaned back in his chair. "I have been directed by the Secretary of War for the United States of America…to buy both you boys a drink, and take the prettiest woman in Mexico out to a very nice supper tonight!"

78

Christmas, 1853

"Is there anything else I can do for you, Father?" Carlos Ropa asked softly as he bent from the waist next to the bed of Cardinal Eduardo Bustamante. "Would you like some fresh water, perhaps?"

"No, my son," Eduardo answered weakly. "Leave me now. You must go and tell them. They will need time to prepare for the Christmas Mass."

"Yes, Father. You get some rest and I will return shortly." Carlos lowered the wick of the oil lamp which burned on the small table next to the Cardinal's bed. The room darkened and the young priest walked quietly to the door.

Carlos walked in silence through the long shadowy halls. He then passed outside under open stone archways and went directly to the National Cathedral. Once inside, he proceeded to the statue of the Virgin Mary, lit a small candle, and knelt before Her. He prayed for Eduardo and asked that the Cardinal's soul would know peace.

Father Ropa made the sign of the cross as he finished his prayer. He remained on his knees and leaned forward, resting his arms on the wooden prayer rail in front of him. The position felt good to his tired body. The solitude of the quiet sanctuary also rested his worn spirit as he gathered his thoughts.

The elderly Cardinal had been right about Santa Anna. From his position at Bustamante's side Carlos had witnessed, from a unique vantage point few could know, the events that had transpired over the past year. He now understood why his aged mentor and friend called Santa Anna '*the Evil One*'.

The government in Mexico City had staged a dramatic ceremonial arrival event the previous April to salute Santa Anna's return from exile. The Church had been called upon to support it and the other elaborate activities produced in the ostentatious show of Santa Anna resuming the Presidency.

Carlos had been present during many conversations between Cardinal Bustamante and different leaders within the congress, in which concern was expressed about Santa Anna's agreement to serve for only one year as President. Lucas Alaman had convinced the Party the he would be responsible for Santa Anna's compliance. Once inaugurated, Santa Anna quickly set about pursuing the Conservative Party's political agenda under the direction of Lucas Alaman and it seemed that *Señor* Alaman was the one person who could control the flamboyant President.

That had all changed seven months ago. On the second of June, forty three days after Santa Anna was inaugurated President of Mexico, Lucas Alaman died.

Political power quickly shifted to a corrupt group surrounding the President. Santa Anna crushed the efforts of Cardinal Bustamante and other leaders who tried to use their influence to limit his control of the government. Santa Anna assumed all authority and once more dominated Mexico.

The political and emotional struggles had been devastating for Cardinal Bustamante. His health began to fail and, as he became increasingly helpless politically, he watched *El Presidente* become more powerful. Santa Anna again ruled the country for his own personal enrichment and that of his small band of corrupt insiders.

Father Carlos Ropa raised his face to the image of the Blessed Virgin as he thought of the upcoming Christmas Mass. He had been helping Cardinal Bustamante prepare for it. Although Eduardo had become increasingly frail and ill, he had been determined to deliver the Christmas service. Both he and Carlos knew, without ever having a conversation about it, that this would be Eduardo's last Christmas Mass to celebrate the birth of Christ.

Now that opportunity was gone as well. Three days ago Eduardo Bustamante had lost all hope. He was in bed now…waiting to die.

There had been a grand ceremony in the plaza of the *Zocalo*. Carlos escorted Cardinal Bustamante to a chair that had been provided for him on the stage. The President arrived amid much fanfare, and then delivered a lengthy energetic oratory about the glory of Mexico and her bright future.

By the end of the speech the skillful Santa Anna had generated a fever within the crowd. There was a roar of cheering and applause from the masses as he finished by declaring himself *Most Serene Highness* and *Perpetual Dictator for Life.*

"Help me find a way to give my friend comfort." Father Carlos Ropa said softly before the statue of Mary. He then quietly rose and made the sign of the cross again before he left the sanctuary to tell the Bishops that in less than a week they would have to conduct the Christmas Mass without Cardinal Bustamante.

Carlos tried to concentrate on his duties of helping serve the Communion at the crowded Christmas Mass, but he couldn't. His eyes kept going to the special elevated pew where *His Most Serene Highness* sat with his young wife and an invited dignitary.

The *Perpetual Dictator for Life* sat with his back straight and stoically watched as the congregation received the Sacrament. The bright late morning sun streamed through the great stained glass windows of the majestic National Cathedral and danced off the gold braiding and medals of Santa Anna's smartly tailored uniform.

Soon Ropa carried the chalice of wine that symbolized the Blood of Christ as he followed a Bishop toward *El Presidente's* special pew. While the Bishop began offering the Sacrament to Santa Anna, Carlos thought of Cardinal Bustamante laying sick, emotionally and physically, alone on his death bed. He wished he held a lesser rank in the priesthood so that he could be out in the *Zocalo* serving the *peons* instead.

After the President and his wife had taken the Sacrament, Carlos offered the chalice to their guest saying, "The Blood of Christ."

James Gadsden took the cup with both hands and drank. He handed the silver piece back to Carlos and smiled. "God bless you, Father."

79

Christmas, 1853

"Would y'all like some more coffee?" Mary Beth asked Walker and Sam from across the large Melendres dining table. She was standing and had just finished pouring a second cup for one of the few men still seated after the Christmas feast. Most of the other men had left the table to get some air.

"I'd love a little freshen-up." Walker smiled back at her.

"Not me," said Sam. "I'm about to pop. I swear there was more food here this year than last year. I've foundered myself."

Mary Beth walked around the end of the table. She put her hand on Walker's shoulder as she filled his cup from the china coffee pot. When she finished she rubbed his back affectionately and said, "Did you get enough to eat?"

"Oh lord, yes. I think I ate enough to hold me 'til late spring, maybe early summer. It was sure good. Thank you."

"I think that's the best part of the Christmas Feast. Everyone brings their best dishes." Mary Beth patted Walker's shoulder again. "I better go help the other women clean-up."

"Boy, this kinda' reminds me of last year. Remember when we had our little talk over coffee and you showed me those letters?" Sam asked.

"Yeah."

"Lot's happened since then," Sam said. "Covered a few miles in just one year, haven't we?"

"Yep, lot's happened, alright." Walker sipped his coffee.

"Listen, Sam, I's kinda hopin' we'd have a little time to talk. Been thinkin' 'bout somethin'…a lot. I need to talk it over with you…an' I guess this is about as good a spot to do it as any."

"What is it, Walker? You got some kind'a problem?"

"Well, don't know that I'd call it a problem. See, the thing is, Sam... well...you see, I love your sister."

Sam smiled, "Yeah."

"Well, I guess you know that. Anyway, I love her more than I ever thought I could love anything in my life. Sam, I wanted to ask you if it'd be alright with you if I asked Mary Beth to marry me? I know I ain't the best husband material there ever was, maybe, but I swear, if she'll have me, I'll be a good husband for her."

Sam leaned forward in his chair. "You haven't asked her yet?"

"No, Sam, wanted to make sure it was all right with you first. I mean, you're her brother, and my friend, an' all. Wouldn't want to do anything to mess up all that, an' all. Shit, Sam, I'm not sayin' this very well...but I love Mary Beth and I want to ask her to marry me! If that'd be all right with you..."

Sam grinned, and then laughed. "Walker, I always hoped my sister would find a good man to marry, but I's kinda' holdin' out for one a little better lookin'."

He reached over and clasped Walker's shoulder. "My friend, I appreciate you askin' me, 'course it's Mary Beth's call, but as far as I'm concerned I'd be happy to have you as part of our family."

"Thank you, Sam. I promise I'll take real good care of her." Walker said sincerely. "But there's one other thing I need to ask you."

There was a sudden apprehension in Sam's voice. "What is it, Walker?"

"If she says yes, will you stand up for me at the weddin' - and be my Best Man?"

* * * * *

James Gadsden stood alone and surveyed the large open room. In the center was a long rectangular oak table with seven fabric covered chairs on either side. At the head of the table was an overstuffed leather chair with the seal of the President of Mexico hand-tooled into its leather back.

From the several big framed maps hanging on the walls, James suspected this place served as a command room during times of war. He walked to one of the maps that showed the boundaries of Mexico before the United States had taken half of her land in the last war. He studied it for a moment and then looked at the cylindrical black leather map cases he held in his hand. He walked to the table and sat them down.

James was satisfied with the negotiations to this point. They had not gone overly well, but he had not hit any impasses either. Santa Anna had taken him to a Christmas Mass at the National Cathedral the day before and he considered that a good sign.

This morning he was asked to meet with the President alone, without any of his American staff. James was apprehensive, but had agreed to the meeting. Now he figured that his being kept waiting was a tactical strategy.

"Good Morning, Sir." A colonel said as he strutted into the room. He wore a well tailored Mexican uniform with many colorful medals decorating its front. The officer was in his late thirties to early forties and walked briskly toward Gadsden.

"*His Most Serene Highness* will be with us soon. He has asked that I join in with all the discussions from this point forward. I will act as special attaché, interpreter and advisor for *His Excellency.*"

"Oh, is that so?" James responded as both his eyebrows raised.

"*Sí.*" The man stopped and stood stiff backed in front of James Gadsden. "*His Most Serene Highness* trusts me implicitly. I have served *His Excellency* loyally for many years. He and I have been discussing this unusual situation of yours.

"Allow me to introduce myself. I am Colonel Denicio Bernillo."

80

January, 1854

"Well, I think you should've asked her before we came on this trip," Sam said. He sat next to Gabriel in the seat of the heavily loaded wagon. They led a column of four other freight wagons on the Camino Real ten miles south of Santa Fe. They were on the way home returning to the Mesilla Valley.

"Yeah, well, maybe." Walker responded as he rode his large paint horse next to Sam's side of the wagon.

"Still can't figure out why you didn't ask her. By the time we get back it'll be over a month since you talked to me about it at Christmas."

"Gadammit, Sam, I told you. I just never did find the right time."

"You could've asked her at the New Year's Fiesta. That would'a been a good time."

"Nah, there was too many people around. Too much goin' on."

Sam turned to Gabriel and nudged him with his elbow. "Don't think a big 'mountain man' would be afraid of a girl, do ya?"

He looked back to Walker and asked, "Well, when are you gonna' ask her?"

"Gadammit, Sam, I'll ask Mary Beth when the time is right. If you don't wart me to death with this shit first! You that anxious to get rid of your sister?"

"Well, not exactly." There was a sudden serious tone in Sam's voice. "See, I been thinkin'. Once you and Mary Beth get married, figure it might be a good time for me to ask Katrina if she'd marry me."

Sam looked at Gabriel. His friend smiled and tears welled up in his dark eyes. Gabriel put both sets of reins into his left hand. With his big right hand he reached over to Sam's shoulder and squeezed it.

* * * * *

Typical for early February, the midmorning air was cool and clear. Despite the mild temperature, the horses were beginning to sweat as their hooves dug into the sand on the last part of the climb to the top of the West Mesa above the village of Mesilla. Mary Beth reined the horse she was riding in behind Walker's big paint and followed him up a small arroyo. The two of them had been in their saddles for an hour.

As they topped out on the escarpment above the Mesilla Valley, Mary Beth could see far out to the west. She looked across tall yellow grasses and mesquite trees on the rolling desert that stretched for miles to the bases of mountains scattered in the distance. She tossed the bonnet off her head and let it hang on her back held by its ribbon around her neck. Now that they were out of the arroyo the light breeze that blew above the valley felt good as it moved through her long hair.

Walker turned his horse back toward the valley and faced the Organ Mountains. Mary Beth followed and rode up beside him.

"Oh, how beautiful," She said as they stopped.

"I thought you'd like this."

They sat silently for a few minutes each taking in the view. The town was directly below them. The small plowed fields all around Mesilla made it look like the adobe buildings and the Plaza were sitting in the middle of a patchwork quilt.

Beyond the town was the mighty *Rio Bravo* snaking its way through patches of thick green *bosque* in the bottom of the valley. The parts of the river where the water was visible were bright blue, reflecting back the color of the clear winter sky. Along the riverbanks in the valley to the north and south, where civilization hadn't cut them down, were huge ancient cottonwood trees.

On the far side of the valley expanses of thick dry grass were made golden by the sunny morning. The many empty arroyos cut into the East Mesa and leading to the river had shadows cast on the south side of their banks making them look like fingers pointing to the majestic Organ Mountains. The craggy peaks of the Organs reflected hundreds of different colors across the valley to the two figures sitting alone on horseback.

Mary Beth turned and looked at Walker as he stared at the vista in front of them. When she caught his eye and he turned, she said, "I'm glad you brought me up here."

He smiled. "Me, too. Let's get down and spell the horses."

He dismounted and then helped Mary Beth down from her horse. They walked to the edge of the short bluff that separated the desert behind them and the valley before them. Walker stood silently for a moment then turned to Mary Beth and took her hands in his.

"Mary Beth, I'm more comfortable out like this than I am in town. Guess you probably know that. I wanted to bring you up here where it was just the two of us…alone."

"What is it, Walker? You need to tell me something?" She was suddenly apprehensive.

"Mary Beth Stevens, I love you. I love you with all my heart…and all my soul."

The bright morning sun made Walker's eyes bluer than Mary Beth had ever seen them before. She squeezed his hands and said, "I love you, too."

The tall man slowly lowered himself to one knee while he smiled up at Mary Beth. "Would you do me the honor of becoming my wife?"

Tears filled Mary Beth's eyes and she began to shake. She sank to her knees in front of Walker as she kept both his hands in hers. She paused and the tears began to trickle onto her cheeks. "Oh, Walker, there are things you don't know about me. Things that happened when I was young, before I met you. Terrible things you…"

"Mary Beth, I love you *now*. The lives either of us had before we met each other are not here now. They don't concern me. Don't let them concern you. The only thing I know, or care to know, is that I love you more than any man could ever love a woman."

"But you don't know…" she started.

"I know…that if you'll have me the way I am, Mary Beth, I'll have you just the way you are. Will you marry me?"

Walker looked at the tears streaming down her face.

Mary Beth pulled Walker to her. As they embraced she whispered, "Yes…Oh…yes."

81

March 5, 1854

"Wonder what he means by 'complications'?" Sam asked as he used his fork to cut into the slice of pie his sister had made from dried apples. They were having an early supper so Katrina could join them and Sam would have time to take her home to the *Melendres' Hacienda* before dark.

"Who knows?" Walker responded. He took a sip from his coffee cup to wash down a bite of the sweet dessert. "You saw the letter."

"All Colonel Davis said was that Gadsden's trip to Mexico City had been successful and that James had signed a treaty to buy the land they wanted. Said that Congress had already churned it up into another slave state issue." Walker put his cup down hard with disgust. "No tellin' what that means. Guess it just shows that a bunch of politicians can mess up damn near anything."

"Yeah, I got that part." Sam said. "They've got to debate it, and vote on it, and accept the treaty, and all that bull. But what was that part about 'significant complications with regard to Santa Anna' that he thought he'd need your help with? Wonder what he's talkin' about?"

"Shit, Sam, ain't no tellin'. I mean, I'll help him out if I can. But, I kinda' got more important things to do right now." He turned to his left and winked at Mary Beth. "Like marryin' your sister here."

Mary Beth reached for Walker's hand. She straightened her back. In a cold stern voice that Katrina and Walker had never heard before Mary Beth said, "I don't want Santa Anna's name used at this table."

Sam and Gabriel looked at one another and then Sam turned to his sister. "Sorry." He said quietly and took another bite of his apple pie.

Mary Beth broke the awkward silence that ensued. "Would you like another piece of pie, Gabriel?"

After supper Sam helped Katrina into the wagon. He then climbed up to sit on the plank board seat next to her and said as he took up the reins, "Guess I'll be back after while." Walker and Mary Beth stood next to one another beside the wagon. Sam looked directly at Walker and shook his head while he said, "Y'all don't want to come along for a little ride, do you?"

. Sam's gesture was obvious and Walker said, "No thanks, Sam. I'm gonna' take your sister on a walk after that good supper she fixed. I got somethin' I want her to see. 'Preciate the offer though. Y'all go on."

"C'mon mules." Sam flipped the reins and gave a little whistle. As the big wagon creaked and the animals pulled it forward, he said, "That was a good supper, Mary Beth. I'll see y'all later. Guess I'll be back around dark."

The wagon moved up the dirt road. Walker and Mary Beth watched Katrina slide close to Sam on the seat and take his arm with both of her hands.

"Are you all right?" Walker asked Mary Beth. He reached for her hand. "What was that thing at supper?"

"I'm sorry," she said. "I shouldn't have been so cross."

"It's all right." He put his arms around her and pulled her to him. "What's the matter?"

Mary Beth pressed the side of her face against his chest. "Oh, Walker, I tried to tell you before. There are things you don't know about me. Horrible things. When Santa Anna invaded Texas and our folks were killed...terrible things happened..." She began to sob.

"Hey now," Walker said softly to the top of her head. "It's all right, Mary Beth." He hugged her more tightly then pulled back to look into her eyes.

He kept his left hand at her waist. His rough-worn right hand came up to her face and he touched it very gently. In a soothing quiet tone Walker said, "Listen, lady, you're here with me now. You're gonna' be my wife. Everything is gonna' be just fine.

"Awful things happen sometimes, they just do. I know the things that happened down in Texas back then must have been very bad. But, that was a long time ago, Darlin'. I promise, the only thing that will ever bother me about it…is that it makes you sad."

Walker's other hand came up and he held her pretty face between his fingertips. He grinned broadly and said, "You see, sweet lady, *my* job is to make you happy, and I intend to be very good at that. Now, if you can work up just a little smile for me, I'll take you to see somethin' I think you'll like."

The corners of Mary Beth's mouth turned up. She reached into the front pocket of her long skirt, pulled out a white handkerchief, and blew her nose. As she stuffed the small handkerchief back into her pocket, she chuckled when she smiled back at Walker saying, "How's that?"

"Damn good start," he said and took her hand and began walking. "Now, come on with me. I wanna' show you something and see what you think."

They strolled down the dirt street away from the Plaza then turned north and walked to the edge of town. When they stopped beside an open field they were less than a quarter of a mile from Mary Beth's house. From where they stood there was an unobstructed view of the Organ Mountains across the valley, their rocky peaks painted purple and pink by the setting sun.

"Well, this is it." Walker said.

Mary Beth, curious, tilted her head. "What?"

"This is where I think I could build you a house."

Her eyes widened.

Walker stepped out into the open area in front of Mary Beth. He began pointing and making large sweeping gestures with his arms as he spoke. "This is a pretty good sized piece and it looks like I can buy it for a decent price. Thought I'd build a house for us right down yonder by those trees. Back over there is plenty of room for some corrals and a barn. I's thinkin', I want to build a really big barn."

He looked at the excitement showing on Mary Beth's face as she started to follow him around the field. It gave him the encouragement he needed to continue.

"Sam and Gabriel have been very good about lettin' me pitch in on their freight haulin' business. But, I's thinkin' that if we build a good barn and some descent pens, it'd give 'em a better place to keep the stock. Also, there'd be room if they ever get other wagons and more mules, or anything.

"Thing is, there's enough freight comin' through here now that if we built a big enough barn, we could start warehousing some of the goods. I could actually start doin' some real tradin' with some of it, maybe. I'm pretty good at tradin', you know.

"Anyway, if we had a place they could use like that I'd feel like you and me were more a part of the whole deal." He stopped. "Am I makin' any sense to you, Mary Beth?"

She smiled, "Yes."

"Well, lady, what do you think?"

"I think it's wonderful!" She ran to his open arms. "I love it. When do we start?!"

"I'll see if I can't work a deal on the land tomorrow." He squeezed her. "An' we'll marry as soon as I get a house built for you."

"Oh, this is perfect." She beamed. "Then Sam and Katrina can have our house, if he ever asks her to get married."

"You know he's goin' to," Walker said.

"I know. Wish he'd hurry up and do it."

"Well, he's waiting on us." Walker backed up and looked at her. "Sam wants our wedding to be perfect for you. He wouldn't do anything to take any of the sunshine off of his sister."

"That's sweet, but it doesn't matter to me," she said. "I say he should go ahead and ask her. What would you think about a double wedding ceremony?"

82

May 9, 1854

"I don't think it needs anymore straw," Mary Beth said to Sam who held a double handful of thick dry grass.

"Yeah, and that's plenty of water," Katrina told Gabriel. He stopped pouring water from a large wooden bucket.

"You sure that's enough?" Sam asked.

"Hey, after stomping a couple thousand miles through this guck, we know our recipe," Mary Beth answered.

"Yeah, Sam," Katrina followed. "It's just like making a cake...or mud pies. You have to know the recipe. Now let us stir the cake and y'all get the baking pans ready."

The boys put down the water and straw they held. They went to the large flat area a few feet away and began lining up wooden forms on the ground. Mary Beth and Katrina stayed knee deep in the pit full of adobe mud.

Each of the women wore large brimmed straw hats. In early May the sun was bright and warm. They had their long skirts pulled up from behind, between their legs and tucked into the fronts of their waistbands. With their bare feet they squished around in a mud pit to mix the straw, water and clay dirt together into the proper consistency to make adobe bricks for the new house and barn.

This mud dance had become a ritual every week or so for the past couple of months. They would mix enough adobe to fill all the forms they'd made. While they waited for the sun to dry the new bricks, they built walls with the previous batch of mud bricks. As each round of bricks was ready, the wooden forms were stripped and a new mud dance began.

"After we get married I suppose our husbands can save a lot of money on mules." Katrina said as she raised her knees high and mashed the straw laying on the surface down into the brown sludge.

"What do you mean?" Mary Beth asked as she did the same thing.

Katrina grabbed both of her thighs and said, "Much more of this and *we'll* be able to pull the wagons!"

When the mix was ready the women came out and washed off their legs. "Guess it's my turn," Walker said. He took off his boots, rolled his pants up, and waded into the pit.

"Oink, oink," Mary Beth said. "When you little piggies get through playing in the mud, we'll have your dinner ready. Have fun."

Walker slopped heavy buckets full of liquid adobe out to Gabriel and Sam. While they poured the mix into the forms and passed the buckets back to Walker, Mary Beth and Katrina put the food out on blankets under the nearby shade trees.

When about half the forms were filled Gabriel stood up and said, "Walker, someone's coming. Three soldiers on horses."

Walker stood up in the pit and saw a U.S. Army Lieutenant flanked by two soldiers ride in. "Hello. What can we do for you?" He said as they approached.

"Mr. Walker, another dispatch has arrived for you, sir. It's from Washington and the order is marked urgent. I am to send back a courier with your reply."

"Well, as you can see, I'm a little busy here, Lieutenant. We gotta' get these forms filled before this mud sets up. You're gonna' have to give me a few minutes, then I'll see what you got there."

"Very well, sir."

Walker scooped another bucket of mud from the pit and handed it to Sam. He looked up at the young officer sitting stiff backed in his saddle.

"Hell, son, get down off your horses and go wait over there in the shade." Walker said. "We'll be over there directly."

"Yes, sir."

Twenty minutes later, while Sam and Gabriel filled the last forms, Walker sat on an upturned bucket and washed himself. After he put on his boots, he slowly poured water from a bucket so that Sam and

Gabriel could wash the mud off their hands and arms. When they finished Walker stretched his back and said, "Guess we oughta' go see what news the shave tail brought from the civilized world, huh?"

The three soldiers stood when Walker, Sam and Gabriel approached. Mary Beth and Katrina remained seated on the blanket and watched Walker open the leather courier's pouch the Lieutenant handed him. He removed a heavy paper envelope and broke open its wax seal. There was a letter inside and he read it in silence.

When he finished he folded the letter as he looked stone-faced at Mary Beth and then at the rest of his friends. Before he could say anything the young officer said, "Sir, the order says that I am to post a courier immediately, as soon as you reply."

"I'll need a pencil and paper, Lieutenant."

"I have pen and ink and paper for you in my saddle bag, Mr. Walker."

"Leave 'em with me. We're gonna' need to talk this over." Walker said as he gestured toward the others around him. "You men come back here in two hours and I'll have an answer for you to send to Washington."

The group waited anxiously for the three soldiers to ride out of earshot. Sam, Gabriel and Walker sat on wooden boxes the women had arranged for them when they'd prepared the area for the midday dinner.

"Walker?" Mary Beth said when she turned back from watching the soldiers ride away.

"What'd Jefferson Davis say?" Sam asked. "What's afoot?"

"Damned if I know," Walker answered. "And this isn't from Jeff Davis. This letter is from John Fremont."

Walker opened the letter and read:

26 April 1854

Dear Walker,
Yesterday the Senate ratified the treaty with Mexico to purchase land necessary for our transcontinental railroad. It has been a bitter debate, the details of which are too complicated to discuss by letter. Much was

changed from the original document James Gadsden signed the end of December in Mexico City, however, we are proceeding.

Now that we have won approval in Congress, there is another extremely significant issue with which we are dealing. It is of a nature and magnitude that are almost incomprehensible, so it is with great anxiety that I write this letter to you.

I have been fully aware, and supportive, of your participation in the early stages of this endeavor. Secretary Davis and I never doubted that you were the right man to be involved. Now we need your help on a much different level and, again, we are in complete agreement that you are the man we can both trust with the responsibility.

Walker, it is imperative that I meet with you to discuss this, and, as time is also critical, we must get together as soon as possible.

Now that the area north of you is a United States Territory, there is a stage line that runs from Independence, Missouri to Santa Fe. I have booked passage to arrive in Santa Fe on or about the ninth day of June. In order to protect the secrecy of what we are doing, I will be traveling alone under the name John Freeman.

Please meet me in Santa Fe and allow me to explain the help we desperately need. Secretary Davis has arranged for military couriers to dispatch your immediate answer.

When we were younger we climbed many mountains together and did things that others thought incomprehensible at the time. This one is a very big mountain. Walker, it is of utmost importance that we climb it and I know I can trust you now, as I did then.

Your friend,

John Fremont

United States Senator
State of California

After Walker read the letter the group sat in silence.

"Guess I oughta' make a trip to Santa Fe," Walker said after none of the others had spoken. "See what John's talkin' about. Sounds like it's something important."

"Sounds like it's something dangerous," Mary Beth said stiffly.

"Wonder what's goin' on?" Sam asked.

"Don't know, but they obviously want help pretty bad," Walker answered while he looked at Mary Beth trying to gauge her reaction.

Everyone else sat quietly while the Mary Beth looked back at Walker. After a brief silence she said, "I know you have to go, but I don't want you going by yourself."

She turned to her brother. "Sam, I want you and Gabriel to go to Santa Fe with Walker."

"Sure," he said. "We might as well make a load goin' and comin' while we're at it. We'll have to get busy if we're gonna' fill out a wagon and be there one month from today." He looked at Gabriel and then at Walker. "We'll plan on leaving the end of next week, all right?"

83

May 19, 1854

"What are you doin' up?" Sam asked, surprised after he'd opened the door from his bedroom and walked toward the kitchen. To light his way he carried a saucer that had a lit and mostly melted candle sitting on it.

"Couldn't sleep. Needed to sit up for awhile," his sister answered. Mary Beth sat in her chair in the living area. On the small table next to her a kerosene lamp was turned down very low and barely illuminated the dark room.

She squinted through the darkness at the wall clock Sam had given her for Christmas a few years before. "It's two o'clock, you should be asleep. You've got a big day tomorrow. You need to get some rest."

"Yeah, I know," Sam said, "I woke up an hour ago and couldn't go back to sleep. Thought I'd try some cornbread and sweet milk. You want some?"

"Sure. That sounds good."

Mary Beth turned up the wick on the lamp and got up from her chair while Sam took two glasses down from the kitchen shelf. She carried the lamp to the table and sat down asking, "Do you have enough light?"

"Yeah, I can see," Sam answered. He reached for the jar of milk sitting in the kitchen window. The window was recessed into the thick adobe wall and the flat spot in front of it made a natural shelf. His sister kept the jar by the cool window at night so the milk wouldn't spoil so quickly.

Sam put the jar to his nose and smelled it to make sure the milk hadn't soured. He lifted the cup towel that covered the plate of left over cornbread and took two large pieces. After he crumbled the cornbread into the glasses he filled each glass with milk and then picked two spoons from the cupboard.

"Here," Sam said sitting a glass and spoon in front of his sister as he sat down beside her. "Are you all right?"

"Yeah, I just can't make my brain stop talking."

Sam smiled. "Know what you mean. Here, try some of this." He pushed her glass closer to her.

Mary Beth took a spoonful of milk and cornbread from the glass. "Mmmm, this is good. Thanks," she said softly.

"Yeah, it oughta' help us sleep, but I don't know if it'll stop your brain from talkin'. What's the matter? Is somethin' wrong?"

Mary Beth put her spoon on the table and looked up into her brother's eyes. "Sam, I'm scared. Seems like whenever things get good...and we have happiness in our lives...it gets taken away. I'm afraid something's going to happen again."

Sam started to say something about having the same feelings, but didn't. He sat quietly and nodded his head.

"You boys are leaving tomorrow and God knows how long you'll be gone. We have no idea what all this is about...and Santa Anna..."

Mary Beth's eyes became teary and she reached into her pocket for a handkerchief. "Oh Sam, I think I'm going crazy." Her nose started to run and she blew it into the handkerchief.

She raised her eyes to the ceiling and took a deep breath in through her mouth before she continued. "I think about Santa Anna destroying everything we had with Momma and Pa and Luke. In San Antonio... and the Seguins...God knows what's happened to them. We haven't heard from Juan and Maria in years.

"With all these things happening now, I feel like he's come back to destroy our lives again. I'm afraid, Sam."

Sam moved his chair next to hers and put his arms around his sister. She cried into his shoulder.

"Sam, we've made a good life here. We're both getting married. I just want to be left alone. I want to have a husband, an' children, an' a home...I want to live my life an' work an' be happy...that's all I want."

"I know," Sam said as he hugged his sister and patted her shoulder gently. "That's all Momma and Pa, or any of us, ever wanted."

"I don't want it to happen again, Sam. Not now…I don't want something bad to happen and take it all away." She pulled back and looked up at her brother. "Do you think I'm crazy, Sam?"

84

June 10, 1854

The stage from Independence, Missouri was a day late getting in. Sam, Gabriel and Walker had been in Santa Fe for three days when it arrived. They already had a full wagon load booked for the return trip to Mesilla by the time the coach rolled in on Saturday afternoon.

"Well, looks like it's finally here," Walker said as the stage came to a stop next to the Plaza across from The Palace of the Governors. He got up from the tree shaded bench in the middle of the Plaza where he and Gabriel had been sitting. "Let's go see if the good Senator survived the trip, an' find out what this is all about."

Gabriel, Walker and Sam strolled to the edge of the Plaza and waited for the passengers to unload. It was a full coach with six men inside the tiny compartment. They watched while the travelers stiffly unfolded themselves from inside the small windowed box and stretched as they stepped outside. When the fifth passenger crawled through the doorway Walker said, "That's him."

John Fremont's legs rebelled momentarily when they finally reached the ground. They had been confined in the cramped space between the stage seats for four hours since the last stop, with ten other legs. He stretched his spine and heard the vertebras cracking as they went back into alignment. Next he heard, "John", and looked toward the sound.

"Walker!" He said, immediately recognizing the tall blonde man dressed in buckskins walking toward him. Fremont smiled broadly as he rushed forward to greet his old friend.

"Damn, it's good to see you, Walker. Thanks for coming," John said as the two reached one another and exchanged a strong, warm handshake.

"Good to see you, too, John. Been a long time." Walker said. "Hear you're an important man now, actually turned yourself into somethin'. Kit's gonna' shit when I tell him that."

"Kiss my ass, Walker," John said grinning and playfully shoved Walker in the chest. "How is Kit anyway?"

"Don't really know," Walker answered. "Hadn't seen him for a long time. He kinda' took up sheep herdin', an' I been down south in the Mesilla Valley for awhile."

"Yeah, that's what I heard. How you like it down there?"

"I like it," Walker said sincerely, and then grinned. "An' let me tell you, it's a helluva lot warmer than some of the country you and I have been in. I like that part a lot!"

"I'm glad," John said and put his hand on Walker's shoulder.

The two just looked at one another for a moment reaffirming the bonds of an old friendship with their eyes. They each saw that the years that had accumulated since the last time they were together were nothing. Each man slightly smiled and nodded, telling the other that they were still good friends.

"It *is* good to see you, Walker. I'm glad you're here."

"Wouldn't miss it," Walker said. "Hey, let me introduce you to my friends." Walker turned and gestured toward Sam and Gabriel.

"This is Sam Stevens and this is Gabriel. Fellas, may I present the Honorable, and I use that term very loosely, John Fremont."

As they exchanged handshakes Fremont said, "It's a pleasure to meet you. James Gadsden has spoken very highly of you both back in Washington."

"We've heard quite a bit about you, too, John," Sam said. "It's nice to finally meet you."

"Let's get your gear," Walker said.

"That's my case there." John pointed to one of the valises in the stack of baggage the driver was unloading. He walked over quickly and picked it up. He hurried back and sat it down saying, "Walker, would you watch this for a minute? I gotta' find a place to make water. I'm about to mess myself. We've been bouncin' around in the back of that stage for hours."

"I'll go with you," Walker said. He turned to Sam and Gabriel. "Would you boys mind keepin' an eye on his bag?"

Walker and John went into an alleyway between two buildings on the side of the Plaza. As they urinated into the trench cut down the middle of the alley Walker said, "You think this is why civilization always smells so bad?"

"Think this is bad, you ought to go to Washington!" His friend said. "There's a lot more people. Open sewers in the street…Jesus, in the summertime the flies are so bad you wouldn't believe people could live around it!"

"Sounds wonderful," Walker said as he finished.

"Yeah, you'd love it there," John said. He began to finish, too. "Listen, Walker, we've got a lot to talk about. We're gonna' need to get someplace where we can be alone."

"If you're talkin' about Sam and Gabriel you can say anything, to 'em or in front of 'em, that you'd say to me. They know everything I know about all this."

"Walker, I'm sure they're good men, but what I've got to tell you is extremely sensitive information. Very secret."

"I'd trust either one of 'em with my life, John, or yours."

Fremont looked at his old friend. "All right, then." He started to walk toward the Plaza. "Let's go find a place where we can talk." Suddenly the Senator stopped short and said as he turned to the mountain man. "Oh, Walker, you're probably gonna' want a drink after you hear this."

That evening the four men had supper in a small private dining room off the lobby of the hotel where they were staying. After their meal was served Fremont asked the waitress to leave them alone for awhile. She closed the door behind her as she left the room.

"Well, Senator, what the hell's goin' on?" Walker asked then took a sip from his coffee cup while he kept his eyes on Fremont.

"Gentlemen, before I begin," Senator Fremont said in a low voice, "I must emphasize the secrecy of what I am about to tell you. This is information potentially damaging not only to the people involved with this, but also to our country itself. Should word of this get out it would almost certainly put lives at risk, as well."

He paused and looked around the table. After each man looked him in the eyes and nodded he said, "Very well, then.

"You are all familiar with James Gadsden's trip to Mexico City and its purpose. James was given the authority to negotiate with fifteen million dollars for the strip of land you helped him investigate for the southern transcontinental railroad. By the time he arrived in Mexico, Santa Anna had assumed control of the country again and declared himself dictator – for life.

"During the negotiations with Santa Anna, James overstepped his bounds in a couple of ways. First, he took the opportunity to include much more land than was planned for. He added into the deal more land to the south, including the entire Baja Peninsula.

"Personally, I don't fault him for it. We have discussed it at length and I believe he used his judgment to do what he thought best at the time. However, many in the Northern States saw it as an attempt to acquire enough land to create another slave state.

"There was bitter disagreement in congress over it." John looked directly at Gabriel across the table. "I am adamantly opposed to slavery. I sided with the legislators from the North in order to keep slavery out of the far West and away from my state of California.

"In the end, after many hard-fought debates, changes were made to the treaty that James signed with Santa Anna. The extra land, including the Baja, was eliminated from the purchase. The price to be paid to Mexico was also reduced to ten million dollars." The Senator paused and looked around the table again.

"Think we're with you so far, John." Walker said.

"Well, turns out, that was the easy part." Fremont said and took a big sip from his coffee cup. He sat the cup down and then leaned both elbows on the table. "This is where it gets salty…the other thing that James did.

"I've heard stories about what a rotten bastard Santa Anna is. After James told me about his dealings with him, I suspect they're all true." John stopped momentarily then said bluntly, "Santa Anna demanded a personal bribe in return for signing the treaty. He decided that ten percent of the purchase price would be an appropriate amount for his services.

"I wish James were here so you could get a better idea of how it really was down there. He spares nothing in describing what a shrewd, heartless son-of-a-bitch Santa Anna was. James told him that the United States government could never be a party to extortion or bribery.

"Santa Anna's response was that the morals of our government were not his concern. The only thing that mattered, if the land was to be sold, was his fee.

"James said that Santa Anna railed on, with jealously, about the fortunes that will be made in commerce from a transcontinental railroad. The stealing bastard's final position was…that the companies and people involved, who would benefit from the railroad enterprise, could provide his payment without Congress knowing about it."

Fremont stopped and took in a breath. He looked around the table to see how the others were absorbing the information.

"Is that what James agreed to do? Walker asked.

"Yes," John said. "That's exactly what he agreed to. It was the only way Santa Anna would sign the treaty."

Sam spoke up. "What's gonna' happen now that Congress has changed the original deal?"

"We're not sure, Sam," Fremont answered. "We've sent word of the changes both officially and privately to Santa Anna. We should have answers to both anytime now. "But, his bribe was for ten percent of the purchase price, not a fixed amount. Even at the reduced amount Congress finally passed, Santa Anna's part will be one million dollars. We think the greedy bastard will gladly take that.

"You see, he may be *Perpetual Dictator for Life*, but, he's been overthrown and exiled before. We think he's just feathering his nest for when it happens again. That could be…when the people of Mexico find out about him selling off thirty thousand square miles of their land to the *Americanos*.

"And get this," John's eyes widened and his head bobbed as he emphasized the words. "He wants all his bribe money in American gold coins!"

"What?!" Walker exclaimed.

"Can you believe that?!" Fremont rolled his eyes. "Gadsden says the man's arrogance is unbelievable. He really does call himself 'The Napoleon of the West'. He said America made arrangements to pay Napoleon in gold when we made our deal with him for the Louisiana Purchase, so by God; Santa Anna wants his fee in gold Double Eagles. Now doesn't that smell just a little bit rotten to you?"

"Damn sure does," Sam said with bile in his throat.

Walker saw Sam's face getting flush. He turned to Fremont and said, "John, what'd you come all the way out here for?"

The Senator took in a deep breath and exhaled it through his mouth. He looked into his old friend's face and said in a flat, serious tone, "We've raised the money for Santa Anna. Steel companies, timber companies, railroad companies and people...it really wasn't that hard. We did it in back rooms and behind closed doors. The President understands the deal, but he can't actually know anything about it."

Fremont waited another moment before he said, "Walker, this is the real salty part. We need your help to get the money to Santa Anna."

85

June 10, 1854

"What in the hell are you talkin' about, John?" Walker straightened his back and sat upright. He put both hands on the edge of the table and used them to push himself back in his chair. "You can't be serious."

"That's why I came all the way out here, Walker," Fremont said. "I've never been more serious in my life. We need your help to get the money to Santa Anna, in secret, without anyone knowing about it."

"I won't have any part of it," Sam said sternly as he looked at the Senator and then at Walker. "I'll be damned if I'm gonna' get involved with anything to do with Santa Anna."

"Yeah, I'm with Sam," Walker said. "Don't think I want anything to do with it either."

"You have to realize how important this is." Fremont leaned forward toward Sam and Walker. "This could be one of the most important moments in the history of our country. It gives us a way to join the nation, and not just commercially. When we are able to move families, information, medicines…from one side of the country to the other…it will change the very nature of our world. We have to make this happen."

Sam also leaned forward and said forcefully, "John, everything bad that has ever happened in my life was because of Santa Anna. In Texas I lost my family, my home, my friends…all because of him. I don't want to get involved. I just want to stay away from that murderin' son-of-a-bitch."

"I can understand that, Sam." Fremont sat back. "But look at it this way, you live in Mexico, and Mesilla's now the largest town in northern Mexico. With Santa Anna declaring himself dictator again, how long do you think you're gonna' stay away from him? How long do you think it's gonna' be before he does something that affects your family?"

Gabriel watched as Sam leaned back in his chair and looked over at him. He could see in his friend's face that the Senator's words had opened a scab from Sam's youth. Gabriel felt the need to comfort Sam, but didn't know what to do, so Gabriel just sat still as Sam turned back.

"John, I'm in a place now where I can be happy," Sam said. "We've made a good life and built up a decent business. I'm fixin' to get married, and all I want to do is raise a family. I don't want to get involved, and I sure as hell would never do anything that would help Santa Anna!"

"To hell with Santa Anna! Do you want your children raised under the rule of a dictator?" Fremont asked forcefully.

"I want to be left alone," Sam answered. "And I want my family to be left alone."

Fremont hesitated, and then said, "If we can buy the land for this railroad from Mexico, then Mesilla will be in the United States. Your children, and their children, will be Americans. Wouldn't you want that for your children, Sam? Wouldn't you rather see your children be American citizens...and be free?"

Sam could feel the other men's eyes looking at him while he looked down into his coffee cup.

After a few moments of silence Walker said, "He's got a point there, Sam."

"Yeah, well, everything I've ever had or loved has been destroyed by that evil bastard, Santa Anna, in one way or another. I won't let him do that to my family anymore."

"Then help us do this," the Senator pleaded. "Help us get a piece of meat to that scavenger and be done with him...for good. Once Mesilla is part of the United States, you and your new family will be rid of him. And, when the railroad goes through, you'll have even more opportunities to make a better life."

Fremont paused and looked at each of the three men in front of him. Then he spoke with deliberation. "Listen, if we can do this, it will make your lives and your family's lives better. And, not just yours, this will affect the lives of literally everyone in the country…and make their lives better, too.

"We need your help." John paused again. "I'd like for you to at least hear me out on this."

Walker looked at Gabriel and then at Sam. When Sam nodded to Walker he turned back to Fremont and said, "All right, John. You came a long way out here. We'll listen to what you have to say."

"Thanks, and believe me, I do appreciate your strong feelings about this," Fremont said looking directly at Sam. "If this weren't so vital to the Union, and our people, I would never ask this of you."

John put his elbows back onto the table. "First, let me say that you men will be extremely well paid. If you agree to serve, you will have the means to create a very good life for the families you are starting.

"The plan is relatively simple. It is the distance involved that makes it difficult. James Gadsden formulated the ideas during his negotiations with Santa Anna. We have refined the details since his return to Washington.

"But, basically, we don't trust Santa Anna. He is an opportunist and a liar, to say the least. Because of that, Gadsden stipulated certain conditions when he agreed to the bribe.

"Santa Anna wanted his gold shipped to Cuba as soon as the U. S. Congress ratified the treaty. James was afraid that Santa Anna would backslide on the agreement once he got his bribe money, especially if Congress changed anything in the original treaty, which they did wind up doing, of course.

"Anyway, James was able to structure the agreement so that there is to be a formal ceremony transferring the land. At the ceremony there will be an official signing of a document recognizing the ratified treaty and a symbolic lowering of the Mexican flag and raising of the American flag. The bribe will be paid when the ceremony is complete."

Fremont stopped talking and looked for a reaction from the others. When no one spoke he continued. "Gadsden insisted that the ceremony take place in Mesilla."

John could see the surprise on the faces of the three other men. He watched as they looked back and forth at one another.

Walker turned to him and said, "You kiddin' me?"

"No," John said. "I think it was actually a very smart move on Gadsden's part. Mesilla's the largest Mexican town in the area being purchased, so Santa Anna had to agree. But, the U.S. Army is just across the river at Fort Fillmore. James also understood that the money would have to be moved secretly and, after his time out there with the three of you, he felt that he knew the right men who could be trusted to do that."

Sam, Gabriel and Walker looked apprehensively at one another. Then Walker said cautiously to the Senator, "What is it you want us to do, and how the hell do you think we're gonna' sneak that much gold to Mesilla?"

"Well, like I said, James came up with the original parts of the plan while he dealt with Santa Anna down in Mexico," John said. "But, it is amazing how well the details just fit together once he got back to Washington.

"The Double Eagles will come from the U.S. Mint in New Orleans. There are a series of rather complex financial transactions going on even now that will mask the sources and purpose of the money. You don't need to know about any of that, but as the uncirculated coins are acquired in relatively small batches they will be specially packaged in New Orleans.

"The money is being disguised as a shipment of books. There will eventually be twenty-one wooden crates. On the inside, each crate will have books packed on the top, bottom, and sides with gold coins hidden in the middle between them. Each crate will weigh one hundred and fifty pounds.

"The books are a gift from 'The American People' to the library of *His Excellency*, Santa Anna, in commemoration of the new treaty. That way it's a very official shipment of something no one would want. It's also not tied to any specific government agency or office.

"The containers will go by ship from the port of New Orleans to Brownsville, Texas, at the mouth of the *Rio Bravo*. Walker, did you ever deal with a riverboat man named Captain Richard King when you were with Jeff Davis during the war?"

"No," Walker said. "Never heard of him. All my time there was down inside Mexico, away from the ports."

"Well," John nodded, "I guess Secretary Davis and Zachary Taylor dealt a lot with a couple of riverboat captains named Mifflin Kenedy and Richard King during the war. The two captains transported the men and supplies up and down the *Rio Bravo* for the army. Jeff Davis apparently got to know Kenedy and King pretty well.

"It turns out; these two have a private steamboat operation, M. Kenedy and Company, on the *Rio Bravo* now. Secretary Davis has communicated with them and this fellow, Captain Richard King, will guarantee that he can get our twenty-one crates of books north up the *Rio Bravo* to the stockade at Presidio - for the right price, of course."

The last of John Fremont's coffee was cold when he stopped talking momentarily and put the cup to his lips, but he took a swallow anyway. He continued. "That's where you all come in. We need for you to ride to the stockade at Presidio and meet Captain King. There will be two wagons with mule teams waiting there for you. You would load the 'books' and drive them to Mesilla. When you get to Mesilla you'd turn the wagons over to the officer in charge at Fort Fillmore with a letter instructing him to present the gift to the Mexican commander as part of the official ceremony after the American flag is raised."

"Don't see why you don't just have the Army go down and pick up that load," Gabriel spoke up.

"Well, Gabriel, like I said, the U.S. Government can't really have anything to do with this. Besides, the closest and easiest way to get heavy wagons from Presidio to Mesilla is up through Mexico, because the U.S. side of the river is too rugged down south.

"Also, we couldn't just prance a company of American soldiers through Mexico. Don't think they'd take too kindly to that. The other thing is…only a small handful of people know about this, and we gotta' keep it that way."

"Well, don't you think we're gonna' need to take a bunch of men down there with us?" Walker asked.

"You'll need a few men, for sure, to help with the wagons and animals…give you a few extra guns," John answered. "But, Walker, the fewer the better.

"Gadsden said you were the one who gave him the idea. He said to tell you this is like getting through Indian country. You either take a whole lot of men…or just a few."

Fremont continued before the others could say anything, "The President won't sign the Treaty until I get back and he is assured that we can do this. Depending on the response we get from Santa Anna, the arrangements will be finalized. We will send a courier to you confirming the date you need to meet Captain King in Presidio, and the date you must be back in Mesilla for the ceremony."

Walker looked around the table at his friends. "Shit," he whispered under his breath, and turned back to Fremont.

"Well, what do you say?" Fremont asked.

"I say you were right, John." Walker threw his napkin onto his plate. "I need a drink!"

86

September 2, 1854

The crowd had been gathering at the *Melendres Hacienda* for over an hour. Women from town brought food throughout the day and the *hacienda's* large kitchen had been active since before daylight. As the evening approached, children hurried around the outside courtyard lighting candles in the *luminarias* in preparation for the party that would follow the double wedding ceremony.

"The men are here. It's time for you two to get ready." Rosa said excitedly as she entered the doorway into Katrina's bedroom.

"Thank God!" Mary Beth blurted like a prisoner whose guards had just opened the cell door. She caught herself and cleared her throat as she said more properly, "I mean, thank goodness it's finally cooling down."

Mary Beth stopped fanning her face and folded the small black lace covered fan. She raised herself from Katrina's bed where she and Katrina had been ordered to rest, for over two hours, by the large battery of older women who had been attending the two young brides. As they had been directed, Mary Beth and Katrina wore only thin camisole tops and their pantaloons so they wouldn't perspire before the wedding.

Katrina also gladly stood up from the bed and looked down at herself. "*Tia*, it has been so hot today. Do you think we could just go to the wedding dressed like this?"

Rosa giggled slyly. "I'm sure Sam and Walker would like that. But, we'd have to bury your mother…and the priest!"

People whistled and cheered as the two grooms approached. Gabriel drove the big wagon with Walker on the seat next to him. Sam rode horseback.

The wagon had been decorated with colorful streamers of ribbon and paper. Four wooden chairs were in the wagon bed with feathers and paper flowers tied to them. On each corner of the wagon a pole held a swinging lantern.

A light evening breeze stirred the streamers when the wagon stopped in front of the Melendres courtyard. Although the day had been a very warm, the desert evening, as always, brought a welcomed coolness.

"Think it's too late to make a run for it?" Sam asked pulling his horse to a halt as people started walking out to greet them.

"Might still be able to make a getaway." Walker answered reaching into the back for his gray suit coat. "What do you think, Gabriel?"

"Wish you wouldn't." Gabriel said solemnly and set the brake. "I made a promise to Miss Katrina and Mary Beth." Gabriel's big smile burst open. "They said if you two took off runnin', I's to shoot you both!"

No altar of any church could have matched the majesty of the Organ Mountains that evening at sunset as they rose like massive stained glass windows in the front of a devine cathedral. While the priest stood before of the *Melendres Hacienda* facing the large crowd assembled for the wedding, the jagged peaks and deep canyons of the Organs framed his silhouette and produced brilliant colors that gradually changed their royal hues throughout the ceremony.

During the service Mary Beth and Walker stood slightly to one side as they faced the priest while Sam and Katrina stood to the other side. Between the two men, directly in front of the priest but one step behind the two couples, stood their Best Man – Gabriel.

It was not a long ceremony when compared to the time and preparation that had been put into making things ready for the wedding. The two couples and Gabriel had spent the summer finishing the new home for Walker and Mary Beth. The large barn and corrals were also completed. Sam and Walker tolerated the countless wedding details that

Katrina and Mary Beth fussed with and, as a result, that night the two young women had the perfect wedding that each had always wanted.

The newlyweds and all their guests enjoyed a grand *fiesta* after the wedding service. The music started as soon as the nuptials finished. Several large tables had been moved outdoors, decorated, and loaded with food. Many of the dishes were made with the fresh green chiles that were only available for a short time before they ripened and turned bright red.

"Are you happy, Mrs. Walker?" Walker asked his new bride as they danced.

Mary Beth squeezed her arms around her husband's neck and said, "This is the happiest night of my life. I want to dance with you forever." She squealed and laughed as he raised her off her feet and spun with her across the courtyard.

Sam turned his head when he heard his sister. He danced with Katrina in his arms and maneuvered his new wife toward Mary Beth. When they got close Sam took Katrina's hand and offered it to Walker. They exchanged partners and Sam started to dance with his sister.

He hugged Mary Beth as they danced and said, "Guess we both got married. Can you believe that?"

"I know. Feels like I'm dreaming…and I don't want to wake up," she said. "Don't you wish Momma and Pa could be here tonight? They'd be so happy. I've been thinkin' about them a lot lately. Momma would love this wedding so much."

Sam pulled back and looked into Mary Beth's face as they kept dancing. He smiled and said, "Hey, don't think they're not here. I got a feelin' they're enjoyin' every minute of this."

A few dances later, at the end when the music stopped, Rosa walked over to Katrina and Sam. She motioned for Mary Beth and Walker to come over, as well. When the two couples of newlyweds were together Rosa said, "It's time for you to leave. Some of the older guests are getting very tired."

"What?" Sam jerked back from her words. "Rosa, the *fiesta* is just gettin' goin' good!"

"Sam, some of the people need to start home," Rosa said.

"Well, hell, let 'em go," Sam replied. "Walker and I are just gettin' started. We still got some dancin' an' visitin' to do!"

"No one will leave before you all do. It's not polite." Rosa said calmly. "It's time for you to go. I've already told Gabriel."

Sam reluctantly followed with Katrina as the two couples said their thank you's and goodbye's to the Melendres family. By the time they finished, Gabriel was waiting in front of the *fiesta* with the lanterns lit on the wagon. After the newlyweds were seated in the chairs in the back of the wagon, Gabriel circled the *hacienda* compound twice so the crowd could cheer, wave, and heckle.

It was a beautifully clear night as they rode slowly through the desert back to Mesilla. The couples relived the ceremony with one another and then talked about all the different conversations each had had with the many people at the party. After awhile there was a stretch of silence.

"Gabriel, thank you for standin' up for me at the wedding," Sam said. "It meant a lot to me. Guess you know that."

"I want to thank you, too, Gabriel." Walker said.

"It was a honor," Gabriel said. "Meant a lot to me, too," he felt his throat get tight. "Pro'bly the biggest honor in my life."

Mary Beth stood up in the bed of the wagon. She stepped up behind Gabriel and wrapped her arms around him. She hugged his stout shoulders and big chest from behind and said, "It meant a lot to me too, Mister. If it weren't for you, we wouldn't be here. We've come a long way from that little homestead in Texas, haven't we?"

Mary Beth put her head next to Gabriel's as he raised his, but kept facing forward. She felt his big right hand come up from the reins and pat the back of both of her hands that were barely clasped together in front of his broad chest. Then she felt his tear splash upon the top of her wrist.

"You've been our 'Best Man' for a long time," she said.

The first stop in Mesilla was Mary Beth and Walker's new home. Gabriel stopped the wagon in front and got out to help Mary Beth down. He stayed by the wagon and held a lantern high for light as they made their way to the front door. They all watched as Walker picked Mary Beth up and carried her into their new adobe home.

Next Gabriel drove to their house off the Mesilla Plaza. He started to get out when Sam said, "Just stay in the wagon, Gabriel. I'll help Mrs. Stevens down."

After he lifted Katrina from the back of the wagon Sam walked to the front. He leaned on the steel rim of the wagon's wheel for a moment with his head down and then looked up at Gabriel.

"Hey, how many miles you think we've been together?" Sam asked quietly.

Gabriel smiled down at his friend. "We traveled some roads, hadn't we?"

"I just want you to know…what Mary Beth said tonight…" Sam started.

"Sam," Gabriel closed his eyes and nodded, "I know." When he opened his big dark eyes again he grinned and said, "Now you better get on in the house. I gotta' go put these poor mules to bed. They ain't used to stayin' out this late!"

Gabriel drove the wagon into the new barn at the Walker's place. He then unhitched the mule team and gave them an extra ration of feed. When he was finished he rode Sam's saddle horse that they had trailed behind the wagon, back to the *Melendres Hacienda*. He spent the night in one of their outbuildings where he had lived when they first arrived in the Mesilla Valley.

Two days later Walker took delivery of another courier's pouch from Washington. The leather satchel held two envelopes. In the first was a short message telling the men that President Pierce had signed the Treaty. It also gave the dates of October 15, 1854 to meet Captain King in Presidio and November 16, 1854 for the ceremony in Mesilla. The second envelope contained a large amount of cash.

87

October 1, 1854

Sam could see the smoke rising from the chimney of their homestead at the bottom of the small west hill. The familiar smell of cedars and live oaks wafted in the air. When the words in his head became louder he turned on the big oak stump on which he was sitting and faced his father.

"…And he's the worst kind. He's a bad man with power," Jonathan said looking into his son's eyes.

"But we're not going to let him get away with it. I promise you that," Pa said with a nod of his head and a soft smile.

"Sam," Jonathan sighed leaning forward and putting his hands just above each of the boy's knees while he kept looking into his son's eyes. "I know you're scared and truth is, I am too. And I'm tellin' you, I don't want to go fight in this damn war. But a man's always gotta' do what's right and sometimes that's not an easy thing. Sometimes, like we're doin' now, that means fightin' against what's wrong. It means standing up against the bad ones and not lettin' 'em have their way."

Jonathan sat up straight and took a deep breath. He said calmly, "That's why we're doin' this, son. If there was a different shot, I'd take it."

Sam looked at his father. "I guess I know that, Pa," He said as tears blurred his eyes. "Just want you to be careful while you're whippin' Santa Anna."

"I will, son, you can count on it.

"You remember all this for when your time comes though. As you go through life your whole world will change, at least a time or two. I know mine has. Everybody's does. But no matter how much the world

443

around you might get twisted up or look different, there's one thing you can hang onto. Right and wrong, *never* change. In your life, when it's your turn, a good man like you can't let the bad ones win. Will ya' promise me that?"

"I promise, Pa," Sam said with all his heart and reached out for his father. He tried to put his arms around Jonathan, but couldn't. Sam reached out farther saying, "Pa...Pa!" Both his arms were outstretched as his head rose from the pillow and Sam awoke.

"Sam, what's wrong?" Katrina said startled as she rose up in the bed and turned toward her husband. "What is it? Are you alright?"

"Yeah, I'm fine, Katrina." Sam said and took in several deep breaths. "Just had a dream. It woke me up."

She cuddled next to him and put her arm around him. "Was it a bad dream?"

"No, just a dream. Sorry I woke you up."

"That's all right. You want to tell me about it?"

"Naw, not really," Sam said quietly, and then continued after a moment. "I dreamed about my Pa. The last time I saw him. We were on the little hill above our old homeplace.

"Everything has been changing so much...guess he's been on my mind lately. Sorry I woke you up. Go back to sleep, lady," Sam kissed Katrina softly on the head as he started to get out of bed.

"Where are you going?" she asked.

"I'm just going to stir the fire. You go back to sleep. I'll get you up in plenty of time to make breakfast with Mary Beth for all the men."

It was still an hour before daylight when Sam woke Katrina and the two of them walked together toward Mary Beth and Walker's place. The crisp predawn air was cold on their faces. Sam held Katrina's hand in his as they strolled, neither wanting to talk about how much they would miss one another over the next month and a half.

Katrina giggled as they passed the corrals and could hear the four mountain men from Taos snoring in Walker's big barn. "Are those men, or bears, that Walker brought down here?" she asked playfully.

"Well, at least I'll be able to get plenty of sleep out on the trail, finally," Sam said. When Katrina gave him a questioning look, he continued, "Now that I've gotten used to your snorin', sleepin' out with those four bears and Gabriel won't be any problem at all!"

Katrina threw Sam's hand from hers and shoved his shoulder with both of her hands. "Samuel Austin Stevens! You lie! I do not snore!" She shoved him again.

Sam laughed and wrapped her up in his arms. "Well, maybe I was exaggerating, just a little bit."

"Sam, I do not snore!" Katrina protested with a soft giggle while she struggled in his embrace.

"You want me to hold him, so you can whip him, Miss Katrina?" Gabriel's deep voice came out of the shadows as he stepped out from behind the corrals. "Is Sam misbehavin' again this early in the mornin'?"

"Yes he is, Gabriel," Katrina said breaking free as Sam released her. "I think he needs a good spanking."

"Now, Sweetheart," Sam said reaching for her hand.

"Don't you try to butter me up, Mister Stevens," Kartina feigned a cold response.

"Gabriel, Katrina heard the boys in the barn snorin'. We were just talking about…"

"Sam!" Katrina burst out.

"Well, they do snore pretty loud," Sam said, and stopped.

"Yeah, they sho' do!" Gabriel grinned. "I could here 'em halfway here from Miss Katrina's folk's place."

"Well, I suspect they probably had another big round at the *cantinas* last night," Sam said.

"Yep," Gabriel chuckled. "I 'magine they did."

After their meeting with John Fremont in Santa Fe, Walker and Sam had made a short trip to Taos while Gabriel stayed with the wagon and mule team. They knew they would need some extra men for the Presidio trip and Walker wanted solid men he could trust. Of the four men they recruited in Taos for the job, three of them were men who had helped Walker bring his horse herd to Mesilla.

Walker had sent for the men as soon as he received the latest dispatch from Washington. The rough hewn mountain men had arrived in Mesilla two days ago. Walker gave them some money when they first arrived. Most of it was now in the hands of bar owners and whores.

"I been waitin' here fo' a little while," Gabriel said. He motioned toward the house with his head. "Looks like they lights're lit in the house now."

Sam and Katrina each put an arm around the other and walked with Gabriel to the front door.

Two hours later the men had eaten a very hearty breakfast. Panniers on the pack mules were bulging with provisions and the horses were all saddled and ready. The animals were tied to the outside fence rails of the large corrals. Riders milled around next to their mounts checking knots, cinches, and gear.

Walker and Sam were standing with their brides close to the front of the new home when Gabriel swung up into his saddle. The mountain men all followed his lead.

"Guess it's time to go," Sam said to Katrina. "I'll be back as quick as I can get here. Don't worry about us. We'll be just fine."

"I'm not worried about you, Sam," she said smiling. "It's all the bandits, and Indians, and rattlesnakes that bother me."

Sam grinned and said tenderly, "I love you, Katrina. I'll think of you every minute 'til I get home." He kissed her. "Then we'll practice makin' babies - a lot. What do you think of that idea?"

"As much as you want," she said. Then they kissed long and hard. Sam released his arms from around her tiny waist, turned, and walked toward the corrals.

Mary Beth and Walker stood looking into each other's eyes with their arms around one another's waists. "You better be careful and come back here to me, Mister," Mary Beth said.

"I don't think there's anything big enough, or mean enough, to keep me from getting' back here to you, Lady," Walker said. He kissed her.

"Walker, you be careful. You're the only husband I've got, you know."

446

"I'll be back before you know it, Darlin'," he said smiling. "Now, don't go getting' sad on me. I need your pretty smile to keep in my head. Got a bit of a ride in front of us. When I get back we'll hole-up in this house together for a month, I promise."

Mary Beth smiled broadly and threw her long hair back. "You just keep your wits about you and come home to me. I'll be waitin' here when you ride in." She put her arms around him and they kissed again.

As Walker left Mary Beth's embrace and turned toward the horses, Sam rode toward him leading Walker's tall pinto by the reins. Sam said boldly, "Got quite a load to pick-up. Let's head south, boys!"

88

October 15, 1854

"Fish-head" Ben Flagg was the first to see the river boats slowly chugging their way north up the meandering *Rio Bravo*. He stood up on the big boulder where he'd been perched. "Yonder comes a pair a strange lookin' creatures," he said and pointed downriver.

"That's likely them, all right." Walker responded, also standing up from a big rock where he'd been sitting. He looked across the river towards the rough-built stockade for Sam and Gabriel, but couldn't see them. They were buying supplies for the return trip to Mesilla while Walker and the other men rested down by the river on the Mexican side to watch for Captain King and his unique cargo.

The group had arrived in Presidio the day before, and as John Fremont had promised, two wagons and mule teams were waiting for them at the stockade. They had forded the river with the mules and wagons earlier in the morning. Although the trip down from Mesilla was uneventful, it had been a long two weeks in the saddles.

"You still got good eyes, Fish-head," Walker said to the other man.

"Yeah, I may not hear for shit, but I can still see things comin' pretty good."

Ben Flagg was called "Fish-head" because he had no ears. Many years before he'd been caught out alone in a high mountain blizzard that caused an avalanche and took his horse, mule, furs and gear. Ben survived in the frozen wilderness for a month with only his knife and a flintlock rifle with a broken stock. After he finally wandered into another trapper's cabin, he lost both ears and several toes to frostbite.

Fish-head met Kit and Walker at a spring *Rendezvous* where mountain men and fur companies gathered to trade goods, exchange news, and usually get exceedingly drunk for about a week. He eventually migrated down to the Taos area and became a regular with the group of trappers and traders who settled there. Walker and Fish-head Ben Flagg had shared many seasons together in the high country.

"Walker, you ever seen boats that looked like that?" Fish-head asked when the odd looking vessels got closer.

"Hell, I've never seen anything that looked like that," Walker answered. The other men laughed.

Dark smoke puffed out of five foot tall smoke stacks that rose from the two approaching boats. As the stacks got closer the pattern of bulges in the smoke stream matched a monotonous *ca-chunk, ca-chunk* sound that traveled up the river from the vessel's small steam engines.

One man stood toward the stern of each boat working a rudder handle. Occasionally, the men would lift a pole from the deck beside them and push off something in the river. When the boats approached within a hundred yards, Walker saw each boatman pick up a rifle.

"Hello in the boats." Walker called out when they were close enough to hear him. "Either one of you Captain Richard King?"

"Who wants to know?" A man yelled back.

"I'm Richard Walker, down here from Mesilla," Walker answered, pausing slightly between words so they would carry over the sounds of the river and the steam engines.

"And who sent you?" The man queried using the same pattern of pauses.

When Walker yelled, "Jefferson Davis", the boatmen put down their rifles and steered the chugging vessels toward the waiting wagons.

The two boats were identical in appearance and very unique in their construction. The pointed bows rose two or three feet above the waterline and the underside of them curved down and became almost flat under the boats. Each vessel flared wide in the middle and tapered narrow in the stern. The sterns were squared, but the bottoms curved up out of the water almost as high as the bows. The small steam engines and smoke stacks were built into the centerline of the boats about two thirds of the way back from the front.

After the mountain men helped beach the two boats, a hard looking man stepped ashore from the first one and said, "I'm Captain Richard King."

"Richard Walker," Walker said and extended his hand. "Looks like you're right on time."

"Yeah, well, this is when I said I'd be here. You men been waitin' long?"

"Nope, we just came in yesterday," Walker said. "These are some unusual boats you got here. Can't say that I've ever seen anything like 'em." He looked over at Fish-head.

"No, you haven't," King said. "I made these two special last year. You have to be tricky sometimes to haul on this river, especially way up north like this."

"Well, looks like you got her figured out"

"Yep, you can ask anybody. If you got enough money for the tare, Captain Richard King can float a load up a dry creek bed, anywhere on the *Rio Bravo*." He turned and pointed behind him across the river at Sam and Gabriel who were leading the pack mules down from the stockade toward the river. "They with your bunch here?"

"Yeah, they went to pick-up supplies for the trip back to Mesilla," Walker answered.

"Well, let's get these gadamn boats unloaded," King said curtly.

As the men unloaded the cargo and started shuttling the heavy wooden crates to the two wagons, Gabriel and Sam forded the river. They tied their horses and the pack mules close to the wagons. Gabriel stayed at the wagons and arranged the load as the mountain men delivered the heavy boxes of books. Sam went down to the river.

"Captain King, this is my partner, Sam Stevens," Walker said standing up after he plopped one of the crates onto the shore.

"Pleased to meet you," Sam said shaking hands with the stern faced boatman. "Did you have any trouble hauling these books up the river?"

"No, just with my conscience," King said. "Guess a man'll do anything for money."

"What do you mean?" Sam responded and cocked his head to one side.

"Well, on the way up here I got to thinkin'. Just a few years ago my partner, Mifflin, and I came out here to haul half the American Army and all their gear up and down this river so they could go kill that worthless piece of shit, Santa Anna. Now we're haulin' fancy presents for that son of a bitch…from the Americans. Ain't that a gadamn stupid thing?"

"Wish they had killed him," Sam said.

"You and me both, mister," King grunted.

When the twenty-one wooden crates were loaded into the wagons, Captain King made ready to launch his boats.

"You headin' back already?" Walker asked.

"Yeah, this time of year you never know what this old river's gonna' do," King responded. "She could be up or down a foot by morning. Without that heavy cargo on board I got plenty of water to float these things. I'm gonna' get my ass back down south while the gettin's good."

He stepped ashore and extended his right hand to Walker and Sam. As they shook hands he said, "Good luck to you and your men. You got a long haul in front of you."

Captain Richard King turned and pushed his boat into the river. He jumped onboard and picked the pole from the deck and used it to push off the shoreline and into the current. Then he turned to Sam and Walker and said loudly as he started to float downstream, "By the way, when you get those books to Santa Anna, tell him I hope he eats shit and chokes to death on it."

The two boats began floating away in the current flowing downriver. Walker turned to Sam and said, "Pleasant, good natured sonofabitch, wadn't he?"

"Yeah, if you like vinegar," Sam chuckled.

"He's pro'bly right about gettin' while the gettin's good, though," Walker said. "This weather's been holdin'. What do you say we try to get some miles behind us before dark?"

"Yeah, I think we should," Sam answered. "Let us see how these new mule teams are gonna' do." He paused and smiled. "You don't think the men are gonna' bitch, do ya'?"

"Oh, hell no," Walker cackled. "They'll pro'bly just tell us to eat shit, and choke on it!"

There were still two hours of daylight remaining that day when their small band started watching for an appropriate spot to spend the night. They had made a good ten miles inland from the *Rio Bravo*, but with the long haul ahead, they didn't want to push the group too hard.

Although the new mule teams were fresh, the men and animals that had made the trip from Mesilla still needed more rest.

"How 'bout that little flat rise up yonder?" Gabriel said. He held the mule's reins in his hands while he stood up tall on the wagon's floorboards and looked off into the distance. "They's some mesquite trees up there, but we'll be able to see what's goin' on all around us."

"That's a good spot, Gabriel," Sam said as he stood from the driver's seat of the other wagon. He pointed to the small hilltop six hundred yards away and raised his voice for all the others to hear, "Let's make for that rise. We'll set our camp there."

An hour later the campfire burned to make coals while Sam and Gabriel cut the fresh meat and late season squash they'd bought at the stockade. One man gathered wood, another got bedrolls distributed, while two men tethered animals. Walker finished hanging the wagon harnesses to dry in the mesquite trees and stepped away to survey the desert around them. He froze with the sight before him.

Walker restrained himself, in order not to alert the approaching horsemen, and walked to the back of the wagon's open tailgate where Sam and Gabriel were preparing the supper.

"We've got company," he said to Sam and Gabriel without taking his eyes from the desert. Walker nodded his head toward the south and said, "Turn real slow."

Sam turned his head to Gabriel and nodded. They stood next to one another and Gabriel kept cutting squash while Sam turned around to look with Walker. "Holy shit," Sam said calmly and leaned back against the open tailgate of the wagon.

"What is it, Sam?" Gabriel asked, still trying to pretend to fix the supper.

"There's a column of Mexican soldiers ridin' in, Gabriel. They're less than a half mile out."

89

October 15, 1854

The twelve mounted Mexican soldiers rode two-by-two in a line as they approached the base of the small rise where the wagons were parked. By the time the soldiers were a hundred yards away and started uphill, the four mountain men and Gabriel had slowly maneuvered themselves behind one of the wagons. They stood with the wagon between them and the approaching force. Each man held his loaded weapon out of sight and ready.

Sam and Walker stood with rifles in hand in front of the wagon and faced the Mexicans. It was obvious that the two riding next to one another in the front of the advancing formation were officers. Soon they were close enough for Sam to tell that the one on the left was a Colonel, and the other was a young Lieutenant. Five regular soldiers rode in line behind each officer.

The Colonel raised his right arm high and commanded, "*Alto*", as he and the Lieutenant stopped their horses ten yards in front of Sam and Walker. The horse soldiers split their column and rode their mounts to a stop in line-abreast positions behind the two officers.

"*Buenos tardes*," the Colonel said when his men were in place facing Sam and Walker.

"*Buenos tardes, Colonel,*" Sam responded.

"I'm glad we caught up to you so soon" the Colonel said in English.

"*Oh. Que paso?*" Sam asked, wondering what was going on.

"This is Lieutenant Benito Chacon." When the Colonel gestured to his left, the Lieutenant straightened his back and saluted.

The Colonel straightened his own back and pronounced importantly, "I am the special *attaché* and advisor to *His Excellency, Antonio Lopez de Santa Anna Perez de Lebron.* My name is Colonel Denicio Bernillo, from *Ciudad Mexico.*

"It is my understanding that you are transporting a very special gift for *His Most Serene Highness,*" the Colonel said smiling. "We have come to ensure your safe passage through Mexico."

Sam and Walker turned their heads slightly and looked at one another.

"I don't trust that Colonel as far as I could piss," Walker said under his breath to Sam half an hour later as the two of them finished filling their plates from the back of the wagon's open tailgate.

"Me neither," Sam said. "We need to keep our men close together 'til we can get this figured out." He turned and both men started walking back toward the fire.

"It is very kind of you to share your meal with us," Colonel Bernillo said when Sam and Walker approached. "This is quite good."

Bernillo sat next to his Lieutenant by the fire. They savored the fresh meat and squash Gabriel and Sam had fixed for their group. The other Mexican soldiers sat next to their own fire thirty yards away eating trail rations.

"Well, we were kinda' surprised when you rode in, Colonel Bernillo," Sam said. "We weren't expecting an escort."

"Yeah, we thought that we were just supposed to come down here from Mesilla and pick up a load, and take it back up there," Walker said.

"You mean you weren't informed about the shipment you are carrying?" Bernillo acted more interested in the bite of squash he put into his mouth than the question he'd just asked.

"Oh, sure," Sam said. "They told us it was a heavy load of books. Very important freight for *His Excellency, Santa Anna,* that we gotta' get back to Mesilla for a big ceremony."

"Ah, yes, the ceremony," Bernillo said. "It will be quite the grand event." He picked up another piece of squash with his fork and asked as he put it into his mouth. "Who was it who hired you, anyway?"

"What was that fella's name? We got it written down back in Mesilla." Walker looked at Sam like a shill wondering how his card shark wanted to play the hand.

"James," Sam looked back. "James Gadsden."

"James Gadsden, of course. Do you know Mr. Gadsden well?"

"No, not personally," Sam responded.

Colonel Bernillo placed his fork onto his plate and straightened his back. "Well, James Gadsden is a very good friend of mine. He and I enjoyed many good times together with *His Most Serene Highness* in *Cuidad Mexico* when James served as the American Foreign Minister."

"Well, ain't that somethin'?" Sam remarked and shot a sidelong look at Walker and Gabriel.

"Yeah, that take's it all, doesn't it?" Walker said.

"Yes, James and I became *compadres* during the time he spent in Mexico. I'm surprised he didn't tell you about arranging for your safe passage through the country," Denicio said sincerely. "After all, it was his idea that you have a military escort provided by *His Excellency.*"

90

October 16, 1854

"This is liable to be somethin' bad," Walker said as he blew across the top of the tin coffee cup in the dawning twilight.

Sam poured himself a cup and sat the pot back on the small bed of coals that had been raked to the side of the morning campfire. He stood up and also blew at the steam in his cup to cool the hot liquid. "Doesn't look good, does it?" he said and tried to take a sip.

The overcast lay like a thick dark blanket in the sky from horizon to horizon. The rising sun hid somewhere behind it in the east, but its brilliant light could only change the darkness of the night into lighter shades of gray. A stiff breeze, of distinctly colder air, blew straight out of the north.

Sam and Walker had been awake in their bedrolls most of the night. They'd watched high thin clouds start blowing across the stars sometime around midnight. Within a couple of hours the stars disappeared and the sky grew very dark.

Colonel Denicio Bernillo walked to the fire and reached out with both hands to warm them. "*Buenos Dias*, Gentlemen," he said smiling. "It appears the weather has decided to change."

"Yep, looks like it could get nasty for awhile," Walker said.

"I think we should wait here until the weather improves, don't you?" Bernillo said and turned to warm his backside.

"Can't do that, Colonel," Sam said. "We got too many miles to cover to get back to Mesilla. We need to get these wagons movin'…and keep 'em movin'."

"Yes, but what about the men?" Bernillo turned and faced the fire again. "Don't you think it would be a hardship on the men to force them to travel in bad weather? Wouldn't it be wise to wait for better conditions?"

"I think our men'll be fine," Walker answered and looked at Sam.

Sam held Walker's eyes for a moment as he took a sip from his coffee cup. He swallowed and said, "Yeah, our boys are used to it, Colonel. But, if you want to keep your men here until the weather blows through, it wouldn't be hard for you to catch up with us."

"Certainly not," Bernillo said, and then smiled. "We are to be your escorts...ensure your safe passage through Mexico."

Denicio Bernillo turned toward the troop of Mexicans huddled around their own fire. He commanded loudly, "Lieutenant Chacon, prepare your soldiers to travel."

The mules did not want to get back into the harnesses and pull the heavy wagons again that morning. After the ordeal of hitching them to the wagons, it was decided that Sam and Gabriel would be the drivers of the unruly teams. After a couple of miles the animals began to settle down.

Drizzle started midmorning. Rain began an hour or so later. The rain and drizzle alternated with one another throughout the day, but the cool north wind never took a break. It blew into the faces of the men and animals mile after mile. By early afternoon they were wet, and cold.

The drizzle began to lighten a couple of hours before sundown. Gabriel found another place to camp that had plenty of mesquite trees for firewood. He and Sam had put some dry wood with the bedrolls and supplies under the tarps with the load in the back of the wagons. When they made camp the first order of business was to use the dry wood to build a fire hot enough to burn the wet mesquite that the men started dragging into the camp.

The slightest hint of sunlight peeked under the clouds to the west an hour before sundown when the drizzle finally stopped. Men alternated between warming and drying themselves by the raging fire and accomplishing whatever camp chores needed to be done before dark. Soon the smell of cooking beans from the big Dutch oven pots filled the cool damp air.

Sam lifted the lid of the big coffee pot and stirred the grounds and water, hoping it would make them boil sooner. While he swirled the coarse ground coffee beans in the heating water, Sam surveyed the camp and watched the men. He noticed Colonel Bernillo standing alone looking off into the distance. Bernillo pulled a watch from an inside pocket and checked it.

"How's that coffee comin'?" Fish-head asked as he hurried up to the fire and extended his hands toward it. "Didn't think a fella could get cold this far south. But I tell ya' what, think I'd trade my last six achin' toes for a hot cup of coffee right now. That damn wind has got me chilled."

"Yeah, me too," Sam said. "This'll be boilin' in a minute. Get your cup ready an' you can have the first go at it."

Both groups sat around the big warm mesquite fire just after sundown and shared a supper of hot beans. Pots of coffee were made, one after the other, until everyone got some. Once everyone was fed and warmed, the Mexican soldiers began to slip off and build smaller fires to keep themselves warm as they slept.

"Another very fine meal, *Señor* Stevens," Colonel Bernillo said as he finished his plate and placed it on the ground next to the fire. "Thank you." He reached into the inside pocket of his jacket and took out a gold watch. He checked the time and started to put the watch away.

"Been noticing your watch there," Sam said. "Looks like it's a nice one."

"Yes, I've had it for many years. It keeps very good time," Denicio replied.

"You seem to check it a lot."

Bernillo paused as though surprised at the comment. "Oh, I suppose it has become a habit. Checking the time. Perhaps I have spent too many years in the Capitol."

"Guess that must be it, 'cause there's not much call for keepin' tight schedules out here," Sam said.

"Of course not." Denicio gave a nervous chuckle.

"Mind if I take a look at it?" Sam asked.

"Certainly," Denicio said and undid the gold chain that was attached to his uniform. He handed the chain and the watch to Sam.

Sam recognized the watch as soon as it was placed into his hand. He swallowed hard before he opened Jonathan's gold watch and saw the fancy script inside which read: *Moses Austin*. His stomach knotted and he clenched his teeth before he looked up and said calmly, "Very nice watch. You say you've had it a long time?"

Denicio reached for the watch and said, "Yes, many years. It is a special momento from our great crusade against the Texas rebels. Spoils of war, as they say. It has actually become somewhat of a good luck charm for me."

Sam felt his face getting flush. With his right hand he rubbed the stubs where the fingers of his left hand had been. His whole body flashed with rage and he looked across the fire at Gabriel. Sam turned to face the Mexican officer. He smiled and said coolly, "So, you served in the war against the Texas Revolution?"

"Yes, I fought at the Battle of the Alamo and at San Jacinto."

"You were at the Alamo?"

"I served with distinction under General Cos. Of course, I was a young Lieutenant then. But, later from the battle in which I acquired this watch, Santa Anna himself decorated me for my service to him," Denicio boasted.

"You got this watch in a battle?" Sam tried to stay under control.

"Well, perhaps it was more of a skirmish, but it brought me great favor with *El Presidente*. I have been a valuable member of his personal staff ever since."

Sam held his hands in his lap and clenched his fists as tightly as he could to help stop his urge to rip out Bernillo's throat. He said slowly, "Guess a little luck goes a long way."

"That must be true," Denicio said as he reattached the gold chain to his uniform.

Gabriel had put Sam's and Walker's bedrolls under one of the wagons with his in case it began raining again. The other mountain men were to sleep under the other wagon. They would each rotate sentry duty throughout the night, along with the Mexican soldiers, as they had done the night before.

When they left the big fire to get in their beds Sam waited until they were out of hearing range. As they crouched down beside the wagon he said, "Gabriel, that's the bastard who killed my Mother and took Mary Beth."

"Oh my Lord, Sam. You think so?" Gabriel had followed the conversation around the campfire, but was apprehensive.

"He's got Pa's watch!" Sam hissed.

"Told you I didn't trust that son-of-a-bitch," Walker said. "What do you want to do, Sam?"

Sam's eyes were steeled as he watched Bernillo walk away from the fire. He said, "Nothin', right now."

Sam had been laying on his back staring up at the bottom of the wagon for an hour when he heard the first scuffles. On either side of him Walker and Gabriel obviously heard the noises, too, because all three men rose up in their bedrolls at the same time. There were grunts and thuds. A gunshot exploded the night air.

"What the hell?" Walker exclaimed. He was on the side closest to the big campfire and turned toward it.

He saw men's dark figures running through the camp in the direction of the Mexican soldiers. Pistol and rifle shots rang out as the figures shot the soldiers who were still trying to rise from their beds. Colonel Bernillo vaulted to a position next to the campfire's light.

Lieutenant Chacon held his pistol in one hand and his saber in the other as he rushed to join the Colonel. The Lieutenant turned away from the colonel. With his pistol Chacon shot one of the dark men. Colonel Denicio Bernillo drew his saber and stabbed the Lieutenant in the back, running his blade completely through the young officer.

One of Walker's men rushed out from under the other wagon. Bernillo pulled his sword from the dying Chacon's back. With one sweeping motion Bernillo swung his saber and slashed the mountain man across the chest. Walker saw the blade flash in the firelight as the Colonel came back with a slicing blow to the side of the man's neck.

"It's a trap! Get to the horses!" Walker yelled at Sam and Gabriel as he rolled toward them and pushed them to get out of the other side of the wagon. Bullets began to ping into his bedroll just when he rolled away. "Get out! Get out!"

Gabriel was the first to his feet on the far side of the wagon. He raised his rifle up quickly and shot one of the assailants in the face. Sam jumped up beside Gabriel and shot another man who was between them and the campfire. Gabriel reached under the wagon and grabbed their powder and bullets then turned to run with Sam toward the horses.

Walker started with them and then turned to the other wagon. He saw Fish-head crouched behind the wagon reloading his rifle. Two men were rushing toward the wagon. Walker shot the one closest to Fish-head. His friend turned with the ram-rod still in the end of his gun barrel. When he pulled the trigger and shot, his ram-rod stuck out of his attacker's chest like a spear.

"Get the hell outta' there, Fish-head! Get to the horses!" Walker yelled.

Fish-head quickly reached under the wagon and pulled out two rifles. "Walker, here! They're loaded!" He called and threw one to his friend. He stooped down again and grabbed his tomahawk before he started running toward the horses.

Sam hacked away at hobbles and pick strings with his knife as Walker and Fish-head ran up. Walker grabbed the lead rope on his big paint and swung up onto the animal's back. The other men each took an animal's lead.

Fish-head handed the lead rope for the horse he took up to Walker and said, "Here, hold him!"

Walker took the line and Fish-head spun around to the remaining string of horses and mules. He rushed to the mesquite where the main tether line was secured and hacked at it with the sharp steel balde of his tomahawk. When the line was cut he waved his arms and spooked the horses and mules. The ones that weren't hobbled ran away.

Fish-head took the lead rope from Walker and jumped onto the horse's back. "That oughta' slow the sons of bitches down!" He roared and bullets began whizzing through the air around them.

"Run!" Walker yelled. "Run, Boys!"

91

October 17, 1854

"Why you suppose he killed all his own soldiers, Sam?" Gabriel asked. "Most these po' boys was still in they beds."

Sam, Gabriel, Walker and Fish-head walked slowly through the carnage that had been their camp the night before. The scattered bodies had finished bleeding out during the night. Now the dead lay in massive pools of dark blood which was drying in the late morning sun. The bellies of most of the victims were distended and swollen as the gasses evolved inside their stomachs.

"Don't know, Gabriel. Maybe they wanted to make it look like a massacre."

"It was one, aw'right," Fish-head said with disgust as he walked toward the bodies of his three companions from Taos. "Damn those murderin' sons-a-bitches to hell!"

"How many of them do you think there were?" Sam asked.

"No idea," Walker said. "But looks like we killed five of 'em." He pointed around to extra bodies that were not dressed in Mexican uniforms.

"They took the wagons south, south-east. Wonder where they're goin'?" Walker asked.

"Don't know," Sam answered thoughtfully. "Maybe back to the river. Maybe down to the coast. No tellin'"

"Well, let's bury our men. Then I guess we might as well start headin' back home," Walker said.

"We're not goin' home," Sam said. "We're goin' after him."

"Sam, we don't know how many men Bernillo has."

"Yeah, I know. But I don't think he's got that many left. That's why they didn't come after us last night or this morning."

"Yeah, maybe, but you think the four of us can just sneak up on 'em and take those wagons back?"

"I been thinkin' about it," Sam answered in a pensive tone. "Bernillo may think we'll come after him, but probably not. He knows there's only four of us. If anything, he'd expect us to try to sneak up on 'em during the night.

"I say we try to get close enough today to get a line on where they're headin', and see how many men they've got. Then we circle around ahead of them tonight. Tomorrow we find a place in front of 'em to set a trap and ambush 'em in the daylight. I don't think they'd expect that."

"You think it's worth it, Sam?" Walker asked slowly.

Sam's eyes narrowed. "It's worth it, Walker. Last night while we were hidin' out, at first all I could think about was getting' back home, and bein' with Katrina...havin' our life together. Guess I was scared.

"Then I got mad. I kept thinkin' about Bernillo and my Pa's watch... and Mary Beth, and my brother. I kept thinkin' about Santa Anna and what we're doin' here."

Sam's eyes hardened and his lower lip peeled back as he began speaking coarsely through his bared teeth. "I've had it. I'm done with the bastards! They're not gettin' their way this time. We're gonna get that gold back and I'm gonna' settle with Bernillo. I know what we're gonna' do with Santa Anna, too. We're gonna finish this, once and for all, and be done with 'em!"

92

October 18, 1854

"There's one man drivin' each wagon. They pro'bly have a couple of guns in the seats with 'em." Fish-head told his three waiting companions as he walked quickly toward them. He had just returned from his scouting position on a small rise a quarter of a mile away to the north. "The other seven are on horseback around the wagons. All of 'em, except that Colonel, are carrin' rifles across their laps."

"They still gonna' come through here?" Gabriel asked.

"Yeah, unless they change direction, through this little low place is the only way they can come with those wagons."

"Alright then, let's get in our hidin' spots," Sam said. "Don't shoot 'til the first mule on the lead wagon gets even with that big rock."

"Yeah, Fish-head and I will get the ones on this side." Walker gestured to his right. "You and Gabriel take the ones on that side. Don't worry about Bernillo. Shoot everyone carryin' a rifle first."

The men took their positions for the crossfire, each with two rifles. There had been plenty of weapons left at the massacre site, but two long guns apiece were all they could readily carry.

Within an hour the horsemen and the slow moving heavy wagons approached the ambush. Sam didn't know if he heard them or felt them first. He was on his stomach lying in the dirt behind the white rocks and scrub brush of a small arroyo. He had been quiet and still in that spot for so long that he sensed the ground vibrations caused by the advancing animals and wagons as they got close.

Sam didn't move, but watched through the brush as the mules of the lead wagon slowly plodded toward the rock that was their marker to start the attack. The hammer of his rifle had been cocked for a long time. He waited.

When the lead mule was a few steps from the rock, Sam took aim on the chest of the first rider on his side of the wagon. As the mule reached the rock Sam fired. Immediately, the report from his gun sounded like one long loud expolsion as it melted into the sound of the other three rifles.

The upper bodies of four of the riders slammed backwards or sideways in odd directions. *"Bastardos!"* one of the other riders yelled. *"Emboscada!"* a wagon driver screamed realizing it was an ambush as Sam looked down the sights of his second gun and fired.

Their small group's next volley was more sporatic, but almost as deadly. The other two mounted riflemen and the driver in the front wagon went down. The second wagon's driver crouched in the floor in front of his seat and fired.

Sam was already trying to reload when he felt the air move as the bullet whizzed past his head. He was dividing his attention between getting another round in his rifle and watching Denicio Bernillo. Sam paid no attention to the wagon driver who reached for another gun.

In the ten seconds it took for the attackers to fire off two well aimed volleys, Denicio Bernillo had been stripped of his defenders. He jerked back with surprise and shock at the first blast. By the time the second rounds were fired he realized what was happening and was totally engulfed with fear. He jerked the reins on his panicky horse and spun it around trying to decide which way to run.

When Denicio Bernillo bolted, Sam hadn't finished reloading. He still had the rifle and ramrod in his hands when he started out of his hiding spot in the small arroyo to cut off Bernillo's escape route.

Gabriel saw the wagon driver watching Sam as the man grabbed his other rifle. Gabriel flew out of his hiding place and his loud voice boomed, "Look out, Sam!" as he sprinted toward the man in the wagon. The wide-eyed man raised his gun and turned it on Gabriel.

Gabriel was almost to the wagon when he heard the loud gunshot and saw parts of the other man's face fly away from the side of the rifle he was aiming. The big black man's momentum carried him to the wagon and Gabriel knocked the gun barrel out of the way to the side. Gabriel grabbed the driver as he slumped sideways and threw him out of the wagon onto the ground.

"You alright, Gabriel?"

Gabriel turned to his right and saw Walker lower the rifle he'd just fired.

They both turned quickly when they heard the loud yell, "Aghhhhh!", coming from behind them. Fish-head Ben Flagg had left his hiding spot and was running, tomahawk in hand, toward the escaping Colonel Bernillo. He was on the side opposite Sam. Bernillo had turned away from Sam and now Fish-head was closer and had the angle to cut him off.

"Yahhhh, you murderin' bastard!" Fish-head yelled as he ran full tilt at the Mexican officer.

Bernillo's horse shied at the screaming wildman and pitched as it tried to turn away. Sam threw his half-loaded rifle toward the animal which spooked it even more.

Denicio was terrified as he fought the confused horse. He breathed in quick shallow pants while his eyes darted between the two attackers. He pulled the pistol from his waist sash and turned toward the closest man.

Fish-head was eight feet away when Bernillo shot him just below the base of the throat. The downward angle of the shot took the bullet straight to Fish-head's heart. Before he died, the earless mountain man buried the entire steel blade of his tomahawk deep into the upper hindleg of Bernillo's horse.

The horse reared and Denicio threw the pistol away as he tried to stay mounted. The animal came back down fighting against its bit. Denicio yanked hard on the reins. They both sensed Sam approaching from the right and while the horse tried to sidestep away from him Denicio drew his saber.

He made a wild wide sweep at Sam's head with his sword. Sam ducked low and jerked the knife from his belt. The saber blade flashed in the sunlight as it went up and over the horse's head.

Bernillo held the reins short in his left hand and came down with a powerful backhanded blow of the sword with his right. Unlike the encounter when Sam was a boy, Bernillo turned his hand so that the weapon came down blade first at Sam's head.

Sam raised his Christmas knife over his head and stopped the saber's blade with it. He used his knife's blade to shove the saber away to the right. Then Sam instantly brought his knife back in one continuous motion and drove it deep into Bernillo's thigh.

The Mexican screamed out with pain and tried to swing back with his saber. As he did Sam grabbed Denicio's fancy uniform and jerked him out of his saddle. Denicio yelled out again as he fell through the air before he crashed hard onto the ground.

Sam sprung toward him and Bernillo rolled over making a quick swipe with his saber. The end of the sword cut Sam across the chest. Sam felt the wound but didn't stop. He went straight for his enemy's throat.

He grabbed the front of Denicio Bernillo's neck with his left hand. The fingers and nubs he had left on that hand forced their way perfectly around the coward's windpipe. All the heartache and pain of a lifetime that had welled up within Sam had now turned into power and rage.

Bernillo gagged for air as Sam jerked him by the neck to his feet. Sam slammed his knife blade deep into the lower end of Denicio Bernillo's abdomen. The Mexican's eyes widened and Sam looked directly into them.

"That's for my mother," Sam growled in slow distinct words. He saw the reaction on Bernillo's face.

In fear Denicio uttered the word, "*Tejas*", as he suddenly remembered the little homestead he'd destroyed in Texas and the young boy who had tried to defend it.

Sam turned the knife in the vile creature's belly to rotate the blade. He yanked the sharp edge upward and split Bernillo to his sternum. "And that's for my sister, you son of a bitch!"

Four weeks later Sam, Gabriel and Walker arrived in Mesilla two days before the scheduled ceremony. They drove the loaded wagons directly into Walker's big adobe barn and closed the doors.

The morning of November 16, 1854 they drove the wagons to the Mesilla Plaza. Sam turned the load of books over to the commanding officer from Ft. Fillmore along with the letter of instruction from Washington.

Mary Beth and Katrina joined their husbands and Gabriel for the ceremony. The five of them stood together at the edge of the Mesilla Plaza and watched as all the territory of what was being called "The Gadsden Purchase" was officially transferred to the United States of America.

Two hours before daylight the next morning the town was asleep after the big *Fiesta* that had followed the historic event. Not one soul saw Sam, Gabriel and Walker leave town again. Gabriel drove the heavy wagon while Sam and Walker each led a string of pack mules with loaded panniers. The small band headed west on the trail toward the Gila.

PART
FIVE

93

On the horizon of the West Mesa thin lenticular clouds haloed the sky above the town of Mesilla. Their undersides were just beginning to turn pink with the early retreat of the late afternoon sun. Behind them giant billowing cumulus rose like white puffy pillows in which the sun would soon rest.

Across the valley the rocky peaks of the Organ Mountains had begun their evening show. The stark midday shadows of the deep canyons had started to soften and become smooth. The massive stone faces of the Organ's taller pipes already reflected the first pink shades from the cloud bottoms.

In their small camp the last of the firewood burned inside the circle of rocks. On the folding table the tin that had held the Dutch oven's early morning pie was empty. A fair amount of the "sweet'ner" was gone, as were most of the other provisions from the ice chests.

Partner sat back in his big padded folding chair and jostled some of the loose papers into place as he closed the heavy leather binder. He squinched his neck back and rotated it while he lifted his tired shoulders. He looked at Sammy and Amanda, adjusted his aged Stetson, and said, "Well, I'm done for today. Think that's as far as we're gonna' get."

"Oh my God, Partner. Is all that really true?" his grandson asked.

"Yes, son, every bit of it. Oh, there's different versions of some of the things I've told you. History's like that. It gets colored up by the contemporary people who are recordin' things, or the ones who come later and try to piece things together. But, this is the way my parents and grandparents told it.

"Besides, I've been able to verify just about every drop of it historically with documents and written accounts and stuff. Well, pretty much everything except the *mordida,* the bribe for Santa Anna."

Partner placed the thick leather binder into the top of the old steamer chest then continued.

"I did try to research that, too, for awhile, in old company business records. Then I realized that even if any of those records had survived from companies back then that might have participated in the bribe… it's not the kind of thing they would have entered in their books. The tracks on bribe money for the head of a foreign country would have been covered up so well you couldn't find 'em even if you knew where to look.

"Anyway, I'd pretty much figured that part was just an old family myth. You know, the kind of things they tell kids at night around the fire. That was…until I started redoin' your grandmother's dress shop.

"Remember I told you my great grandfather had apparently built a fireplace in the original part of the room where you kids are stayin'?" Sammy looked at his wife then turned back to Partner and nodded.

"Well, when I started the remodel, I found where water was gettin' behind that wall and the old adobe mud bricks in there were beginnin' to melt. When I tore into the wall to rebuild it, I found what was left of the old fireplace. Behind the rocks, above what had been the mantle, I found this."

Partner reached into the chest and lifted out a dark box. He handed it to Amanda. When she took it he saw in her face that she was surprised at its weight.

Amanda turned the small box and showed it to Sammy. On the top in very ornate script they saw engraved, "*JMS*". Amanda looked up at Partner and said softly, "Jonathan Michael Stevens".

The old man nodded. "Yup, it's Jonathan's lead box…from the miners in Missouri." He paused while the two young people reverently examined the old container.

"And I found some interesting things inside it, too," Partner said.

He reached into the steamer chest again and retrieved a small plastic bag. He opened the bag and unwrapped a piece of cloth from inside it. "This is yours, son," he said and handed a gold watch to Sammy.

Sammy gingerly took the watch and held it for Amanda to see also. He looked up and said, "Oh Jesus, Partner. Is this the watch?"

"Open it," his grandfather said.

Sammy gently opened the watch cover and read aloud, "Moses Austin." He turned and looked at his wife. When she looked up from the watch and into his eyes he couldn't speak.

"Wait 'til you see this, son," Partner said, and then smiled slyly.

From the antique steamer chest Partner took three sheets of heavy plastic that looked like the insert pages for a photo album. Two of the sheets had rows of small clear pockets. Large coins had been placed into each of the pockets. Partner handed a coin filled sheet carefully to each of the young people.

Sammy took his and said, "These are heavy. They're not..." He looked up with wide eyes.

"Gold Double Eagles," Partner said boldly. "Sam put those in his Pa's old box hidden in the fireplace."

"You think these could be from Santa Anna's bribe?" his grandson asked.

"Look at 'em, Sammy. There's hardly a scratch on any of 'em. Those coins have never been circulated," Partner said smiling. He waited while Sammy and Amanda looked at the coins before he said, "And then there's this."

The old cowboy held up the third plastic sheet. Inside its large clear pouch was pressed a piece of yellow-white paper. "This is how I know it's all true," Partner proclaimed proudly. "This is Sam's map to where they hid Santa Anna's bribe money. That's his handwriting and signature right there." Partner pointed to a bottom corner.

"What!?" Sammy exclaimed open mouthed.

"Yeah," Partner grinned, "Sam, Gabriel and Walker filled Santa Anna's book boxes full of lead, rocks, and adobe bricks. They took all his Double Eagles way up in the Gila...and buried 'em!

"I know the area he's got on his map here, but I've never been back in there. It's really rough."

"You're not serious, Partner!?" Sammy exclaimed again.

"Yes sir, a hundr'd percent."

"And they never went back to get it?"

"Nope, they left it there. Sam didn't take it for himself. He just didn't want Santa Anna to have it, I guess. Anyway, I'm pretty sure nobody in our family ever went up and got it."

"What about Santa Anna?" Sammy asked.

"Oh, he had his hands full after the Gadsden Purchase, once his people found out about him sellin' off so much of their country. Ya' see, when Santa Anna first took over the Presidency, back when Jonathan and the other colonists supported him, Mexico was the second largest country in the world.

"Under his rule, Santa Anna either lost in battle or sold off over half of Mexico's sovereign land, basically down to the size she is today. 'Course, if it weren't for the partisan politicians in the United States Congress, a lot more of what is now Mexico, including the entire Baja, would be part of the U.S.

"Anyway, the Gadsden Purchase ultimately finished Santa Anna politically. It's what finally took him out of power for good." Partner tilted his head down slightly and looked at Sammy from under the brim of his old cowboy hat as he said grinning, "Besides, who was he gonna' tell that he'd been double crossed on a million dollar bribe?

"He probably never knew if the money was even sent at all. And, the people in the states who put the bribe together - just assumed he got it."

"You think the money's still up there, Partner?" Sammy asked slowly.

"Don't know, son, but I'd say there's a better than even chance it is. For the first seventy-five years it was buried, the Gila was either hostile Indian country or very sparsely populated. For the past seventy-five years that part of the Gila has been a National Wilderness Area, and the only way to it is on foot or horseback. The area it's in is some tough country. You can bet there haven't been many people back in there."

"A million dollars...buried in the Gila," Sammy said and smiled.

Partner chuckled. "Hey, Sammy, think about it for a minute." He bumped back the brim of his old Stetson. "It was a million dollars in twenty dollar gold pieces back in the 1850's. The Democrats did away with the Gold Standard in 1933 when Franklin D. Roosevelt outlawed the private ownership of gold. Everyone in the country had to turn in their gold coins and they were all melted down.

"About the only Double Eagles that survived were ones the overseas banks or people in Europe had. They're rare coins now. I checked the Internet yesterday. Coin dealers are tradin' Double Eagle twenty dollar gold pieces for twenty-eight hundred dollars...per coin!"

"Jesus Christ!" Sammy said and looked wide-eyed at Amanda.

"Yeah, takes awhile to cipher it out, but it runs into a hell of a lot of money pretty quick," Partner smiled.

"That's unbelievable," Sammy sat back in his chair.

"Well, this is all yours now, Sammy boy," Partner said proudly and gently placed the map into its place inside the strong old steamer chest. "Y'all can decide what you want to do with it."

"Partner, what happened to them?" Amanda asked in a quiet, sincere voice. "Mary Beth and Sam, and the others?"

"It's all here...in these binders, darlin'. The generations after them, too." The old man said and then smiled when he saw the disappointment his answer brought to Amanda's face.

"Well, let's see." Partner paused in thought for a moment. "Because of his strong anti-slavery feelings, John Freemont founded the Republican Party and was their first candidate for President of the United States. 'Course, he didn't win.

"And, ultimately, Freemont lost all his fortune from his gold strike in California. It was kinda' too bad. After everything I've told you about what happened, John Freemont lost everything he had investing in the railroads. In the end he and his wife survived off money from books she wrote about her husband's adventures in the days when he was charting the West with Kit Carson and Walker.

"Oh, that old river boat captain, Richard King, turned out to be a pretty interesting character, too. He and his partner, Kenedy, wound up owning some of the largest spreads in South Texas. The King Ranch still exists down there." Partner smiled. "It's just a little bigger than the state of Rhode Island."

Partner paused again and looked into Amanda's eyes before he continued in a kind voice.

"Mary Beth and Sam got to have their own families with their own children. Guess you figured out that part, or else we wouldn't be here.

"From the money the government paid them, Gabriel was able to buy his own farm in the valley. He got to have dogs again, too.

"Sam and Gabriel lived for another ten years…up into the time of the American Civil War. Mary Beth lived longer than that. Walker didn't make it as long as she did.

"Like I said, it's all here…in these binders. There's so much more you need to know about."

Partner sat back and gave them a quirky grin as he raised his eyebrows. "If you thought the first part of the story was somethin', just wait 'til you hear the other parts. I'll go over it all with you sometime, if you want. But, I had to tell you about this part while I had you both here. I hope you understand now."

"I had no idea, Partner." Sammy rose and stepped over to his grandfather. "This has been the most remarkable day of my life."

The old man stood up and hugged his grandson to him. As they embraced he said, "Remember, son, all the things our family's done… the things we've been a part of…they can't be forgotten. Now you, and Amanda, know. Now you're a part of it, too."

When they finished Partner pulled a red bandana from the back pocket of his worn Levi's and blew his nose. After he stuffed it back he sat down and reached for the sweet'ner. As he poured a small taste into his coffee cup he looked at the brilliantly lit clouds of the sunset and proclaimed, "Boy Howdy, what a day!"

Amanda smiled over at him and said, "Partner, I have to know. What happened to Juan Seguin?"

"Well, that's a sad one, darlin'," Partner replied. "He had to serve in the Mexican Army and did see some action in the Mexican American War. But, mostly he served on frontier defenses guarding river crossings and protecting against Indian attacks. When they let him out of the army he got permission to return to Texas and did settle for awhile on land by his father's ranch.

"However, the anti-Mexican sentiment and prejudice among the people back then eventually chased him and his family back to Mexico.

He died in Mexico, in Nuevo Laredo, just across the river from the *Tejas* he loved and fought for.

"The people of Texas today do recognize him as a patriot though. In the mid-1970's his remains were moved back to Texas. During the Bi-centennial Celebrations on July 4th, 1976 they were buried in Seguin, Texas - which was, 'course, named after him.

"People just don't realize the scars Santa Anna left on the southwest, especially in Texas after two big wars. To give you an idea, Juan Seguin was the last Texan of Mexican descent to be elected as Mayor of San Antonio until the 1980's. That kinda' tells you somethin', doesn't it?"

"What did finally happen to Santa Anna, Partner?" Sammy asked as he sat down in his chair next to Amanda.

"Well, think that's my favorite part of the story. I kinda' feel like that's where Sam kept the promise he made to his Pa on that little hill the last time they saw each other." Partner leaned back in his chair and took a sip from his coffee cup. He showed his broad grin and cocked his head slightly to one side. "When it came Sam's turn, he didn't let the bad ones win.

"*Antonio Lopez de Santa Anna Perez de Labron,* the man who called himself 'The Napoleon of the West'...the cruel dictator who ruled Mexico eleven times during the 1800's...was a blind, one legged pauper...when he died in the *barrios* – the slums of Mexico City."

CPSIA information can be obtained at www.ICGtesting.com
Printed in the USA
LVOW080843070612

285055LV00001B/334/P